"It's a [illegible] tasy novel that combines storytelling verve with inventive turns of phrase."

SFX Magazine

"Gives Shakespeare's London an alternate-history twist ... A lively, readable debut."

David Langford, The Daily Telegraph

"Terrific... A great new talent in the fantasy field."

Mark Chadbourn, author of The Sword of Albion

"Murder, mayhem and intrigue at the court of Elizabeth I. All this and magic too makes for a great read."

Mike Shevdon, author of Sixty-One Nails

"An outstanding debut and Lyle is certainly a name to watch for the future. I thoroughly enjoyed it."

The British Fantasy Society

"Anne Lyle's *Alchemist of Souls* [is] an outstanding debut!"

Lynn Flewelling

"I would definitely rate *The Alchemist of Souls* as one of the best novels of the year."

The Founding Fields

"With an effective mix of espionage, backstage drama, and mystery, Lyle provides compelling drama in an intriguing setting."

Publisher's Weekly

BY THE SAME AUTHOR

The Alchemist of Souls

ANNE LYLE

The Merchant of Dreams

Night's Masque Vol II

ANGRY ROBOT
A member of the Osprey Group

Lace Market Hous
54-56 High Pavem
Nottingham,
NG1 1HW, UK

www.angryrobot
They stumble tha

An Angry Robot p
1

Anne Lyle asserts the moral right to be
identified as the author of this work.

A catalogue record for this book is available
from the British Library.

ISBN: 978 0 85766 277 4
Ebook ISBN: 978 0 85766 279 8

Set in Meridien by THL Design.

Printed and bound by CPI Group (UK) Ltd, Croydon, CR0 4YY

"The man that hath no music in himself,
Nor is not moved with concord of sweet sounds,
Is fit for treasons, stratagems and spoils;
The motions of his spirit are dull as night
And his affections dark as Erebus:
Let no such man be trusted. Mark the music."

William Shakespeare, THE MERCHANT OF VENICE

CHAPTER I

Mal leant over the ship's rail, scanning the shore for any sign of a wreck. The mistral had swept the sky bare, leaving the coast etched in hard lines by the cold clear light of a January morn.

"There," he said at last, pointing to a dark shape on the beach.

Coby joined him at the rail. "Are you sure it's the skrayling carrack, sir? Those timbers could belong to any ship."

"You still don't believe me."

"I..." Her head drooped, expression hidden by the hood of her cloak. "It's been more than a year, sir. I thought... I thought all that was over."

It'll never be over, he wanted to tell her. *Not whilst I have this thing inside me.*

The ship tacked westwards, closer to the pale sands. A rocky headland loomed to their left, the prevailing winds threatening to dash them onto its rocks as it had the ship they sought. Ahead, the northernmost tip of Corsica rose in low hills seared to colourlessness by the mistral. As they drew nearer, pieces of flotsam dashed themselves against the bow, as if clamouring to board a sound vessel. A scrap of dull red sailcloth tangled in rigging confirmed Mal's suspicion. This was the skrayling ship from his dream.

"I don't see any bodies," Coby said after a while.

"No, thank the Lord." He made the sign of the cross, then addressed their captain in French. "Set us ashore here."

"Is that wise?" the Moor replied in the same language, his native accent heavy. "Just the two of you?"

"Would you rather come with us, and be mistaken for a corsair raiding party?"

Captain Youssef waved to two of his men to lower the jolly-boat. Mal glanced at his companion. Dressed in masculine attire, she easily passed for a boy of fifteen or so, and a hard life had given her a toughness beyond that of most young women. Still, he worried every time he took her into peril.

As if guessing his thoughts, she grinned at him and patted the knife at her belt.

"If any are left alive, we'll find them," she said. "Ambassador Kiiren would never forgive us if we did not."

They poked amongst the wreckage on the beach, but found no one either dead or alive, nor any sign of the ship's cargo.

"You think the islanders already picked it clean?" Coby asked, straightening up and brushing sand from her breeches.

"They've had a good couple of days," Mal replied. "I doubt this is the first vessel to fetch up here, nor will it be the last."

"No footprints besides our own."

Mal shrugged. "Erased by the mistral's dying breath, perhaps."

They found a narrow track leading up from the beach and followed it over the ridge. A village, little more than a hamlet, lay in a sheltered hollow of the hills, surrounded by the chestnut trees for which the island was famous. No smoke rose from its chimneys, no cry of children or bark of dogs disturbed the morning air. Coby glanced at Mal but said nothing. He drew his rapier and continued down the track, scanning the buildings for any sign of life.

As they came closer they realised the houses were falling into ruin, their silvery thatch half gone, interiors standing open to the sky. Doors hung askew on their hinges or lay on the threshold in splinters.

"Corsairs?" Coby whispered.

"Long gone, by the looks of it." Mal sheathed his sword. "We should search the houses. If there are survivors of the wreck, they could have taken shelter here."

It did not take long to search the entire hamlet, but they found no sign of the skraylings, only half a human skeleton well-gnawed by dogs. An old man or woman, judging by the shrunken, toothless jaw. Mal pointed out the blade-marks on the ribs.

"They take the able-bodied villagers for slaves," he said, "and kill everyone else."

Coby stared at the pathetic remains, hand on her throat where a small wooden cross hung on a cord. He wondered if she was remembering other deaths, of those far closer to her than this unknown Corsican.

They followed the track out of the other side of the village until they came to a fork. One path wound southwards through a chestnut wood carpeted in golden leaves, the other led back northeast, towards the coast.

"Where now, sir?" Coby asked.

Mal searched the ground for a short way along each road, though he was not hopeful. The earth was too dry and hard to take prints. He was about to give up when a dull gleam caught his eye: a bead about the size of a pea, made of dark grey metal. Hardly daring to trust his luck, he drew his dagger and touched it to the bead. When he lifted the blade away, the little sphere clung to it like a burr.

"Lodestone," he said with a smile. "The skraylings came this way, and left us a clue."

He gathered up all the beads he could find, and they set off down the coastal path. A chill northerly breeze, no more than a faint memory of the mistral, tugged at their cloaks and ruffled their hair. They had still not seen a living creature apart from the ever-present gulls.

"Youssef told me the citadel of Calvi lies not far from here," Mal said. "If the skraylings were taken by the islanders, my money is on Calvi. The Genoese would pay handsomely for intelligence of the New World."

"You think Youssef will wait for us?"

"Until noon tomorrow, at least. So he swore." He looked at her sidelong. "You do not trust him?"

"No more than I trust any man in our line of work."

Mal grinned. "Very wise. But he has not failed us so far. I think he has earned such trust as we can spare."

His hand closed around the beads in his pocket. They were already starting to take on some warmth from his flesh, and there was something comfortingly familiar about the way they clung together as he rolled them over one another. Perhaps it was only an echo of a memory, of playing with his mother's rosary as a child. Though her beads were of amber, not cold steel.

"There," he said a few moments later. "The citadel of Calvi."

The broad promontory stretched northeastwards away from them, covered in more of the bare-branched chestnut trees. At its farthest point it rose to a hill encased in walls of pale stone, rising sheer and impregnable from the cliffs. Within, tall red-roofed buildings clustered about a domed church. It made the Tower of London look like a child's toy.

"If they are in there," Coby said, "how in the name of all that's holy do we get them out?"

• • • •

Above the open gates of the citadel was carved a motto: *Civitas Calvis Semper Fidelis*. Faithful to whom? Mal wondered. Their Genoese overlords, or their own self-interest?

A lone guard, slouching in the meagre warmth of the noonday sun, detached himself from the wall as they approached and looked them up and down. He was a good six inches shorter than Mal, with greasy black hair and a gap between his front teeth.

"Who are you?" he asked. "And what is your business in Calvi?"

Mal hesitated. His Italian was a little rusty, and the man's accent was not easy to understand.

"Our ship is damaged," he said, pointing back northwards. "We need to buy nails and rope for repairs." Just enough truth to give his story verisimilitude, that was the trick of it.

"You are English," the guard said, his eyes narrowing.

"I was born in England," Mal replied, "but I have family in Provence. We were sailing to Marseille–"

"Not a good time of year to be sailing anywhere."

"My father is dying," Mal said with a shrug. In truth his father was some years dead.

"There is a chandlery down by the quay." The guard gestured over his shoulder.

"Thank you. But first I would light a candle for my father's soul, and give thanks for our own safe landing. There is a church in the citadel?"

"The Cathedral of Saint John the Baptist," the guard said, drawing himself up to his full height. "Go to the top of the hill; you cannot miss it."

Mal thanked him again, and they went through the gate. A steep cobbled street wound upwards, turning into a broad flight of steps that led past the ochre-and-white stucco façade of the little cathedral.

"Now what?" Coby asked in a whisper.

Passers-by were eyeing them suspiciously. Mal might be taken easily enough for a local, apart from his height, but Coby's blond hair and pale skin made her stand out in any crowd south of Antwerp.

"We do as we said, and go inside," Mal replied.

Coby halted and stared around as they stepped through the cathedral doors. Perhaps the plain exterior of the cathedral had led her to expect a similarly austere interior. Instead, the light of hundreds of votive candles gleamed on the pale curves of alabaster carvings and reflected off the gilding of a hundred statues and icons of saints. The elegantly vaulted ceiling overhead was punctuated by oval panels painted with scenes from scripture, as fine as any work Mal had seen in Italy. An enormous crucifix, taller than himself, stood on the altar.

Mal genuflected, dropped a handful of *sou* into the collection box for the ransoming of Christian slaves, and lit a candle, placing it before a statue of Michael, his own patron saint. Coby remained near the door, looking uncomfortable in the opulent and, no doubt in her eyes, all-too-Papist surroundings. Mal turned back to the alabaster saint and murmured a prayer. For her soul, his own, and most of all that of the brother lost to him.

A chill of unease ran over him as he thought of Sandy. Touching his finger to his forehead in a hurried gesture, he returned to the cathedral door.

"Let's get out of here," he told Coby.

"What's wrong, sir?"

"I don't know. Something…" He shook his head to dispel the uncomfortable feeling. "Let's go down to the harbour. We might be able to pick up some gossip at the chandler's."

A long flight of stone steps led down from the citadel to the quayside, where housewives haggled with fishermen over baskets of the morning's catch. Flocks of gulls screamed overhead; their more cunning fellows sidled around the stalls, yellow eyes fixed on the fishermen's baskets. Mal looked around for the chandlery, but his eye was caught instead by a squat stone watchtower at the end of the quay, connected to the citadel above by a length of wall that ran up at a sharp angle. No entrance was visible from this side, nor any windows, and yet the islanders were giving the building a wide berth.

Mal looked out to sea, shading his eyes as if looking for a ship, and drummed his fingers thrice on his dagger hilt. Coby halted at the signal and waited expectantly.

"There," he said, glancing sidelong towards the tower.

She nodded, following his gaze discreetly.

"The skraylings?" she whispered.

"I'm sure of it." He could not say how, but he was as certain as if someone had just told him. "Where better to lock up a score or two of unexpected prisoners?"

"How are we to get them out?"

"Our only hope lies in stealth. We'll return tonight, after dark; a few hours will make little difference."

Youssef's ship, the *Hayreddin*, was a sleek galleass of the sort popular with both Turks and Christians. As well as its three triangular sails, it had two dozen oars on each side, the better to manoeuvre in battle – or sneak into a harbour against the wind. However it was too large to go unnoticed on a moonlit night, so they dropped anchor and went the rest of the way in the ship's boat.

Though they rowed as slowly and carefully as possible, the splashing of the oars sounded over-loud in the night air. Their course was not easy, hugging the foot of the citadel's hill as close as possible so that anyone on the walls above would have to look over and down to see them, instead of out across the water. The darkness that concealed them came at a price, however; it also concealed the rocks near the shore, and one of Youssef's keenest-eyed men was obliged to crouch in the bow, raising a hand now and then to steer them away from destruction. On several occasions Mal thought they were about to be dashed against the rocky shore, but the sailors' skilled rowing thrust them back out to sea. He wondered how often they had done this kind of work before. Best to be grateful they had, and not ask questions.

The harbour was not unguarded, of course. Torches burned in cressets at intervals along the waterfront, and a sentry paced back and forth. Not, Mal noted, too close to the little tower. His conviction that the skraylings were held within deepened.

Their little craft slipped from one fishing boat's shadow to the next and into an empty berth. Mal scrambled ashore, signalling for the rest of them to stay put. He waited until the sentry was nearing the far end of his course, then slipped silently across the quay and hid in the alley between two warehouses. Long moments passed, punctuated only by the sentry's receding footsteps and the occasional hawk-and-spit. Then the feet turned and began to approach. Mal edged closer to the alley mouth and drew his dagger.

As the sentry drew level, Mal stepped out behind him, clamped his left hand over the man's mouth and slammed the dagger up under his ribs towards his heart. The sentry writhed in his grasp, stubble grating against Mal's palm, then sagged to the ground. Mal wiped his blade on the man's clothing, sheathed it and hurried back to the waiting boat.

At his signal, Coby clambered ashore, followed by Youssef and two of his men. The sailors scattered to keep watch, whilst Mal and Coby ran towards the tower. A large arch pierced the connecting wall. Mal paused in its shadow, scanning the shrub-covered slopes between the waterfront and the base of the citadel, but could see nothing moving. He beckoned to Coby and slipped round the far side of the tower.

To his relief there was a double door at ground level on this side, its rusty handles secured with a new steel chain and padlock. Any doubts that they might have the wrong place vanished. Why lock up a watch tower so securely, unless you were afraid of what was inside?

Coby uncovered a small lantern as she neared the door. Handing it to Mal, she rummaged in her satchel and produced a canvas roll. Mal positioned the lantern so that its beam fell on the enormous padlock, and Coby began probing the workings with the largest of her skeleton keys. Mal kept watch as she worked; they were well hidden from view here, but also cut off from their allies if things went wrong.

Coby muttered under her breath and blew on her fingers to warm them. Mal glanced back down at her and she made an apologetic face. Biting her lip, she twisted the key again – and the padlock gave a satisfying click and sprang open. Mal took hold of one end of the chain with his free hand whilst Coby gently unwound the rest from the rough, flaking handles of the tower doors and lowered it to the ground. Mal seized the handles, and a shudder of unaccountable dread swept over him. He took a deep breath and hauled the doors open.

A rush of warm air swept their faces, an ancient maritime scent of salt and seaweed, laced with a familiar musky scent: skraylings. Mal gestured for Coby to raise the lantern and stepped forward, expecting to see chained captives blinking back at him. He was partly right. At his side, Coby whimpered and clapped a hand to her mouth.

"Dear God in Heaven," he murmured, making the sign of the cross.

The bodies of about two dozen skraylings lay on the floor of the tower in a pool of dark blood, still roped together. Their wrists and fanged mouths were bloody, as though they had torn open their own veins – or one another's. He began methodically examining the bodies in case any of the victims had survived, but they were already beginning to stiffen. This must have happened hours ago. Was that the cause of the unease he had felt back at the cathedral: the skrayling soul trapped within him, mourning for the snuffing out of its fellows? He shuddered, not liking that line of thought.

At that moment he caught sight of a dark head amongst the white-streaked hair of the other skraylings. Short black hair. He frantically pulled the dead bodies aside until he had uncovered the dark-haired one and turned him over.

It was not Kiiren. Yes, the face lacked the tattooed lines of skrayling traders, and when Mal lifted the upper lip, the canine teeth had been removed; but this was not the ambassador. Another Outspeaker, then?

A scuffle broke out away to his left and he sprang up, drawing his sword. Coby's lantern shattered on the stone floor as she grappled a slight figure who barely came up to her shoulder. More than that, he could not make out in the darkness.

"Kuru tokh nejanaa sjel! Kuru tokh kurut siqirr kith-gan nejanaa sjel, nej nejt adringeth dihaaqoheet-iz aj-an."

Though Mal could not understand the words, the frightened, pleading tone was unmistakable.

"Hush!" Coby replied. "Friend, no hurt you."

As Mal's eyes adjusted to the faint moonlight, he realised she had hold of a young skrayling, probably no older than herself though his hair was already striped with silver like his elders. When he caught sight of Mal, the boy froze and stared.

"Erishen-tuur?"

"In a manner of speaking," Mal replied, sheathing the rapier. Seeing the boy's confusion, he racked his brains for what little Vinlandic he knew, and inclined his head in greeting. *"Kaal-an rrish."*

"*Kaal-an rrish*, Erishen-tuur," the boy replied, bowing back. "*Nejanaa Ruviq*."

"Ruviq-tuur." Mal guessed it was the boy's name.

Ruviq grinned, revealing his eye-teeth, then looked guiltily back at his dead comrades. Coby said something to him in an undertone and put her arm around his shoulder.

"Come on, we'd better get back to the ship." A thought struck Mal. "Wait. Help me collect the necklaces from all the bodies."

"What? Why?"

"Just do it. Quickly."

It was a grisly task, but Mal's instincts were correct. After a few moments the boy Ruviq began to help, and they quickly gathered them all into Coby's satchel.

"I can manage," Coby said as Mal took the satchel from her and slung it over his shoulder. "It's not that heavy."

"It will be if you fall in the sea with it weighing you down. Look to the boy."

He led them back round the tower and signalled to Youssef. The Moor raised a steel-grey eyebrow at the lone skrayling youth but did not ask for an explanation. Mal's respect for the man's professionalism increased, and he wondered if he should bring Youssef into his cadre of regular informants. Perhaps later, when this business was dealt with. He helped Ruviq into the jolly-boat and sat beside him; the boy seemed to take comfort from the presence of a familiar face. Mal smiled to himself. Sometimes being mistaken for his twin brother had unexpected benefits.

At that moment a bell tolled somewhere in the citadel high above them. Rapid footsteps echoed down the long stair leading to the quay, along with shouted Italian. Youssef pushed off as muskets popped and flashed in the dark and bullets whistled overhead. Mal scrambled to help the rowers, whilst Coby pulled the boy down behind the flimsy shelter of the bulwarks. The jolly-boat lurched against the tide, moving agonisingly slowly into the lee of a fishing boat. Soldiers were pouring out onto the quay and boarding the boats. Bleary-eyed fisherman trailed in their wake, swearing at everyone indiscriminately.

As the jolly-boat pulled steadily out of the harbour, the soldiers appeared to be squabbling with the fishermen over who was in charge of putting to sea in pursuit. A few musketeers lined up in the sterns; the rising wind had scattered the clouds and the fleeing rescuers were an easy target. Youssef yelled at his men to row faster as the first fusillade peppered the water around them.

The fishing boats cast off at last, but the wind was in the west and they would have to tack hard to get round to the *Hayreddin*. Youssef's men laughed until a lucky shot caught one of their number in the head, sending him sprawling back against the gunwales. Coby pulled Ruviq close, not letting him see the man's body; she looked as if she was going to throw up herself. The rest of the crew bent to the oars and pulled as if the Devil himself were after them.

They reached the *Hayreddin* without further casualties, and climbed the rope ladder one by one. Ruviq moved slowly as if in a dream, or a nightmare. Mal beckoned to Coby, and together they took the boy into the small side-cabin in the stern.

Mal could tell she was eager to question the boy, but he stalled her with a gesture. She took the hint and with signs and a little Tradetalk encouraged Ruviq to lie down and rest. When he was settled, she followed Mal back out onto deck and they stood at the rail, staring out across the moon-limned waves.

"You needn't have killed him," she said. "The harbour watchman."

And here he was, thinking she was worried about the boy.

"Perhaps not," he said. "But you well know how chancy a business it is, to knock a man senseless. Too hard, and you may kill him anyway; too soft, and you might as well not bother. Would you rather I had taken that chance, and he had raised the alarm before we could rescue the boy?"

"No, of course not."

He put an arm around her shoulder and she leaned into him, though as much, he suspected, for warmth as any other reason. Still, it eased his own heart a little.

"So what do we do with the boy, sir?"

The note of formality in her voice brought him back to the present, and his duty to his masters in England.

"We take him back to Sark," he said. "And then we try and find out why the skraylings were here in the first place."

CHAPTER II

They sailed back to Marseille with Youssef then rode to Mal's estate near Aix with the boy. At this time of year the roads were so empty of traffic that three travellers on horseback attracted curiosity, so Coby used a little of her stage makeup to cover the tattoo lines on Ruviq's brow and cheeks and hid the rest of his face with a hood and scarf. Only his amber eyes threatened to give him away, and he kept those fixed on his hands where they rested on the pommel of his saddle.

Concealing Ruviq's identity from the servants was a different matter. They were only just coming to terms with having an English-born master, and Mal did not trust them to keep quiet about a skrayling visitor, however well-disguised. He therefore rode ahead and ensured the entire household were too busy lighting fires and preparing supper to notice Coby smuggling Ruviq into the house as dusk was falling. She had her own apartments with a lock on the door to keep out prying eyes when she was undressing, so hiding the boy for a short time would be little problem. There were however a few suspicious glances when she appeared later that evening, and not a few mutterings when she asked to eat in her room.

After supper she came down and sat by the fire with Mal. The servants brought mulled wine laced with honey and lavender to aid sleep, and then left them alone. Coby knelt before the hearth and stared into the flames, her hands wrapped around the steaming mug. Mal coughed to get her attention, and she looked up, half her face red-gold in the firelight, the other in darkness. It took all his self-control not to fall to his knees beside her and drink from those wine-hot lips until…

"How are things?" he asked instead, glancing up at the ceiling. One could never be quite certain the servants were not eavesdropping.

"As well as can be expected," she replied, taking the hint. "But the sooner we leave, the better."

Mal nodded. "Pack tonight, and we'll be away at dawn. The days are short enough as it is."

He drained his own cup, bade her goodnight and retired to his own chambers, before he could do something they might both regret.

"It would have been safer to go by sea," Coby grumbled one day as they rode through yet another small village where people stared at the three of them as they passed.

"The boy has been through one shipwreck already. I didn't want to alarm him with another long sea voyage, especially at this time of year. The weather out in the Atlantic is far worse than our crossing to Corsica."

Coby nodded. She still had nightmares about the storm in which she had lost her parents, on the crossing from Neuzen to Ipswich. All she remembered was cold salt water coming at her from every direction, and then a chill worse than midwinter snows eating into her bones as everything went black. She shivered at the memory.

"Where do you think the skrayling ship was headed?" she said. "Marseille?"

"Perhaps. Though if they were dealing with the French, why not go straight to Paris from Sark?"

"Mayhap they prefer to trade in Marseille. The markets there are full of goods from Africa and the East."

"As are those of London. No, they had a reason to come further south."

"Italy, then?"

"Possibly. Though if they hoped for a warm welcome in Genoa, they were disappointed."

"The boy might know." She looked over her shoulder. Ruviq's pony had stopped and was tearing mouthfuls of grass from the roadside. Ruviq seemed not to have noticed; he slumped in the saddle, his face hidden by his hood. Coby reined her own mount to a halt and clucked to the pony.

"I asked him, back in Provence," Mal said, "but he just mumbled something in Vinlandic and would not say any more."

"Perhaps he needs more time," she said. "After everything that's happened to him... to find himself amongst strangers who do not even speak his tongue... I remember how horrible that was."

"You ask him, then. He may confide in you."

She turned her mount and trotted back down the road. Ruviq looked up in alarm, as if he'd quite forgotten where he was. Coby gave him a reassuring smile and reined in beside him, then they rode knee to knee for a while, out of earshot of Mal. At first Coby made small talk, asking Ruviq how he liked the horse and apologising for their campfire cooking. When he seemed at ease, she brought up the subject of the voyage.

His expression instantly became guarded.

"I do not know."

"You must have overheard someone say something, surely? I remember when I was a child, I used to crouch on the stairs, listening to my parents talking to visitors–"

"No. There were *qoheetanisheth* on the island, but I was too young."

"Co-what?"

"Elder talk. In here." He tapped his temple.

Coby raised a hand to the cross at her throat. It sounded like more witchcraft to her. She kicked her pony's sides gently until it caught up with Mal's gelding.

"So," she said, after relating the conversation, "we are no wiser than before."

"For now, at least. But we have the advantage of a true friend amongst the Vinlanders. If anyone knows what the skraylings are up to, it's Kiiren."

The island of Sark had been given to the skraylings of Vinland by Queen Elizabeth in return for their services in keeping the Narrow Sea free of pirates. The fact that the island had itself been a haven of pirates played no small part in its selection. That and it annoyed the French, who also liked to lay claim to Sark and its larger neighbours.

Still it was now to all intents and purposes an independent realm, a little piece of the New World tacked to the edge of the map of Christendom, and English ships were only slightly more welcome than those of any other Christian nation. It took Mal a whole morning of negotiation to persuade a Cherbourg fisherman to sail them the forty miles to the island. Whether he would return in two days to take them back to France remained to be seen.

As they got nearer, Coby realised she could still see no sign of buildings apart from the crumbling harbour wall, which must have been constructed long before the skraylings' arrival. Within it a copse of masts sprouted, yardarms bearing the square reddish sails typical of skrayling vessels, most of them tightly furled against the spring gales. The only other sign of the Vinlanders' presence was a cairn at the seaward end of the harbour wall, out of which thrust a great branch of driftwood hung with yellow and blue ribbons and strings of shells that rattled in the sea breeze. Some of the ribbons were faded to colourlessness by the salt air, whilst others were as bright as spring flowers. The fisherman muttered and crossed himself as they passed this heathen-looking monument, and his passengers were barely given time to scramble ashore before he turned the boat around and headed back out to sea.

They were greeted by a stout, elderly skrayling with white shell beads woven into his braids. He bowed to them in the skrayling manner, arms at his side with palms facing forward.

"My master desires to visit the Outspeaker," Coby said in Tradetalk, after the introductions were over.

"Of course. The brother of Erishen-tuur is always welcome with us. Kiiren-tuur's tent is over the next ridge, downstream from the *hendraan*."

"*Hendraan*?" Coby asked. Another Vinlandic word to add to her vocabulary.

"Place of staying, with many tents," the harbourmaster said.

She thanked him, and conveyed the directions to Mal. As they left she could feel the harbourmaster's eyes boring into her back. He must be curious as to what a boy of his own people was doing in the company of two English visitors, but evidently the outspeaker's business was not his to question.

A steep path led up from the harbour to the interior of the island. Steps had been cut into the cliff face, but like the harbour wall they had not been maintained well. Several times Coby lost her footing on the weathered stone and had to steady herself by grabbing a handful of the coarse weeds that had sprung up by the path. At last they reached the top, where they were buffeted anew by the powerful westerly winds that swept the island. A dry, dusty track led across short turf peppered with rabbit droppings.

In a sheltered hollow about half a mile to the west, the skraylings' striped tents rose out of the surrounding bracken and gorse like an unseasonal flush of toadstools.

"Take the boy to the camp and see if you can find his kin." Mal gave her the pouch into which they had gathered all the intact necklaces. "I'm going to look for Kiiren."

She nodded, guessing it was his brother Sandy he really wanted to see. If it had been her own lost brother waiting in the next valley, no amount of curiosity about the skrayling expedition could have kept her from him. She waved Mal away, then set off towards the main camp.

As they drew nearer, she could hear the sounds of raised voices. She glanced at Ruviq, but the boy only grinned and quickened his pace. Coby hurried after him, wondering what could be causing such a commotion amongst the normally peaceful skraylings.

On the seaward edge of the camp a wide circle of ground had been stripped of its turf and dozens of skraylings were clustered around the perimeter, stamping and cheering. Through a gap in the crowd Coby could make out two figures within the circle, locked in a wrestling hold. Patches of dust stuck to their grey-and-pink skins, adding to the mottled effect of their natural colouring, and their long hair was tied back with coloured ribbons like the ones on the harbour monument. Both were naked as savages. A blush rose from her suddenly tight collar and she made to turn away; too late. She stared in horrified fascination at the stubby, hairless tail extending from the base of the nearest wrestler's spine until her view was thankfully blocked by the shifting crowd.

She shuddered. There were rumours, of course, but she had dismissed them as ignorant gossip like all the other tall tales circulating back in London: that the skraylings bound elemental spirits into bottles, sacrificed human infants to their dark gods – though to Coby's knowledge the skraylings acknowledged no gods, heathen or Christian – and that they had no females and were born from the bark of trees, which was certainly nonsense. Master Catlyn had explained that skrayling females preferred the safety of their island cities and did not wish to undertake the long and hazardous journey to Europe.

Her train of thought was interrupted by a roar from one of the wrestlers, followed by the thud of bodies hitting the ground. A few moments later the crowd erupted into whoops of victory on one side and groans of disappointment on the other, and the match was over.

The spectators began to disperse, only to come to a halt when they caught sight of the new arrivals. Or rather, Ruviq. Coby realised they were all staring at the boy in surprise and alarm. One of them, whose facial tattoos were almost identical to Ruviq's, pushed through the crowd and threw his arms around the boy, exclaiming loudly in Vinlandic. Others crowded around them, their tone of voice questioning.

She tried to explain in broken Tradetalk what had happened, but when she came to the part about finding the bodies, her throat closed around the words and tears began to stream silently down her cheeks. She held out the pouch.

"These are all?" one of the skraylings asked.

"Yes." The word came out as a croak. She swallowed and tried again. "Yes. All."

Ruviq said something to the others in Vinlandic, miming pulling at his throat.

"It was your necklace we found," she said to him. "I think Mal – Catlyn-tuur – has some of the beads. Do you want them back?"

"Blue-stones?"

"No, only the lodestone ones."

He shook his head sadly. "Only the blue-stones were given to me by my father. I must make new."

"He would be proud of you," Coby said, patting him on the shoulder.

Her business completed, she bade farewell to the skraylings and set off to look for Mal. The light was already fading, and an icy wind whipped the waist-high bracken into a dark, rattling sea. Behind her, the skraylings' voices rose in an eery song of mourning.

The harbourmaster's directions proved easy enough to follow. Mal skirted the coastward edge of the settlement and soon found a little stream, swollen now with winter rains, cutting through the thin skin of earth to reveal the island's rocky skeleton. Soon it descended into a narrow defile that opened out into a sheltered dell looking out to sea. A single tent stood well back from the cliff edge. Sheltered behind it from the constant winds, fist-sized stones ringed a circle of ash.

"Holla! Kiiren! Sandy!"

After a moment a short, slight figure emerged from the tent and shaded his eyes to look up at where Mal was standing.

"Catlyn-tuur!"

Mal scrambled down the last few yards and Kiiren met him halfway across the dell, teeth bared in a very human smile. For a moment Mal saw again the unknown outspeaker lying dead with his shipmates in the Corsican tower. Kiiren hesitated, his concerned expression betraying the change in Mal's own demeanour. Mal forced a smile.

"Well met, old friend," he said, and stepped forward to embrace the former ambassador.

"There is not bad news about your young friend?" Kiiren asked, pulling back and peering around Mal, as if expecting the girl to be hiding behind him.

"Hendricks is well. I came on ahead, to see my brother."

It was Mal's turn to look around. "Where is he? How... how is he?"

"He is much better since last time I wrote to you. Healing almost done."

Healing. Well, that was one way of looking at it.

"He went down to shore," Kiiren went on, "to gather food. Perhaps you would like to go to him?"

"Sandy can wait. There's something we should talk about, first."

Kiiren frowned. "It is so important?"

"Yes."

Kiiren led the way to his tent. It was the same one the ambassador had occupied back in Southwark, a small domed affair with bright blue silk panels adorning the interior. It even smelt much the same, a mixture of smoke, skrayling musk and *shakholaat*. Bedding enough for two was piled on top of a richly carved sea chest of dark wood, but there was no other sign that his brother had been here. Mal was not sure what he expected to see; when Kiiren had taken charge of him, Sandy had owned nothing but the clothes he stood up in and a few books.

Whilst Kiiren brewed fresh *shakholaat* over a charcoal brazier, Mal considered how to broach the subject of the Mediterranean expedition. He had rehearsed this conversation so many times on the journey from Provence, but now it came to it he hardly knew where to start. Before he could frame a strategy, however, the tent flap opened and Sandy ducked inside.

Mal scrambled to his feet and stood eye to eye with his twin. Sandy gazed back levelly for a moment before breaking into a smile and hugging him. Mal patted Sandy's back, swallowing tears of relief. For a moment he had been afraid Sandy wouldn't even recognise him; odd as that would be, since apart from Sandy's clean-shaven chin they were as alike as two peas in a peascod. At that thought he released his twin and looked at him afresh. Sandy was looking better than Mal had seen him in years, suntanned and flushed with the exertion of climbing up from the beach. He was dressed in a loose tunic and breeches like a skrayling, and his hair hung in braids past his shoulders. He hefted a net full of mussels, grinned at Kiiren and said something in the ancient tongue of the skraylings. The words tugged on the sleeve of Mal's memory, but without the skrayling drug to help him, he could make out only fragments.

"Speak English, *amayi,*" Kiiren said.

"Sorry, brother." Sandy ducked his head, sheepish. "I… I have not spoken our father's tongue in such a long time, I forget."

Kiiren gestured for them to sit on the cushions scattered around the tent. "You had something important to say, Catlyn-tuur?"

"It can wait until later," Mal replied. He wasn't about to distress Sandy with talk of mass suicides. "Nothing is more important than my brother."

Sandy poured three cups of *shakholaat* and passed them round.

"Why are you here?" he asked Mal without preamble.

"I'm returning to London on Walsingham's business." It wasn't exactly a lie; if the skraylings were up to something in the Mediterranean, the spymaster would want to know. "And since I would be passing the island anyway–"

"You must have been this way before." Sandy's tone was even, but Mal's guilt supplied the unspoken accusation.

"I didn't want to interfere with your healing. Kiiren indicated it would take a long time."

"But you came anyway."

Mal put down his cup. "I came to see you as often as I could, when… when we were both in London. Do I need a reason to visit here?"

Kiiren reached out and put a hand on Mal's arm. "Do not be offended, Catlyn-tuur. We live apart here and are not accustomed to company. We are both made disagreeable by it, I think."

Ever the ambassador. Mal lowered his eyes and let his hands fall into his lap.

Kiiren turned the conversation to less prickly matters, like the best way to cook mussels, and after a few minutes Sandy excused himself and went outside to start building a fire for supper.

Keeping half an eye on the tent-flap in case Sandy returned, Mal told Kiiren about their discovery on Corsica.

"Why would they do such a thing?" he asked Kiiren when he was done. "To live as a slave is terrible, I know, but–"

"It is not this life they feared, but next."

"I thought you skraylings didn't believe in Hell – or Heaven."

"Next life in this world. As humans."

"As guisers."

"Yes. It is not just against our law, but against our beliefs. Skraylings are skraylings, humans are humans; that is how it should be."

"Could they not choose to just... die and not be reborn?"

"Perhaps. Not all are reborn, even if they wish to. But to die in fear and pain brings..." He shook his head. "I do not know English word. Perhaps you have none."

"English word for what?"

"Creatures that haunt dreamlands, lurking in shadows."

"I know the things you mean." He shuddered. He well remembered the creatures he had seen – or rather not seen. They lurked on the edge of vision, filling their victims' hearts with the terrible certainty that to look upon them was to go mad. "I don't think we do have a word for them."

"*Hrrith*, they are called in Vinlandic. It holds meaning of hunting, and hunger, and emptiness beyond death."

"That's a lot to put into one small word," Mal said. "Hunting and hunger, eh? Perhaps we should call them 'devourers'."

It felt good to pin them down with a name. Naming a thing gave one power over it in the old stories his nurse had told him.

Kiiren nodded his approval. "You remember Erishen's murder, how his soul – your soul – fled into the darkness, seeking haven from *hrrith*."

"They would have destroyed Erishen. Devoured his soul."

He wished they had, then none of this would have happened. Erishen's soul would not have tried to take refuge in unborn twins, and he and Sandy would both have been whole and sane and spared this damnation.

"Erishen would have truly died that night," Kiiren said, echoing Mal's thoughts. "If his murderer had not first stolen his spirit-guard."

"Like the earring you gave me, back in London." He fingered his left earlobe, though he had not worn the pendant for some months. "That's why Ruviq is still alive. He lost his clan-beads, or threw them aside on purpose, and so he dared not take his own life."

"Yes."

The coals settled in the brazier with a sigh, making him start.

"What about the outspeaker?" he asked. "What was he doing on that ship?"

"I do not know. Mine is not only clan here, and since I took over care of Erishen, I have little time for worldly business. I am not privy to elders' counsel any more."

"And now?"

"Now I will have to serve my people, if they need me."

"And what about Sandy? He still needs you."

"He is much recovered. Better even than I had hoped."

This was his chance. He drew a deep breath. "I want to take him home, to Provence. He has spent too long amongst strangers; he needs to reacquaint himself with the manners of his own kind."

"He is already amongst his own kind."

"So you say. But Erishen or no, he is still my brother. Still one of my people, as well as one of yours. And..." He lowered his voice. "And if anything happens to me, he is sole heir to my estate."

"You do not intend to marry your girl Hendricks, then, and make children?"

"I–" He stared at Kiiren. 'How did you know?"

"I have made much study of your people. I know man from woman, even if many of my companions do not. And like her, I am both in spirit." He grinned. "Besides, she does not smell like man."

"I should hope not," Mal replied with a laugh. Then he recalled Kiiren's earlier question. "No, we are not betrothed, nor even lovers. She will not give up her male garb, and French law is very harsh on the subject of masculine love."

"But she is woman, not man."

"And for that transgression also, she could be punished. Even if we were to move back to England, it would not be simple..."

Kiiren clicked his tongue. "My people were wise not to ally themselves with France. I think we would not be welcome there."

"That is as may be, but it has nothing to do with my brother," he said, unwilling to let the subject drop now he had dared to broach it. "May I take him back with me, at least for a while?"

Kiiren's mouth curved downwards, and he shook his

head. "I am sorry, my friend. I think this is not good time. Not yet."

"Then my business here is done," Mal said, getting to his feet. "I will seek passage to London in the morning."

CHAPTER III

Coby strode through the dusk, hoping she had chosen the right direction. She could hardly return to the skrayling camp in the middle of a funeral.

The wind rustled the gorse bushes, and the last rays of the setting sun caught the tips of their thorny branches, gold and… lilac? She turned, and saw three figures striding across the rough ground towards her. Skraylings, carrying coloured lanterns. She was not keen to speak with them, but they appeared to be heading towards Lord Kiiren's camp, and at least with them to guide her she wouldn't have to worry about getting lost and falling off a cliff. She waited patiently for them to catch her up.

The three skraylings halted a few yards away and raised their lanterns, peering at her through the gloom. She thought she recognised one of them from the crowd at the wrestling match, but she couldn't be certain. All three had iron-grey hair and wore the elaborately patterned tunics and jewelled hair-beads of senior merchants. The swaying lamplight distorted their tattooed faces, and for a moment Coby could almost believe the story that they were born from the bark of trees.

"You go Kiiren?" one of them asked.

"Aye."

He gestured somewhat to his left. "Here. We too go."

Coby bowed her thanks and followed the elders across the heath. Thankfully they did not speak to her further, though they exchanged a few words in Vinlandic. She thought she caught the word *senlirren*, which she knew meant "outspeaker", since it had been Lord Kiiren's title in London.

They followed a small stream to where it disappeared over a lip of stony ground into a narrow defile. The south-east-facing hollow was already as dark as night, lit only by a fire over which a large pot bubbled, giving off an enticing savoury smell. Mal and Sandy were hunkered down by the fire; they both got to their feet as the elders approached, and bowed. The skraylings returned the gesture, then without another word ducked into Kiiren's tent.

"Where on Earth have you been?" Mal asked Coby, draping an arm about her shoulder. "You nearly missed supper."

They sat down opposite Sandy, who stirred the pot with a wooden spoon, seemingly oblivious to their presence. Coby studied him discreetly as they waited. Last time she had seen Sandy Catlyn, he had been in the grip of whatever fiendish enchantment the late Duke of Suffolk had inflicted on him in that cellar. He appeared sane enough now, though he was still quiet and withdrawn even compared to his brother.

A few moments later Kiiren and the elders emerged from the tent.

"Please forgive me, Catlyn-tuur," Kiiren said to Mal. "I am called away on clan business. Please, enjoy your supper without me. I will return in the morning."

Kiiren embraced Sandy, then the four skraylings departed in silence.

"I wonder what that was all about," Coby said, watching them leave.

Mal told her about his conversation with Kiiren. He said nothing about their findings on Corsica, however, and Coby guessed he had not yet broken the bad news to Sandy. She wondered if the ambassador had known any of the dead skraylings.

"Then Lord Kiiren was right," she said when Mal finished. "Whatever this other clan are up to, they expect him to help."

Across the fire Sandy tasted the pottage, nodded to himself in satisfaction, and ladled some into a wooden bowl.

"We will have to share," he said, passing it to Mal. "Kiiren and I have only the two."

Mal handed the bowl and a spoon to Coby. The pottage was thick and salty, made with mussels and the fat yellow corn the skraylings brought with them from the New World. After a few greedy mouthfuls she remembered her manners and passed it back to Mal.

Whilst she waited for her next turn, she took off her shoes and put her feet as close to the fire as she dared. The flames had died down, but the damp wood still popped and spat occasionally. She wriggled her toes, frowning at the hole in one stocking.

"I suppose you two have had a lot to catch up on," she said as Mal passed the bowl back.

They shrugged in unison. Mal grinned, but on catching Sandy's eye he sagged, expression grave again. Coby bent her head over the soup bowl. Well, that went really well. She racked her brains for a subject that might provoke more than a shrug.

"Perhaps you can help me with something, in the morning," she said to Sandy.

Both men looked at her quizzically.

"Master Catlyn has been teaching me to fire a pistol," she went on, "but I can barely hit a target once in five shots. I thought that if I could understand how the bullet moves, I might be able to improve my aim."

Sandy sighed. "Alas, I can no longer read half the books I brought from England, and I forget much of what I read before. Kiiren's healing has... changed me."

"Oh. I'm sorry."

"Don't be." He smiled. "There may be other ways I can help you. Some adjustment of the gunpowder mix–"

"No!"

Mal put a hand on her arm. "It's all right. There's no need to change anything. You just need more practice with the pistols."

He took the bowl from her unresisting hands and she wrapped her arms about her knees. Learning to fire a pistol had been easy enough, but every time she loaded it she thought of the adulterated flash-powder that had made the stage cannon explode, killing her previous master. She suspected this was the reason Mal made her continue with the training, to inure her to such thoughts, like making someone get back on a horse after falling off. Knowing it was for her own good didn't make it any easier.

She couldn't blame Sandy, of course. Why should he know about the fire at the theatre? He and Mal had seen so little of one another since they rescued him from Suffolk's clutches. What the brothers needed was more time together.

"I would like to come to England with you," Sandy said, as if reading her thoughts.

She looked up, startled. Could he do that? If Mal could dream of things that really happened, anything was possible.

"You overheard?" Mal said. "Then you know Kiiren said no."

Sandy smiled. "He said no to you taking me. He did not say I cannot go of my own will."

"All right. If you think he'll agree, we'll ask him in the morning."

• • • •

Mal woke to discover that Coby had hogged the blanket in the night, leaving his back exposed. He sat up, rolling his shoulders to work out the stiffness. Perhaps a few fencing drills would loosen him up a bit and get the blood flowing again.

He scrambled out of the tent on hands and knees and stood to stretch in the icy morning air. Across the slate blue sea, a distant line of mist marked the coast of France. Skraylings might not be welcome there, but as long as Sandy behaved himself he should be quite safe. Safer than in England, at any rate. Jathekkil might be out of the game for a while, but there were other guisers in England who might wish to take up his cause against the Catlyn twins. No, best to complete their business in London as fast as possible and then put a few hundred miles between themselves and their enemies. In the meantime, he needed to keep his wits sharp and his blades sharper.

Drawing his rapier he adopted a *seconda guardia* stance, blade at chest height and horizontal with the ground, left hand raised defensively, weight on his forward foot. Footwork first: forward, then back. Again. Now with the blade: forward and lunge – and back. As formal and controlled as a courtly dance, and as well-practised. One should be free to study one's partner, without having to give a thought to the steps…

A rattle of stones to his left sent him whirling about, sword raised, but was only Sandy coming up from the beach with a string of brown eel-like fish. Mal quickly sheathed his blade.

"Breakfast," Sandy said, grinning.

He knelt and gutted the fish and threaded them on sticks, whilst Mal fetched dried bracken from the canvas-covered store behind the tent and laid a fire. Coby emerged a few minutes later, yawning and combing her fingers through her pale hair.

"Did someone mention breakfast?"

Soon the fish were giving off a mouthwatering aroma. Sandy left them to keep an eye on the cooking and returned after a few minutes with cornbread and a jug of *aniig*. Mal couldn't help but notice that Sandy had now put aside his skrayling garb and was dressed in his old clothes, the ones he had been wearing when Mal rescued him from Suffolk. The faded doublet was tight across the shoulders where Sandy had filled out in the past year and a half.

"Is that a good idea?" Mal asked him. "Kiiren won't be happy if he thinks I put you up to this."

"I am the elder by many lifetimes. I go where I will."

Mal had no answer to that. It was too easy to forget he was talking to an ancient skrayling, not the brother he had known since childhood.

"I should warn you," he said slowly, "when we get to England, we'll be staying in Ned Faulkner's house."

Sandy's eyes narrowed.

"I know that name." His expression hardened. "He delivered me into the hands of our enemy."

"He was forced into it," Mal said.

"So many men claim."

"Do you remember the others who took you from Bedlam? It was they who forced him."

"My memories of that time are unclear," Sandy replied.

"But you remember me."

"We share a soul. I cannot forget that."

"Then you know you can trust me," Mal said. "And I trust Ned."

Sandy bent his head to his breakfast, though Mal could tell from the set of his brother's shoulders that the discussion was not over yet. He looked over at Coby, but she was licking the fish grease from her fingers and studiously ignoring both of them. Perhaps they should take lodgings elsewhere, despite the expense. He wondered if he could persuade

Walsingham that news of the skraylings' voyage was worth a pound or two of the Queen's money. Probably not.

They were just tidying away the remains of breakfast when Kiiren appeared at the lip of the dell. His expression was as guarded and inscrutable as Mal had ever seen it. Mal braced himself for an argument over Sandy's leaving.

"I have spoken with kin of those who died," Kiiren said, when he had joined them by the hearth. "They have sung mourning, and will take news back to our homeland."

"And the bodies?" Coby asked.

Kiiren sighed. "It is unfortunate. But many die far from home; it is our fate." He glanced at Sandy, and his brow furrowed.

It was something Mal had never considered before. What had happened to Erishen's previous body, or to the unfortunate skrayling he and Sandy had seen murdered that night over a decade ago? Was Europe strewn with the lost bones of Kiiren's people?

"Sandy has asked to come to London with me," he said, wanting to get this over with.

"Very well," Kiiren replied.

Mal stared at him, all arguments dying on his lips.

"Mourning is private time," Kiiren went on. "It is best if you leave as soon as possible. One of our ships will take you over to France; we cannot spare time for journey to England."

Sandy hugged the skrayling, grinning at Mal. "Of course. Thank you, *amayi*."

Mal quickly retrieved his and Coby's packs from the tent.

"Let's leave them to say their farewells," he said, and ushered her up the path out of the dell.

"Lord Kiiren gave in very easily," Coby said when they were out of earshot.

"Too easily. If I were of a suspicious turn of mind, I'd think he wants to be rid of us for reasons of his own."

"Such as?"

"Now that is the question. And unfortunately, on an island inhabited by none but skraylings, we have no means of spying on him to find out."

"What if Kiiren changes his mind about Sandy coming with us?"

"Then I will go back down there and beat some sense into him."

Coby broke into a grin and he smiled back, not certain how seriously he meant it. To come this close to getting Sandy back, and then fail? No, he would not accept that. His left hand strayed to his sword hilt, thumb rubbing the pommel absentmindedly as they walked back towards the main camp.

Erishen ducked into the tent and scanned its contents. Apart from his clothes, everything here belonged to Kiiren, or was shared between them.

"You must take silver, to buy new garments," Kiiren said, entering the tent behind him. "The less the humans notice you, the better. And you must remember to call yourself by your English name."

"Sandy. Short for Alexander. I will remember."

Kiiren squatted in front of the chest and lifted the lid. For a moment he just crouched there, his hands grasping the front of the wooden box tightly, then he moved a pile of linens aside and pulled out a string of silver ingots. They rang like festival chimes, a cheery sound at odds with Kiiren's solemn mood.

"You can exchange these for English coins at the guildhouse," Kiiren said, handing them over.

Erishen looped the cord over his head and tucked the ingots inside his doublet.

"You will also need to cut these." Kiiren reached up and touched his braids. "Sit down, I will see to it."

Erishen knelt on a mat whilst Kiiren fetched an obsidian blade from the chest. Skraylings had little need of razors, since they grew no facial hair, but their healers had many uses for the slivers of black stone and Kiiren had been obliged to trade for one after he complained once too often about Erishen's beard. Erishen winced at the tearing sound as each braid was severed. It felt like Kiiren was cutting them close to the scalp; he would be as crop-headed as a girl at this rate.

At last it was done, and Kiiren put the severed locks aside.

"Will you burn them?" Erishen asked, running his fingers through his shorn locks. He felt naked with his head so bare.

"I thought I might make a keepsake from them, as humans do," Kiiren said softly. He went back to the chest and took out a small leather pouch decorated with tiny white shell beads. "Take this also."

Erishen took the pouch from him, loosened the neck-strings and peered at the contents. His eyebrows rose.

"Use it only at need," Kiiren said. "I had hoped to keep you here until all danger was past, but–"

"You think Jathekkil was not working alone?"

"I think it is best not to make assumptions."

"Thank you, *amayi*." Erishen pocketed the pouch.

They stood awkwardly for a moment, then Erishen held out his arms and enfolded the skrayling in a gentle embrace. This was not the first time they had been parted, nor would it be the last. He laid his cheek against Kiiren's hair, which was nearly as short as his own.

"You're leaving the island too," he murmured.

Kiiren shifted in his arms and looked up. In the dim light of the tent, his eyes were like a hunting cat's: pupils round and black as obsidian spheres, irises topaz-dark. "How did you know? Did you spy on the *qoheetanishet*?"

"No," he said with a smile, "but you would not give me up so readily unless you had plans that did not include me."

Kiiren looked abashed. Erishen bent to kiss his brow. *Dear, innocent boy. It is always so easy to get the truth out of you.*

"How long will you be gone?" he asked, letting a plaintive note creep into his voice.

"All summer, perhaps."

"You are going home?"

"No, not so far." Kiiren stood on tiptoe and whispered a name in Erishen's ear.

"I do not know the place."

"No, but your brother does."

Erishen grinned at him. Perhaps his *amayi* was not so innocent after all.

England was still in the grip of winter when they arrived in Southampton. Mal, never the best of seafarers, hired horses for an overland journey to London rather than spend another day on a cramped and freezing ship. At Coby's insistence he bought a cloak for Sandy and riding gloves and woollen caps for them all in Southampton before they set off, and was vastly grateful for them himself before they were halfway to Winchester. Even at noon, patches of hoar-frost lingered in the shade, and the horses' breath steamed in the still air.

They spent their first night at the Dragon in Petersfield, after a gruelling day's ride along roads slick with ice-puddles. In the inn yard Mal dismounted stiffly then held the reins of Sandy's horse, ready to catch his brother if he fell.

"I was riding horses long ere you were born," Sandy muttered. "Though this body is out of practice, I confess."

"Hush!" Mal stepped closer. "Do not let anyone hear you talk like that. Or do you wish to be locked up in Bedlam again?"

Sandy narrowed his eyes, but said nothing. Mal suppressed the urge to cross himself. Back on Sark he had begun to hope that Kiiren was wrong and Sandy was cured after all, but this was almost worse than the raving. At least in Bedlam he had been his old self between attacks. This Erishen was a stranger in his brother's skin.

When they entered the inn, the locals stared and muttered into their ale. Mal hoped it was only surprise at seeing identical twins, and not darker suspicions. Both he and Sandy favoured their French mother too well in their looks: an advantage for an English spy in France, a liability here in England.

Mal paid for a private room on the upper floor, big enough for the three of them. There was one large bedstead and a servant's palliasse, a wash-stand with a cracked basin, and a couple of pisspots.

"Not exactly the best welcome back to England," Mal said.

"We've stayed in worse," Coby said, peeling back the bedsheets. "That inn outside Paris, for one."

"Don't remind me. I think I was picking lice out of my breeches for a week."

He threw his saddlebags down and sat on the edge of the bed to let Coby pull his boots off. She wrinkled her nose at the state of his stockings.

"I'll go and ask for hot water to be sent up, shall I, sir?" she asked, setting the boots to the floor.

"Aye. And order supper, if we're not too late."

After she had gone, Sandy rummaged around in his saddlebag and produced a small leather pouch. By the way he handled it, Mal guessed it contained something heavy and perhaps fragile. Sandy sat down on the end of the bed and stared at it, a frown creasing his brow.

Mal leant on the bedpost and cocked his head on one side in a silent question. Sandy looked up.

"A gift from Kiiren," he said, tipping the contents onto the worn coverlet beside him as if reluctant to touch whatever it was.

Kiiren's gift turned out to be a string of the same beads Mal had found beside the road on Corsica. Perhaps larger, and certainly rather more of them, enough to go right round a man's neck. A spirit-guard.

"I thought wearing iron made you soul-sick?" Mal forced the words out.

"It does, in time. But I must wear it, or leave myself defenceless." Sandy sighed and prodded the necklace with a fingertip. "I do not think Jathekkil was the only guiser in England, do you?"

It was something Mal had thought about a lot in the past year and a half. Particularly in the small hours, when he couldn't sleep.

"You didn't put it on when we landed."

"I doubt there are any guisers this far from London. Nor are there enough dreamers in these small towns to disturb my own sleep. But in the city... How soon will we be there?"

"At this pace? Perhaps the day after tomorrow, if we suffer no mishaps."

"Then I should get accustomed to the feel of it, at least when I sleep."

"You expect something... bad?"

"It has been a while. I really do not know." He unbuttoned his doublet and loosened the drawstring on the neck of his shirt. "Will you help me? I am afraid I..."

Mal picked up the necklace. The metal beads were ice cold after the journey, and he breathed on them to warm them a little. Sandy pulled the neck of his shirt open, and Mal knelt on the bed behind him and slipped the loop of beads over his head. His brother flinched and his breath caught.

"Sorry! Did that hurt?" Mal asked, fastening the catch.

"No," Sandy replied after a moment, and with a flush of joy Mal recognised something different in the timbre of his voice, something more like the brother he knew.

"Alexander?" He scrambled off the bed and moved round to get a clearer view of his brother's face. "Is that you?"

"Of course it's me," Sandy replied with a smile. "Who were you expecting?"

"But… Erishen…"

"He is still inside me. He… we are still me." He grinned at Mal's puzzled expression. "You remember when we were fourteen? We broke into the cellar and drank father's best muscat until we were sick."

"Do I ever!" Mal laughed. "Between the hangover and father's beating, I thought I was going to die."

"And you know how, when you're drunk, you say and do things… things you would never dream of when you were sober?"

"Aye." *All too well.*

"It's like that. I remember saying and doing things, but it doesn't feel like it was me who did them. And yet it was me. Well, that's what it's like. Being Erishen."

"And now?"

"Now I'm sober, for a while. Until I take the spirit-guard off."

"Then he comes back."

"No. Then I am him again."

"How is that different?"

"I don't know. It just is."

"I don't understand, and I'm not sure I want to. As long as you're back…"

Footsteps sounded in the corridor, and a moment later Coby came in, carrying a jug and three leather tankards.

"Supper is on its way, and hot water in about an hour."

She rubbed her arms. "It's a bit cold in here, isn't it? Why don't we go back down to the common room?"

"No," Mal said, as she turned to leave. "Sandy's not in the humour for company. Are you, Sandy?"

Sandy appeared about to say something, but shook his head.

"Very well," Coby said, and set about filling the tankards.

"I suppose," Sandy said, when they were all settled on various corners of the bed, "you want to know what the skraylings were up to, on that ship you found?"

"You know?" Coby asked, leaning forward. "Why didn't you say sooner?"

Mal hushed her. "Go on."

"They were sailing to Venice."

"Venice? Why Venice?"

"I don't know. Something to do with a new alliance, I think."

"But the Vinlanders are allied with England," Coby said.

"Those you know as Vinlanders consist of many clans. Kiiren and the merchants in Southwark come from the same clan, the Shajiilrekhurrnasheth, but there are others on Sark now. Or hadn't you noticed?"

Mal snorted. "I can barely tell one skrayling from the next."

"Is that why there was another outspeaker there?" Coby asked. "The one we found–"

"Dead? Yes."

"And these other clans," Mal said. "They want an alliance with Venice?"

"Yes, I believe so."

"But their outspeaker is dead now, so there's nothing to worry about," Coby said. "Is there?"

Sandy pulled a face. "They have requested Kiiren's services as outspeaker, so they can mount another expedition."

"But he isn't a member of their clan."

"No," Sandy said, "but as an outspeaker, it is his duty to–"

"–to be a 'vessel for words, nothing more'," Mal said. "Yes, I remember."

"So what do we do?" Coby asked.

"We tell Walsingham and let the Privy Council decide," Mal said. "We are intelligencers, not politicians. Like Kiren, we are simply vessels for words."

CHAPTER IV

Ned stirred the pottage again and lifted the ladle, blowing away the wisps of steam that rose from the surface. After a moment he took a cautious sip and grimaced. Too much rosemary, his mother would have said, but at least it gave the thin broth some flavour. He put the ladle down and set about laying the table. Gabe would be back from Shoreditch soon, and he was always ravenous after a day's work. Ned smiled to himself. They'd settled into quite the domestic routine in the last two years, like an old married couple. It was a reassuring counterpoint to their other, secret lives, as informants in the pay of Sir Francis Walsingham.

Footsteps sounded on the garden path and Ned looked up, expecting the door to be flung open by a bright-eyed but weary Gabriel. Instead the owner of the footsteps halted and knocked, in a pattern he had not heard in many months. He all but ran to the door.

"Mal!"

His old friend grinned back at him, then engulfed him in a rib-crushing, horse-stinking embrace. Memories stirred, and old desires with them, but Ned pushed the thoughts aside. Their lives had gone separate ways long ago.

"God's blood, it's good to see you again," he said when

Mal finally released him. "What are you doing back in England, anyway?"

"Someone's got to keep an eye on you. Sandy, you remember Ned, don't you?"

"Ned Faulkner. Good to see you again."

Mal's brother bowed in that stiff way the skraylings had. Still as mad as a March hare, then, but not by the looks of it in a vengeful mood. And at least he was speaking English again.

"And my servant, Coby Hendricks." Mal gestured to the slender figure at his side. The boy had grown, but was still as beardless as a eunuch. Perhaps he *was* a eunuch. That would explain a lot.

"How could I forget?" Ned replied. "Well met, Master Hendricks. So, how long are you here for?"

"Not long." Mal took a coin out of his purse and tossed it towards Hendricks, who caught it with practised ease. "I don't suppose Ned here made soup enough for five. Get a pie from Molly's ordinary; I doubt she'll have any meat this time of year, but ask anyway. And don't eat it all on the way back, hollow-legs."

The boy grinned, sketched a bow to his master and left.

"So..." Mal swung one long leg over the kitchen bench and sat down near the fire, "what's the latest news from London?"

Ned stood with his back to the hearth, hands clasped in the small of his back like a boy reciting his lessons.

"Frobisher's dead; caught a bullet besieging some Spanish fort in the Netherlands. They brought him home, but he died in Southampton."

Mal nodded.

"You knew him?" Ned asked.

"Only by reputation. Go on."

"Some Jesuit fellow, Southwell, was arrested late last year." Ned watched his friend for a reaction, but saw nothing suspicious. Not that he was about to betray Mal's Catholic sympathies to Walsingham, but it never hurt to keep your eyes open. "Been in the Tower since then, under Topcliffe's tender care–"

"He confessed," Mal said with a grimace.

"What do you think? Anyway, he's up for trial next week. Sentence is a foregone conclusion, of course."

"Of course. Anything else?"

"Just the usual: another half-arsed plot on Her Majesty's life, thwarted by her loyal servants..." He tried not to look smug; somewhat unsuccessfully, it would appear. "Oh, and–" He glanced at Sandy. "Your skrayling friends have been quieter even than usual."

Mal leaned closer. "Has there been trouble?"

"No, not that. But they're seldom seen on the streets or at the theatre. They come out of their camp to do business, and go back again as soon as it's over." He cocked his head. "You're not surprised."

"It's all of a piece with my own news–"

The back door flew open, bringing a gust of icy air that sent sparks flying up from the fire, and Gabriel strode into the kitchen. The actor's thin cheeks were flushed with the cold and his cloak dripped half-melted snow into the rushes; he removed it in a swirl of forest-green wool and hung it on a peg by the door before turning to greet their guests.

"Catlyn!" Gabriel embraced Mal, and then his brother. "Good to see you both again."

Ned went to shut the door, only to have it pushed open again by Hendricks. The boy muttered an apology and stamped his boots on the threshold. Crossing to the table he took a small pie from under his cloak and set it down.

"Salt cod and onion, sir," he said. "It was the biggest I could get for the money, I'm afraid. Molly says it was such a bad harvest, flour is nearly twice the price it was last year."

Mal looked at Ned for confirmation, and he nodded glumly.

"No matter," Mal replied. "Come, sit down."

The boy took off his cloak and gloves and sat down next to Mal. Gabriel joined them, and Ned spooned a little of the pottage into each bowl. Even with their whole loaf of bread, it would have made a meagre supper for five.

"You were about to tell me your own news," he said to Mal, taking his place on the bench opposite Gabriel.

Gabriel shot him a reproving look and folded his hands on the table. Mal followed suit; Hendricks' head was already bowed over his clasped hands. Whilst Gabriel said grace, Ned couldn't help but notice out of the corner of his eye that Sandy just sat there, watching them all curiously.

Mal cut the pie into five wedges.

"Cod and onion, eh? Looks like it's mostly onion."

He helped himself to a piece and passed the plate around.

Ned tried to raise the subject of Mal's news from abroad several times during the meal, but Mal always neatly deflected his questions and instead took more than his usual interest in the doings of the theatre company. Gabriel, of course, was more than happy to be the centre of attention.

"Shakespeare says he's nearly finished Romeo and Juliet," Gabriel said, setting down his spoon, "so we will be playing it this summer."

"Shakespeare says that every winter," Ned replied. "How long has he been writing that play?"

Gabriel ignored him.

"I am to play Tybalt, Juliet's cousin, and die in a duel with Romeo. Burbage will be Romeo, of course."

"I would like to see that," Sandy said. "I have not been to an English theatre before, and we do not have anything quite like them in the New World."

Away with the fairies after all then. Ned stirred his pottage, biting his lip lest he say something discourteous. Poor Mal. He had had such high hopes of the skraylings being able to cure his brother.

"I doubt we are staying that long," Mal said, breaking the awkward silence. He rose from his seat and beckoned to Hendricks. "My apologies, gentlemen, but we have urgent business in the city."

"Tonight?" Ned said. "In the dark and the snow?"

"We're only going across the river, not back to France." Mal turned to Sandy. "Make yourself comfortable. We'll be back before curfew."

He patted his brother on the shoulder and departed with Hendricks in tow. Gabriel helped Ned to clear away the dirty dishes then excused himself, saying he had some sides to learn for tomorrow's rehearsal.

Ned sluiced the bowls clean in a bucket of water and wiped each one dry with a rag, all the time feeling as though Sandy's eyes were boring into his back. He still wasn't entirely clear what had happened in that cellar two years ago, and he wasn't sure he wanted to. Mal had said something about the duke having drugged everyone by burning a skrayling herb so they imagined things that weren't there, but Ned knew what he'd seen. One moment Sandy had been bound back-to-back with Mal around a pillar, the next he was gone. If that wasn't skrayling witchcraft, he was a Dutchman.

He looked up with a start to see Sandy standing over him.

"You're afraid of me, aren't you?"

"No," Ned replied, glancing around the kitchen in the hope of spotting a handy weapon. The carving knife was still on the table, and the fire irons out of reach on the hearth.

"Yes you are."

"All right, yes, dammit." Ned straightened up, putting as much distance between them as he could without actually retreating. "Now say what you have to say and be done with it."

"Good. We understand one another. So understand this." Sandy leant closer, fixing Ned with his dark eyes that were so like Mal's – and yet unlike. "If you ever betray my brother again, I will come for you."

Ned swallowed, unable to tear his gaze away.

"In the night, whilst you sleep," Sandy went on. "And if you are very lucky, I will only kill you."

Coby followed Mal through the darkening streets, her stomach churning in nervous anticipation. This was the first time she had accompanied Mal to Walsingham's house, and she had no idea what to expect. The Queen's spymaster had a formidable reputation as a man of brilliance, cunning, and dogged devotion to the Crown.

Their route took them over London Bridge and along Thames Street almost as far as the Tower. The streets were empty, most citizens having the good sense to stay at home on a night like this. A freezing east wind blew gusts of tiny snow pellets into their faces, and Coby bent her head against the onslaught, pulling her cloak tighter around her shoulders.

Just before Petty Wales they turned aside into Seething Lane, a narrow street lined with tall timber-framed houses. Mal went most of the way to the end and knocked on a door. It was opened almost immediately by a servant, who frowned at the two visitors in suspicion. Coby wondered if the Queen herself would come under the same scrutiny, if she turned up on the spymaster's doorstep unannounced.

"Maliverny Catlyn, to see Sir Francis," Mal said.

They were ushered inside and left to wait in a black-and-white panelled atrium whilst the servant went upstairs.

"Should we take off our cloaks, sir?" Coby asked in a whisper, conscious that she was dripping on the tiled floor.

"Best to wait until we know we are to be admitted," Mal replied.

A voice sounded from the floor above: a woman, quietly insistent. Coby couldn't hear whoever it was she argued with. A few moments later the servant returned, took charge of their damp cloaks and directed them up the stairs towards a half-open door. Before they could reach it, however, the door opened and a woman – *the* woman? – came out. She was about Master Catlyn's age, small and dark-haired, with a heart-shaped face and shrewd dark eyes. Mal bowed deeply.

"Lady Frances."

"Master Catlyn." Lady Frances blocked his way into the bedchamber. "I suppose you are here to see my father on the usual business."

"Yes, madam."

"He is… not a well man. I will not have him troubled by ill news from abroad. You bring ill news?"

"There is seldom good news in our line of work. Please, Lady Frances; I swear I will not keep him long."

She sighed, but bowed her head and let them pass.

The bedchamber was warm and stuffy despite the cold winter evening. Sir Francis Walsingham lay in the great carved and canopied bed, his face as pale as the candles that burned on the table nearby. Like the candles his flesh had a translucent appearance, as if he were already insubstantial as a ghost. Coby regarded Lady Frances in renewed sympathy; she had not been exaggerating her father's illness.

The spymaster's heavy-lidded eyes opened.

"Catlyn?" His voice was barely above a whisper.

"Sir Francis." Mal knelt by the bed. "Sir, I will be brief. I bring grave news; the skraylings are planning an alliance with Venice."

Walsingham's expression became more alert, and he

struggled to sit up. His daughter hurried to help him, propping him up with bolsters. "Are you sure?"

"I have it on the best authority," Mal replied.

He began telling Walsingham about the shipwreck and their journey to Sark. Coby noticed he said nothing about the dream that had led them to the wreck, or his unease in the cathedral. She could hardly blame him; men had been burned at the stake for less.

Lady Frances resumed her seat by the bed, and busied herself sewing a sleeve onto a new linen shirt. Coby couldn't help noticing that, although she never once looked in their direction, her expression changed from moment to moment, as if she were listening to every word and filing it away. Her father's daughter in more than looks, it seemed.

"This bodes ill for our kingdom," Walsingham said when Mal finished his tale. "If the skraylings take their trade elsewhere, Her Majesty's coffers will be much the emptier. But what do you make of the business? You seem very certain of your informant."

"We are but one small island," Mal said, "and the New World is very large. It was inevitable, I think, that the skraylings would not be content with our friendship alone. The Spanish they despise, and with good reason: King Philip's hubris in claiming the New World for the Pope was not well-judged. The French crown is..." He broke off with a laugh. "I've lost count of how many assassins have tried to murder King Henri. My... ah... manservant and I stopped at least two during in our time in Paris."

Walsingham's expression grew distant, and Mal glanced at Lady Frances briefly before continuing.

"The Holy Roman Empire is too strongly allied with the Pope," he said, "as is much of Italy. And then there is Venice."

"Ah, the Serene Republic." Walsingham turned his attention back to his visitors. "Yes, they have long been out of favour with His Holiness. The enemy of our enemy should be our friend, but when it comes to business, a Venetian would sell his own grandmother. An alliance with the skraylings would allow them to reclaim their position as the trade centre of the Mediterranean."

He coughed, each spasm racking his frame. Lady Frances poured wine and passed the cup to her father.

"I confess I have been expecting something like this for a while," Walsingham went on when he had recovered his breath. "Ever since Naismith's theatre burnt down, relations between England and the skraylings have cooled. At first I hoped it was a temporary setback, a misunderstanding over our ability to control seditious elements within the realm. After you left for France, the Privy Council ordered a great many arrests and executions, and yet the number of skrayling ships coming to London continues to decline."

Coby bit her lip, wanting to interject but knowing her comments would not be welcome. Arrests and executions? No wonder the skraylings were unhappy, even if it was not their own people being punished. She knew what it was like to be a stranger in London, only grudgingly accepted for the work she could do. They must be wondering when the Queen's anger would turn against them instead of her own people.

"Then you will bring this matter before the Privy Council, sir?" Mal said.

Walsingham smiled ruefully. "Alas, I am in no condition to attend the council, nor am I like to be. Besides, we – or perhaps I should say, they – are not due to meet again until after Easter, and by then it may be too late."

"Then what are we to do?"

Walsingham waved a trembling hand at his daughter. "Letters of introduction, my dear, for Master Catlyn. One to Sir Walter Raleigh, and one to Sir Geoffrey Berowne. The usual cipher for the latter, in case the Venetians try to intercept it."

Lady Frances put down her sewing and went to the desk by the window.

"You look surprised, Catlyn," Walsingham said.

"All London wondered why she did not marry the Earl of Essex," Mal said in a low voice. "Has she been working for you all this time?"

"They say women's tongues are loose and prone to gossip; where better, then, to place an informant than amongst the women at court? Essex would have had her with child and packed off to his country estate for the good of her health. I needed her here."

"An obedient woman is prized above rubies," Mal said.

Coby wondered if the comment was directed at herself. She stared at the floor, her jaw tightening. He was her employer, and she owed him obedience, she knew that. Would he now expect her to follow Lady Frances's example? Resuming female garb was one thing, but how was she to converse with other women and learn their secrets, when she had spent the past seven years trying to forget her sex and pass as a boy?

"Raleigh is one of yours also?" Mal asked.

"Not precisely," Walsingham said. "But he seeks to win his way back into favour with the Queen, so he is grateful for any service he can do her."

"And Berowne?"

"He is Her Majesty's ambassador to Venice. A dull fellow, but until now we have had no need of anyone better."

"You want me to go to Venice, sir?"

"You are the trusted friend of the former ambassador of Vinland. You must find out if the skraylings have made any trade agreements with the Venetians, and if so, to what end."

"Yes, sir." Mal paused, and exchanged glances at Coby, who nodded encouragement. "Sir… in France I made good use of local men, those dissatisfied with their king or simply out for themselves. A little money for bribes would not go amiss..."

"I... strongly advise against it," the spymaster wheezed. "The Venetians are proud of their loyalty to their republic, and do not take kindly to dissent." He paused for a sip of wine. "Keep a civil tongue in your head when you are there. God knows I have been ruthless in dealing with those who speak out against Her Majesty, but I learnt by the Venetians' example."

"You have been to Venice, sir?"

Walsingham shook his head. "Only as far as Padua. I studied at the university there."

"Padua belongs to the Republic."

"Yes."

"Then you can teach me all I need to know," Mal said, leaning closer.

Walsingham slumped back against his pillows and his eyes closed.

"I think you have wearied my father more than enough," Lady Frances said. She got to her feet and crossed to her father's bedside where she stood like an angel at the gates of Eden, arms folded and eyes narrowed as if daring them to challenge her authority. "Come back tomorrow, Master Catlyn, and you shall have your letters."

Walsingham stirred. "One more word, my dear, before they go."

He beckoned to Mal, who leant over whilst Walsingham whispered in his ear. Coby strained to hear what they were saying, but the old man's voice was too faint. Mal nodded several times, then straightened up.

Lady Frances showed them out of the house herself, summoning a servant to return their cloaks. As Mal crossed the threshold, he ventured one last question.

"It would be helpful to my mission to learn as much of Venice as I can. Perhaps Lord Brooke–"

"Alas, Brooke is no longer with us," Lady Frances replied. "An ague took him, the winter before this."

"A pity."

Lady Frances inclined her head in mute agreement, and closed the door.

"Lord Brooke?" Coby asked as they walked away.

"The former ambassador to Venice; he was with Effingham's party, that day you came to the Rose to find me. I thought he might have some useful insights into Venetian politics."

"We shall have to make do with our own wits, then," she replied with a grin.

"Aye." He smiled back, and pulled up his hood against the cold. "Come, let's take a wherry back to Southwark. It'll be curfew soon, and I don't want to get caught on the wrong side of the city gates."

They made their way to the docks where a few wherries still lingered, hoping to make a last penny or two at the end of the day. The snow had abated, but it was even colder out on the river than in the city streets, and they huddled shoulder to shoulder for the crossing. At last the wherry bumped up against Battle Stairs and Coby scrambled up the ice-slick steps, groping for the rail with reddened, nerveless fingers. As they emerged into St Olave's Street, she gave vent to the irritation that had been gnawing at her all the way from Seething Lane.

"Why Raleigh, of all people?" she asked of the night air. "That pompous, arrogant, narrow-minded... heretic!"

"You don't approve of our captain?"

"No I do not."

"But he's one of the heroes of the age," Mal said. "He's been to the New World and back, quelled the Irish, fought the Spanish–"

"Hero of the age indeed! He's naught but a pirate with charming manners."

A trio of drunken tanners staggered across the street towards them, the stink of their trade unmistakable even in the chill air. Mal threw back his cloak to reveal the hilt of his rapier and they backed off, swearing.

"What reason have you to dislike him so?" Mal said, when the tanners were out of earshot.

She sighed. "Perhaps you don't remember. No reason you would, it wouldn't have mattered to you."

"What wouldn't?"

"About three years ago, before we met, Raleigh was very active in Parliament. He's a member for Devon, you know."

"So?"

"So there was a motion to grant wider privileges to the immigrant communities in London. My people were overjoyed to be accepted at last, to have the same opportunities as native-born merchants and craftsmen, to be able to own their workshops and join the city guilds. Little things, perhaps, but they meant a lot to us." She drew a deep breath. "Raleigh spoke against the bill."

"Oh."

"It did him no good, of course. Parliament was united in favour. But it made Raleigh's name a byword for prejudice in our community. He hates the Dutch, the Jews, everyone who is not English."

"And the skraylings?"

She shrugged. "I cannot suppose him to be a friend of the skraylings, for all his travels in their country."

"Why did you not mention this to Walsingham?"

"We need to get to Venice, don't we? My dislike of Raleigh is neither here nor there."

"But you think we should keep an eye on him."

"I think we would be fools not to."

She quickened her pace. If only Mal had not had that ill-fated dream, they would be back home in Provence now, snug in their respective chambers. Not running around

Southwark in the cold and the dark, and certainly not chasing skraylings to the far side of Christendom.

CHAPTER V

The next morning, Ned was surprised to be asked to ride out to Hampton Court with Mal.

"Not taking Hendricks with you?" he asked as they set out for the livery stables.

"He's taken against Raleigh," Mal said, "and I want to give a good first impression. It's a long voyage to Venice."

"You're too soft on the boy." He glanced at Mal sidelong. "Always were."

Mal said nothing, but his jaw tightened in that way Ned knew so well. The conversation was at an end, for now at least.

The snow flurries of the previous night had given way to a crisp, clear morning, every fencepost, roof-tile and blade of grass limned with frost. Bankside stood silent, its inhabitants huddled in the warmth of their beds. Ned envied them, and cursed Hendricks silently. If not for the boy's sulks, he could have stayed snug in his own bed, at least until Gabriel had to leave for the playhouse.

At the livery stables Mal chose a bay gelding for himself and the most placid pony they could find for Ned, who still wasn't used to riding. It was occasionally useful in his work, though, so he had had to learn. Truth was, he'd had to learn a lot of new skills in the last year.

There had been a time when he resented playing the servant, tagging along at Mal's heels and deferring to him in public. But Baines had taught him the importance of invisibility. No one paid attention to servants, so they could eavesdrop on their betters in places other men could not go without comment, and pass unnoticed even in the halls of power. And he was curious to see the palace Gabriel had told him so much about. Ned tried to keep his jealousy in check, for fear it would only make matters worse, but it gnawed at him to think of his lover surrounded by rich powerful men who expected everyone to pander to their needs without question. How many of the men they were about to meet had bedded his precious boy? His hands tightened on the reins, and the pony shook its head in protest.

Mal looked back at the sound.

"Not giving you trouble, is she?"

Ned shook his head and forced a smile.

They came within sight of the sprawling red brick palace just before noon, skirting round the north side of the royal park to approach the enormous gatehouse from the west. Ned dismounted awkwardly, stiff with cold and more than a little sore in the seat.

"Raleigh had better have a roaring fire and a jack of mulled ale waiting for us," he said as they walked towards the gates.

"This is a royal palace, not the Bull's Head. Now mind your manners."

The porter asked their names and business, and Mal showed him his letter of introduction. After glancing at the address the porter turned it over and raised an eyebrow at Walsingham's seal, then jotted something down in a ledger. Ned tried to read the list upside down, but could not get close enough for a good look.

"Dinner is in an hour, sir," the porter said, handing the

letter back. "Across the courtyard, take the staircase on the left under the archway."

"I'd like to see Sir Walter first," Mal replied. "It is somewhat urgent."

"I'm afraid Sir Walter rode out to Syon House this morning."

"Will he be back?"

"Aye, like as not. The steward might know for certain."

Their footsteps echoed from the surrounding walls as they crossed the courtyard. With the Prince of Wales and his court still in London the palace was largely deserted. A lone guardsman in royal livery stood in the far archway, his partisan planted solidly on the paving.

"I don't like the idea of my comings and goings being written down like that," Ned muttered, glancing back at the gatehouse. "I'm supposed to be the one watching people, not the other way round."

The guard looked Mal up and down then waved them both through. A staircase broad enough for several men to walk abreast led up to the Great Hall, where servants were laying trestle tables with snowy linens and bright pewter dishes. Ned tried not to gawp at the tapestries, twice the height of a man and woven in vivid hues of red, blue and gold, or at the elaborately carved hammer beam roof far above them.

"Let's not get in the servants' way," Mal said loudly.

He winked at Ned, and led the way towards a door on the far side of the hall. Unfortunately the next room was just as busy, with more servants coming up the back stairs from the kitchen with baskets of bread and jugs of ale. Ned resisted the urge to steal a piece of bread as they passed; the royal steward would probably have his hand cut off, or worse.

Beyond the service room lay a grand presence chamber, smaller than the great hall, but still resplendent with tapestries. A fire had been lit on the wide hearth, but the room was empty.

"Should we be in here?" Ned whispered.

"No one is stopping us, are they?" Mal said.

Ned paused to warm his arse at the fire, but Mal was intent on exploring further. With a sigh Ned followed him, and found himself in a gallery lined with portraits of the royal family: Queen Elizabeth and her late husband Robert, with the infant Prince of Wales; the prince as a youth in a magnificent suit of engraved and gilded armour; and a more recent portrait of his wife Juliana, surrounded by her four children. The youngest, hardly more than an infant, sat on her lap gazing out intently at the viewer.

"Is that–?"

Ned broke off at the sound of a girl's voice, raised in laughter.

"Back to the hall!" Mal hissed.

Too late. A wooden ball painted with red and blue stripes came bowling round the corner, followed by a child of about eighteen months old in an embroidered linen smock from which trailed leading strings of ivory silk ribbon. The child from the portrait.

"Harry! Come here!"

A dark-haired girl of about ten or eleven skittered along the polished floor, arms outstretched to catch the boy. She skidded to a halt upon seeing Mal and Ned and put a hand to her mouth. The little prince also paused and looked up at them. For a moment Ned thought he saw an expression of loathing cross the boy's chubby features, then Prince Henry burst into tears and buried his face in his sister's skirts.

Mal bowed.

"Forgive us for the intrusion, Your Highness."

Gesturing for Ned to do likewise he backed out of the gallery, head still bowed.

"What was all that about?" Ned asked when they were out of earshot.

"That… child is the creature who pretended to be Suffolk. His plan was to be reborn as Princess Juliana's child, and it appears he succeeded."

"You don't really believe that, do you?"

"I told you as much, after you and Hendricks helped me escape."

"Yes, well, as I recall, in the preceding two days you'd been abducted, tortured, drugged, shot, drugged again – I thought it the ramblings of a tormented mind."

Mal didn't seem to appreciate the jest.

"So…" Ned lowered his voice, "the Prince of Wales' son is a changeling?"

"I suppose you could put it that way," Mal replied.

"Shouldn't we tell someone?"

"Who would believe us? I've seen enough of the inside of the Tower for one lifetime, thank you."

Ned glanced back towards the entrance to the gallery. Either Mal was as insane as his brother, or he had fallen into a web of conspiracy that would put the most intricate Catholic plot to shame. He wasn't sure which alternative was the more terrifying.

After the encounter with Prince Henry Mal felt disinclined to explore further, so after dinner he and Ned lingered in the Great Hall over a flagon of beer and swapped tales of their doings since they had last seen one another. By 3 o'clock Raleigh had still not returned, however, and Mal began to grow restless. Any chance of getting back to London before dark was long gone, and though he had warned Sandy not to expect him until the morrow, it irked him to be idle for so long. He had almost decided to go down and ask the porter again when a page in royal livery approached them.

"M... Maliverny Catlyn?"

"I am he," Mal replied.

"I have been sent to invite you, sir, to take supper with Sir Walter Raleigh."

Mal bowed curtly, and turned to Ned.

"Speak to the steward about lodgings for the night, will you, Faulkner?" He gave his friend a wink which he hoped would be interpreted as "and see if you can get any interesting gossip out of the servants whilst you're at it."

"Aye, sir." Ned ducked his head in obeisance, but not before Mal had caught a glimpse of his sly grin.

He considered telling Ned not to get into trouble, but knew that would only have the opposite effect. Instead he turned away and followed the page through the palace to one of the private apartments off the main courtyard. Not for the first time he wondered what Raleigh was doing here, so far from the court. Was he in league with Jathekkil, perhaps even a guiser like the infant prince?

The page conducted him through an anteroom into a large bedchamber that doubled as a parlour. Firelight gleamed on linenfold panelling and on the rich brocades worn by the men gathered around the hearth, and the air was thick with the scent of tobacco.

"Maliverny Catlyn, sir," the page said with a bow.

Raleigh looked up. Dark eyes met Mal's own, narrowing in appraisal. Raleigh was about a decade older than himself and surprisingly handsome, with a broad brow and dark hair turning grey at the temples. His elegant pointed beard was likewise touched with silver, and he wore a pearl earring the size of a robin's egg. Only his wind-burned cheekbones hinted at a more active life than most courtiers. Mal sketched a bow.

"Sir Walter."

He handed over Walsingham's letter. Raleigh broke the

seal and scanned the contents, nodding to himself and frowning slightly in concentration. At last he looked up.

"So you're the hero who toppled the mighty house of Grey," he said in a soft Devonshire accent. He drew on his pipe and after a moment breathed a halo of smoke across the space between them. "I expected at least a Samson, if not a Hercules."

"Hardly toppled, sir. Brought to its knees, perhaps."

"A David, then." Raleigh laughed. "Come, join us. You will not find any Philistines here."

A servant pulled up a stool, and Mal seated himself on the edge of the company.

"I was just telling Harriot here 'twas time for a new venture," Raleigh said, gesturing to a plain-garbed man with receding hair seated on the opposite side of the fire. "And now Her Majesty wishes me to ferry you to Venice with all haste."

"Indeed."

"Venice?" Harriot leant forward, his eyes fixed on Mal. "Does Her Majesty seek to create a royal observatory?"

"An observatory?"

"I have certain theories regarding the use of glass–"

"Come now, Harriot," Raleigh said, "Catlyn is a man of action, not of science. He is not here to discuss optics and mathematics, are ye?"

"No, sir," Mal replied. "That is more my brother's realm of knowledge."

"Really? I should like to meet your brother," Harriot said.

Mal inclined his head politely. He already regretted mentioning Sandy. "I'm afraid neither of us will be in England long. The weather here is not good for my brother's health." He looked around the company for any sign of displeasure that might give away a guiser, but saw nothing untoward.

"So what are you here for?" a voice from the shadows drawled.

Mal turned towards his interrogator, a pale young man of eighteen or twenty whom he recognised with a start as Josceline Percy, younger brother of the Earl of Northumberland. Not that he should be surprised. Raleigh and Northumberland were as thick as thieves, so what was more natural than that the earl's brother should be of their fellowship?

"I'm afraid I'm not at liberty to say, my lord," Mal replied.

Percy got to his feet, eyes glittering in the firelight. Mal realised his own hand had gone to his rapier hilt. Last time he had run into Josceline Percy he had managed to avoid getting drawn into a duel; this time he might not be so lucky. He leant back on his stool, feigning to adjust the lie of the weapon in this confined space.

"Peace, boy," Raleigh said with easy familiarity. "Master Catlyn is my guest tonight."

Percy bowed curtly to his host and sat down, though his expression remained alert and disdainful.

"All I can say," Mal told the assembled company, "is that my mission is for the good of the realm."

"No loyal Englishman can have quarrel with that," Raleigh said.

There was a murmur of agreement, though Mal noticed that Percy's voice was not amongst the loudest. A sign of guilt, or was the boy canny enough not to be seen to be trying too hard?

"Still, a strange time of year to be undertaking a sea voyage," Percy said, picking up his wine cup and swirling the contents ostentatiously.

"Frobisher risked the North West Passage and returned safely," he said, matching Percy's casual tone. *I hope the arrogant little prick turns out to be a guiser, so I have an excuse to run him through.* "The journey to Venice will be a stroll in St James's Park in comparison."

"Frobisher's dead."

"Of a Spanish bullet, not by Poseidon's hand."

"Percy has a point. I would counsel against a winter voyage–" Raleigh held up his hand to forestall interruption by the younger man "–except in this case. The letter makes it clear that this mission is of the utmost urgency."

"Whose letter?" Percy held out his hand.

Raleigh pointedly threw the paper onto the fire and prodded it with a poker until it was burnt to fragile wafers of soot.

"As Catlyn says, he is not at liberty to reveal such information."

Mal inclined his head in thanks.

"I fear, sir," he said to Raleigh, "that others may be curious as to our purpose. Perhaps Master Harriot is right; we should put it about that you are on Her Majesty's business. We could even take Harriot along, to be our guide in matters optical."

The philosopher turned pale. "Oh goodness me, no. Please excuse me, my lords, I am no traveller. You should take Shawe here." He gestured to his companion, a thin-faced man with faraway eyes. "What say you, Shawe? Would you like to go to Venice?"

Shawe turned slowly towards Raleigh, as if only just awakened.

"I regret I cannot be spared so long."

"No, I suppose not," Raleigh said. "Northumberland keeping you busy, eh?"

"Just so."

Mal offered up a silent prayer of thanks. Neither Harriot nor Shawe were the kind of men he wanted to be stuck on a ship with for weeks on end. One would likely never stop talking, and the other was about as cheery as a November afternoon.

"Well then, we must away with all dispatch," Raleigh

went on. "The *Falcon* has been berthed at Deptford these past months and wants only provisions to be ready to sail whither you will. Be there for the morning tide on the day after tomorrow, and I'll have ye in Venice by Easter."

The steward had assigned them lodgings on the north side of the palace, where the servants of the royal household lived when the court came to visit. The chamber was barely large enough to hold the vast, ancient bedstead, which must have been old in Wolsey's day. No doubt the Tudors had spurned it in favour of more modern furnishings, but such a grand edifice was too valuable to discard entirely.

"I suppose we'll be sharing, then," Ned said cheerily, leaning on a bedpost. "There's scarce room to use a piss-pot, never mind set out a cot bed."

Mal grunted an affirmative, stifling a belch. Raleigh's supper had been so generous, it was easy to forget there were food shortages back in London.

"Just like the old days," Ned went on. He pulled off his boots and threw himself down on the bed. "If only my old mam could see me now, sleeping on a feather bed in a royal palace…"

"Ahem."

"What?"

"You're supposed to be my manservant, remember?"

Ned stuck out his tongue.

"In public, perhaps." He propped himself up on one elbow and looked Mal up and down appreciatively. "Or would you like me to undress you… my lord?"

Mal gave him a withering look, turned his back and began unbuttoning his doublet.

"Did you discover aught useful?" he called over his shoulder.

"Not much. Plenty of gossip about Lady Dorothy; she and Northumberland do not get along, and there's some doubt as to whether they've even consummated the marriage yet."

"Servants' tittle-tattle, and naught to our purpose," Mal replied. "Go on."

Ned listed a few more rumours, none of them of any great interest. Mal finished undressing and crossed to the tiny washstand, where a number of toothsticks stood in a pewter beaker. He picked through them, looking for the least well-used one.

"Is that all?" he said, when Ned fell silent.

"Just one thing. Though it's probably nothing."

Mal turned back to the bed, toothsticks forgotten.

"Tell me."

"Walsingham's dying–"

"I know that already," Mal said, getting into bed. "Tell me something I don't know."

"So guess who's courting his daughter in secret."

"Who?"

"Blaise Grey. Duke of Suffolk, as he is now."

"What?" Mal stared at him. "But if Grey marries Lady Frances–"

"She'll be a duchess. It's a good match for her, especially as she's older than him."

"Is that all you can think about? If Grey marries her, he'll have access to all Walsingham's papers. He'll find out everything. The intelligence network, the ciphers… all our secret dealings, here and in France."

"It's only a rumour."

Mal stared up at the carved canopy. This was all he needed. Bad enough to lose his mentor, but to have his affairs put into the hands of the man who had tortured him and Sandy… and now he would be leaving England in two days, not to return for months. He muttered a string of curses, then blew out the candle and lay down with a sigh. There would be no sleep for him this night.

Walsingham kept asking him the same questions over and over. Why wouldn't he stop? He should know by now that Mal didn't have the answers. The questions didn't make sense anyway. Mal looked up, squinting; his eyes refused to focus, as if they did not want to see. No, not Walsingham. It was Grey in the spymaster's black robe and skullcap.

"I'm afraid this may be a little painful," Grey said, holding up an obsidian blade.

"No!"

He blinked, and his interrogator's features changed again, to the sallow complexion and hooded eyes of Josceline Percy.

"So what *are* you doing here?" Percy drawled. He gestured around them, and Mal realised they were no longer in Walsingham's study. They stood on a rutted track, hemmed in by drystone walls. Night was falling, or so Mal thought at first.

"What were you doing here, Erishen?" a voice whispered in his ear. "What did you find out?"

He spun around but there was no one there. The walls were gone too, leaving him exposed in a vast expanse of dark grass. Overhead the sky swirled in hues of pewter and lead as if a storm were brewing. This was not a dream any longer – or at least, not just a dream. This was the night realm of the skraylings, an almost-place beyond the waking world. When he had been here before, it had always been at the instigation of Kiiren or Erishen, but who was it this time?

Jathekkil.

He dared not say the name aloud, but even the thought of it sent ripples across the dreamscape.

"Not he," the whisper came again. "Did you think my *amayi* was alone?"

"Who are you?"

His invisible tormentor only laughed.

Ned woke with a cry as something hit him in the face. Mal's arm. He scrambled out of the way as his bedfellow thrashed in his sleep. The moon, not long past its full, streamed in through the narrow window to reveal Mal's twisted features.

"Who are you?"

The cry was loud enough to wake the household. Ned launched himself across the bed and clamped a hand over Mal's mouth. Mal struggled for a moment, then his eyes snapped open.

"Hush!" Ned tightened his grip as Mal writhed underneath him. The movement made him suddenly, inappropriately aware that only a layer of sweat-soaked linen separated their flesh, and he eased backwards a little. Now was not the time. "You were having a nightmare."

Mal nodded, and Ned cautiously removed his hand.

"Guisers," Mal hissed. "Here."

He looked around wildly, as if expecting to see them lurking in the shadows.

"It was just a bad dream," Ned said. He laid an arm across Mal's chest and squeezed his shoulder. "You're safe now."

Mal turned and caught Ned's gaze with his own. His eyes were wells of dark water, reflecting Ned's face back at him.

"I know what I saw," Mal said. "Trust me, they are here."

"All right, whatever you say. Now go back to sleep."

"No, I mustn't sleep. That's when they come for you."

Ned sighed. "Then we'll stay awake. Light the candle, and I'll get my cards." There were other ways to stay awake, but they usually made them both sleepier afterwards. Pity.

"You have your playing cards with you?" Mal asked.

"Of course. Never know when they'll come in handy. People talk a lot more freely when their minds are taken up with the game."

He scrambled past Mal and retrieved the pack of cards from the pocket of his slops.

"We'll play until it gets light, and then get out of here."

"Thank you," Mal said. "You're a true friend."

"You may change your mind before dawn. Now, what game shall we play?"

CHAPTER VI

When Mal did not return that night, Erishen feared the worst. Something was wrong, and it was all his fault; he should have not let his brother ride out to the prince's palace without protection. Jathekkil was too young to threaten them, but he must surely have an *amayi* to watch over him. Though the guisers flouted skrayling law and went against their people's deepest beliefs, some traditions could not be put aside so easily.

The girl Hendricks and Faulkner's lover tried to persuade him there was nothing amiss, it being usual for great men to keep supplicants waiting, but Erishen was uneasy nonetheless. He spent a restless night with the spirit-guard coiled around his wrist in half-hearted defence, wishing he dared venture into the dreamlands to search for Mal but fearing to attract the guisers' attention. The less their enemies knew of their whereabouts, the better.

By dawn he was ready to ride out to Hampton Court and damn the guisers, but he did not know the way and he doubted he could convince the others to accompany him. So he went up to the attic, where a front window gave him a good view of the street, and waited. Hendricks came looking for him after about an hour, saying breakfast was ready, but he waved her away and she left him to his vigil.

The church clocks had struck ten before he finally spotted a pair of men turning the corner into Deadman's Place. After a moment's hesitation to make sure it really was Mal and his friend, he ran down to the kitchen to greet them.

When Mal entered the kitchen, one look at his brother told him his report of the night's events would not be news. Sandy clutched the spirit-guard in one white-knuckled fist, but it was Erishen who looked out through his eyes.

"We knew there must be more guisers than Jathekkil in England," Sandy said as they sat down to a late breakfast. "You should have worn the earring that Kiiren gave you."

"A little late to remind me now." Mal warmed his hands on the bowl of barley gruel, but his appetite had fled.

"The hole looks half closed up, you've not worn anything in it so long." Coby said. "It needs re-piercing."

"Come then, you can do it for me now." He got to his feet. "Before I run afoul of the guisers a second time."

They left Sandy and Ned to finish their breakfast in mutually hostile silence, and went up to Mal's chamber. Whilst Coby sought the necessary equipment in her own room, he rummaged in his saddlebags until he found the velvet pouch, and shook out a baroque black pearl on a hoop of dark metal. The hoop was made of the same stuff as the skraylings' spirit-guards, and he wondered for a moment why they did not wear such things themselves. Come to think of it, he had not seen a skrayling with piercings of any kind, for all their love of tattoos. Perhaps they saw it as a human fashion.

Coby poked her head through the open door. "I'm ready. Come in here, the light is better."

Mal slipped the earring back into its pouch and went through into her chamber, feeling oddly self-conscious.

Coby dragged a short bench over to the window and laid out a bodkin, some scraps of clean linen and a small bottle.

"Before we begin, I have a favour to ask." He paused, hands in pockets, his eyes alighting anywhere but her face. "I need you to take Sandy back to Provence, as soon as the weather is good enough for travel. It's not safe for him here with so many guisers around."

Her eager smile faded. "But... I thought we were going to Venice."

"I am still going. I've decided to take Ned in your place; he might be glad to widen his horizons."

"Ned? Is that wise?"

"He made one foolish mistake, and that only when threatened with harm to those he loved most."

"So with his mother dead and Master Parrish safe here in London, you think him trustworthy enough."

"That was unkind, and unworthy."

"Sorry, sir. I hope you're right." She ducked her head in contrition. "How... How long will you be gone?"

"All summer, I suppose. It's a good month's sailing to Venice and the same back, and I know not how long in between to discover what the skraylings have agreed with the Venetians."

She stared down at her bitten nails.

"There is more that I would have you do before you leave England," Mal said. He told her of the rumour about Blaise Grey and Lady Frances Sidney. "We must know if it is true. If Grey were to take up the reins of Walsingham's network after his death, that would make him our master."

"We could refuse to take his orders," she replied.

"And risk being accused of treason?" He shook his head. "I fear we are mired too deep in Walsingham's intrigues to escape so easily."

"We could give up this mission to Venice altogether, return to France and never come to England again."

Mal sighed. "It may yet come to that. But while Walsingham lives, we must do his bidding. I owe him my life."

"How am I to discover the truth of this rumour?" Coby asked. "Grey will not tell me, I am sure of it."

"You must speak to Lady Frances, woman to woman."

"But..." She folded her arms and frowned at him. "This is some ruse to get me back into women's clothing, isn't it?"

"No, I swear. But this is too important not to try every approach at our disposal."

She drew a deep breath. "Very well, I shall consider it."

"You will?" He wished he could be there to see the attempt. He had always wondered what she would look like in proper clothing.

"As a last resort. Now, come, let me deal with this earring."

She motioned him to the bench, then perched next to him. Taking hold of his earlobe, she pushed the blunt needle through the piercing.

"Owww!"

"Big baby. What must you have been like on the battlefield, if you complain at such a tiny scratch?"

Before he could reply, she swabbed the wound with *ashaarr*. He gritted his teeth as the pungent fluid seared his flesh, bringing back the memory of Grey's voice in his ear, asking the same questions over and over. Sweet Jesu, it had been more than a year; he should be over it by now, not shivering like a whipped cur at the very thought. He slipped his arm around Coby's waist and leant his head against hers. She froze, but did not pull away, and the blood stirred in his veins at the memory of their first and only kiss, half an age ago or more.

"I need to put the earring in, sir," she said after a few moments.

He gave her the pendant. The touch of her fingers on his were sweet torture.

"Hold still," she muttered. "It's bleeding again."

"Good. Blood on iron–" he gasped as the hoop caught on raw flesh "–breaks any enchantment."

When she was done, he turned his head slightly so that their eyes met. His arm was still around her, though she was as tense as a deer poised for flight.

"How do I look?" he asked.

"As handsome a rascal as ever," she said, the quaver in her voice belying her bold comment.

He leant in to kiss her, but she wriggled out of his grasp and went to stand by the door, hugging herself and not looking at him.

"I can't," she whispered. "We can't."

"Why not?"

He crossed the room and took her in his arms again. She rested her head against his chest, but would relent no further.

"You know why," she whispered.

"We are not in France any more," he said, trying to keep the anger out his voice. "We are among friends. Who is there to betray us?"

She muttered something into his doublet, but he could not make out the words.

"Please, Jacomina. I am going far away and… and I cannot be sure of coming safely back to you."

"Don't say that."

He bent and kissed her brow. "You know it for the truth."

She looked up at him and a moment later they were kissing, though he was not aware of having moved. Desire for her threatened to overwhelm him but he reined it in, unwilling to spoil this moment. It was enough to hold her, feel her lips warm and soft against his own.

How long they stood there lost in anguished pleasure, whether moments, hours or days, he could not say. Releasing her was the second hardest thing he had ever done, after giving Sandy into Kiiren's care. For a moment his resolve wavered. All he had to do was change his mind, take both her and Sandy on Raleigh's ship as far as Marseille... but he had to know the truth about Grey. Otherwise he could be coming home to worse than guisers.

After supper that evening Coby boiled some water and took a cupful upstairs to her room. From the chest at the foot of her bed she brought out a pouch of coarse cotton and sprinkled a generous pinch of dried herbs into the hot water. The skraylings called it "desert fire" and sold it to women who wanted to avoid conceiving a child – and those like Coby who wished to stop their monthly flow altogether.

When the herbs had steeped long enough she dragged the bench over to the chimney breast that took up most of the back wall, sat down and leaned back against the warm bricks. Cupping her hands around her drink, she breathed in the steam. At first she had found the taste unpleasant, but brewing it had become a treasured ritual, a quiet moment in many a hectic day.

Tranquility evaded her tonight, however. All she could think about was this morning: the pleasure of that kiss, and the pain of knowing she would not see Mal again for months. *Go to him tonight,* a voice seemed to whisper in her ear, *lie with him. You may never get another chance.*

"Satan, I abjure thee," she breathed into her cup. "I will not lie with him until he marries me."

She laughed bitterly at herself. Small chance of that, unless she were to put aside her disguise for good. And what then? Would she have to be the dutiful wife, staying at home to cook and sew and raise his children? She thought again of Lady Frances Sidney, who had refused an earl in order to serve her queen – but would she refuse a duke, especially one with ambitions to continue her father's work? Perhaps, if he forbade her to continue with her spying.

Coby put the cup down and began to pace the floor. Lady Frances could prove a valuable ally, could perhaps even teach her how to behave in a more womanly manner. There was only one thing for it. She would visit Goody Watson on the morrow and buy a gown for herself. No, not tomorrow. She would wait until Mal left for Venice, the better to surprise him on his return.

Sandy slept more soundly that night, knowing both he and Mal were safe from the guisers. In the morning he delayed longer than usual before removing the spirit-guard; he wanted to say farewell to his brother in his right mind, not through the mist of skrayling memories that filled his thoughts during daylight hours.

By the time he had reached this decision, Mal was out of bed and sorting through the chest at its foot.

"What are you doing?" Sandy asked, throwing back the covers.

"What do you think?" Mal pulled out a pile of underlinens and began sorting through them. "Why does the laundress never send stockings back in matching pairs? I swear there's another man out there with an identical set of odd ones."

"There's something we need to talk about."

"Oh?" Mal looked up, then appeared to notice his brother was still wearing the spirit-guard. He closed the lid and came to sit on the bed. "What is it? Nothing's wrong, I hope?"

"No." Sandy shook his head. "At least, not yet."

He tried to find the words. Erishen would be able to explain it better, but Erishen might not put it right.

"It's... this voyage," he said at last. "It's dangerous, isn't it?"

"All sea voyages are dangerous. But yes. I'm going a long way away, to a far-off land where I have few friends."

"So you might not come back. You might… die."

"Yes."

Sandy nodded. "Erishen doesn't like that."

"Well, neither do I."

"You don't understand. Erishen wants to be reborn as a skrayling. He… I am not sure he can do it, if we die apart. If your half of our soul is lost."

"If I die wearing this earring, you mean. My soul bound in iron, like those skraylings we found."

"Yes."

"And if I do not? Will I have to face the devourers?"

Sandy looked away. He had no answer for his brother.

"It seems to me," Mal said slowly, "that Erishen is doomed either way."

"I know," Sandy whispered.

Mal put an arm around his shoulder.

"We are no worse off than we ever were. Far better, in fact. If you had died in Bedlam in shackles, Erishen would have been destroyed for certain. Now, at least he has a chance. And I have no intention of dying in Venice, or anywhere else. Not yet."

Sandy hugged him, blinking back tears. "I believe you, brother."

He reached behind his neck, unfastened the spirit-guard and let it fall into his lap. The world shifted, the ordinary surroundings of the bedchamber now unfamiliar, the man before him too pale of skin and dark of eye.

"Erishen?" Mal said softly.

"Our fate is in your hands, *rehi*. Do not fail us."

It was a mere four miles from Southwark to Deptford, a pleasant enough walk on a bright spring afternoon. Mal strolled along the Kent Road, eager to be off at last despite his dislike of travelling by sea. Coby walked at his side, uncharacteristically silent, whilst Sandy trailed just behind them, stopping to examine every new sight by the way. Ned and Parrish brought up the rear.

"This reminds me of being on tour with Suffolk's Men," the actor said. "Though 'tis far more pleasant."

"Aye," Coby said, emerging from her reverie. "No heaving the wagon out of potholes every half-mile, nor walking all day only to sleep in a barn at the end of it."

"With Naismith's snoring to keep us all awake. May God rest his soul."

Coby fell silent again. Mal knew the girl blamed herself for Naismith's death, even though it had been the work of anti-skrayling seditionists. He draped a companionable arm around her shoulder. She looked up at him with tired grey eyes and seemed about to say something, but evidently thought better of it.

As they passed Deptford Strand, Ned pointed to a handsome timber-framed house backing onto the river.

"Isn't that where Marlowe was murdered?"

Mal halted, curious. So this was where his fellow intelligencer had met his end. Hardly the low tavern of popular rumour, it looked to be a respectable establishment, a rooming-house or perhaps a private ordinary where a gentleman of modest means could hold a dinner for his friends. Or his enemies.

"Something wrong, sir?" Coby asked as they set off again.

"Just this chill morning air. I've become too used to the warmth of Provence."

Beyond the Strand lay the King's Yard, where the navy berthed its ships. A forest of masts, bare as winter trees or laden with snowy sails, showed above the warehouses and boat-sheds of the dockyard. Mal wondered if the *Ark Royal* was still there, a sleeping giant waiting out the spring gales before venturing back into the Atlantic. He did not relish the thought of sailing on such a large vessel. Even on his short dock-bound visit with Ambassador Kiiren, the navy's flagship had rolled disconcertingly in the river swell. He didn't like to think of what it would be like at sea.

The *Falcon* rode at anchor in the mouth of Deptford Creek, a short way further downriver. The galleon was not so large as the *Ark Royal*, but its clean lines spoke of greater speed and manoeuvrability. Mal counted eight gun ports along the near side, in addition to the smaller swivel-guns on poop deck and fo'c's'le. Creamy white sails flapped lazily in the rising wind, ropes rattling against the canvas.

He caught Ned eyeing the vessel nervously.

"You've seen plenty of ships before, surely?" he said.

"Aye, but I never stepped aboard one in my life."

"Lucky you," Mal muttered, hoisting his knapsack higher onto his shoulder.

He left Ned to bid his farewells to Parrish, and turned to Coby, but there was nothing to say that they had not said already. The girl stood with hands clasped behind her back, her mouth tight with emotion. Sandy stepped into the awkward silence.

"Tell my *amayi* I long to see him again," he said to Mal.

"I shall," Mal replied, and embraced him. "Take care of my… companion."

"Ah, Catlyn!" Raleigh was striding along the riverside towards them, but came to an abrupt halt as Sandy turned to face him. "Two of ye? The letter said naught about that."

"I came only to bid my brother farewell," Sandy put in before Mal could explain. He bowed. "Alexander Catlyn, at your service, sir."

Raleigh returned the courtesy. "Your brother says you are a mathematician."

"It interests me, yes. Though I am no expert."

"You must call by Durham House and introduce yourself. My friend Thomas Harriot would be glad of another man of learning to talk to." He turned to Mal. "Well, we must be away, sirs. Time and tide wait for no man."

Mal beckoned to Ned, who was deep in conversation with Parrish. The lovers embraced and exchanged discreet kisses, then Ned picked up his knapsack. Mal said farewell to Sandy, then there was only time to clasp hands with Coby and kiss her on the cheek before Raleigh pressed them once more to join him in the skiff that would take them out to the *Falcon*.

They climbed into the boat, though there was scarce room aboard for three men in addition to the rowers. Ned perched on a barrel of salt beef whilst Mal tried to make himself comfortable on a sack that crunched slightly as he shifted on it.

"Chunny," Raleigh said, indicating the sack. "Keeps better than ship's biscuit, or so I'm told."

"Dried potato?" Mal peered down at the sack. A wooden plaque carved with a distinctly skrayling emblem had been tied to the string around its neck.

"You know of it?"

"I accompanied the Ambassador of Vinland to a meeting with the guild-masters once," he said with a grimace. Soldiery could be dull, but listening to merchants' discussions was enough to send any man to sleep at his post.

"I'm trying it out in the hope of using it on my next long voyage. I've begun growing potatoes on my own estates in Ireland, but the drying of it is an art my tenants are still mastering, so I've had to buy this lot from the skraylings."

"Since they are already experts in the craft, would it not be easier to leave it to them?" Mal asked.

Raleigh smiled. "And give them all the profit on't? Certainly not."

A few minutes later the skiff bumped against the hull

of the *Falcon* and they climbed the rope ladder to the rail. The sailors paused in their work to touch their woollen caps in acknowledgement of Raleigh's arrival. Mal noticed a few of them surreptitiously studying him and Ned when they thought the captain wasn't looking.

Raleigh showed them into the poop, a long narrow cabin with a ceiling barely high enough for Mal to stand upright without scraping his scalp on the planks of the deck above. A row of bunks were built into each side of the cabin under small arched windows, and the rest of the space was taken up by a great table and benches.

"My officers of marines sleep here in times of war," Raleigh said. "You and your man may make free with it."

He disappeared through a door at the far end, which Mal guessed led to the captain's cabin.

The bunks' sides were built high enough to stop a man falling out as the ship rolled. Two had bedding piled on them: sheets, thin blankets and a bolster, all stained with long use. Mal unstrapped his rapier and stowed it between the mattress and the ship's side, where it wouldn't roll around, then set about exploring the confines of their new lodgings. There wasn't much to inventory: a small locker beneath each bunk, a barrel of what looked to be wine, several lamps hanging from hooks and a storage chest full of pewter tableware.

"This isn't so bad," Ned said, looking around. "You told me ships were wretched places."

"They are, for the most part. The rest of the crew will be crammed cheek-by-jowl belowdecks, sleeping in hammocks and breathing the stink of the bilges."

"What are hammocks?"

"I'll explain later. Come, let's go out on deck and wave farewell to our friends."

"Tide's turning, captain!" one of the sailors called out as they emerged from the cabin.

"Raise the anchor, Master Warburton!" Raleigh called up to the poop deck. "All hands, prepare to make sail!"

Canvas tumbled down from the yardarms and caught the wind, and the ship began to move downstream. Mal stood at the frost-rimed stern rail, watching Deptford shrink slowly into the distance. Before they were more than a hundred yards from the creek he saw Sandy put an arm around Coby's shoulder, and for a moment it was as if he was seeing himself, watching his old life recede into memory. He shivered, and not just from the cold. The two figures on the shore were the most dear to him in all the world; what if he never saw either of them again?

CHAPTER VII

Coby hardly slept that night, so sick she was with fear of what might happen to Mal. A storm could pound Raleigh's ship onto the cruel rocks of the Normandy coast, or blow them westwards into the endless ocean. Barbary corsairs could capture them and sell them into slavery. She tried to cheer herself up by imagining leading a rescue party, but it was one thing to venture into Middlesex, barely a dozen miles from home, and quite another to brave two thousand miles of ocean and the unknown perils of Moorish Africa.

When dawn finally came, she gave up on sleep and took herself down to the kitchen, though she had little stomach for breakfast. She hoped Sandy would find some occupation around the house today so that she could get on with her mission. Mal had left her plenty of money for the journey back to Provence, so she easily had enough for a secondhand gown plus some new linen to make head-coverings. Sandy however had other plans. As soon as they had eaten, he put on his cloak and hat and strode out of the back door without a word.

"Where are you going?" The cinder path crunched under her feet as she hurried after him with her own hastily snatched-up cloak over her arm.

"I wish to see London," Sandy replied.

He paused to open the garden gate, giving her a chance to catch up with him.

"All right, but I'm coming with you." Mal would never forgive her if Sandy got lost or hurt.

They walked side by side towards London Bridge, their breath frosting in the air.

"You have been to Whitehall Palace?" he asked, as they passed the church of St Mary Overie.

"Once or twice," she replied, instantly wary.

"Then you can take me there?"

"Why do you want to go to the palace?"

He smiled down at her. "To see an old friend."

"Very well." They were almost at the bridge, so they might as well go that way and save on the wherry fare.

As they walked, Coby racked her memory. Whom at Court could Sandy possibly call a friend? Until he had been abducted by Suffolk's hirelings, he had been locked up in Bedlam, for several years at least. Before that... Mal had said he was too ill to attend university, so he couldn't have made friends that way. And after they rescued him from Suffolk, he went straight into Ambassador Kiiren's care. The only Englishmen he had met outside Bedlam were his captors: the late duke, his henchmen, and... oh no.

She halted abruptly, earning muttered curses from other pedestrians. Sandy walked on a few more paces before realising he had left her behind.

"What is it?" he asked.

"You're going to see Blaise Grey?"

"Yes."

"But... His father wanted to kill you. And he tortured your brother."

Sandy's expression hardened. "He knows a great deal more than he guesses. I have need of that knowledge."

He set off again down the Strand.

"What knowledge?" Coby asked, catching up with him.

"Knowledge I have sought for many years. Or so I hope."

Coby did not enquire further. It was bad enough when Mal spoke of dreams and portents, but his brother acted as though being possessed by a skrayling was the most normal thing in the world. They walked in silence the rest of the way, giving Coby plenty of time to mull over all the unpleasant possibilities ahead of them. She prayed their quarry would be away from Court, preferably far, far away where even a madman would not seek him out. Having inherited his father's considerable estates, the young duke could be anywhere in the kingdom.

As they approached the eastern gate of the palace, Sandy murmured, "I think it would be wise for me to pretend to be my brother, at least until we find Grey."

"And if I refuse to go along with this charade?" she replied in the same quiet tone. "I am his servant, not yours."

"Do as you wish. But I am going to the palace."

She sighed and fell into step at his heels, slipping into the familiar role of silent, unregarded manservant. Sandy gave their names and business at the gate, and they were waved through by a guard.

"Where now?" Sandy asked.

"I don't know," she replied. "Mal sometimes reported to Sir Francis Walsingham at his office, but that's the last place you want to go if you don't wish to be caught masquerading. Ask a porter."

To her dismay they were told that the duke was indeed present at Court, though he was at a meeting of the Privy Council all day.

"Then we shall wait," Sandy said.

"All day?"

"You have something else to do?"

She considered telling him about her mission, but decided that the less he knew, the better. The thought of wearing women's clothes again, of going out in the streets to visit Lady Frances, terrified her enough; facing her friends in such garb was a prospect that turned her bowels to water.

"I hear there are bowling alleys," she said. "We could go and watch a game for a while."

Sandy agreed, and they headed into the maze of palace buildings. More than the game itself, such a gathering was a good place to observe the undercurrents of court politics. There might even be some more accurate intelligence to be gleaned regarding Lady Frances and the duke.

Their forward progress was interrupted, however, by a great mass of people crowding the hall they were trying to cross. Coby was all for back-tracking and finding another route, but then a trumpet sounded and cries of "Make way for His Royal Highness the Prince of Wales" rang out. The crowd parted, the nearer half pushing Coby and Sandy back towards the wall, where they were trapped in an alcove against a suit of rusting armour. Coby could see little over the heads of the crowd, so she boosted herself upwards using the plinth of the armour-stand and the nearby wall.

The prince strode through the crowd, face dark as a thundercloud. Petitioners clutched their papers to their chests as he passed, but even the most desperate had more sense than to importune his future monarch in such a mood. A few moments later the councillors emerged from the chamber in twos and threes. Coby recognised the Earl of Essex, and that short, almost hunchbacked figure with him must be Robert Cecil, the Queen's private secretary. Unlike the rest of the council, the two men looked rather pleased.

The crowd began to disperse, some trailing after the Privy Councillors, the rest resuming whatever business had been interrupted by the prince's passage. As Coby stepped down from her vantage point, she saw an all-too-familiar figure leaving the council chamber.

Blaise Grey was a good four inches taller even than Mal, though he stooped a little these days, leaning on a silver-topped cane that rapped on the tiles in counterpoint to his footsteps. He resembled his father more than ever, though his curly hair was a lighter shade of honey brown. Coby froze. Last time she had brought news to Grey, he had struck her and then apologised for his burst of temper. A man of such mercurial, choleric humour as Grey needed treating with caution.

"Catlyn." Grey looked Sandy up and down. "I thought you'd sailed with Raleigh?"

Before Sandy could reply Coby stepped forward, scarcely believing her own temerity.

"A rumour put about to confound our enemies, Your Grace," she said. "Master Catlyn has far more important business in England."

"And you." Grey glared at her. "You are the ungrateful whelp who nearly got my father killed."

"N… no, Your Grace. It was the work of Huntsmen sympathisers. The man responsible was caught and hanged."

At the mention of Huntsmen, Grey's expression changed. "What do you know of the Huntsmen?"

"More than you, I think," Sandy said. "And I am willing to help you, if you will help me."

Grey gave a short laugh. "Why should I believe you, when you would not speak under duress?"

"I had nothing to gain then. Would you have spared me if I had told you?" When Grey made no answer, he went on. "I can translate your father's notes."

"What do you mean?"

"My… That is, I saw you with certain papers, covered in skrayling writings."

Coby breathed a sigh of relief. She thought Sandy was about to bring up her own role in all this; she had no desire to attract Grey's wrath a second time.

"They were written in Aiyalura," Sandy went on, "an ancient tongue of the skraylings."

"What nonsense. They look nothing like any skrayling writings I have seen."

"That is because you have only seen Vinlandic. Does the script of the Moors resemble that of the Christians?"

Grey considered, tapping one finger on the silver head of his cane.

"You seem very knowledgeable about these foreigners and their outlandish tongues, Catlyn. Anyone would think you had been working with them all along. Is that why Leland appointed you?"

"Do you want my help or not?"

"Why should I trust you? You could claim it says whatever you please, and I would be none the wiser."

"Very true. But since you do not go forward with it yourself, you will be no worse off than before."

The duke's eyes flicked towards Coby, then back to Sandy.

"Come to Suffolk House after 4 o'clock." He turned on his heel and limped away before either of them could frame a reply.

"What are we going to tell Mal?" Coby muttered as they walked back through the corridors of Whitehall Palace. "He'll have apoplexy when he learns you've made a deal with his mortal enemy."

"My brother is not here to find out – and you will not tell him. Ever. Now, let us enjoy the rest of the day. I still have a mind to see the city."

Their tour did not take as long as Coby feared, since the theatres were closed until Easter and Sandy had no interest in the hangings, bear-baitings or other bloodthirsty entertainments enjoyed by most Londoners. She left him at the skrayling guild-house trading news with Kiiren's kinfolk whilst she slipped away on her own errands, then when the clocks tolled four they set off for Suffolk House together.

They were admitted immediately and led through the main courtyard to a suite of rooms on the upper floor. Coby stood in the middle of the antechamber, making a swift inventory of possible exits and weapons, whilst Sandy drifted over to a cabinet where fine china and silverware were on display. The apartment was not so grand as the reception chamber Coby had seen on a previous visit, but nonetheless designed to show off its owner's wealth and taste.

A few minutes later Grey himself appeared, bearing a small book bound in red leather. Coby recognised it as the one he had been perusing when she went to Ferrymead House to rescue Mal. Sandy accepted it graciously and began flicking through the pages, his brow creased slightly as he read. If it had been Mal, Coby would immediately have guessed there was something wrong. She was careful to keep her own expression blank, however. After a moment he looked up.

"This is in a very old dialect," he said to Grey. "It may take me a few days to translate it properly."

Grey nodded curtly. "Very well. But do not think to cozen me; I expect results by the end of the week."

Sandy returned the book to its owner, and they made their obeisances and left.

"Is there something wrong?" Coby asked as they made their way back to Southwark.

"It is in a language I do not recognise," Sandy replied.

"What?" Coby halted, heart sinking. "You can't translate it?"

"I can transcribe it, and then perhaps someone else can be found to translate it."

"I don't understand."

"The document is written in the Aiyaluran script, but the language is not Aiyalura as I had thought. There are many languages in the New World, and I know only a few of them."

"And if we can't find anyone else who knows this tongue?"

Sandy shook his head. "There must be a solution. I did not come all this way for nothing."

Sewing a coif and hemming other pieces of linen for kerchiefs took Coby until well after nightfall, and she fell into her bed too exhausted to worry about the morrow. It was full light when she woke, and she dressed hurriedly and ran down to the kitchen, fearing that Sandy might have left without her. Instead he was stirring a pot of barley gruel over the fire and whistling a strange melody.

"You're cheerful this morning, sir."

Sandy put down his spoon and straightened up.

"Last night, whilst I slept, I remembered," he said. "I remembered where I had seen the language in the duke's book."

"Where?"

"It is Latin."

"Latin? But why Latin?"

"I think it is intended as a cipher; a cipher within a cipher, in fact." He passed her a sheet of paper, which she recognised as the copy of Grey's notes she had made from memory to show Mal. "Imagine for a moment that you are a scholar well-versed in Latin. What would you make of that?"

"It's nonsense," she said. "Just squiggles."

"Indeed. And whilst the 'squiggles', as you call them, mean something to me, the words do not."

"But you and Mal both went to school," she said. "Do you not remember your Latin?"

He took the sheet of paper back, looked at it, and sighed. "Kiiren could not heal me completely. I am… in two pieces. As I am now, I am Erishen, and can read this script, but not the language. And if I were to put on a spirit-guard again, I would forget how to read the script. Now do you see why it is a double cipher?"

"No one can read it," she said, with a shiver of excitement. "Not Christians, and not skraylings. Only guisers. If they've been to school, of course."

"Exactly. And being drawn to power, they will seek out any opportunity to gain knowledge. Latin is essential for any learned man, is it not?"

"So what do we do?"

"We will have to transcribe the original, of which this is but a crude imitation. I will read out the words to you, as best I can, and you will write them down."

"But I don't know Latin."

"Just do your best to represent the sounds in your English letters, and we will hope to make sense of them later."

"I'll try."

She made her way back upstairs, deep in thought. If they were to go back to Suffolk House, perhaps she could turn the situation to her own advantage. Grey might not be willing to confess to a liaison with Lady Frances, but there were other ways to glean intelligence. Time to put her skills to good use.

This time they were shown into a book-lined room on the ground floor of Suffolk House and Grey was not present, only a middle-aged man in dark blue servant's garb with a gilded unicorn badge on a chain about his neck. Coby's heart sank.

"Master Dunfell," she said, bowing. She turned to Sandy. *Please let him remember he's supposed to be Mal.* "Sir, I don't think you were introduced to the late duke's secretary, were you?"

"We met at the theatre," Dunfell said with a sniff. "Briefly."

To her relief Sandy inclined his head in acknowledgement and managed a polite bow.

Dunfell went over to the desk and opened an unlocked cupboard, from whence he took a sheaf of blank paper and some uncut quills. He set them down next to the enciphered book and fussed with the inkwells.

"His Grace instructed me to provide you with all the materials you may need," he said. "Dinner will also be provided, in the servants' hall. I will send someone to fetch you at 1 o'clock."

"Of course, sir," Coby said. "Thank you, sir."

Dunfell favoured her with a brief, icy look and left without another word.

"He doesn't like you," Sandy said.

"He asked me to spy on Mal, back when I worked at the theatre. I'm afraid I disappointed him." She picked up a quill and searched on the desk for a pen knife. "What are we going to do about the book, sir? Lord Grey expects a translation."

"We will make the true transliteration first," Sandy replied, "then if need be I will invent something to satisfy Grey."

It took them a good hour to transcribe the first page, by which time Coby's head was aching. This was more difficult than any cipher Mal had taught her.

"May we rest a while?" she asked Sandy, flexing her cramped hand. "I have business of my own here."

"Oh?"

"Your brother's business." It was enough of the truth for now. "Please, stand watch at the door, will you?"

"What are you doing?"

"You'll see. Just cough loudly if you see anyone coming, all right?"

She unbuttoned her breeches, ignoring Sandy's curious

gaze, and thrusting a hand into her drawers retrieved a small canvas roll about four inches long and an inch thick. She untied the cord holding it closed then with a practised flick of the wrist unrolled the bundle across the desk, revealing a set of miniature skeleton keys, perfect for opening desk drawers and other small locks. Smiling to herself she set to work.

The locks were old and of a simple design, but rather stiff. She cursed her ill luck in having no oil to ease the movement, but it would only leave telltale stains anyway. Instead she patiently probed the wards until she found a skeleton key that fitted, then twisted with all her might. After a few moments' grimacing and cursing, the key turned in the lock.

The desk drawers contained a number of letters addressed to the duke, but none in the same hand she had seen on the letters of introduction written by Lady Frances. If Grey were indeed pursuing the lady, either their negotiations had not reached the stage of exchanging love-letters, or he kept them somewhere more private than his library. An absence of evidence was not evidence of absence, Mal had often told her. Still, it eliminated one line of enquiry.

Just then the bell rang for dinner. Coby carefully rolled up her lock-picks and stowed them in her drawers, along with the folded sheet of transliteration. Best not to leave it lying around for inquisitive servants like Dunfell to find, or the game would be up.

After dinner they returned to the library and Coby retrieved the sheet of paper from her codpiece. Sandy took a beaded pouch from his pocket and shook the contents onto the table. It was the skrayling necklace that Mal had said protected him from the guisers as he slept. Sandy fastened it about his neck and drew a deep breath. His features softened, as if another soul looked out of his eyes. Not Erishen, but Alexander Catlyn once more. Her throat tightened in sympathy for Mal.

She swallowed and looked away, pretending a sudden interest in the contents of the bookshelves. Her mother had taught her to read and write – a useful skill for a tradesman's wife, and an essential one when Coby had worked in the theatre – but reading for pleasure was a luxury she had never picked up the taste for it. She drifted around the library, running her fingers over the leather bindings.

Sandy coughed. She looked round, but he had gone back to his reading. She made another circuit of the room. Another cough.

"Sorry, am I distracting you, sir?"

"Only a little."

She went and stood by the window. The library was positioned about halfway along the southernmost range of buildings, where its tall windows could catch the best of the daylight. From here she had a fine view of the gardens sloping down to the river, the palace of Whitehall and beyond that the delicate stonework of Westminster Abbey. Spring sunlight glittered on the water and warmed the panes of glass that separated her from the outside world. She watched the boats heading downstream towards the sea, and wondered where Mal was, and what he was doing. Being seasick, no doubt. She smiled to herself and tried to pretend it was only the dazzling light that made tears well in her eyes.

"No. Oh no no no no no." Sandy leapt to his feet and backed away from the desk as if the book were about to burst into flames. "No. Not that."

"What's wrong, sir?"

Sandy muttered something in a garbled mixture of English and Latin.

"Here, let me take that off," Coby said, remembering Mal's warning. "You've been wearing it far too long."

She thought he was going to fight her off, but he stood meekly and allowed her to remove the spirit-guard. Just in time she thought to pull up a chair as Sandy's knees gave way.

"Sir, are you ill?"

Sandy was as white as a sheet, and looked as though he was going to faint. Coby ran to the door and called for a servant.

"Quickly, fetch some wine! My master is unwell."

She returned to Sandy's side and hurriedly stowed the necklace in her pocket, then took his left hand in her own. His flesh was cold and unyielding as marble.

"I'm sorry, sir," she whispered, though it was not the man before her she was apologising to.

A few moments later the servant arrived with a flagon and a silver cup. The look he gave Coby as he left suggested he thought she might run off with it if not watched.

She filled the cup and held it out to Sandy. When he did not respond, she lifted it to his lips and urged him to drink. He took a sip, and then another.

"Erishen?"

Dark eyes turned upon her, solemn and thoughtful.

"I have found what I sought," he said. "And now I wish I had not."

"What do you mean?"

"This is not just any guiser's journal. This is a copy of a much older document, a record of the journeys made by the Birch Men, five hundred years ago."

"Birch Men?"

"From your northern lands, or so they said." Erishen closed his eyes for a moment. "Tall, fierce men, with white skin and yellow hair like birch trees in autumn. Men like you."

Coby frowned. The Dutch had not travelled to the New World so long ago.

"You mean the Danes? Master Catlyn told me how they sailed to the New World and brought back stories of the skraylings."

"Not just stories," Erishen said. "They took some of our kinfolk with them. This book was written by those captives, after they escaped. Several lifetimes after."

Sweet Jesu. "Guisers here in England, hundreds of years ago?"

"Yes."

"And do they still live?"

"I think it unlikely, but I cannot be sure until I have translated the rest of this book."

"Then we must do it, as fast as we can." *And pray that you are right.*

CHAPTER VIII

Ned ducked into the cabin, kicking the door shut behind him to keep the weather out. Rain sluiced down the diamond-paned windows and seeped through the gaps around the frames, adding to the perpetual dampness of the ship's interior. Shaking the water from his hair he made his way to the far end of the dining table, where he set down the covered plates he had brought up from the galley.

"There you go," he said, removing the pewter lids to reveal mounds of pinkish grey mash. "Sir."

Mal looked up from the map he had been studying and gave him a wan smile.

"Where's that?" Ned asked.

"Venice."

Ned pushed the unwanted plate aside and leant over Mal's shoulder. The details of the map were hard to make out in the gloom. "Looks like a fish to me."

"It's a fanciful map of the city," Mal replied, "but I'm told the island is more or less this shape." He traced a broad blue line that curved like an S, cutting the island into two unequal halves. "See, that's the Grand Canal, and there's the Piazza San Marco, Saint Mark's Square. They say the basilica is beyond compare."

"What's this place?" Ned pointed to an over-large building south of the basilica with rows of round-topped arches drawn across its façade.

"It says..." Mal referred to the numbered key in the corner of the map. "Palazzo Ducale. The Doge's Palace."

"What's a 'doge' when he's at home? Some sort of duke?"

"Not exactly. The Doge is of noble birth but is elected by his fellow citizens, like the Lord Mayor of London."

"Huh. Is that why it's called a republic?"

He listened with half an ear whilst Mal described the workings of the Roman senate and speculated on the similarities with modern Venice. It seemed to take Mal's mind off his seasickness; now, if only he could be persuaded to eat. Perhaps if he were set an example? Ned straightened up and went round to the other side of the table.

"Do you reckon the skraylings are there yet?" he said, sitting down.

Mal looked off into the distance, his fingers twitching as he did the reckoning in his head. "No. They cannot be many days ahead of us, even if they left Sark when we did."

"I can't wait to see Lord Kiiren's face when you turn up hot on his heels. He's bound to know you're up to something."

"It's not him I'm worried about."

"Oh?" Ned scooped up a spoonful of the salt-beef-and-chunny mash. It was plain fare, but filling, and at least there was some meat in it.

"The other skraylings are from a different clan," Mal said. "They aren't going to like me talking to Kiiren, not if they think I'm in Venice on the Queen's business."

"Then you'll have to convince them you're there for some other purpose."

"Yes, but what?"

"I thought that was what Raleigh was for? To be your Trojan horse."

"That ruse may fool the Venetians – with any luck they've never heard of me, and won't connect me with Kiiren – but the skraylings are another matter." Mal stared at the map, tracing the contours of the island with one finger. "Fear not, I'll think of something before we reach Venice."

"And if not?"

"We are in God's hands, and can only do our best."

"Easy for you to say," Ned replied around a mouthful of mash. "I don't fancy going back to London to tell Walsingham we've failed."

"We haven't failed yet. And I don't intend to."

The ship lurched over the crest of another wave, and Mal's plate slide a few inches along the table.

"I hope my brother is faring better than we are," Mal said. His face was pale in the cabin's gloom. "I swear I would rather face a dozen guisers than another Atlantic storm."

"No more nightmares, then, since we came aboard?"

Mal shook his head. "Not of that sort."

"I don't suppose there's likely to be any guisers on board anyway. Are there?"

"It's not impossible, but no, you're right. Why would they risk one of their own on a hazardous sea voyage, when there's plenty of mischief they could be getting up to in England?"

"Such as?"

"Whatever manoeuvring at Court will bring them the most power, I suppose."

Ned muttered a curse under his breath. God-damned monstrous witches, they should be rounded up and burned, and their skrayling friends sent back to the New World with their tails between their legs.

"Still, they can work magic from afar, can't they?" he said after a moment, glancing at the rain-blurred window. "That's how you were spirited away."

"True. But over hundreds of miles of ocean? I pray they do not have that kind of power."

"So do I. Though I'd be happier if I had some kind of protection like yours."

"Oh I'm sure something could be found," Mal said with a shadow of his familiar grin. "Master Warburton is certain to have some leg irons around."

"I'm not that desperate," Ned replied hurriedly.

Mal sipped his watered wine and glanced at the plate of mash. A moment later he was leaning over the edge of the table, retching up what little he had eaten this morning. Ned sighed and went to fetch a bucket of sea water.

Mal folded up the map and stowed it in the pack in his locker, then threw himself onto his bunk. He cursed Walsingham for pressing Raleigh upon him, Raleigh for his eagerness to set sail, and most of all himself for agreeing to this voyage. They should have gone overland, through France and northern Italy, despite the risk of spring floods. But Ned was not accustomed to hard riding, and he needed Coby to… His heart contracted at the memory of her in his arms, her mouth on his, her slender body warm against his belly… His hand strayed down to his groin, but the seasickness had robbed him of even that small comfort, and he abandoned the attempt with a curse of frustration and rolled over in the bunk.

The pearl earring pressed against his cheek, and after a moment's indecision he took it out. Surely there were no guisers here on the ship? And if there were, better to know of it than remain ignorant. He hauled himself out of his bunk, retrieved his knapsack and stowed the earring in its pouch. It would be a pity to lose such a rich jewel, and he would need it when he returned to England.

The sound of someone singing a bawdy ballad filtered down through the poop deck overhead, and Mal smiled to himself. Enough of such fretting! It gained him naught but to sour his stomach further. He needed something wholesome to occupy his thoughts. As soon as this weather abated, he would teach Ned how to handle a sword.

Rain lashed down as Ned leant over the rail, hauling on the thin rope. At this rate he might as well stand on deck and let the bucket fill by itself. Or wring his clothes into it. His woollen doublet and hose had soaked up rainwater like the earth after a drought, and they now hung in leaden folds that encumbered his every move. He pushed wet hair back from his eyes and thought longingly of his own warm bed in Southwark.

Above and behind him the sailors went about their mysterious tasks amongst the rigging, seemingly oblivious to the rain. They had scarcely spoken a word to Ned since he came aboard, apart from the ship's cook, who joked about Mal's poor appetite and advised Ned to eat his master's dinner for him.

As he hauled the bucket up the last few feet, he became aware of someone standing over him. Looking round he squinted up into the broad, weatherbeaten face of the second mate: Handsaw, Hangnail, or whatever he was called. Hard to make out names over the roar of a gale.

"Still throwing up, be he?" the sailor asked.

"What is it to you?" Ned lowered the bucket to the deck, never taking his eyes off the man.

"You look to have your sea legs already. Been on a ship before?"

"No."

"Natural-born sailor, then."

Ned shrugged. "I couldn't say."

"Well, ye've taken to it quicker than your master. Not missing your own varlet back in London, then?"

"What?"

"I saw ye, afore ye came aboard. Both o' ye, kissing those pretty yellow-haired lads. Or were they your whores?"

I know your sort of old. Think you can goad me into a fight, eh? "Is that what you ask for, when you visit a stew?" Ned replied. "Girls in breeches?"

The second mate roared with laughter. "Not I! Can't get at her cunt fast enough that way, can ye?"

He elbowed Ned, who laughed with him, though mostly out of relief. The other man had height and reach on him, and fists like half-bricks.

"Master Hansford!" Raleigh bellowed down from the poop deck. "I thought you were taking the whipstaff?"

"Right you are, captain!" Hansford glowered at Ned. "Don't think that's an end on't. I got my eye on ye, ye fish-bellied knave..."

Ned waited until the man was halfway up the stairs to the poop deck, then made the sign of the fig at his back before snatching up his bucket and heading for the cabin.

He stepped through the door and pulled up short. Mal was sitting on his bunk with his sheathed rapier across his knees, dangling the matching dagger from one finger by the ring on its hilt.

"You're looking more cheerful," Ned told him. "Stopped feeling sick?"

"No," Mal replied, getting to his feet, "but I weary of letting it rule me. I shall be the master of my stomach from now on."

"Glad to hear it. I weary of being your nurse."

Mal flipped the dagger upwards and caught it by the hilt. "How would you like to be my sparring partner instead? I grow restless, mewed up like this."

"Me, fight you? With a sword?"

"Don't you want to learn?"

"I..." *Had Mal overheard?* "I reckon I can handle myself

well enough in a tight spot. I'm not one of your milk-livered courtiers, you know."

"I'm not talking about tavern brawls. Real fighting, against men armed with steel. You never know who or what we might come up against on this expedition."

"I've fought an armed man before. And killed him, too." He tried to sound as if it was nothing though, truth be told, if it hadn't been for a lucky throw of a piss-pot he would have been the victim, not the victor.

"Once. And that only by great good fortune," Mal said, echoing his thoughts.

"I told you many a time, I have the Devil's own luck."

Mal shook his head in despair.

"I cannot go into a fight knowing you can't guard my back – worse, that I must defend you as well as myself."

"All right, all right. Tell you what: if you can go an hour without puking, you can teach me what you will."

He held out his hand, and Mal clasped it. "Done."

Ned retrieved his bucket and swabbed up the vomit, then went back out on deck and threw the bucket's contents into the sea, being careful to choose the leeward side so that it didn't blow straight back in his face. Hansford might be a ill-favoured lout, but he was right about one thing: he really was getting the hang of this sailing business. And now he was to become a swordsman too. *Well, they do say that stranger things happen at sea.*

Ned woke with a start, and for a moment wondered where he was. Why was the house creaking like a ship in a storm? Oh, yes – because he was on a ship. Probably in a storm. And his bladder was as full as an alderman's belly.

He climbed out of his bunk, cursing as he banged his shins on the raised side. Mal muttered something in his sleep and rolled over. Ned staggered across the cabin, still barely half-awake, and fetched up against the table. He was sorely tempted to piss on one of the unused mattresses and save himself the bother of going out on deck, but he'd heard alarming tales about naval discipline. He'd rather get soaked again than endure a flogging.

He pulled on his still-sodden hose, groped his way to the door and heaved it open. Thankfully the rain had stopped, though the westerly wind drove the *Falcon* onwards as swiftly as her namesake. The only light came from a couple of lanterns, barely enough to pick out the sheen on wet timbers and the pale faces of the men on duty. It was enough. Ned wove across the deck to the welcome cover of the forward cabin.

The darkness within stank of sweat, tobacco and stagnant seawater, and only a narrow gangway was left between the rows of hammocks. Ned sidled down it, praying he wouldn't disturb any of the sleeping sailors. He didn't know if Hansford was on duty tonight or asleep in one of these canvas swaddlings, but either way he had no wish to encounter him. He had nearly made it to the far end, and the tiny jakes-cabin they called the heads, when his nemesis stepped out in front of him.

"What be ye doing abroad at this time o' night?" Hansford growled. "Come looking for a pretty boy to fuck?"

"I've come for a piss, nothing more."

"Hear that, lads?" Hansford laughed softly, and two other sailors materialised out of the blackness, no more than shapes against the pale bulks of hammocks. "This 'un's come to get his prick out for us."

Ned tried to run for the cabin door, but one of the sailors blocked his way. Someone – Hansford? – grabbed his shirt from behind and pulled him backwards. Before he could cry out, a fist connected with his belly and his aching bladder shed its load.

"Aw, the little babby pissed 'unself," Hansford crooned. "Better get him into the heads, boys, before he shits his breeches as well."

"Bastards!" Ned panted, catching the doorframe with one flailing hand and bracing his feet against the deck.

One of the sailors ducked and grabbed his ankle, hauling it up so that Ned was now suspended between his captors like a sack of turnips. He struggled as if the very devils of Hell had hold of him, but the doorframe slipped from his grasp and he was carried into the fetid blackness beyond.

Mal twitched awake and heard the cabin door creak shut.

"That you, Ned?"

There was no answer. Mal hitched himself into a sitting position, noting that he felt less queasy than he had done for a while. He turned to see a dark shape moving about the cabin.

"Ned?"

The figure leapt towards him, the sweep of his arm alerting Mal to his intent. Mal dodged and rolled over the side of the cot, landing heavily on the deck as the blade thunked into the wood where he had been lying. He carried on rolling until he was sure he was out of reach, then leapt to his feet. The assassin was between him and his blades, damn him. Mal dodged back around the table. The man hesitated, and Mal cast his mind about the cabin in search of a weapon. A lantern, on the hook behind and to his left. No point in a feint; they could barely see one another in the darkness.

He stepped back and reached up to his left, fingers brushing the lantern's greasy exterior. In a moment he had it unhooked, and transferred it to his right hand. Throw or swing? The assassin chose that moment to dash around the end of the table. Swing it was, then. He parried the incoming blade and continued to back away around the table. Just a little further, then he could get back to his bunk before his opponent and retrieve his weapons.

A cry rang out in the night air, distant but shrill. Ned?

Mal threw the lantern at the assassin and ran for his bunk, scrabbling at the back of the mattress until he found his rapier and dagger. He turned just in time to catch another downward-angled thrust, this time on the sheathed rapier. Seizing the scabbard close to the tip with his other hand, he pushed his opponent backwards. The man staggered and almost fell, giving Mal time to draw both blades.

"That evens the odds, eh?"

The assassin began backing towards the cabin door. Mal lunged, driving the forty-inch blade across the space between them. The man cried out; a hit! Then his heavier blade crashed down on the rapier, driving it towards the deck.

Before Mal could pull the rapier back for another strike, light flooded the cabin.

"What's all this?" Raleigh bellowed. "Catlyn? And who are you?"

But the would-be assassin had already fled through the other door.

"He won't get far." Raleigh crossed the cabin and was out of the door after him with scarcely a glance at Mal. "Master Warburton! Belay that miscreant!"

Mal followed him, blinking against the lantern's after-images that danced before his eyes.

Out on deck, his assailant had already been apprehended by three of Raleigh's men. He cowered back from the captain but did not struggle to break free. There was little point, unless he preferred drowning.

"Who is this man?" Raleigh asked Warburton as the first mate clumped down from the poop deck.

Warburton looked the man up and down, his white eyebrows twitching.

"Smith, isn't it?" he said to the man. "Tom Smith."

Smith said nothing.

"Why were you attacking my passenger?" Smith looked pointedly away, and Raleigh cuffed him round the temple.

"Look at me when I'm talking to you, man. Who are you, and what is your purpose on my vessel?"

Smith spat at Raleigh's feet.

"Take him away," Raleigh said, gesturing to his men. "He hangs at dawn."

As the prisoner was led towards the hatch down to the lower decks, the door of the forward cabin opened and Ned limped out. His clothing was torn and half undone, and he sported a split lip and several bruises.

"Dear God in Heaven!" Mal crossed the deck to his friend and slipped an arm under his shoulder to support him. "Who did this?"

Ned shook his head. Mal looked around at the crew, but no one would meet his eye.

"Seems our friend there had accomplices, distracting your manservant so you could be attacked with ease," Raleigh said. "Master Warburton, half rations for all the men in the third watch until we find out who it was."

Hansford glowered at the captain.

"I heard Smith whispering and joking with some of the crew," he said slowly. "Mocking the lad here for being a mite too fond of his master, if you know what I mean, sir."

"I hope you're not insinuating anything unseemly about my passengers, Master Hansford."

"Nay, sir, not I. I'm just saying what I heard."

"Do you know who these men were?"

Hansford shook his head. "'Twere dark, cap'n."

"I see."

"As for allies, I couldn't rightly say. We took a few new men on, just afore we sailed."

"Very well, we'll look into it further in the morning." Raleigh looked around at his crew. "Well, what are you waiting for, ye lubbers? Back to work."

Seeing there was no chance of further progress tonight, Mal helped Ned back inside. They sat on one of the benches in silence until Raleigh had retreated to his own cabin, then Ned began stripping off his soiled clothing. Mal found flint and tinder and lit one of the lanterns, then hung it from a beam where he could get a better look at Ned's injuries. His friend stood naked and shivering, not meeting Mal's eye. Dark fingertip-sized bruises were already blooming on his arms where his assailants had seized him, and larger ones marred his back and chest.

Mal retrieved some clean under-linens from his own knapsack and handed them to Ned.

"I should bind your chest," he said as Ned pulled on the drawers. "You've likely cracked a rib or two."

He took one of the sheets and began ripping it into strips with his dagger.

"You don't have to–"

"Yes I do. I asked you on this expedition, and if it wasn't for that assassin wanting to get me alone, you wouldn't be in this state."

"Don't be too sure of that. Hansford was just looking for an excuse–" Ned winced as Mal wound the first bandage around his chest. "I've come across his kind before."

"It was Hansford? The lying bastard."

"Aye, and a couple of his mates."

Mal recalled some of the rougher sorts he'd met on campaign, men who took out their frustrations on anyone weaker than them, by any means that amused them. He swallowed.

"Did they…?"

Ned shook his head. "Just roughed me up a bit."

"I'd like to rough *them* up. With the edge of my blade." He tucked in the loose end, and tore off another strip of linen. "Hansford will get off scot-free, I suppose. No man is like to betray his superior or his comrades, not for a stranger."

Ned grunted his agreement.

"Still," Mal went on, "as Raleigh said, it's too much of a coincidence that we were attacked at the same time."

"Perhaps yon assassin did egg them on, then took advantage of the distraction."

"Perhaps."

He finished up the bandages, then helped Ned back into his shirt. On impulse, he leaned in to kiss his friend's temple.

"Don't," Ned muttered, pulling away.

Mal nodded in understanding. The last thing Ned wanted to think about was the suspected sin that had earned him this beating. He sheathed the dagger and laid both weapons along the outside edge of the bunk, between him and the door, then settled down next to them.

He lay there for hours, listening to Ned's breathing slow into sleep, wondering who had sent the assassin aboard. Plenty of people knew he was leaving with Raleigh: Jos Percy, the astronomer Harriot and his friend Shawe, indeed everyone at Raleigh's supper. Then there was Walsingham and his daughter, and perhaps through her, Grey. Dammit, it could hardly have been more public if he had printed a broadsheet and had it cried through the streets of London. There were too many connections at Court, too many threads linking him to his enemies. Perhaps exile was the only answer after all.

CHAPTER IX

When they got back to Deadman's Place, Gabriel was in the back garden cutting kale for supper. Coby stopped to help him, glad to be free of Sandy's company for a while. The kale plants stood in neat rows, their lower leaves yellowed with frost. Most of the other beds were bare, or covered with half-dead weeds.

"Ned tries his best with the garden," Gabriel said, "but it was such a bad summer we scarcely had a harvest, never mind seed left over for spring. I dare say it'll turn to wilderness now he's gone."

His carefree tone had a brittle edge; Coby guessed he shared her loneliness.

They walked to the end of the garden. Over the hedge they could see the Rose Theatre, taller than any other building in Bankside, and beyond it and to the left... Her breath caught in her throat. A familiar-looking timber framework loomed against the evening sky. With the sun behind it, it almost looked like it was on fire.

"What's that?"

"Didn't I mention? They're building a new theatre on the site of the Mirror."

"Oh."

"Apparently it's going to be called the Swan. Everyone says it's a pity the name 'Fortune' was already taken, since that's what it's costing."

He laughed, and she couldn't help but smile back. They carried the piles of kale leaves into the kitchen, and Gabriel began tearing them up to add to their pottage. Sandy was sitting at the table with his back to them, reading by candlelight. Probably another of those mathematical treatises they had brought back from Sark. He usually read them at night, since they were in Latin.

Latin. Why would he be reading Latin so early in the evening? Had he put the spirit-guard on already? She moved round to the other side of table, and her guts twisted in panic. It was the red book from the library.

"Grey's book?" she cried out. "You stole Grey's book?"

Sandy looked up. Or rather, Erishen. She was already beginning to tell the difference.

"It's of no use to him."

"But… You stole it."

"I believe you already mentioned that." He turned his attention back to the ciphered text.

"When he finds out, we'll all be arrested." She went to the back door and looked out at the darkening sky. "There's still time to take it back, curfew isn't for at least another hour. We'll pretend we left something behind at Suffolk House and–"

"No, I will not give it back. It was not rightfully his to begin with."

"What's going on?" Gabriel said, looking round from the hearth. The firelight limned his delicate features, turning him into the image of his namesake, stern and beautiful.

"Master Alexander–" she spat out the formality "–has stolen the book we were supposed to be translating. It belongs to the Duke of Suffolk."

"It belongs to one of my kinsmen," Sandy said.

"Your dead kinsman. Long dead."

"But reborn. According to our laws–"

"I don't give a fig about 'your' laws. This is England. You've stolen the duke's property; that's a felony, and you will be hanged for it."

"Enough!" Gabriel said. "Is this true, Catlyn?"

"The book was in the possession of the duke," Sandy conceded.

"You brought stolen goods into my home?" He seized Sandy by the front of his doublet and hauled him to his feet. "Christ's bones, man, we could all hang for this."

"Then we had better leave for France before they come for us," Coby said.

"Now?" Gabriel said. "It's almost dark. Where would we get a ship at this time of night?"

"Leave that to me," Sandy said. "My kinsmen–"

"A pox on your so-called kinsmen!"

"Wait!" Coby cried. "He has a point. The skraylings aren't happy with all the spy-hunts and executions as it is; I'm sure they'd give Lord Kiiren's friends sanctuary."

Gabriel released Sandy, none too gently.

"So I am supposed to abandon my home and friends and flee into exile," he said in ominously quiet tones, "all because of a madman's whim?"

"You work for Walsingham too," she replied. "You know our lives could be forfeit at any moment. Look what happened to Marlowe."

Gabriel sighed, and shrank from wrathful archangel to a tired, frightened young man.

"I shall go and pack my belongings straight away," he said, heading for the stairs.

"He will be safer with us," Sandy said when he was gone.

He would have been safer if we had never come back to England. He would have been safer if Mal and Ned had never met. But she had not the heart to say so out loud.

• • • •

Coby went over and over the contents of her knapsack in her mind, afraid she had forgotten something vital. Changes of shirt, drawers and stockings, all of which would no doubt be filthy by the end of the first fortnight; lock-picking tools; paper and a stick of black lead; wash-ball and flannel; comb; her precious supply of desert fire. And of course the knife on her belt and the pair of pistols Mal had given her for her birthday, along with a flask of gunpowder and a small bag of shot.

The gown and small-linens were laid out on the bed. Should she put them on now? Grey was looking for three men, so two men and a woman might evade the search better, but that would mean revealing her sex to her companions. After a moment's prevarication she folded them up and stuffed them into another sack. That was a decision she wanted to put off as long as possible.

The door opened, making her start.

"Come," Sandy said. "The guild-house will be closing soon. And bring your belongings. I do not intend to come back here."

"You will have to learn better manners," she muttered, swinging her knapsack over her shoulder, "if you are to spend time amongst good Christian folk."

"Then you can teach me on the way to France."

Gabriel was waiting for them in the kitchen, already wrapped in a threadbare cloak of ruby velvet lined with silvery rabbit fur.

"Don't leave anything valuable behind," Coby said to the actor. "Grey is going to tear this place apart looking for us."

Gabriel looked about the house. "A good point. I will ensure he finds nothing else of interest here."

"Be quick about it," Coby said, following Sandy out of the back door. "I doubt I can delay Master Catlyn."

Though it was nearly dark, the curfew bell had not yet rung and the suburb's streets were still busy. Coby kept glancing over her shoulder as they hurried along St Olave's Street, expecting to see armed men in the duke's blue-and-white livery in pursuit.

The skrayling guild-house stood on the corner of Bermondsey Street, at the easternmost edge of Southwark. From the outside it looked much like any other mercantile establishment in London, except for the skrayling writing on the sign over the door. Coby had been here once before, on theatre business with Master Naismith. For a moment she saw again the actor-manager lying dead at her feet and smelt the acrid tang of flash-powder, and a cold weight of melancholy settled on her heart.

The main hall of the guild-house was much as she remembered it, though quieter owing to the late hour. Sandy approached one of the benches and spoke in Vinlandic to the skrayling merchant seated there. The skrayling put down his counting blocks and gestured to one of his colleagues. Sandy went over and repeated his question. The second skrayling inclined his head in a gesture Coby had come to recognise as one of cautious agreement, and they proceeded to talk in low tones. Not that she could have understood them, even if they had been talking loud enough. She thought she heard Lord Kiiren's name mentioned at one point, but it was impossible to be certain.

Sandy pulled a string of silver ingots from his doublet and handed them over to the skrayling, who examined them and then counted out a heap of silver coins of various sizes. Sandy scooped them up into a purse, bowed to the merchant and came over to Coby.

"Our business here is done," he said. "The ship leaves on tonight's tide, though we should be aboard before curfew. I think it is safer if we stay hidden here in the guild-house until then."

Coby nodded, relieved at the short delay. It would give Gabriel time to catch them up, and yet was soon enough for them to escape Grey. Or so she hoped. Her prayers had been answered so far, but God's plans were seldom so straightforward.

The hour passed, and still there was no sign of Gabriel.

"We have to go," Sandy said, getting to his feet, "or we may miss the tide."

"What about Gabriel?"

"He is a grown man, is he not? He will have to fend for himself."

"But–"

"It was you who insisted we flee to France. Have you changed your mind?"

"No."

Coby picked up her belongings and followed him out of the guild-house. No sign of the duke's men, thank the Lord, but no Gabriel either. Unless... A figure shrouded in a red hooded cloak was making its way towards them in the wake of a group of labourers. Eventually the labourers turned down Bermondsey Street, leaving their companion behind. Coby embraced Gabriel briefly, then Sandy led them across the wooden bridge at the end of the street and out onto the downs where the skrayling camp stood.

Surrounded by streams and a wooden palisade, the camp was forever isolated from the city. However it seemed to Coby that there was less smoke rising from within than last time she was in London, and fewer lights glowing amongst its trees. Perhaps it was just the cold weather keeping the skraylings subdued, but she remembered Walsingham's comments. If the skraylings and their silver stopped coming, things would go badly for England.

They did not enter the stockade but continued round to Horseydown Stairs on the banks of the Thames, where a small gull-prowed boat waited to take them out to the ship anchored further downriver: a typical skrayling carrack, broad in the waist, two-masted and sturdy to weather the Atlantic crossing. The trip to France should be a Sunday afternoon's stroll in comparison.

Soon their little boat was bumping against the timber side of the ship, and they climbed the rope ladder to the deck. Sandy was greeted warmly by a stout skrayling whose amber-and-turquoise-beaded hair marked him out as a person of status. They spoke briefly in Vinlandic, then Sandy introduced his companions.

"This is Trader Hennaq," Sandy added in English. "He is brother to Chief Merchant Hretjarr, and a distant cousin of Kiiren."

Hennaq bowed to each of them, then beckoned to one of his men, who gave Sandy a round glass lantern that glowed a cool blue-green. Lightwater. He passed it to Coby.

"This vessel does not normally carry passengers," he said, ushering her towards an open hatch. "I am afraid we will have to take shelter in the hold."

"I've had worse accommodations," she said, climbing down into the darkness. "Anyway, it's a short enough crossing to Calais. We'll be there in a few hours at most."

She found a hook to hang the lantern on and settled down on a pile of sacking. Best to get some sleep, if she could. The more miles they could put between themselves and Grey once they landed, the better.

Despite her best intentions, Coby did not fall asleep straight away. What if Grey caught up with the ship before it sailed, or managed to blockade it? She lay awake listening to the creak of timbers, until at last the nameless vessel began to move. How the skraylings could possibly navigate in such darkness she did not know, but perhaps their cat-like eyes could see as well by night as humans could by day. Distracted by these musings, she at last drifted off to sleep.

When she woke the hold was empty of her companions,

but she could hear voices overhead. She pulled on her shoes and hurried up the ladder onto the gun deck. And stumbled to a halt, her companions forgotten.

In the pitch blackness last night she had not noticed the guns, but now with the late morning sun shining down through the hatch they were an extraordinary sight. Though shaped much like English cannons, they were not of bronze or iron but some peculiar glassy stuff that gleamed with an unearthly opalescence. As for the shot, it consisted of equally strange spheres of what appeared to be glass, partially filled with a liquid that sloshed around inside. What use they would be in battle, she could not imagine. They looked like they would sooner explode than trouble an enemy.

Shaking her head over these strange artillery, she climbed up to the deck. The sun was high in the sky, or as high as it got this early in the year. To the west lay the Kent coast, with its ploughed fields rising gently above the shoreline. A blur on the eastern horizon must be France. At this rate they would be at Calais long before dark.

"Good afternoon, sleepy-head!" Gabriel called out to her.

She went over to join him at the rail.

"Why didn't you wake me sooner?" she asked.

"And deny the skraylings the pleasure of your snoring? Not likely."

She pulled a face at him.

"Careful, the wind might change, and then you'd be stuck like that," he said. "Would you like some breakfast? Hennaq seems well supplied; there's cornbread, some kind of fish fritters, and plenty of *aniig*."

He produced a plate and jug, seemingly out of nowhere, and Coby sat down on the deck with her back against the gunwales. The fritters were cold and a bit greasy, but she wolfed it all down and licked her fingers clean. Gabriel leant back on the rail, watching her with an amused smile.

"What's so funny?" she said at last.

"Not very ladylike, I must say."

"What?" She felt herself flush. "What business is that of yours? I thought you'd given up female roles."

"*I* have." He grinned again. "Have you?"

She jumped to her feet.

"Have you been rummaging through my belongings?"

"You brought a great deal of baggage on board, much more than you arrived in London with. That made me curious."

She looked around in case anyone was listening. Few skraylings spoke English, but Tradetalk was similar enough for them to pick up the gist of many a conversation. Fortunately the crew were all some distance away and busy at their posts.

"And?"

"And it occurred to me, as it apparently has to you, that if we are to be sure of evading Grey then a few disguises may be in order."

Coby forced herself to breath slowly. "You're right. I should have told you earlier."

"That you're a girl?"

"No, I meant the disguises. Where's Sandy, anyway?" she said, hoping to change the subject.

"Off talking to the captain, I believe. So you're not a girl, then?"

"No."

"Hmm. Well, Ned always was prone to lie about such things."

"Ned? How did he find out?" she muttered, more to herself than Gabriel.

"Oho, so it is the truth!" Gabriel looked smug. "Does Walsingham know how easily you confess your secrets?"

Coby sighed. "Is there anyone who doesn't know?"

"Are you accusing me of spreading gossip?"

"Well, have you?"

"No, of course not. I know how to keep a secret. Besides, I'm hardly in a position to lecture any man on how he should live a virtuous life. Or woman, for that matter." His mischievous grin faded, and he leant closer. "So, does your master know you're a girl? Mal, I mean."

"Mal's known for a long time," she replied. "Since before we left England together."

"Oh."

"I don't really want to talk about it."

"Suit yourself," Gabriel replied with a shrug. "It's no business of mine."

"You seem to have made it your business."

Gabriel sighed. "Let us not quarrel, my dear. We are in the same boat, you and I, if you'll forgive the pun. Placed in peril of our lives by the actions of yon holy fool."

Coby nodded. She couldn't blame Gabriel for being scared and angry, not after what had happened yesterday.

"There is something I would like to ask you, now that you know." She cleared her throat. "You used to play women's parts, and then when you were too old for that, you managed to change over to men's roles. It must have been difficult."

"It was, at first. I had to unlearn everything I had been taught about acting. How to walk, how to speak, even how to think of myself."

"Do you ever regret it?"

"A little, perhaps. But I had no choice. It was that or starve. Why do you ask?"

"Oh, nothing."

"You're thinking of giving up your male disguise for good."

"Perhaps. But I'm scared. I know it's the right and proper thing to do, but…"

Gabriel put his arm around her shoulder.

"I'm sure you'll make the right choice in the end. But perhaps the moment for choosing has not yet come."

She nodded, biting her lip. What use was there in being a woman, if Mal was not around? She was safer as she was, and far better able to keep an eye on his brother for him.

"I think we should get under cover," Gabriel said. "I can see a squall blowing in from the north."

They spent a dull afternoon in the gloom of the hold, then as night fell a sailor brought them a lamp and a dish of stewed beans and corn for supper. At length the rain eased off, and Coby went back up on deck, hoping to see the lights of Calais. Only impenetrable blackness met her eye. Most likely they had been blown off-course, and would have to make land further south. Perhaps Hennaq would take them to Le Havre, where they could get a boat up the Seine to Paris. Mal had friends there, or at least allies. She went back down to the hold and settled into an uneasy sleep.

Next morning they were invited up to the captain's cabin to take breakfast. Coby looked around curiously as they entered. The carpenters had done their best to mimic the inside of a skrayling tent, lining the walls with cabinets on whose doors were carved elaborate patterns of intersecting triangles like the ones on the merchants' tunics. Spherical bottles of lightwater hung from the ceiling in nets, casting a watery blue glow. Captain Hennaq rose from his cushion to greet them.

"You have good night?" he asked.

"Great good, thank you," Coby replied.

They sat down to eat. This morning it was a sweet yellow porridge and some kind of bean dumpling rolled in chopped nuts. She wondered if the skraylings were keeping Lent, or if they usually carried no meat on their ships. Dried vegetables would certainly keep better, or at least not go rancid.

"I want to thank you, captain," she said in Tradetalk, "for agreeing to take us to France in our hour of need."

"It is my pleasure," Hennaq replied, pouring *aniig* for them all. "Erishen-tuur told me you are fleeing the wrath of our enemy Grey."

"Your enemy?"

"Aye. His father was the leader of the Huntsmen, was he not?"

Coby inclined her head. A convenient fiction to explain his involvement in the attack on the Catlyn twins. Jathekkil's true motives could not be revealed without endangering them all.

"Are we near Le Havre yet?" she asked. She had no idea how far away the port was from Calais, nor how fast this ship had travelled in the night.

"We are not going to Le Havre," Sandy said.

"Where then? Cherbourg?"

"I have decided to take you home, to… Nar-say," Hennaq said.

"You mean Marseille? That is a great voyage, and far out of your way."

"Not so far, perhaps. And safer for you."

Coby doubted it, but did not gainsay him.

"Grey may send men after you by land, may he not?" Hennaq went on. "And they may thus happen upon you, alone on the road."

"Yes, this is true."

The skrayling gestured around him.

"Here, you are not alone. And since he does not know you are on my ship, how can he find you?"

Gabriel frowned at her and she translated for him.

"He has a point," Gabriel said in a low voice. "We are none of us great fighters like Mal."

"I have my pistols, and you your cudgel," she whispered back.

"Against men armed with steel? I do not fancy our chances."

Coby rose and bowed. "Thank you, captain. We are grateful for your protection."

"And you may repay the favour when we near the end of the journey," he said, baring his teeth slightly. "I am minded to treat with the lords of Corsica for the bones of my countrymen."

Coby took a sip of *aniig* to hide her discomfiture. She had no intention of returning to Calvi; the lords of the citadel would probably arrest her on sight. But that was an argument for another day. It would be some weeks before they reached Corsican waters, and by then they would be nearly home.

CHAPTER X

Mal had hoped to question Smith again, but the assassin was hanged at dawn on Raleigh's instructions. Two other newcomers to the crew were accused of being his co-conspirators, since no one could vouch for them. They protested their innocence most piteously, and in the end Raleigh relented and had them put ashore at Bordeaux to find their own way back to England.

As the *Falcon* made her way down the coast of Portugal the weather improved, and Mal was able to think about teaching Ned swordplay as they had agreed.

"We'll be in Venice within the month at this rate," he said, as they ate breakfast one morning. "That's nowhere near long enough to teach you the finer points, but at least you can learn how to block a blow and give one back."

Ned made a noncommittal noise around the hard biscuit. *Probably afraid of making a fool of himself in front of the men who assaulted him.* The bruises were faded to yellow, but he grew quiet whenever Hansford was around.

"Wasn't that the bell for first watch?" Mal went on. "Perhaps we should wait until the crew have changed places before we get in their way."

After a moment Ned took the hint. Hansford and his accomplices were in the third watch, and would be going to their hammocks soon.

"All right," he said. "But we only have one sword between us. How will we manage?"

"I don't trust you yet with edged steel," Mal said with a smile. "I've no wish to die of a festering cut before we reach Venice. There's bound to be something on board we can use as wasters."

He got to his feet and went in search of the ship's carpenter. Half an hour later he returned with two short poles, similar in size and weight to cudgels.

"I'm afraid you'll get a few bruised knuckles, since there's no cross-guard," he told Ned, tossing one of the poles across the table.

Ned caught it easily.

"I've had worse," he replied with a grin.

They practised every morning on deck after that, starting about an hour after breakfast and stopping only when the sun got too high in the sky. Their route had taken them south of Spain, within sight of the North African coast, before heading northeastwards into the heart of the Mediterranean, and the weather was now as hot as a summer's afternoon in England, though it was only the middle of March.

Mal was right about the rapped knuckles, Ned thought ruefully as he braced himself for another attack. He had always wondered if the fancy hilt of Mal's rapier was just for decoration, but he was beginning to appreciate how its graceful curves might deflect a blow away from its wielder's fingers. He was not as badly outmatched as he had feared, though; Mal was still unsteady on the pitching deck, and had been impressed by the ease with which Ned had mastered his footwork.

"Good," Mal said, after another repeat of their usual drill. "Now, I'm going to come at you and I want you to defend yourself. Don't try to hit me back; you're not going to kill a man in a fight if you get killed first."

Ned tried to relax into the stance he had been taught: right foot forward, waster level with the ground and pointing inwards towards his opponent, left hand raised close to his body to stop a backhand blow. Mal kept his weapon low, his eyes never leaving Ned's, challenging him to guess where the next attack would come from.

Mal's cudgel moved in a blur, but somehow Ned blocked it, his arm seeming to move of its own accord.

"Very good. Again."

Each time the blow came in at a different angle. Sometimes Ned parried; often he did not. At least these bruises were well-earned.

At last Mal called a halt.

"I think that's enough for one day," he said, tossing his cudgel to Ned.

Ned caught the weapon and sagged against the rail. Both their shirts were soaked with sweat and sticking to their backs, but Mal was otherwise as fresh as when they'd begun. Ned watched in mingled admiration, envy and lust as his former lover strode, slightly unsteadily, across the deck to their cabin.

"Fancy a trial o' the ratlines?"

Ned looked around sharply, fearing to see Hansford, but it was just one of the younger sailors, a man of about his own age with spiky blond hair and a powder-burn cutting a swathe through his scrubby beard. He stood on the rail, holding onto the rigging, as if it were the most natural place in the world.

"The what?"

The sailor indicated the rigging: a set of seven or eight stout cables, joined by horizontal lengths of rope to make a crude ladder. They were hitched somewhere on the outside of the ship and converged on a tiny platform high above them. It made Ned dizzy just to look at it. He swallowed hard.

"A jest only," the man said, leaping down onto the deck. "Captain Raleigh won't thank us if one of his passengers is tossed into the sea."

"Are you saying I can't do it?"

"Well..."

"You're on."

He put the cudgels down and went back to the rail. The ratlines were just within arm's reach, out beyond the safety of the deck, and he quickly scrambled up, standing on the rail with his hands clenched on the cross-ropes. The ship rolled gently beneath him. *Best get this over with.*

He swung his feet out towards the ratlines, trying not to think of the fact he was now hanging over the side of the ship. His feet caught, and he clung to the lines for a moment, muttering prayers he thought he'd forgotten. Taking a deep breath he began to climb.

It wasn't so bad once you got going. There was a rhythm to the ship's movement, and the cross-ropes were spaced close enough together to be an easy reach for all but the smallest cabin boy. If it weren't for the prospect of having to do this kind of thing in a gale, he could almost see himself taking up a sailor's life.

He managed to get a third of the way up before he made the mistake of looking down. And saw nothing but sea below him.

It was some moments before he opened his eyes again and realised he was clinging to the tarred rope so tightly his hands had started to bleed. To calm his nerves he forced himself to breathe deeply and focus on the horizon. There. A ship, smaller than the *Falcon*, with triangular sails on its foremast, coming towards them.

Coming towards them.

"Sail ahoy!" cried the lookout. "Corsairs!"

Ned's stomach turned over. The crew whiled away their rare moments of leisure by swapping tales of the corsairs' cruelty and the various horrible fates awaiting those taken captive. Most able-bodied men ended up in North Africa, labouring in quarries or worse still chained to a bench on a galley, with no choice but to eat, sleep, piss and shit where they sat. Either way they would be worked to death in the space of a couple of years.

Cursing under his breath he scrambled down the rigging as fast as he dared. At last he glimpsed the rail just below him. With a last burst of bravado he swung his feet back onto the rail, jumped backwards and spun in mid-air to land on the deck, then sprinted for the cabin.

"Mal, get up! Corsairs!"

Mal groaned. "What?" He propped himself up on his elbows and squinted at Ned.

God's teeth, I thought he was over the seasickness. He looks like the day's leftovers at Billingsgate fish market.

"Corsairs. Slavers, like as not."

Mal climbed unsteadily to his feet. "How far off?"

"I don't know. Not far enough."

"All right." He leant against the bulkhead for a moment, his expression distracted. "We'd probably best get up on deck, but try and stay out of the crew's way."

"Can't we stay in here?" Ned replied, looking around him. The cramped, stuffy cabin suddenly felt as welcoming as his own bedchamber back in Southwark.

"If the corsairs fire on us, we're better up there being shot clean dead than shredded by splinters from a cannon hit."

Ned retrieved Mal's sword belt and dagger from the bunk, feeling as sick as his friend looked. Mal threaded his rapier hanger onto the belt and cinched it around his hips.

Ned swallowed. Now there was a sight to stiffen a man's sinews.

"Take your waster," Mal said. "It's not much of a weapon, but at least you know its weight and reach. We'll get you a sword if Raleigh has any spare."

Footsteps thudded overhead as men ran back and forth, putting on sail in an attempt to outrun the corsair ship. Mal and Ned left the cabin and made their way up to the poop deck. Raleigh was directing his men with calm efficiency, as if being attacked by pirates were an everyday occurrence.

"Ah, Catlyn," he said as they approached. "Ready for your first sea-action?"

Mal's reply was drowned by a shout from aloft. "Enemy coming about, captain!"

"So, they have made their decision," Raleigh said. "May God protect us."

They all crossed themselves.

"Sure I can't persuade ye to exchange that hat-pin for a more fit weapon?" Raleigh asked Mal, patting the hilt of his own backsword.

"Thank you, no," Mal replied. "I'll take my chances with the blades I know."

"Please yourself; it's no loss to me." Raleigh turned back to his crew. "All hands to the guns!" He patted his first mate on the shoulder and added in quieter tones, "More speed, Master Warburton. As much as she can give us."

The corsair galley was running before the wind at alarming speed, her oars shipped but ready to be deployed at a moment's notice. As she came nearer, Mal could make out the crew leering at them from the rigging, sun-darkened faces contrasting with the bright colours of kerchiefs or half-concealed by wild black hair. Not all were Moors, however; here and there he spotted the bleached hair and reddened skin of men from lands far north of Africa. Dutch, probably, or perhaps even renegade Englishmen. There were always a few who sought mayhem like others sought wine or women.

"Remember what we practised," he told Ned. "Keep your weapon low and close. Don't be tempted by anger to raise it up and leave yourself vulnerable."

"I'll try," Ned muttered.

Mal caught his gaze. Ned was terrified, but trying very hard not to show it. *Of course. He's never been in a real fight before, not one with guns firing and deadly blades on all sides.* Mal chuckled ruefully.

"What?" Ned glowered at him.

Good. A little anger will take the edge off his nerves. Just not too much. "Don't worry. You'll do better than I did in my first battle."

"Why? What did you do?"

"Very nearly shat myself with terror, for one thing," Mal replied with a smile. "And dropped my pike on the sergeant's head. Twice."

Ned laughed. Into silence.

Raleigh's crew watched in fascinated horror as the corsair ship changed course again, heading straight for their stern.

"What's it going to do? Ram us?" Ned asked.

The galley was barely a hundred yards behind them now, and sat so low in the water that Mal could look down onto its bow deck from his position in the stern. The mouths of two large cannon stared back at him.

"Jesu help us," one of the nearby sailors muttered, turning his swivel gun as far on its mount as he could, in an effort to train it on the galley.

"What is it?" Mal asked.

"They're going to rake us." When Mal gave him a puzzled look he added, "Fire on our stern."

"And that's bad, is it?"

"It's the weakest part of the hull. Any shot that hits us will tear the length of the lower decks."

"Hard a'larboard!" Raleigh yelled at the helmsman. "All larboard guns prepare to fire!"

The galleon heeled to the left, lines thrumming like lute-strings as the sails fought the wind. Slowly, too slowly. Puffs of white smoke issued from the corsair cannons, followed a moment later by a low thunder – and Mal staggered against the rail as the poop deck bucked underfoot. Behind him men screamed.

"Get down there and help carry away the injured," Raleigh told Mal. He turned to his crew. "You there, fire on their gunners at will."

The swivel gunners obeyed, the higher pitched bark of the small cannon ringing out as Mal and Ned clattered down the steps to the weather deck. The door to their own cabin lay in splinters, and a trail of destruction down the starboard side of the deck revealed the cannon-ball's flight. The remains of a man, cut almost in two, were bleeding copiously onto the deck.

"God rest your soul," Mal muttered, stepping over the corpse. "Here, Ned, help me with this one."

Another man was lying face down, groaning, his leg bent at an unnatural angle. He screamed when they hauled him upright, and Ned nearly dropped him.

"Steady," Mal told him. "No point in making it worse."

Ned said nothing, only took a firmer grip of the man's arm.

"Get him down to the bilges, out of the way," one of the survivors shouted at them.

"But–"

"Just do it!"

They lowered the man down the ladder to the gun deck. Any moment Mal expected another cannonball to rip through the hull and smash them all to pieces. They shuffled through the gloom, dodging the cannons that rumbled gently back and forth with the motion of the ship and the men scurrying around them with ramrods and match-cords.

The wounded sailor began to struggle as they half-carried, half-dragged him towards the ladder leading down into the belly of the ship.

"Not the bilges!" he moaned. "In God's name, don't leave me to die, not in there!"

Mal glanced at Ned, who shrugged, his expression bleak. He halted and leant close to the man's ear.

"Just as far as the main hold, eh? We can't leave you up here."

The sailor nodded, his face white with pain. Mal and Ned helped him down the ladder and made him as comfortable as they could on a pile of empty chunny sacks. The stink of the bilges was strong down here, but at least this level was dry.

The *Falcon* shuddered again as her own cannons fired, and dust rained down from the planks overhead. The three men waited, hardly daring to breathe, but there was no answering response from the corsair galley. Ned let out an audible sigh of relief.

"Come on, there's nothing more we can do here," Mal said, wiping the sweat and grime from his brow with the back of his sleeve.

He scrambled up the ladder and ran the length of the gun deck. At the foot of the next ladder he put out a hand to stop Ned.

"Hear that?"

Shouts and the clash of steel sounded from the deck above.

"Corsairs?" Ned asked. "They've boarded us already?"

Mal put a hand to his sword hilt – and halted with the blade half-drawn. Dammit, Raleigh was right. A ship was no place to be carrying a rapier. He slammed it back into the scabbard and drew his dagger instead. Ten inches of cold steel. It would do for now. He ran up the ladder two rungs at a time and leapt out onto the deck in a fighting stance. Immediately he found himself facing a heavily built Moor almost his own height. The corsair's falchion came round in a belly-slicing arc and Mal sprang back, tripped over Ned and sent him tumbling back down to the gun deck. The falchion smashed into the deck inches from Mal's head as he rolled aside and scrambled to his feet again. Mal switched the dagger to his left hand and drew his rapier. The corsair laughed at the sight of the slender blade.

In that brief distraction Mal lunged, simultaneously raising his dagger to deflect another blow from the falchion. The Moor stared down at the red stain blooming across his white tunic, then sagged to his knees as Mal withdrew the rapier blade and closed in to slash his throat open with a backhand sweep of the dagger.

Another corsair prepared to leap across the hatch towards Mal, but the end of Ned's cudgel slammed into his groin and he collapsed, moaning in agony. A moment later Ned popped his head up.

"Stay below!" Mal yelled, and stabbed the corsair through the heart before he could recover.

The enemy had not yet gained the upper hand, but far too many of the men lying helpless or dead were English. He roared and ran at the nearest corsair, a giant of a man made taller by an elaborate turban topped with red and black plumes. His falchion had a deep-toothed edge to its blade, designed to latch onto a ship's rail as well as cause unpleasant puncture wounds. They danced back and forth for long moments, Mal dodging the shining arc of his opponent's weapon rather than risking a parry, trying to coax the man to move in closer. There. He leapt into the opening, bringing his rapier round – and skidded in a pool of blood as the ship rolled.

The falchion whistled down and caught on the elaborate curves of the rapier's hilt. Mal swore and released his grip before the toothed blade could sever his fingers. The corsair shook the rapier aside with a grin and moved in for the kill, but before he could do so, his head exploded in a spray of blood and splinters of bone. Mal looked up to see one of the swivel gunners grinning at him from the poop deck.

"Christ's holy mother!" he yelled up at the man. "That could have been me!"

The sailor made an obscene gesture and set about reloading his gun. Mal got to his feet and retrieved his sword. The remaining corsairs were fleeing back to their ship, diving into the water to avoid being shot by the English sailors. With her sails still unfurled to catch the wind, the *Falcon* was being blown further away from the galley with every moment, unable to turn back and pursue the oared vessel. Mal watched in frustration as their enemy slipped beyond the reach of cannon fire, though in truth Raleigh had barely enough men left whole to crew his ship, still less take the corsairs on for a second bout.

He wandered into the shattered remnants of the poop. The table and benches lay in ruins, and the dividing wall between their cabin and Raleigh's was gone, only a few splintered timbers showing where it had been. Beyond it, the stern was a gaping hole, floorboards shattered and sloping precariously down towards a drop into the sea. If he had not persuaded Ned to join him on deck, his friend would likely be dead right now. For the first time in weeks he was glad he had not brought Coby. The thought of her cut in half like that poor bastard out there... He put the grisly image aside. Where was Ned anyway? With a pang of guilt he headed back to the gun deck.

When he found Ned at last, the younger man rushed to embrace him, muttering curses over and over like prayers as he buried his face in Mal's shoulder. Mal rested his chin against Ned's brow, fighting down his own post-battle shakes. Around them the gunners were slapping one another's shoulders and laughing, even as their injured fellows groaned in the hold below. They had lived to see another day, God be praised. No man could ask for more than that.

CHAPTER XI

Coby stood on the after-deck, staring up at the red sails that bellied above her. Nearly three weeks into their journey and they were still zigzagging down the coast of Portugal. The same westerly winds that hindered their own progress would be blowing Mal's ship around the coast of Spain and into the Mediterranean. She kicked the rail irritably, as if the ship were a lazy pony needing to be spurred on by its rider. The skrayling at the ship's wheel turned to stare at her, and she muttered an apology in Tradetalk.

She looked around for Sandy, and presently spotted him sitting on a coil of rope with a book of mathematics open on his lap. She pattered down the steps to the weather deck and crossed the ship's waist in long, slightly erratic strides.

Sandy looked up as her shadow fell across the pages.

"We left England only a day or so after Mal," she said. "Do you think we might catch up with him?"

"The *Falcon* is a fast ship, made for war. They are well ahead of us by now."

"But you cannot be sure, can you?" She squatted next to him so that they were eye to eye, and lowered her voice. "You have not… spoken to him yet?"

"I have tried." He stared southwards, as if he could see

Mal's ship in the distance. Coby had to admit that he looked like a man who had not slept well in days. Or rather, nights. "But most likely he still wears the earring Kiiren gave him. At any rate, I have searched all night, as far as I dared to go, and found no sign of him."

"You are right, I suppose," she said, standing up. Though she strained her eyes, she could see nothing in any direction except miles of empty ocean. "It's almost Easter, and still we sail south. Surely we must be nearing the Straits of Gibraltar?"

Sandy got to his feet. "I will speak to our captain, if that will soothe your spirit."

"Thank you, sir."

"And you should take cover, like your friend Gabriel," he added. "The sun is far stronger in these parts, and will burn you before you know it."

Since the hold was now hot, stuffy and stinking of the bilges by day, Hennaq had rigged up an awning on deck between the two masts so that his passengers could shelter from the sun and keep out of the way of the sailors. Gabriel was lying on his stomach stripped to his shirt and hose, a sheaf of paper before him and an ink-pot wedged into a gap between the mats that covered the bare deck. He looked up with a frown, and Coby tried not to smile at the ink stain down the side of his nose.

"Sorry, I didn't mean to disturb you."

"No, don't go." Gabriel laid down his pen and pushed himself up off the matting, twisting round to sit cross-legged. "I want your opinion on something I'm writing for Ned."

Coby sighed. "I know little of love poetry, sir."

"This isn't a love poem. At least, not in the usual sense. It's a play."

"Oh." She sat down on a cushion next to him. "What's it about?"

"It's..." He cocked his head on one side, his features twisted into a caricature of frustrated thought. Coby suppressed a laugh. Gabriel was ever the actor, on or off stage.

"There's this young man and his sweetheart," he said eventually, "but her father wants her to marry a rich old merchant, so they trick the old man out of his fortune and get married anyway. I'm calling it *A Bear-baiting in Bankside*, because that's where it's set. And the old man is the bear, do you see?"

"Oh. That's... different."

"Tales of kings and princes and foreign lands are all very well," Gabriel said, "but what man – or woman – does not enjoy scandal and gossip? And one's neighbours cannot be relied upon to follow lives of constant wickedness."

"No indeed."

"So I thought, why not put it in a play? A comedy about men's foibles – with a moral ending of course."

"That could work. And the Master of the Revels could have no objection to such a trifle."

"My thoughts exactly." He grinned and passed her a handful of papers. "Here, tell me what you think."

Coby began to read. The handwriting was dreadful, and the page a mess of crossings-out with corrections written very small between the original lines, but she had seen enough such drafts in her time at the theatre to be able to make sense of it. She read on to the next page. It was hardly Marlowe, but the words had a lively spirit to them, the humour sharp-edged without being malicious. She found herself smiling at a line here and there.

When she got to the end of the first scene, she looked up to see Gabriel gazing at her anxiously.

"Well?"

"It's... promising," she said.

"You truly think so?"

"Truly. But if I were you, I'd make sure to put your

name on every page. And burn the ones you mean to discard, or tear them up and throw them overboard."

"Why so?"

"The skraylings are mad for stories; they're as good as money to them. Which means that ownership is important."

Gabriel held out his hand for the script. "Thank you for the reminder. I'll do it right away."

She settled down on the cushions to doze the heat of the day away. Sandy was right. Mal was probably almost to Venice by now. Perhaps he would come to Provence on his way back to England. She smiled to herself at the thought, and closed her eyes.

Erishen waited until he was sure the girl was busy talking to Gabriel, then made his way to the bow. He had not wanted to alarm her, but she was not alone in her concern over their slow progress. The captain owed them a clearer explanation at the very least.

Captain Hennaq was conferring with his quartermaster over their supplies, so Erishen waited at a respectful distance until they were done. This would have to be handled carefully if he were not to cause offence. Though Hennaq had agreed to help them, he made it clear he did so for his cousin's sake alone. As a law-breaker, even an unwilling one, Erishen had no place in the clan hierarchy.

From the little he could overhear, Erishen was able to gather that the captain was concerned about their supply of fresh water. It was always a problem on long voyages, and with enemy lands on either side, finding somewhere they could safely refill their barrels would not be easy. After some debate they agreed they would consult the navigator on the best place to land, and the quartermaster left the foredeck.

"You wish to speak to me?" Hennaq said, seeming to notice Erishen for the first time.

"I bring a request from my Christian friends." It was not the ideal topic, but it had the advantage of having some truth behind it. "It is their custom at this time of year to celebrate their spring festival, and they seek your permission to do so."

The captain glanced towards the passengers' tent.

"What does this festival entail?"

"The first three days require only quiet contemplation, then it is customary to hold a celebratory feast."

Hennaq hissed his amusement. "It does not sound like much of a festival."

"It is their tradition, not ours," Erishen replied, softening his reproving words with a stance of submission.

"Very well. They may proceed, though we have few enough supplies for a feast. I will instruct the cook to do his best." He paused. "I think there can be no harm for us all to eat well together, eh?"

"No, indeed. Thank you, sir."

"However your Christian friends must not interfere with the work of the crew, nor importune them to join in the other ceremonies."

"Of course, captain." The skraylings had listened attentively to the first missionaries to the New World, paid them generously for the stories they told, then told them very politely to go home. Those that did not take heed had soon fled in terror from visions of Hell out of their own sermons. "I think the Christians have learned their lesson."

"Is that all?"

Erishen bowed. "My friends also asked me to enquire whether you or any of your crew possess a copy of the Christian book of stories they could borrow."

"I shall make enquiries amongst the crew. But any such copies will be in our own tongue."

"I will read it to the Christians, putting it into English," Erishen replied. It would be good practice of his language skills, as well as another way to pass the time.

"When is this… festival to take place?"

Ah, now we get to it. "That is the difficulty. My friends have lost track of the count of days since we left England, and it is important that they celebrate on the same day as other Christians."

Hennaq looked up at the sky. "Please, excuse me."

He hailed the first mate, then made a complex series of arm movements, signalling his commands to the crew. Something about the ropes, or the sails…? Erishen had little idea; he had never been much interested in sailing.

"We have been at sea for twenty-two days," Hennaq went on. "Do you not agree?"

"That is what I thought, but I did not trust my own reckoning. I have been studying an English book of mathematics and astronomy, and also following our voyage on one of their maps."

"And?"

"And I am perplexed. Either the map is wrong, or we have sailed much further south than the gateway to the Inner Sea."

He watched the captain's reaction, expecting bluster or denial. Instead Hennaq smiled, baring his fangs.

"The map is not wrong, nor your calculations."

"What?"

"I have changed my mind as to our destination."

The captain nodded absentmindedly. Erishen turned in alarm; too slow. Powerful hands seized his arms and a sack was thrown over his head. He struggled and cried out, but to no avail. There were at least three of them, maybe more, and though he was a good head taller than any skrayling, he could not fight blind. And even if he did break free, where would he run to?

Coby woke from a dream in which she was wrestling shadowy figures who jabbered incomprehensibly at her, only to discover it was not a dream. The skraylings seized her arms and legs, pinning her to the matting. She screamed, as much in fury as in terror, and kicked out. The grip on her right leg momentarily loosened, and she lashed out again. This time her foot connected with the skrayling's jaw, sending him tumbling across the matting onto the deck.

"Hendricks?"

It was Gabriel's voice.

Before she could answer him she was cuffed around the temple and her head snapped sideways, making her gasp and retch at the pain.

"Silence!"

She licked her lips and looked around for the speaker. In the shadowy confines of the hold, the tattooed faces looked too alike for her to distinguish individuals. What was this nightmare? Why had the skraylings turned on them?

The sailors hauled her to her feet and bound her hands in front of her. She could see Gabriel now, standing calmly defiant between his captors, his fair hair in disarray and a smear of blood across his chin.

"What…?"

A hand clamped over her mouth, rough fingers smelling of seaweed and tar.

"I say silent, you are silent," a voice growled in her ear. "See you it?"

She nodded as best she could.

"Good."

The voice barked orders in Vinlandic, and the captives were pushed out of their shelter into the blinding gaze of the sun.

They removed the sack, and Erishen spat pita fibres, blinking in the dim dusty light of the hold.

"What is this, Hennaq? Where are you taking me?"

He was tied to the main mast where it penetrated the hull, hands bound before him and ropes around his ankles, knees, hips and chest so that he could scarcely move. Beyond Hennaq, he could see the girl and the actor being helped down the ladder.

"Leave my English friends out of this," he said. "If any offence has been caused, I will bear the responsibility alone."

"It is a little late to take responsibility, Erishen." The captain leant close, hissing his name in his face. Erishen resisted the urge to return the gesture. Without fangs, it would be about as threatening as a child sticking out his tongue.

"Responsibility for what?" he said instead.

"You don't remember, do you?"

"There are many things I do not remember."

"I was but a boy when you first came to England, in proper shape–" Hennaq looked him up and down disdainfully "–and told the council how you were going to find our kin, stolen by the Birch Men long ago. I thought it a fool's errand, even then, but my heart-mate Tanijeel…"

Hennaq stood silent for a long moment, staring at something in his hand. Erishen grasped at the name, sought it amongst his shattered memories, but found nothing. The captain cleared his throat.

"Tanijeel was smitten with you: one of the oldest of our kind, who had walked with the stolen ones and spoken with the Birch Men, come to our humble settlement in a far-off land! He wanted to accompany you on your quest, but you would have none of it. He was heartbroken."

Erishen remembered now. A young man of perhaps eighteen or twenty summers, judging by the extent of his clan-marks, with bright eyes and a breathless enthusiasm that reminded him all too much of Kiiren.

"It was too dangerous."

Hennaq laughed sharply. "In that at least, you were correct."

"What happened?"

Hennaq stared at him, golden eyes full of hatred. "When you did not return, he went looking for you. The first time, when he came back empty-handed, I thought that would satisfy him. But he never gave up. The last time he went looking, he did not come back."

A sick feeling twisted Erishen's guts. "When was this?"

"Eleven years ago." Hennaq's eyes narrowed. "Why do you ask?"

"No reason. What did you mean, you've changed your mind about our destination?"

Hennaq smiled. "I'm taking you home, honoured one. To Vinland."

"Vinland? What about my *amayi*? He is your cousin–"

"And many miles away. No. Too many have died already on this quest of yours."

Hennaq carefully unfastened the top two buttons of Erishen's doublet and loosened the neck of his shirt, then took something out of the pouch at his waist and held it up for Erishen to see.

"We found this in your baggage." He unfastened the spirit-guard and reached around behind Erishen's neck. "I cannot let you roam free."

"No!"

Coby did not struggle as they tied her to one of the upright timbers that supported the deck. The last thing she wanted was for them to bind her so tightly she had no chance of escape. But escape from a ship in the middle of the ocean required planning, and planning required time and a clear head.

To her relief Gabriel appeared to have come to the same conclusion, and was meekly standing against his post whilst the skraylings fetched another length of rope. Somewhere behind them, Sandy was talking to the captain and it didn't sound good. The captain was angry and upset by turns, and Sandy kept asking him questions, or so she guessed from his tone of voice. But if the captain was not interrogating his prisoner, what was he up to? Why bring them all this way, if he was not their ally? They must be near the coast of Africa by now...

She swallowed against the sick feeling in the pit of her stomach, and glanced at Gabriel. Two healthy young people, fair of hair and skin, would fetch a high price in the slave markets of Moorish Africa. But on the other hand a shipful of skraylings was worth a hundred times that. Surely their captors would not risk enslavement themselves, just for the money they could get for her and Gabriel. Not if the reaction of the crew they had found on Corsica was anything to go by. It must be something else, then; something to do with Sandy and Kiiren and skrayling politics. Quite what, though, she could not fathom.

The skraylings finished tying them up and departed with their captain. Coby called out to Sandy, but he didn't respond. Maybe the captain had gagged him, or fed him a sleeping draught to keep him quiet. She realised she had no idea how the skraylings dealt with their prisoners. They did not seem like a cruel people, and yet she had heard some blood-curdling stories of the New World, of human sacrifice and mutilation. If the skraylings inscribed their flesh with needles for mere decoration, what might they not do to their enemies?

"Hendricks?"

She turned at the sound of her name. Gabriel grinned at her, his face a mask of blood, bruises and shadows. No, the skraylings would not have been so rough if they had intended to sell their human passengers to slavers. She took a sliver of comfort from the thought.

"You're not badly hurt?" she asked Gabriel.

"I gave as good as I got. You?"

"The same. I'm not sure about Sandy, though. He's been silent since the captain left."

She craned her neck. Sandy was trussed up tighter than his companions, and by the looks of it only the ropes held him upright. His head lolled forward, his features slack and eyes closed.

"Have you any idea why we've been taken prisoner?" Gabriel asked.

She shook her head. "It makes no sense. If the captain isn't our friend, why did he bring us all this way? Did he change his mind?"

"He could be taking us somewhere else."

"But where? Not Africa. I've seen for myself how much the skraylings fear slavery."

"Spain, then. You and I both work for Walsingham; I am sure King Philip would pay a bounty for the likes of us."

Coby shuddered. "They'd torture us for information."

"I dare say they would."

"You aren't afraid?"

"Terrified, to be frank. But we're not betrayed to the Spanish yet, so there's no point worrying about it, is there?"

"I wish I could be so sanguine."

The deck above them trembled with the passage of footsteps, and dust sifted down, sparkling in the thin beams of sunlight that pierced the planking. The captain shouted orders, and the entire vessel creaked and groaned as it shifted to starboard.

"What? Why are we heading west?" Coby cried out.

"West? Are you sure?" Gabriel looked around. "Perhaps we're turning back for England."

"Perhaps." It was a thin hope at best. "I think I can get

out of my bonds. Mal's taught me a few tricks in the last year, and I have one or two of my own."

"Such as?"

She strained to look around. "I'd rather not say out loud. We can't be sure who's listening."

"Good point."

"Anyway, there's no use our getting free until we have a plan."

"And do you have one of those?"

"Alas, no."

Sandy sagged against his bonds, his stomach churning, though whether that was revulsion at the memories flooding his mind, or just the usual disorientation he felt whenever he put a spirit-guard on, he could not decide. Perhaps a mix of both. What had the captain said the young skrayling's name was? Daniel, or something like it. And Daniel had gone into the lion's den and not come out.

It had been a winter's night, eleven years ago, when Sandy and Mal had been woken by their elder brother Charles and taken on a midnight ride across the hills with the Huntsmen. A ride that ended in fire and mutilation and murder, an act intended to strike fear into the hearts of the skraylings and ensure they never ventured outside their enclave again. It was also the initiation of the two brothers into that secret order, against their will.

His memories blurred into a parade of images as unreal as the flickering shapes seen in a fire: distorted faces leering at him, candlelight that burned his eyes, houses flashing past the window of a coach… and through it all, the memory of the skrayling's cries of agony. He had not recognised him as the boy from the council meeting, of course – the trauma of rebirth had locked most of Erishen away in the depths of his mind –but seeing Tanijeel tortured and murdered by the Huntsmen had broken through the scars.

Now the wounds bled afresh and he wept with guilt and grief. Hennaq was right. Too many had died already, and it was all his fault.

CHAPTER XII

They had fought off the corsairs, but it was a Pyrrhic victory. Nearly a third of the crew were either dead or so badly injured that their lives hung in the balance, and few had escaped unscathed. Every man who could walk and use at least one hand found himself doing double watches, including Mal and Ned. As far as possible they were given the simplest tasks: hauling on the sheets under the guidance of more experienced sailors, tending the wounded, fetching and carrying anything that was needed by Raleigh or the crew.

Unfortunately the ship's carpenter was one of the casualties, and without him the crew were able to make only the most basic repairs. The stern was the highest priority, and by the end of the first day after the attack the rear wall of the captain's cabin had been cobbled back together, enough to keep out the worst of the wind and sea should they hit a storm. However they had to break up most of the remaining bunk beds for planking, so Raleigh moved into the forward cabin and Mal and Ned joined the common sailors below. There was plenty of space now that so many of the crew were gone, but with the moans of the dying echoing up from the hold and only a few unbroken lanterns left to light the pitch darkness, the lower decks might as well have been some forgotten corner of Hell.

"What now?" Ned asked one morning, as he and Mal squatted on coils of rope in the shade of the mizzenmast, stealing a moment's rest between errands. He stretched out his legs, knowing that his aching feet would be even more painful once he stood up again, but the chance of a respite was too good to resist.

"Raleigh's set a course for Sardinia," Mal replied, staring off into the distance.

"Where's that?"

Mal shook out a length of rope and arranged it in the rough outline of the Mediterranean.

"We were about here when the corsairs attacked," he said, pointing to a spot well north of the African coast, "and Sardinia is here, halfway between France and Italy. It's not too far out of our way, at least."

"You don't sound very happy about it."

"Sardinia is ruled by Spain. Even if we can recruit more crew there, can we trust them?"

"Do we have a choice?"

Mal shook his head. "Another corsair attack, and we're dead. Raleigh will never surrender to slavers."

"Is that likely?" Ned asked.

Mal didn't answer. Ned swallowed past a sudden tightness in his throat. He'd known this voyage would be dangerous, but until now he hadn't understood just how great that danger might be. And if he died here at sea, so far from home, how long would it take for the news to reach Gabriel? Gabriel, whose face he might never see again... He felt tears prick his eyes, and cleared his throat noisily in an attempt to force them away.

"Come on," Mal said, scrambling to his feet. "No use in fretting about what may never happen. We have work to do."

• • • •

The *Falcon* limped into Cagliari harbour two days later, her crew capable of raising only the faintest of cheers. Mal paused for a moment on his way to the rail, and then slumped back onto the fo'c's'le stair, his blistered hands falling into his lap. A moment later Ned slithered down the stair behind him and clapped him on the shoulder.

"Soon be back on dry land," he said, his voice as raw as Mal's palms.

"You'll have to winch me ashore," Mal groaned, leaning his cheek against the rough planking. "And hire a wheelbarrow, to tip me into bed."

By the time they weighed anchor Mal had rallied somewhat, and was persuaded to gather his belongings and stagger down the gangplank with the rest of the crew. They followed Raleigh across the too-bright quay and through winding streets to an inn, where they were shown into a courtyard filled with tables and benches. Mal sagged onto a bench at Ned's side, and laid his head down on folded arms. He could swear the cobblestones were rolling underfoot like waves. It felt like only a moment later when someone shook him awake.

"Mal? Supper."

He raised his head. The courtyard was half in shadow, and though his shirt had dried on his back as he slept, his shoes and stockings were still damp and stiff with salt water. He straightened up and rubbed a hand over his sunburned face. Someone had mentioned supper?

On the table in front of him sat a bowl of stew and an earthenware cup of velvet-red wine. Suddenly aware he'd not eaten since breakfast, he pulled the bowl towards him and dipped the spoon into the broth. The dull green ovals of broad beans bobbed amongst hunks of dark fish-meat, along with what looked like a slice of lemon. Mal tasted it cautiously then, hunger roused, wolfed the contents of the bowl, wiping it clean with a hunk of coarse bread.

Ned grinned at him across the table. "Better?"

"Much." He drained his cup and refilled it from a jug. "Where are we?"

"Some hostelry in the backstreets. I just followed the rest of them."

He looked at the surrounding building in curiosity, and Mal followed his gaze. Thick walls of whitewashed cob surrounded them on all sides, pierced by round-arched windows and roofed with terracotta tiles. Olive trees stood in huge green-glazed pots at intervals around the courtyard, and over the rooftops they could see more buildings in the same style, rising up into the darkening sky where the waning moon gleamed like a well-used English penny.

"First time on foreign soil, eh?" Mal said.

"Yes." Ned looked back at him. "Is it all like this?"

"Like what?"

"So… bright and dark at the same time. Blinding sun, and shadows like drowning pools…"

"How much have you had to drink?" Mal asked, taking another sip of his own wine.

"No more than you."

"Enough then, on an empty stomach."

A dark-haired girl sauntered over with a flagon on her hip. As she set it down on the table, she leant forward rather further than was necessary, giving them a fine view of sun-tanned breasts plumped up by a tight-laced bodice. Smiling at Mal she slowly stepped back a pace, as if inviting him to follow. He grinned, stood up rather too quickly, and threw up his fish supper at her feet. The girl pulled a face and flounced off in search of a less inebriated sailor.

"Come on, let's put you to bed," Ned said, taking him by the arm.

Mal wiped his mouth on the back of his hand, took a last gulp of wine to wash away the sour taste of vomit and let himself be led away from the now-raucous party of sailors. Ned steered him around a potted olive tree, through an archway and along a short passage. At the far end was a sturdy oak door with iron staples either side and a length of timber leaning against the wall nearby. Mal stared at it for a moment, fuzzily certain there was a reason for a door being like that.

Ned fumbled with the latch for a moment before getting it open, and they stumbled through. The passageway was narrow, with blank whitewashed walls on either side that caught the moonlight so that Mal could easily see the ground ahead. Fortunate, since it still felt unsteady under his feet. He followed Ned down the passage and out into a street running along the back of the inn. Ah, that was the reason for the bar on the door. They were outside the inn.

"I think we came the wrong way," Ned said, voicing his own thoughts. "Let's go back."

As they turned to retrace their steps, two men stepped out of the shadows of a doorway opposite. Mal froze, instantly far more sober than he had been moments before. Neither of the men appeared to be armed, but both were broad of shoulder and hard of eye. Mal decided he had enough aches and pains already, without adding fresh bruises to the list.

"Can I help you, gentlemen?" he asked in Occitan, the nearest dialect he knew to the local language.

The Sicilian drawled a reply; Mal could only make out something about "English", and possibly an obscenity involving his mother and overweight poultry. To emphasis his point the Sardinian followed it up with a raised middle finger.

"Fuck yourself, sirrah!" Ned returned the gesture.

The Sardinian spat on the ground and assumed a fighter's stance, knees slightly bent and fists at the ready. When Mal held his ground, the man made a beckoning gesture, tilting his head back. Mal caught movement out of the corner of his eye.

"Forget it, Ned," he murmured. "Go on, back down the alley."

"But–"

"Just do it."

He heard rather than saw his friend comply. All his attention was on the Sardinians, who were grinning now. Mal sighed and drew his rapier.

"Go home, lads," he said in English, circling round towards the alley mouth, "unless you want your kidneys served up on a platter."

The Sardinians eyed the yard-long blade for a moment, then melted into the night.

"What was all that about?" Ned asked as Mal followed him down the alley to the inn door.

"Just drunkards on the lookout for trouble," Mal replied, sheathing the rapier. Even their assassin's unknown master could surely not have discovered them here, so far off their intended route.

He ducked through the doorway back into the inn and the safety of several dozen of his own countrymen. Rather than trust to Ned's sense of direction he hailed a passing serving girl.

"Our room?" he asked, miming laying his head on his hands to sleep.

She smiled and gestured to herself. Mal shook his head; after what had just happened, he was reluctant to put himself in a position of vulnerability with any stranger, no matter how comely. He made the sleeping gesture again, and she pointed to an outside staircase in the far corner of the courtyard.

At the top of the stairs, Mal signalled to Ned to halt and took the lead, rapier drawn once more. Though it seemed unlikely they would meet any more trouble tonight, it never hurt to be careful. Pushing the door open with the point of the blade, he looked inside without stepping over the threshold.

Moonlight etched the bedchamber's scant contents in lines of silver and black: a wide bed, a washstand with a basin but no ewer, and a short bench under the window. Mal kicked the door wide and entered, sweeping the rapier in an arc at waist height. No Sardinian brigands leapt out at him, however, and he beckoned for Ned to follow. A few moments later they had a candle lit and were able to assure themselves that they were alone in the room. Mal bolted the door and closed the shutters on the window.

A room to ourselves, eh? I suppose Raleigh didn't want any more trouble between Ned and the crew, although this is just going to stir more rumours.

Ned placed the candle in a smoke-blackened niche near the bed and sat down to pull off his boots.

"Almost like home," he said.

"Aye, it does take me back."

Mal sat down on the bed next to his friend and pulled off his own boots, dropping them noisily on the floorboards. They both undressed to shirt and drawers and lay down side by side, staring at the ceiling. Mal groaned. The bed seemed to sway underneath him like the deck of the *Falcon*. He knew he ought to sit up, but it was too much effort.

"You and me. Mates again," Ned murmured.

"Aye."

Ned rolled over and propped himself up on one elbow. "Really?"

"Of course. Why do you think I asked you along?"

Ned leant closer. "I've missed you," he said, and kissed Mal on the cheek.

Mal turned his head towards him, acutely aware now of Ned's closeness, the warmth of another body only a finger's breadth from his own. Ned kissed him again, on the mouth this time, and a shiver of lust passed over Mal's skin like a hot breeze. He pulled away reluctantly.

"Don't be a damned fool, Ned. Raleigh's crew have already put two and two together and made five."

Ned made a rude noise. "They're going to think it anyway, be we chaste as virgins."

He sat up and pulled his shirt over his head. In the candlelight his skin was smooth and golden, as flawless as Mal's had once been, long ago.

"What about Parrish?" Mal asked, groping for another objection. He really didn't want this. Did he?

"What about him?"

"Aren't you and he…?"

"We have this agreement," Ned said. He lay back down on his side, head cradled on an arm grown hard with muscle from their recent labours. "What with him disappearing off on tour with the Prince's Men for months on end and all. Private performances for Lord This or Earl That, know what I mean? So, I don't ask him who he's fucked, and he doesn't ask me. Only difference this time is, I'm the one who's far from home."

"I see."

"What about you and Hendricks?"

"I told you, I'm not–"

"–interested in young boys. I know. But Hendricks isn't a boy, is she?"

Mal stared at him. "You know about her? How?"

"Your brother told me, back in London."

"Oh." He muttered a curse under his breath. It had never occurred to him that Sandy might find out, or need warning not to tell anyone.

"You worried he might take your place?" Ned asked with a sly smile.

"No." His brother only had eyes for Kiiren, that was obvious. Or rather, Erishen did. What Sandy's feelings were on the matter, he had no idea. He swore again. Just thinking about Erishen made his head ache.

"Well, then. Forget about it." Ned shuffled a little closer. "Anyway, you never answered my question."

"About Coby? What do you expect me to say?" He sighed. "She refuses to wear women's garb, and I cannot make love to her as she is, for fear the servants would see us and gossip. I have no desire to be burned at the stake."

Ned made a dismissive noise. "Barbarians, the lot of them. You should come back to London for good."

He took Mal's unresisting hand and kissed each knuckle in turn, then made his way back across the finger joints, one by one. Mal clenched his fist, then shook Ned's hand away.

"We can't go back to the way things were."

"Come on, just for one night. You know you want to." Ned ran his fingertips up the inside of Mal's thigh, making him gasp in anticipation. "You know you want *me*."

Mal closed his eyes, caught between desire and guilt, but the phantom movement of the floor made him want to throw up again. He opened his eyes, and blinked. For an instant he thought the dark-haired figure leaning over him had mottled skin and golden eyes, then the illusion passed. This was just Ned, as human as ever. Wasn't it? Heart pounding, Mal slid his hand around Ned's waist and down the back of his drawers.

Ned chuckled. "That's better."

There. The rounded end of a human spine, not the stubby tail he had feared to find. But the image persisted in his mind's eye. Kiiren. He released Ned and pushed him away.

"Mal?"

Mal ignored him. He staggering over to the window and flung the shutters open, sucking in deep lungfuls of cool evening air to try and clear his head. What in God's name was happening to him? Was this some vision seen through his brother's eyes? Or were Erishen's memories of another life surfacing once more?

He recalled Sandy's words. Like being drunk. Could drink itself have the same effect? Was he Erishen right now? He didn't feel any different. He stumbled over to his knapsack, pulled out the earring and with trembling fingers fastened it in place. No, still no different.

He looked down at Ned, who had turned away, the taut muscles of his back as eloquent a statement of frustration and disappointment as any words. Mal found his eyes tracing the lines of the other man's shoulder-blades, down his spine to… No, he could not blame Erishen for his own feelings towards Ned.

He lay back down, the space between them now a chasm. For a moment he considered apologising to Ned, perhaps even trying to explain, then thought better of it. He rolled over, wincing as a piece of straw stabbed through the mattress into his hip, and prayed for the room to stop moving.

Ned leant against the windowsill, basking in the warmth of the newly risen sun. Back home it would still be cold at this hour, and summer only a distant promise. Mal's estates were somewhere north of here, he recalled, on the mainland. No wonder Mal was so tanned, and Hendricks so sunburnt.

Thoughts of Hendricks only served to remind him of last night. He didn't know who he was most annoyed with: Mal for rejecting him, or himself for making such a dog's dinner of the whole thing. He was out of practice at seduction, that was the trouble. Not that he regretted devoting his attention to Gabriel these past two years, but Gabe was home, security… routine. With Mal around, anything could happen, and usually did. Admittedly it had been rare for their lives to be in serious danger like this, but even the most trivial escapade had lent a delicious edge to their carousing.

He cursed softly. That was why Mal couldn't give Hendricks up. Surely they must have had far narrower escapes together than he and Mal ever did – and yet she denied him the celebration of life he craved. Uptight little puritan! She hadn't changed a bit. Not that he could entirely blame Mal for desiring her. He himself had been fooled into trying to kiss her once, back when he still thought her a boy – though she had responded by biting him, the venomous bitch! If God had not ordained it, surely no man of sense would choose to consort with women.

Mal stirred and rolled over.

"Who's there?" He sounded wide awake already, and in no good humour.

"It's only me." Ned held up his hands as Mal groped for his blades. "Good day to you too."

"Why's the window open?"

"You opened it last night, remember? Besides, I thought we needed some fresh air in here. Even your would-be footpads aren't going to be attacking us in broad daylight."

"Dawn is one of the best times," Mal said, sitting upright and retrieving his breeches. "Your victim is drowsy, the light dim and shadowless..."

"Another of Walsingham's lessons?"

"Something I learned on campaign."

"How's your head, by the way?"

"Don't ask." Mal finished dressing and strapped on his sword belt. "Come on, let's find a serving wench. I need breakfast."

CHAPTER XIII

Coby spent a sleepless night considering and discarding half a hundred plans for escape. Unfortunately most of them depended on the ship being in harbour, and there was no way of knowing how near or far that day might be. Even if the skraylings were taking them back to London, it could be another week or more. And the alternative, that they were being taken to the New World, did not bear thinking about. Her body already ached in every joint from being immobilised; how she would endure days or weeks of it, she did not know.

Her own suffering was a small thing, though, compared to Sandy. Late in the evening two of the sailors had come down to the hold to check on the prisoners and give them a little water to drink. As they had lifted Sandy's head to try and force some water between his lips, Coby had caught a glimpse of metal at his throat. The spirit-guard. She had seen what happened when he wore it for more than a few hours a night. And now he was likely to be wearing it for weeks. She had failed in her duty to Mal twice over.

By the time the sun rose, she was dizzy with hunger and lack of sleep, but still determined to find a way out of their predicament. When she heard movement above and feet on the ladder, she instantly roused. To her left, Gabriel stirred against his own bonds. She waited, heart pounding.

Half a dozen skrayling sailors entered the hold, came straight over to the two younger prisoners and began untying their bonds. Coby would have fallen if one of them hadn't caught her, wedging his shoulder under her armpit and wrapping both of his arms about her waist. Even as she slumped with her chin on the skrayling's shoulder, a small part of her mind reflected that this would be a good opportunity to relieve the sailor of his belt-knife. Of course it would be a lot easier if she had any feeling in her limbs.

The sailor tried to walk her to the ladder, but her legs were not her own and refused to obey. He gave up and sat her on a pile of empty sacks with a growled warning not to move. It was hardly necessary. She lay sprawled like a discarded doll, biting back tears as the feeling began to return to her limbs in a flood of fire.

She looked across at Gabriel, who was being led up and down the deck with his arms round the shoulders of two of the skraylings. They looked like a trio of drunks on their way home from the alehouse, and she would have smiled if it had not been for their dire situation. Instead she chafed her hands and feet and endured the pain.

One of the other sailors brought them cornbread and watered *aniig*. By the time Coby had broken her fast, her strength was beginning to return. The skraylings appeared to have anticipated this, however, and stood ready with staves to beat the prisoners back. They had still not untied Sandy, she noticed, though they had attempted to feed him; not an easy task since he was the best part of a foot taller than any of them.

A shadow fell across her lap and she looked up to see a skrayling standing over her. She recognised him by the pattern of beads in his hair as the one who had supported her weight when she was untied. He held out his hand.

"You walk," he said. "See sky."

She was not about to turn down a chance at a walk in the fresh air, so she reached out and let him help her up.

"Thank you."

It was slow, painful going, climbing first one ladder to the gun deck and then a second to the weather deck, and by the time she emerged into the sunlight she was shaking like a man with the ague. She slumped against her guide once more, squinting against the brightness and trying to take stock of her surroundings. Beyond the ship's rail, dark blue waters stretched as far as the eye could see. She turned her head, but the view was no different. No chance of escape here.

After a short walk around the deck and a visit to the jakes – a tiny, well-scrubbed cabin in the bow – it was time to go back to the hold. At the bottom of the ladder she shook off her guard and stumbled over to Sandy. His eyes were unfocused, and he was mumbling under his breath.

"Sandy?"

His eyes sought hers. "Prove thy servants, I beseech thee, ten days, and let them give us pulse to eat, and water to drink. Then let our countenances be looked upon before thee, and the countenances of the children that eat of the portion of the King's meat: and as thou seest, deal with thy servants."

"Which servants?" It was a verse from the Old Testament, she was certain, but she could not place it.

"And the King said unto them, I have dreamed a dream, and my spirit was troubled to know the dream."

"Daniel," she cried. "You speak of King Nebuchadnezzar, in the book of Daniel."

Sandy lifted his head, staring fixedly at the underside of the deck above.

"And at the ninth hour," he said, his voice rising to a wail, "Jesus cried with a loud voice, saying, *Eloi, Eloi, lama sabachthani*? 'My God, my God, why hast thou forsaken me?'"

"Hush, Sandy, be still!" She glanced back over her shoulder, expecting the skraylings to haul her away any moment. "He hasn't forsaken us. Sandy, trust Him. We will be delivered, like Daniel. I swear it."

Sandy ceased his moaning, subsiding into glazed-eyed silence. With a heavy heart she allowed the skraylings to lead her back to the wooden pillar.

"Need I talk to high-fellah," she told them as they secured her once more. "Erishen-tuur is sick, go die soon."

The nearest skrayling cocked his head, tattooed brow creasing.

"He die?"

"Aye. Hurry!"

It was an exaggeration, but she couldn't think what else would persuade them to give her the chance she needed. A chance to talk some sense into Captain Hennaq, before Sandy was beyond her help.

Slow hours passed, and the sun was approaching its zenith by Coby's reckoning before the skraylings returned. There were only two of them this time, and neither was her friend from breakfast. Perhaps it was mere chance, or perhaps his small kindnesses to the prisoners had been noted.

She stumbled a little as they removed the ropes binding her to the upright beam, and noticed that they stepped backwards as if expecting this to be the first feint in an attack. They waited for her to steady herself against the pillar, then closed in and bound her wrists in front of her. Quite what they thought one lone youth could do against a shipful of men, she could not imagine.

On cue, Gabriel shouted after them, just as they had planned.

"Where are you taking her?"

The skraylings ignored him. Coby wondered how much English the sailors understood, and whether they had noticed that Gabriel had revealed her true sex. She hoped so. It would lend weight to the argument she was about to unfold.

Her escort led her up onto the weather deck as before. The sun was dazzling now, and hot as an English summer day. Coby squinted at the horizon, but it was as empty as ever. She wondered how far they were from land. Too far, that was for certain.

The captain's cabin was as dark as a cave after the sunlit deck, and she stood blinking for several moments as coloured shapes swam across her vision. Voices spoke in Vinlandic; the captain questioning her escort, perhaps? At last her vision cleared, but the sight that met her eyes was not encouraging.

Captain Hennaq stood on the opposite side of the cabin, his pose one of extreme formality: arms by his side, palms turned forward in a greeting that was barely more than an acknowledgement of her presence. One of the sailors pressed her shoulder, and she knelt on the matting. The captain gestured to his men, who backed off but did not leave.

"You asked to speak to me," Hennaq said in Tradetalk, his accent heavier than normal, as if deliberately straining her comprehension.

"Yes, sir. As one leader to another, I ask that you show mercy to my men."

"Your men?" Hennaq gave a hissing laugh. "You are but a boy."

"No, sir." She looked him in the eye. "I am a woman of my people."

She got to her feet and made a formal curtsey as best she could. It would hardly pass muster at court, but the skraylings were unlikely to know the difference.

"A woman?"

"I am sure you have searched our belongings by now. Did you not find women's clothing amongst them?"

"One of your party is an actor. How am I to know the clothes were not his? And if you are a woman, why do you not dress like one?"

"I..." She took a deep breath, and then another, as she had seen the actors do before going on stage. "Your physician, if you have one, may examine me to find the truth."

The captain gestured to one of the men, who left the cabin. The other sailor spoke to the captain. Coby wondered if he was relaying Gabriel's words. Perhaps so, since Hennaq nodded and looked at her more closely.

"Even if this is true," the captain said at last, "it is no proof you are their leader. I am not ignorant of human custom, here or in the New World."

"You concede that we English are ruled by a queen?"

"Of course. But no other woman sits on your great councils."

"True." She thought of Lady Frances Sidney. "But women serve our country in many ways, not always openly."

"Women like you."

"Yes."

"Is this why you pass yourself off as a man?"

"It is safer when travelling, especially in strange lands where I have few friends."

The cabin door opened, and the sailor entered with an older skrayling in dark blue robes, carrying a wooden workbox. The newcomer spoke to the captain in low tones, both of them eyeing Coby from time to time. She swallowed and pressed her shaking hands together. The physician.

"This is Elder Gaoh," the captain said. "He will examine you, as you have offered."

The old skrayling knelt down on the mat at her feet and opened his workbox. From it he took a bulbous glass flask, into which he poured a little liquid from a sealed ceramic bottle, and swirled it around. The liquid began to glow like a miniature sun. Lightwater, but stronger than any she had seen before. He held the lamp up to Coby's face and examined her skin through a lens set in a bone handle. Coby hardly dared to breathe. He lifted her upper lip to examine her teeth, and ran a thumb up and down her throat until she could not help but cough.

Next he unbuttoned her doublet. She trembled, fearing he was going to strip her, but he merely unfastened the neck of her shirt and lent close, sniffing delicately at the exposed flesh. Coby felt a blush rising from her throat at this strangely intimate gesture. Gaoh hummed to himself and refastened her clothing.

At last the physician gestured for her to show him her hands. He turned them over, examining front and back minutely, though for what she could not imagine. He said something to the captain in Vinlandic and put away his instruments. Coby breathed a sigh of relief, hardly able to believe she had avoided a more intimate exploration.

"It appears your story is true," the captain said. "Please, sit."

Coby inclined her head and obeyed.

"You said you were the leader of the two men," Hennaq went on. "The pale-haired one I concede is no leader, though I am told he is a fine actor. But Erishen-tuur is one of our *qoheetajeneth*, and has seen many lifetimes. I cannot believe he would submit to the leadership of any human, even a female."

"He is not himself, sir," she replied. "Indeed, this is the matter on which I wanted to speak to you."

"Ah, yes." Hennaq scratched his chin. "You told my men that Erishen-tuur was going to die."

"I... Perhaps it was not the right word to use. But he is very sick, as I am sure they have told you."

"I shall have Elder Gaoh attend him."

"This is not a sickness of the body, sir. The lodestone necklace upsets his mind."

Hennaq frowned at her.

"How is that possible? It is meant to protect, not harm."

"I don't really understand it myself. But you have to take it off, or he will get worse."

"I cannot. It would not be safe for anyone on board."

"You think he would attack you with his... sorcery? I will gladly vouch that he would not."

A lie, and she feared the captain could see it in her eyes. She was not at all confident that Sandy would listen to her, not after this.

"Do you know what he can do?" Hennaq asked.

"Some of it." She shivered, remembering Suffolk's man hacking one of the other servants to death. What had that been, if not bewitchment? "Will their own spirit-guards not keep your crewmen safe?"

Hennaq's expression hardened. "And why should I punish my own men for his transgressions? No, I will not do it."

"Punish them? I don't understand."

"No, you do not. I cannot expect a human to understand our customs. And I cannot free Erishen now that he knows my purpose."

"What purpose?" A sick feeling roiled in her stomach.

"I am taking him back to our people, to answer for his crimes."

"His crimes?" She leapt to her feet, not caring any more about etiquette. "It is you who have lied to us, stolen him away–"

"And your people stole ours away. You and your companion are descendants of the Birch Men, no?"

"No."

"I think yes. You look just like the Birch Men in the old tales, and England was part of their domains, was it not?"

"Yes, but–" She broke off, trying to marshal her thoughts. "You can't take us all the way to the New World. It's not fair."

"I am sorry," the captain said, "but I have made my decision. Erishen will stand trial."

One last try. She would not give up on Mal.

"For what crime?" she said, trying to keep the anger and frustration out of her voice.

"For leading my heart-mate and others astray."

"How? He has been locked up in a sanctuary for the sick of mind since he was a boy. Or is this some more recent crime, since he was taken to Sark?"

"No, I speak of long ago, when Erishen was one with our people."

"When he was a skrayling."

"Yes."

"But..." She was out of her depth now. "But the man you have captured did not commit those crimes. He has a new life now."

"Nonetheless, he is still Erishen. The soul is accountable, as well as the body." Hennaq spread his hands.

A desperate thought struck her. "If you want to try Erishen," she said slowly, "you need the whole man, not half a one."

"What do you mean?"

"Erishen has a brother. Lord Kiiren's former bodyguard, Maliverny Catlyn."

"I know of this man. He is the one whom Kiiren-tuur brought before the council of elders. What of him?"

"Have you not heard? They are not merely brothers, they are twins."

Hennaq muttered something under his breath in Vinlandic. "You are sure?"

"Certain. That's how Master Catlyn found the skrayling captives on Corsica. He and Sandy are two halves of a fractured soul. They are both Erishen."

"This complicates matters," Hennaq said, shaking his head.

"Yes it does. You need both of them if it is to be a fair trial."

"And you know where to find this other brother?"

"Of course. He is going to Venice."

Hennaq laughed, setting his beaded hair rattling. "Oh, very clever. You think you can trick me into taking you to Kiiren?"

"It is the truth, I swear. Do what you will to me, let your sorcerers probe my secret thoughts if you must. But I swear in the name of all that is holy, I speak the truth."

The captain stared into the middle distance for a long moment, running his tongue around one fang thoughtfully.

"Very well," he said at last. "I will take you to Venice, and you will bring this other brother to me."

Coby nodded, though she had no intention of doing so. "And you will take the spirit-guard from Sandy?"

"That remains to be seen. How do I know I can trust him not to turn on me and my crew?"

"He wishes to be with his brother, more than anything in the world. And the sooner you take that thing off him, the saner he will be, and the less likely to harm you."

"I will order my men to do so, and to replace your bonds with ones less confining." He stepped around the cushions so that he was only an arm's length away. "But I warn you, human. If you pay back my kindness with treachery, I shall throw all three of you into the ocean without a second thought. Do you understand?"

"Yes, sir."

One moment he was gasping for breath, pulse hammering in his ears; the next, his lungs filled with air and he was blinking away salt water. Had he been rescued from drowning? Two pairs of eyes, grey as the sea in winter, blue as summer sky, stared down at him. Human eyes.

"Sandy?"

That was what they called this incarnation, wasn't it? He drew breath and whispered: "*Hä*. Yes."

"Thank God." The grey-eyed one, the girl, lifted his hand and kissed it.

"Something is wrong?"

"No, no. You had a seizure, and we feared you might hurt yourself."

He tasted metal now, as well as salt. The young man, Gabriel, helped him to sit up. Erishen spat blood on the deck, squinting as a bright yellow light loomed before his eyes. Gentle fingers took hold of his jaw and examined his mouth.

"Nothing worse than a bitten tongue," the owner of the hands said.

It was a moment before Erishen realised his examiner had spoken in Vinlandic. The light receded, and he made out the features of an ancient skrayling with faded clan markings on his cheeks and forehead.

"Hennaq–" Erishen looked around. So, still in the hold. "Where is that misbegotten son of a raccoon?"

"Calm yourself, honoured one, or you will have another seizure."

"I'm fine."

He got to his feet, too quickly. The world pivoted and he stumbled, banging his elbow painfully against the mast as he tried to steady himself.

"Please, sir, sit down," the girl said, catching hold of his other arm.

He allowed her to help him back down, irksome as it was to display such weakness in front of others.

"I thought I saw you captured and bound, both of you." He looked from one to the other.

"I… made a deal with the captain." She stared pointedly at the old skrayling, who clicked his tongue but packed his medicine chest and left them. When they were alone, she told Erishen about Hennaq's plan to take them all back to the New World, and how she had persuaded him to go after Mal instead.

"You–" He lunged for her, knocking her down onto the deck.

Gabriel caught him by the arm. "Dammit, Sandy–"

Erishen turned and snarled at him, and the actor backed off, hands held up defensively. The girl took advantage of the distraction to twist underneath him, trying to throw him off. He caught hold of her wrists, but she brought her knee up between his legs. Erishen howled.

"Stop it!" Gabriel fell to his knees and tried to push them apart. "Look at the two of you, fighting like dogs in the street. How does that help Mal, or any of us?"

Erishen shot him a warning look, but the man was right. With a sigh he released the girl. Hendricks, that was her name. She scooted away across the deck until her back was against a stack of crates and crouched there, eyeing him sullenly.

"You really think I would betray Mal?" she said in a low voice. She glanced up towards the hatch, then back at Erishen.

"Then what do you intend to do when we get to Venice?" he replied, matching her tone. She was right; Hennaq could have set someone to spy on them, and some of his men likely knew English, even if they refused to speak such an effete tongue.

"I don't know yet," she said. "But it's still going to take us several weeks to get there. We're bound to come up with a plan by then."

Erishen made a noncommittal noise. The three of them against a shipful of skraylings? He did not like those odds at all.

CHAPTER XIV

Hiring enough crew in Cagliari to get them to Venice proved difficult, especially once the name of their captain got about. Many of the locals were reluctant to sign on with the man who had time and again led victorious forces against their Spanish overlords, nor was Raleigh keen to hire them. In fact their captain proved to be so choosy about whom he would consider, Mal despaired of ever reaching their destination.

"Raleigh knows the urgency of our mission," he said for the hundredth time. He and Ned were sitting on the harbour wall, watching Master Warburton supervise the repairs. "We need a full crew, or..."

"Or what?" Ned asked.

"Or we leave here on another ship. Today."

"Today? Why today?"

"Why not today? At this rate, the skraylings could have completed their negotiations and be on their way back to Sark by the time we reach Venice."

"Or they could still be cooling their heels in the... What did you say the ruler was called again?"

"The Doge."

"Aye, him. Anyway they could still be cooling their

heels in this Doge's antechamber," Ned replied. "Or on their way home with nothing to show for it. We won't know until we speak to Lord Kiiren."

"If he'll even tell me."

"I thought you two were friends." Ned snickered. "Practically brothers-in-law."

"I thought so too," Mal replied, ignoring the jibe. "But if so, why was he so secretive about this mission? Did he think I was spying on him?"

"You are spying on him."

"Well, yes, but..." He shook his head. "There's something else going on, just like there was back in London."

"Such as?"

"I have no idea. Last time, Kiiren was trying to hide the truth about Sandy and me from his kinsmen. As to what he's hiding this time..." He shrugged.

He took out Walsingham's second letter, which he had taken to carrying in his pocket at all times. A name and directions were written on the outside:

Sr. G. Berowne
Salizada San Pantalon
Venezia

Mal wondered what the ambassador was like. A country knight of no account, perhaps, sent overseas to serve his Queen with few thanks and fewer rewards. Much like Mal's own father. He was tempted to cut the seal, but doubtless there was nothing of real interest in there anyway, since Walsingham would expect him to open it.

"Ahoy there! Catlyn!"

Mal turned to see Raleigh waving at him.

"What does he want?" Ned muttered.

"I suspect we are about to find out." He jumped down from the harbour wall and strode towards Raleigh. "Sir?"

"You mentioned you are acquainted with a sea-captain in Marseille."

"Aye, that's true."

"Good. I want you on the next ship thence. Bring me back carpenters and crew, as many as you can." He pressed a heavy purse into Mal's hand.

"Aye, sir. Thank you, sir."

Raleigh frowned at him. "I'm not doing it for you. I need my ship repaired, and these damned Sardinians are worse than useless. I fear the governor has sent out word that we are not to be helped."

"Surely it's in his interest to see the back of us."

"It would be, unless he's stalling because he's sent for Spanish reinforcements to capture us."

"You think that likely?"

"I think it is not wise to discount it. And you are, I'll warrant, as anxious to be done here as I."

"Yes, sir."

"Good. Then get to it. There's a ship sailing north this afternoon."

Mal bowed and headed back to the inn, Ned trailing at his heels.

"Of course," Ned said as they crossed the market square, "we could just take Raleigh's money and sail to Venice on the next boat heading east, like you said."

"We could, but we're not going to."

"Why not?"

"Because I don't need Raleigh as an enemy. I have enough of those already."

"Who is this friend of yours?" Ned asked as they disembarked in Marseille.

The harbour was thick with fishing boats, and the skies even thicker with gulls. They picked their way around piles of netting, baskets of silver anchovies and dark blue mussels, and squirming sacks of live octopus.

"His name's Youssef," Mal replied. "A Moorish merchant."

"You, dealing with a heathen? I thought you fought in the wars against them, the Moors or Turks or whoever?"

"So I did, years ago. But the French have allied themselves with the Ottoman Empire against the Hapsburgs, and men like Youssef can pass easily between Christendom and the Barbary Coast."

"He's a spy?"

"No." Mal caught his arm. "And do not imply any such thing within his hearing. Not if you wish to go home with all your members intact."

The *Hayreddin* stood at anchor at the end of the quay, its triangular sails reefed and its oars drawn in with only their blades protruding from the rowlocks. Men were carrying barrels up the gangplank in a steady stream, then jogging back down empty-handed.

"I thought you said he was a merchant," Ned said in a low voice as they drew nearer. "That looks a lot like the ship that attacked us."

"Oared vessels are common in the Mediterranean. The seas are gentler, and slaves plentiful."

"Slaves? Are you sure he's not a corsair?"

Mal laughed. "Calm yourself. There are no slaves aboard the *Hayreddin*. Captain Youssef considers them an unnecessary expense, since God provides the wind for free. The oars are for manoeuvring into harbour, that is all." *Well, mostly all.*

Ned muttered something under his breath.

"Of course," Mal added, "if you'd rather be imprisoned by the Spanish..."

"No. It's just... not what I expected. Your life in France, I mean."

"You thought France was exactly like England, only with more wine and garlic?"

Ned pulled a face. "Now you're mocking me."

Captain Youssef greeted them courteously in French and invited them into his cabin, where he served them sweet mint tea and honeyed pastries. Mal told him about the attack on the *Falcon* and his own need to reach Venice as quickly as possible.

"Perhaps the ship is not so badly damaged," Youssef said. "Danziger's a good shipwright, *inshaallah* he would have it repaired in no time."

"Perhaps. But if he cannot?"

"Then you have a difficulty," Youssef said, leaning back in his seat. "Is the *baklava* not to your liking?"

Mal glanced down at the half-eaten pastry, fearing he had offended his host.

"It's very good, but the sea has not agreed with my stomach."

"Has it ever?" Youssef laughed. "Your companion there seems little afflicted."

They both looked over at Ned, who was licking the last crumbs of pastry from his fingers. *Glutton,* Mal mouthed at him. Ned had the grace to look sheepish, and put down his empty plate with an apology.

"Tell him he may have as many pieces as he wishes," Youssef said. "He looks as though he needs a good meal."

Mal translated the first part, and after a moment Ned loaded his plate and settled back to enjoy this rare luxury. Mal turned back to Youssef and cleared his throat.

"We have not known one another long, sir," he said, "and yet I feel I can call you a friend."

Youssef inclined his head in acknowledgement.

"And, as a friend," Mal went on, "I hope you will consider a humble request. You do owe me a favour, after all."

Youssef leaned forward, but it was only to pour more tea.

"Was helping you rescue the child of the painted ones not enough?"

"I thought it more of a... down payment. After all, I did

save your life that one time. Or was it twice? Anyway, surely that's worth more than one skrayling boy?"

"It was once. The second time was by Allah's blessing. And it was your manservant's doing, in any case."

"It was a lucky shot," Mal conceded. "Though I had to buy Madame Félice a new warming-pan."

"I doubt she needs you to warm her bed, my friend. So." He leaned back in his seat. "What is this great favour that will wipe out my debt?"

"Will you take me back to Sardinia on the *Hayreddin*, and if the *Falcon* cannot be repaired soon enough for my needs, would you take me on to Venice?"

Youssef appeared to consider the request for a moment.

"To the first part, yes. I was going to leave port in a day or so in any case."

Mal began to smile, but Youssef held up his hand.

"I am sorry, my friend, but I am bound for al-Jaza'ir. I have a cargo of pitch and timber in my hold, and a buyer waiting."

"You could take it to Venice instead," Mal replied. He sipped the scalding tea. "The Republic always has need of shipbuilding materials."

Youssef spat on the deck. "I would as soon sell my cargo to the Spanish."

"That would make a pleasant change. As I recall you stole your last cargo from them."

Youssef's eyes narrowed, then he burst out laughing.

"Very true. But I still don't see why I should help you."

Mal lowered his voice. One never knew who was listening.

"I am on a mission to discover the Venetians' plans for regaining influence in the Mediterranean," he said. "Is that not worth a little of your time?"

Youssef shrugged. "The empire has been at peace with Venice for a generation. Who am I to stick my oar in those waters?"

Mal raised his tea glass to the light, admiring the delicate pattern of gilding around its waist. Only the Venetians made glass this fine.

"Peace has its benefits," he said. "Trade with old enemies, for one."

"You do not give up easily, do you, Englishman?"

Mal suppressed a smile. *The tide turns.*

"And then of course there is Raleigh's ship, the *Falcon*," he added. "Even now, the Spanish may be closing in on Cagliari."

Youssef grinned, his dark eyes glinting like Sandy's obsidian blade.

"Now you are talking, my friend. It will be my pleasure to snatch such a prize from the grasp of my old enemy – and yours."

As they neared Cagliari, Youssef sent all his lookouts aloft to keep an eye out for the Spanish. Ned half-expected to find the *Falcon* taken, but as they entered the harbour he spotted the galleon at anchor where they had left it. Still, it would not do to be seen coming to Raleigh's rescue, so he and Mal disguised themselves as members of Youssef's crew in baggy calf-length breeches and canvas shirts, barefoot and with kerchiefs tied about their heads. Mal even removed his earring and stowed it in his discarded boot; the black pearl was too distinctive and valuable a bauble to be worn by a lowly sailor.

Captain Youssef chose a berth not too far from the *Falcon*, from which vantage point they were able to see Raleigh's crew at work on the repairs. There was no sign of Spanish soldiers on board.

"A pity," Ned muttered. "I should have liked to see that bastard Hansford taken by the Spanish. With any luck they'd hang him, like his assassin friend."

"You'd rather travel with Youssef, then?" Mal said with a smile as they disembarked.

Ned shrugged. "He's all right, for a foreigner."

They blended into a group of sailors leaving one of the other ships, then slipped down a side-alley and headed for the inn where Raleigh was staying.

Ned trailed after Mal, still feeling a little queasy. The rich pastries had sat like a stone in his stomach on the journey back from Marseille, and it had taken all his self-control not to throw them up again. To make matters worse, when they found Raleigh in the inn's courtyard he was smoking his foul pipe and playing cards with Warburton and Hansford. Ned wasn't sure which of the two made his stomach curdle the most. He wandered over to stand in the shade by a potted olive tree whilst Mal told Raleigh about their business in Marseille.

Raleigh's face darkened, and the two sailors put down their cards.

"A damned Turk?" Raleigh bellowed. "You may go with him if you will, but I shall stay with the *Falcon* – and have my gold back."

Mal replied in placating tones and sat down on the bench next to Raleigh. The captain glowered at first, but his expression softened at every word and eventually he smiled and nodded. They shook hands and Mal came over to Ned's shady corner.

"You persuaded him to go with us?" Ned said as they headed up to their chamber.

"I reminded him that the Queen herself had commanded this service. I also suggested that, when we get to Venice, he puts it about that he captured the *Hayreddin* in a mighty sea-battle. There are enough Christians in Youssef's crew to make it look like the truth, if we have them all manning the ship when we arrive."

Ned chuckled.

"You've turned quite the cunning rascal, you know that?"

"I learned from the best," Mal replied with a grin.

Ned hid his delight at this compliment with an elaborate

bow. If only some of that persuasive power could be his, the remainder of this voyage would be a lot more enjoyable.

"Monsieur Catlyn! Monsieur Catlyn!"

Mal levered himself up on his elbow and squinted at the door.

"Who is it?"

He got to his feet and gingerly crossed the rough floor. The voice came again. Mal wrenched the door open and was almost hit in the face by a frantic sailor.

"What is it?"

"Monsieur! Captain Youssef sent me to fetch you. The Spanish have been sighted, four galleons flying the royal ensign."

"We'll be right there." He went back inside and woke Ned. "Come on, lazy bones! Time to go."

As soon as Ned was on his feet, Mal went to find Raleigh. The rest of the crew were soon roused and sent to rejoin their fellows on the *Falcon*, and the three Englishmen headed for the *Hayreddin*. The harbour lay in shadow still, and a chill breeze blew down off the hills.

"Take my ship back to Marseille," Raleigh told Warburton, "then come to Venice as soon as she's fully repaired."

"Aye, captain."

They boarded the galleass, and Mal and Ned went to change back into their familiar English garb. They had been assigned a tiny cabin in the fo'c's'le with no bunks, only three paillasses that covered most of the floor. The sturdy lock on the door suggested this was normally used as a storeroom for valuable cargo.

"Damned uncomfortable way to spend the rest of our journey," Raleigh muttered.

He gestured for Mal and Ned to place his sea chest on the only remaining piece of bare floor, and stumped back out on deck.

"This is going to be cosy," Ned said, throwing down his own small knapsack.

"We can spend most of the day on deck," Mal replied. "At least the weather is better than in the Atlantic."

They went back up to find the oars shipped and the crew preparing to row out of the harbour. Mal shaded his eyes and gazed southwards. Four white sails in the distance, though he could not make out their flags. Youssef's lookouts must have the eyes of hawks.

"We'll tow the *Falcon* out to sea," the captain said as the *Hayreddin* began to move. "This land breeze is too feeble to get her going fast enough to outrun the Spanish."

"Can we help?" Mal said, looking down at the men straining at the oars.

Youssef shook his head. "My men know the rhythm; you would only break it and slow us down. Do you know how to work the sheets?"

"A little."

He sent Mal and Ned to help unfurl the sails, and they hauled on the ropes until their hands were blistered. The *Hayreddin* slipped past the *Falcon* and threw her a line, then the two ships moved out of the harbour together, veering eastwards out of the path of the oncoming galleons. The Spanish changed course to intercept, fanning out in a line that spanned the bay.

"Do you think they'll fire on us?" Ned asked when they paused for breath.

"Probably," Mal replied, wiping his forehead with the back of his shirt sleeve. His left shoulder ached and his palms felt like they'd been burned with brands. "They have more sail as well."

"And that's bad, is it?"

"They're faster, but less manoeuvrable. It's going to be close."

The westerly wind caught the *Falcon's* sails at last,

and she slipped her cable and drew alongside the *Hayreddin*.

"The sooner we split up," Raleigh yelled across to Warburton, "the harder it'll be for the Spanish to catch us both. Run before the wind, then turn back north as soon as you can."

"Aye, my lord. I'll see ye in Venice – or take a few Spaniards down with me to Hell!"

The *Falcon*, true to her name, sped eastwards. Her transom was still a patchwork of salvaged timbers, but she was otherwise sound and fled the confrontation without further damage. Youssef steered the *Hayreddin* to starboard, on a heading that would take them between two of the Spanish galleons.

"Is that wise?" Mal said, joining him on the poop deck.

"They will have to turn to fire on us," he replied, "and they risk hitting their own ships if they do so."

"And if they don't turn and we time it wrong, the starboard one could ram us amidships."

Youssef nodded. "And we could rake the other in the stern."

The Spanish had clearly come to the same conclusion, for the more easterly of the two began to turn north whilst its companion continued on its course. Mal and Ned could only watch anxiously from the rail as the *Hayreddin* drew closer to the galleons.

The easterly galleon opened fire, but the wind had already taken them too far away and their shot fell shot, splashing into the waves a ship's length short of their target. A few of Youssef's sailors jeered, but the rowers only pulled harder. They were getting close to the second galleon now, close enough to see the faces of the men hauling on the sheets and the mouths of the cannons within the gun-ports.

"To larboard!" Youssef shouted, and the galleass heeled as the wind caught her sails and drove her on a slanting course ahead of the Spanish galleon.

Mal clung to the rail, unable to look away as the galleon bore down on them. Surely she would ram their stern? But the rowers and the wind between them pulled her clear. The *Hayreddin* bucked as the galleon's wake buffeted her stern, then they were free of the cordon. Mal watched in mingled relief and anxiety as the Spanish, assuming that Raleigh was aboard his own ship, headed east in pursuit of their original quarry.

"It looks like you may get your wish," he said to Ned.

"If it were only Hansford and his cronies aboard, I'd be cheering the Spanish on," Ned admitted, "but the rest of the crew don't deserve to be drowned or imprisoned for Raleigh's sake."

"True enough."

Mal grimaced as he peeled his hands from the rail. He had been clutching the wood so hard the blisters had burst.

"Here, let me see to those," Ned said, taking him by the elbow. "You'll not be fit to carry a sword if they fester."

Mal let himself be led away. It would be a blessed relief to be back on land, where he could take on enemies on his own terms.

Ned took Mal belowdecks and bound his hands.

"A pity," he said. "I was looking forward to practising my swordplay again."

"True. You still need to work on your parry." He flexed his bandaged hands experimentally. "Give me a day or two, and I'll be fit enough."

Mal's prediction turned out to be accurate. With his riding gloves for extra protection, he was soon able to hold a weapon again. They spent every morning drilling and sparring, and the afternoons watching the Italian coast drift past. At first Ned felt uncomfortable showing off his skills, or lack thereof, in front of Youssef's crew, but the sailors paid the passengers little mind and went about their business with a quiet efficiency that made Raleigh's men look like an ill-disciplined mob.

Youssef allowed them to study his map of the eastern Mediterranean and, with little else to occupy his thoughts, Ned tracked their route along the northern coast of Sicily. Soon they reached the Straits of Messina, slipping between the city of the same name and the toe of Italy, and then steering north-eastwards towards the heel. The waters hereabouts were thick with ships, mostly fishing vessels of all sizes, but a good many merchantmen too, of all nations: Italian, Greek, English, French, Dutch, Spanish, Portuguese, Turkish. Ned had seen many such vessels moored at the London quays at one time or another, their crews filling the air with a babel of tongues, but seeing them here on the sunlit waves where they belonged was somehow different. They reminded him of wild beasts set free, beautiful but deadly.

"Should only be three or four more days," he said to Mal as they limbered up one morning. "We're in the Adriatic Sea now."

Mal laughed. "You're becoming quite the navigator."

"Have you thought about what we're going to do when we get there?"

"I've thought of little else," Mal said in a low voice.

"And?"

"A good commander doesn't make decisions until he's seen the lie of the land."

"In other words, you have no plan at all yet."

Mal threw him a cudgel and gave him one of those lopsided grins that stirred his blood in delicious but frustrating ways. "Pretty much, yes."

CHAPTER XV

The city of Venice lay at the centre of a large rectangular lagoon, protected from the sea by a line of narrow islands. The entrance to the lagoon, a gap between two of the larger islands, was guarded by towers on either side, and galleys patrolled the waters without. One of them came swiftly towards the *Hayreddin*, oars flashing in the spring sunlight. Mal prayed the Venetian officials would not ask to search the vessel, or they might wonder why Raleigh had a couple of dozen Moors lurking belowdecks.

"What is your business in the Republic?" the captain of the galley hollered in Italian once they were in range.

Time to play the ignorant foreign visitor, foolish and harmless.

"I beg your pardon?" Mal shouted back in English.

"Ah, *inglese!*" The captain repeated his question, this time in English.

"We are come to buy lace ruffs for Queen Elizabeth of England," Mal told him.

The Venetian laughed. "You expect me to believe you came all the way from England, *signore*, for a few yards of lace?"

Raleigh stepped forward and leaned over the rail.

"Do you know who I am, sir? I am Sir Walter Raleigh,

Lord Warden of the Stannaries and a trusted advisor of Her Majesty Queen Elizabeth."

Mal suppressed the urge to kick Raleigh. The title was legitimate enough, but "trusted advisor"? This was not the plan they had discussed on the voyage.

"I beg your pardon, Signore Raleigh," the Venetian replied. "We are honoured to have so famous an English hero in our city. Please, proceed."

Raleigh, looking pleased with himself, gave the order to enter the lagoon.

"What are you doing, sir?" Mal hissed, drawing Raleigh aside. "Our story is that you are out of favour with the Queen and here to buy gifts to win her over."

"Tush! It sufficed to get us past that jumped-up harbourmaster, did it not?"

"Well, yes, but that's not the point. If this plan is to work, the Venetians must not suspect us of being here to spy on the skraylings."

Raleigh sighed. "Very well, I will play your part if I must."

"Thank you, sir."

The *Hayreddin* had passed into the lagoon now and was making its slow way towards the distant city. Countless vessels rowed back and forth across the calm waters, from tiny rowing boats to massive oared galleys, single-sailed fishing smacks to mighty galleons bigger than the *Ark Royal*. Beyond them all, the city shimmered above the water like a heat haze, its pastel-coloured buildings as insubstantial as mist.

"So that's Venice, then?" Ned said, joining Mal at the rail.

"Indeed. *La Serenissima*. The Serene Republic."

"You seem to know a fair bit about it, considering you've never been here before."

Mal turned his gaze westwards, towards the mainland. "There was much talk of Venice when I fought in the north of Italy. It stands between Christendom and the Turkish

Empire, owing scant loyalty to the former and ever at war with the latter."

"But they are Christians here, Catholics?"

"Of a sort. But they do not like the Pope. The Venetians dislike being under the thumb of any foreign lord, spiritual or temporal."

"I like them already."

Mal laid a hand on his shoulder.

"Just mind your tongue, all right? If there is one thing they do not tolerate, it's insults to the Republic. You think what happened to Kyd and Marlowe was bad? The English are amateurs compared to the Venetians."

Ned turned pale. The events of two years ago had cast a long shadow over Bankside.

"No one must suspect our business here," Mal added in a low voice. "I shall adopt the manner of a gallant, that thinks of naught but fine Italian doublets and the latest fashion in shaping his beard."

"You, play the coxcomb?" Ned burst out laughing. "I shall enjoy seeing that."

As they drew closer they could make out the main landmarks of the southern side of the island: the pale façade of the ducal palace, the gilded domes of the basilica behind it and, most prominent of all, the campanile in St Mark's Square, rising above the surrounding buildings like a *digitus impudicus*, defying the world. To the right of the palace, a long quay stretched the length of the shore towards a vast red brick walled enclosure at the tip of the island: the Arsenale, the Venetian state shipyard.

"I heard they once built an entire ship in two hours," Mal said, "whilst King Henri of France was eating dinner with the Doge. Mind you, they have thousands of men working there."

"They would have made short work of the *Falcon*, then."

"They do not repair anyone else's ships. The whole place is locked up as tight as a nunnery, to preserve the secrets of their craft, and all foreign visitors to the city are watched closely."

"It's not going to be easy, this job, is it?"

"No, it's not."

The *Hayreddin* dropped anchor some hundred yards offshore and Ned brought up their baggage ready to disembark. He deposited it on the deck at Mal's feet with a thud.

"Where now?" he said.

"We find the English ambassador's house," Mal replied, "and give him Walsingham's letter. After that... I need to see the lie of the land first."

"Right." Ned shaded his eyes and scanned the docks. "Well, that answers one question."

"What's that?"

"We know the skraylings are here." Ned pointed out a red-sailed vessel, half hidden behind an enormous brig.

"Either that, or there's more than one skrayling ship come to Venice in the past month." It was not an encouraging thought.

Before the jolly-boat could be lowered into the water, the *Hayreddin* was approached by one of the many gondolas plying their trade along the waterfront.

"I take you somewhere, *signori*?" the gondolier called up. "My cousin has the nice taverna, very cheap."

"Do you know the house of the English ambassador, my good man?" Mal said. He took the letter from his pocket and pretended to read the address with effort. "It's in the, um, Salizada... San... Pantalon."

The man's expression changed very slightly, no doubt recalculating how much he dared charge this wealthy but ignorant milord for his services.

"Of course, *signore*. The district of Santa Croce. How many of you am I to take?"

"Two. And my servant and baggage."

They climbed down into the slender craft, which rocked alarmingly as if determined to throw them into the emerald-green waters. Somehow they managed to manhandle Raleigh's sea chest aboard without anyone falling in, and they were soon skimming westwards towards the mouth of the Grand Canal.

The gondolier took them past a succession of elegant palazzos, every one different: plaster painted white or rose or honey-yellow; windows with round arches, pointed arches, with or without little stone balconies; shutters on upper windows thrown open to greet the day or latched tight. In one respect, however, they were all alike. Every one had ground-floor windows protected by thick iron grilles to keep out robbers. Mal had seen similar arrangements elsewhere in Italy, but in Venice the contrast with the airy buildings was particularly striking.

Just as the Grand Canal turned back on itself their gondolier heaved on his oar and continued on westwards down a tributary. The houses here were less grand, though still three or four stories tall with bronze doors and painted plaster walls. A bridge crossed the canal, barely high enough for the gondolier to go under without ducking; it had no parapet, as if the citizens of Venice were so accustomed to the water that they gave it no thought.

A little further on they passed under a second bridge and then turned aside into a yet smaller canal, perhaps twenty feet across. The houses bordering it were more modest in proportion, mostly no more than two or three stories, with simple arched windows edged in white stucco. The gondola snaked around a dogleg bend and stopped at the foot of a weed-encrusted stair leading up to the *fondamenta*, the canal-side walk.

"Here you are, *signori*," the gondolier said, gesturing to the building on their right. "This is the residence of the English ambassador."

The house sat on the bend in the canal, a fine specimen of Venetian architecture with walls painted a deep terracotta red and arched windows decorated with white plaster mouldings. Two sides faced the canal, the third gave onto a street that merged into the *fondamenta*, and the fourth was joined to its neighbours. Mal's thoughts were already occupied with assessing its entrances and exits.

He scrambled ashore, relieved to be back on solid ground again, and waited with studied indifference whilst Ned heaved their belongings onto the *fondamenta*. Raleigh paid the gondolier, strode up to the house's street entrance and rapped on the handsome panelled door. Mal joined him, signalling to Ned to wait with the baggage. Several minutes passed, and Mal began to think they had the wrong address. He was just about to ask a passing Venetian for directions when the door opened and a manservant peered out.

"Sir Walter Raleigh, to see the ambassador," Raleigh barked.

The servant blinked at them, then opened the door with a bow.

"Please, come in, sirs."

They followed him into a small but elegant atrium with a floor of grey marble tiles. The servant left them there and made his way slowly up a narrow staircase of the same stone, clutching the balustrade with an age-knobbed hand. No wonder it had taken forever to open the door. Mal wandered over to a gilded side table and leafed through the pile of handwritten notices: announcements of executions, the election of citizens to public office, and all the other doings of a well-run state that might be of interest to diplomats and men of business.

Above the table hung a portrait of a gentleman in recent English fashions; the ambassador himself? Mal's guess was proved correct when the man from the painting descended the stair. A little older and stouter, perhaps, but undoubtedly Sir Geoffrey Berowne in the flesh.

"Sir Walter!" The ambassador bowed. "How wondrous unexpected! How is Her Majesty?"

Raleigh bowed in turn. "In good health, God be praised. And yourself?"

"The damp plays hell with my joints in the winter, but the summers make up for it." He looked from Raleigh to Mal and back. "Have I been recalled?"

"Not at all," Mal said, bowing and holding out Walsingham's letter. "Maliverny Catlyn, at your service."

Berowne took the letter and peered at the seal, then turned away as if he had quite forgotten their presence and headed back towards the stairs. Raleigh gestured for Mal to follow.

The stairs opened out into an antechamber hung with English tapestries. The one bare section of wall bore a portrait of the young Queen Elizabeth in a scarlet gown trimmed with gold, and below it stood a high-backed chair of dark wood. There was no other furniture.

"This is what they call the *piano nobile*, the noble floor," Berowne said, seeming to remember his guests at last. "No Venetian lives on the ground floor of his house. No cellars, you see, because of the canals, so the street level chambers serve as storerooms and shops."

He ushered them through a door into a smaller, more intimate chamber, more like an English parlour. A chair and footstool, both upholstered in tapestry-work, waited by a small fireplace, though most of the space was occupied by a dining table of polished marquetry with an enormous gilt-and-glass candelabrum in the centre. Berowne went over to the window and cracked the seal of the letter.

They waited in silence until the ambassador had finished reading.

"Well," Berowne said, and put it down on the table top. "Well, well."

"Sir Geoffrey?" Mal took a step towards the ambassador. "Can I be of assistance?"

"I take it you are here to spy on the skraylings."

Mal inclined his head in acknowledgement.

"Well," the ambassador said, "I fear you have come all this way for naught."

"What? Have they left already? But we saw one of their ships–"

"Oh no, they are still here. But how you are to spy on them, I cannot fathom. No one may speak to them without the permission of the Ten, not even the Doge. I doubt they will extend that privilege to a visiting Englishman."

"Even one who is a personal friend of the skrayling ambassador?"

"Especially one who is a personal friend of the skrayling ambassador."

"I see. That does present a difficulty. However Sir Francis has put his trust in me, and I must do what I can."

Berowne squinted at him. "What did you say your name was?"

"Catlyn, sir. Maliverny Catlyn."

"Catlyn… Catlyn." Berowne went over to a bureau that Mal had not noticed before, hidden as it was in a shadowy corner. "I know that name from somewhere."

Mal exchanged glances with Ned.

"Mayhap you received news from England, sir," Mal said, "of how I saved the ambassador of Vinland's life the summer before last."

Berowne unlocked the bureau and sifted through some papers.

"No, no, that was not it. There was something in dispatches, about a fire in Southwark and the death of Sir Anthony Grey, but no mention of a Catlyn. What was it now? Ah, here it is." He held up a sheet of paper. "A census of Englishmen living in the city. Another damn fool imposition, if you ask me, but it doesn't do to question the Ten."

Mal took it from him and scanned down the list. His heart lurched as he read the name: Catalin, Carlo.

"Charles." He bit back a curse.

"You know him, then?"

"If it's the same man, yes. He's my older brother. I knew he had fled abroad, but had no idea of his whereabouts. In truth I thought him dead."

Wished him dead, more like. What in God's name was that base, shameless villain doing in Venice? He turned away, pretending to re-read the list. He tried to tell himself it was mere chance, that Charles had naturally been drawn to a city infamous for its whores and gambling dens, but he couldn't shake off a feeling of unease. The bonds between the Catlyns and the skraylings ran far too deep for this to be a coincidence.

Next morning, Mal and Ned accompanied Raleigh to the Mercerie, the mercantile district of Venice. A series of narrow thoroughfares leading from St Mark's Square to the Rialto Bridge, it was lined with shops selling every luxury the Serene Republic could provide. The upper stories of its buildings were draped with tapestries and lengths of silk and cloth of gold, so that the Mercerie looked more like a royal presence chamber than a city street. Cages of nightingales hung from shop fronts, adding their piercing notes to the clamour of voices, and the scent of ginger, cloves and attar of roses vied with the stink of the crowds. Ned stared about him, dazed by the assault on his senses. Now he knew how countryfolk felt upon arriving in London.

"Come on, snail!"

Ned turned to see Mal beckoning to him through the crowd. Raleigh was standing outside a haberdasher's shop admiring a display of lace. Ned caught them up just as Raleigh went inside.

The interior of the shop was dim and cedar-scented, its walls lined with shelves on which a king's ransom in fine fabrics lay neatly folded: cloth of gold and silver; silks of every colour imaginable, satin-smooth or cut velvet; rolls of ribbon, braid and of course Venetian lace. Some of the latter was made up into ruffs and collars, arranged on wooden half-dummies to display them to advantage. The black-clad proprietor stepped forward, like a shadow come to life.

"Good day, sirs!" he said in perfect English. "Welcome to my humble establishment. What is your desire?"

"How did he know we were English?" Ned whispered to Mal.

"Does Raleigh look Italian? Or French?"

Ned had to admit that the captain looked like neither, any more than the haberdasher looked like an Englishman. It was an odd sensation, finding himself the foreigner in town, and he decided he didn't like it.

Raleigh pointed out a roll of lace, and the haberdasher gestured to an assistant to take it down and unroll it. Mal stood at ease nearby, the very picture of a discreet retainer waiting to attend on his master. Ned wandered around the shop, ignoring the venomous glances the haberdasher's assistant threw his way. Gabriel would love this place; a pity Ned couldn't afford so much as a handkerchief to take back as a gift. He reached out to touch one of the ruffs, but froze at a hiss of disapproval from the assistant and shoved his hand back in his pocket. Today was going to be about as pleasant as escorting his mother on a visit to the parish priest.

Behind him he could hear the haberdasher singing the praises of various samples, and naming prices that would have made the Queen herself turn pale. Raleigh made noncommittal noises, and eventually bowed and made his excuses, leaving the haberdasher and his assistant to tidy up the mess of unrolled finery. Ned hurried after Mal and emerged blinking into the street.

They repeated the process in half-a-dozen shops along the Mercerie, until Ned was yawning with boredom. Even Mal was looking rather less at ease, a slight frown creasing his brow in that way Ned always found so charming. Tonight he would convince Mal to stay in, share a couple of bottles of wine, and then… perhaps his friend could be persuaded to enjoy himself for once.

"Have you seen any skraylings yet?" Mal asked him as they followed Raleigh towards yet another shop. This one had a glazed window made up of rectangular panes as big as the pages of a book, so clean and clear they were almost invisible. Just beyond the glass was an elaborate silver-cased clock on a display table.

"Not a one," Ned replied.

"I suppose it's not surprising," Mal said, "if no one is permitted to speak to them. Hardly any point wandering the city being shunned like lepers."

"Perhaps we should scout out this lodging-place of theirs, see if there's a secret way in–" He yelped as Mal clipped him round the ear.

"I thought I told you to mind your tongue?"

Ned hung his head.

"We can discuss strategy in the safety of Sir Geoffrey's house," Mal went on. "In public, pray restrict yourself to the most inoffensive of observations, or keep your mouth shut."

Mal peered in through the shop window as if admiring the clock and Ned leant against the nearby wall, hands in pockets, chewing the lower edge of his moustache. A trip to the barber's was in order and soon, unless he wanted to look like a beggar. Or a sailor on shore leave. Much as he longed to go home, he wasn't looking forward to another month at sea.

To distracted himself from his ill humour he turned his attention to the passing crowds. Most of the men were dressed in sombre black, and practically all the women were of the lower sort: suntanned peasant women in brightly coloured skirts, or whores with bare breasts and painted faces, their yellow hair piled high on their heads. He had heard Berowne say that the Venetian nobles kept their womenfolk locked up like virgins in a brothel, but had discounted it as exaggeration. Perhaps the bumbling old maltworm was not entirely ignorant after all.

Raleigh appeared at the shop doorway.

"Ah, Catlyn! I shall be dining with Signore Quirin today, so you are free to go about your own business."

Mal bowed and thanked him, then beckoned to Ned.

"Come," he said in a loud voice, "let us stroll around this magnificent city a while and enjoy its sights."

Ned detached himself from the wall and trotted after him. "So where are we going?"

"I thought we might take in the Rialto Bridge and buy dinner at the fish market." Mal replied with a wink.

Ned grinned. According to Berowne, the skraylings' lodgings were along the Grand Canal from the fish market. Time for a bit of intelligence work after all.

CHAPTER XVI

Like the Thames, Venice's main waterway had only one bridge, lined with shops on either side to catch the ever-flowing foot traffic. But whereas London Bridge was a long level street supported on massive piers, the Rialto Bridge leapt the Grand Canal in a single arch of dazzling white stone.

"Is it not splendid?" Mal said, as they climbed the broad, shallow steps to its summit. "Berowne says it was only completed a handful of years ago."

Ned had to admit that it was very grand. After the oppressive narrowness of the Venetian streets it felt good not to be hemmed in by strangers, if only for a short while.

"I thought Raleigh wanted to buy lace for the Queen," he said. They paused to take in the view of the Grand Canal, glittering in the mid-morning sun. "He seemed a lot more interested in those clocks, though."

"I think it is not only Her Majesty he plans a gift for," Mal replied with a smile.

"No?"

"There is much in Venice to interest a man of scholarship, and a gift like that astronomical clock would be well received by Northumberland, I think."

Ned shrugged. He cared little for the doings of the high

and mighty, although somehow he always managed to get entangled in them anyway. Another hazard of keeping company with Mal.

It wasn't hard to find the fish market. Not because it stank like Billingsgate; on the contrary, the cobbles were as clean as any in Venice and the fish looked fresh-caught that morning, their scales glinting in the sun and their eyes plump and clear. Rather it was the cooking smells that alerted the nose; the scent of fish fried over charcoal with onions and spices. Ned's mouth began to water.

"Dinner?" Mal said, grinning down at him.

"Dinner."

Mal bought two plates of fried sardines and they ate them standing a short distance from the stall.

"We could always send a letter," Ned said after a while. He inclined his head towards a large red brick building across a side canal from the market, which had a sign bearing the word "Poste" hung over the door. When Berowne had told them about the city's public postal service over supper the night before, Ned's first thought had been to send a letter to Gabriel back in London.

Mal gave him a sarcastic look.

"All right," Ned muttered. "It was just an idea."

"And not a very good one." Mal's eyes narrowed as he stared across the Grand Canal. "And yet it is not wholly without merit..."

"What are you thinking?"

"Later. I need to mull it over. Let us continue with our tour of the city for now."

Ned finished off the last of his fish and licked his fingers clean, then took Mal's plate and his own back to the stall-holder.

"We should take a gondola," Mal said. "We'll get a much better view of the palaces from the water."

• • • •

For an extra lira, the gondolier was happy to give them a tour of the Grand Canal and point out all the places of interest.

"And there, *signori,*" he said, gesturing somewhat dismissively to a marble-fronted palazzo on the lefthand bank, "is the Fondaco dei Sanuti, residence of the ambassador from the New World."

Mal made no reply. The swaying of the gondola was making him feel seasick again. However it was a far less conspicuous way of reconnoitring the skraylings' residence than on foot, and there was no chance of getting lost either.

He fixed his eyes on the palazzo façade in the hope that it would quell his nausea a little. The prospects for getting into the *fondaco* unseen were not good. Like most grand buildings in Venice its main entrance opened onto the canal bank, where a short flight of steps led up from the water to its colonnaded porch. A smaller canal ran down the lefthand side of the building, and a broad street along the right. As they passed the latter, Mal caught a glimpse of another, narrower street running directly behind the *fondaco*. No chance of getting in over the roofs, then.

As soon as they were far enough away to allay suspicion, Mal ordered the gondolier to let them ashore. It was not difficult to convince the man that he felt too water-sick to continue. Even Ned looked a little worried as they disembarked.

"Where to now?"

"I think," Mal said, looking around, "we should try to find our way to Berowne's house on foot."

The walk took them a lot longer than he expected. The city was a network of alleys, bridges and canal banks punctuated by small tree-lined squares, each with its church. It was not that they looked the same – indeed every square was different, some paved, some cobbled, some with market stalls, some empty – but there was no pattern to the layout of the city. In London the river flowed straight east-west from the Tower to Lambeth Palace, and most of the main streets ran parallel to the river or down towards it. In Venice, the Grand Canal curved through the city in the shape of a letter S, and the streets and lesser canals filled in the spaces like scrollwork on an illuminated manuscript. It made him dizzy just trying to remember the way they had come.

Late in the afternoon they finally emerged into a familiar-looking square where workmen were laying the foundations of a new church, and took the correct turn along the canal bank to Salizada San Pantalon.

They were greeted at the door by Jameson, Berowne's ancient steward, who conducted them up to the parlour. Berowne was not there, only Raleigh, pacing before the hearth.

"About time, Catlyn. I have an invitation from Quirin to accompany him to a supper party, and I want you to come with me."

"Of course, sir."

"It doesn't do for a gentleman of my station to go abroad without a retinue." Raleigh said, adjusting the drape of his half-cloak. "Even a retinue of one."

Ned pulled a face behind Raleigh's back. Mal managed to keep his own expression respectful, though only with great effort.

"I trust you have suitable apparel, Catlyn," Raleigh went on. "I am told many of the city's eminent men will be present."

"I packed my best suit, sir," Mal replied, "in expectation of just such an opportunity. I wore it at the French court on several occasions."

"I dare say it will suffice," Raleigh sniffed, and wandered back out into the antechamber, muttering under his breath.

"No point me coming along anyway," Ned said when

Raleigh had left the room, "seeing as how I can't speak the language. Still, it must be a grand do if Raleigh wants to act the English lord."

"Don't worry, I'll bring you back some sweetmeats," Mal said, punching him playfully on the arm. "Just don't get into trouble whilst we're out, all right?"

As they made their way downstairs, Raleigh handed Mal a white half-mask.

"I am to wear this?"

"Apparently everyone else will be wearing them," Raleigh said, settling his own in place and tying the ribbons behind his head. It covered his face from his temples down to his upper lip. "You'll have to leave your rapier behind, though. Venetian law."

Mal gazed down at the smooth white visage before him. It ought to have been a reassurance, to be able to hide behind this expressionless shell, but instead it brought back memories of the Huntsmen in their black leather hoods with slits for eyes. Death walked in a mask like this. He shook off the grim thought and followed Raleigh through a heavy door at the foot of the stairs.

He found himself in a vaulted storeroom like a cellar, and recalled Berowne's words. Ripples of light, reflections from the canal outside, played over the walls, so that it felt more like a sea cave than a man-made structure. At the far end, steps led down to a small dock in which sat a plain black gondola. Wooden gates, descending into iron grilles underwater, closed the dock off from the canal.

"How very cunning," he muttered, wishing the ambassador kept horses rather than boats in his undercroft.

The gondola took them out onto the Grand Canal, across that great artery of the city, and into another maze of waterways. Eventually they arrived at a house far grander than Berowne's, though not as large as the skrayling residence.

"This is the clockmaker's house?" Mal asked in surprise as they disembarked.

Raleigh smiled. "Nay, Quirin is merely our passport. This is Ca' Ostreghe, the palazzo of Olivia dalle Boccole."

"A woman?"

"The most beautiful woman in Venice, by some accounts. They call her an 'honest courtesan'."

Before Mal had a chance to ask what that meant, they were ushered into the *palazzo* under the watchful eye of a tall black servant in scarlet livery. Judging by the man's soft, hairless face he was a eunuch, and therefore a slave, though no less fearsome for that. Mal had faced Turkish officers, some of them eunuchs, during his service in Italy and had a cautious respect for their skills.

Feeling uncomfortably aware now of the absence of his rapier, he followed Raleigh through the echoing atrium and into the garden beyond. White marble statues of Greek and Roman goddesses gleamed against a background of dark clipped hedges, and dozens of blown-glass lamps hung from the gnarled branches of olive trees. Hidden by a crowd of admirers, someone was playing a lute. Mal was reminded of the skrayling camp in its heyday, though the music here was far more familiar and homely.

As they moved through the throng of visitors, Mal realised that there were no women to be seen, only black-clad Venetian men, chattering like a flock of jackdaws. Then the crowd around the lutenist parted, revealing their hostess, Olivia dalle Boccole. The young woman looked up from her instrument and Mal halted in his tracks, transfixed.

Eyes green as fine jade gazed back at him from a mask of creamy silk trimmed with gold braid. Below the mask, carmine-dyed lips curved in a welcoming smile against umber skin. The courtesan's yellow silk bodice was cut more modestly than those of the tavern whores, though it was low enough to reveal half-circles of dusky skin above her nipples.

"Signore Raleigh!"

She set aside the lute and rose gracefully from her seat. Her eyes were now almost on a level with Mal's, though with her black hair braided with strings of pearls and twisted into fantastical shapes, she topped him by several inches. "How good of you to come! And who is this you have brought to me?"

"This is Maliverny Catlyn, a companion on my voyages," Raleigh said, sounding somewhat irritated at being passed over.

Mal bowed low, holding the pose a moment whilst he regained his composure. He had been too long at sea, he decided, if the sight of a beautiful woman unmanned him so.

"Maliverny," the courtesan purred in a rich alto as he straightened up. "That could almost be an Italian name."

"It's French, my lady. My mother was from Provence."

"*C'est vrai? J'adore les Français*. Now, gentlemen, please make yourselves at home." She gestured towards a nearby table, where refreshments were laid out.

Guessing they were dismissed for now, Mal drifted over to the table. Flagons of wine stood on silver trays surrounded by delicate glasses with gilded rims, amongst a sea of small dishes containing olives, almonds and morsels of fish fried in batter.

"Can I pour you wine, sir?" Mal asked his companion.

"Yes, do." Raleigh practically snatched the glass from him, and drained it in one go. "Most beautiful woman in Venice? She's naught but a Moorish whore."

Several of the guests turned towards them. Apparently many Venetians spoke at least a little English.

"Keep your voice down, sir," Mal hissed. "We are the guests here. It does not behove us to cause offence."

Raleigh shot Mal a venomous look, refilled his glass and stalked over to a statue of Diana, where the clockmaker Quirin stood with a number of other men.

"Good evening, *signore*," a voice rumbled at Mal's elbow.

Mal looked round to see one of the guests who had bridled at Raleigh's comment: a heavyset man with thick iron-grey hair curling around the edges of his mask, and a steady, genial gaze.

"Good evening."

"Please, allow me to introduce myself," the Venetian said with a bow. "I am Giambattista Bragadin, Signorina Olivia's patron."

Time to play his part. "Maliverny Catlyn, at your service, sir."

He sketched an elaborate bow, flourishing the ruinously expensive lace handkerchief he had bought in the Mercerie.

"Delighted, Signore... Catalin." Bragadin's hesitation was so brief, Mal could not be sure it was not his imagination, or merely a stumbling over an unfamiliar name. Or was his brother well known in the city?

"You speak English very well," Mal said. "I have noticed that a number of your people do."

"We get many foreign visitors here, and the English are especially welcome."

"How so?"

"We are both maritime nations, proud of our independence, and have many enemies in common. And we are too far apart to be rivals."

Mal smiled. "Very true. And of course we have money to spend on all your wonderful goods."

"Indeed. In fact I understand that is the purpose of your visit?"

Mal told him about their morning's expedition to the Mercerie and subsequent invitation to Ca' Ostreghe.

"And what do you think of La Margherita herself?" Bragadin asked, picking up an olive and popping it into his mouth.

"She's not at all what I expected. I thought golden hair and pale skin were esteemed the height of beauty in Venice, as in England."

"So they are. And yet who does not welcome cool shade after the day's heat, eh?"

"Indeed." Mal helped himself to one of the fried delicacies, which turned out to be a surprisingly tender piece of squid. "Sir Walter told me she is what you call an 'honest courtesan'. Have to say I'm not acquainted with the phrase."

"It is a new fashion of our city. The honest courtesan is a beautiful, accomplished woman, skilled in music and poetry and all the graces of civilised discourse; the perfect companion to ease a man's soul."

"And you are her... patron."

"Yes. It is my honour to support her. Our city would be much duller without such jewels to ornament it."

A wealthy man, then, to support a mistress in such style. "And in return she entertains your guests?"

"With her music and poetry, yes." Bragadin's manner remained courteous, but there was no mistaking the steel beneath the velvet scabbard.

Mal took the hint and allowed Bragadin to usher him over to a group of other men, all alike in their white masks and black gowns. Whilst his host rattled off introductions, Mal tried in vain to match names to... faces? Hardly. A distinctive chin here, white hair there... but how could he match those with certainty to their owners' faces at a later date? The work of an intelligencer in Venice required very different skills.

"Forgive my ignorance," Mal said when the introductions were over, "but what is the purpose in wearing masks, if everyone knows who everyone is?"

Bragadin chuckled. "You Englishmen like to wear swords to your Queen's court. Do you intend to kill someone there?"

"No, it's…" Mal smiled, understanding. "It's the fashion."

"Just so," Bragadin said.

"We were just discussing yesterday's vote," the white-haired man – Venier? – said. "Quite a turnabout from old Pasqualigo, eh?"

"Anyone would think his hand was forced," muttered another patrician. "He never favoured Grimani before now."

Mal sipped his wine and pretended disinterest. If he were patient the conversation might turn to the skraylings eventually.

"You think Grimani will be the next Doge?" Bragadin said.

"At this rate, yes," the first man replied. "He carries all before him. A 'gift' here, a word there…"

"*Il Mercante di Sogni,*" someone muttered.

"Nothing but a rumour," a fat man with heavy gold rings on his fingers said, tucking his pudgy hands into his belt. "A name to frighten the guilty with."

"Who is this '*Mercante*' fellow?" Mal asked. The epithet meant "the merchant of dreams"; an ill-omened name, given his recent experiences. *Must I start at every shadow, like a guilty man?*

"No one knows. It is a rumour, as Dandolo says–" Venier glared at the fat man "–but no less true for that."

"An assassin, spy and extorter of favours," the man who had first mentioned Il Mercante added. "It is said he can get you whatever you desire: the love of a woman, the downfall of your enemy, the favour of the Ten. No doubt Grimani has been using his services liberally."

"Enough, gentlemen," Bragadin said. "La Margherita will not thank us for speaking treason under her roof. Or in her garden."

The other Venetians laughed nervously.

"No, there is no possibility of corruption," Bragadin went on. He turned to Mal. "Do you know how the Doge is elected?"

Mal shook his head.

"Thirty members of the Great Council are chosen by lot," Bragadin said, "and those thirty are reduced by lot to nine; the nine choose forty and the forty are reduced to twelve, who choose twenty-five. The twenty-five are reduced by lot to nine and the nine elect forty-five. Then the forty-five are reduced to eleven, and the eleven finally choose the forty-one who elect the Doge."

Mal stared at him. "You just made that up. It's ridiculous."

Bragadin looked affronted. "Certainly not, *signore*. It is a grand and ancient tradition, designed to absolutely ensure that no one can influence the elections."

"I'm sorry, I meant no offence, gentlemen. I fear I have no head for politics."

"Then you had better go home, *signore*, or you will have no head at all," Venier said.

Mal swallowed, wondering if he had gone too far, but then the Venetians burst out laughing. He forced himself to join in. They were a strange folk, and no mistake; merry one moment, and deadly serious the next.

The conversation turned to less controversial matters, and after a while Bragadin and his friends began to disperse, some to the card tables, others to take their leave of their hostess. Mal took advantage of the confusion to slip away in search of Raleigh. Instead he found himself drawn back towards the music. He caught sight of Signorina Olivia again, a gilded lamp against whose beauty these black-clad admirers battered themselves in vain. And yet he could not blame them. Almost against his will he made his way towards her through the throng.

Her hands moved over the neck of the lute, strong but

graceful, and she sang more sweetly than the caged birds in the trees. It was a moment before he realised she was singing in English.

"Flow my tears, fall from your springs.
Exiled, forever let me mourn.
When night's black bird its sad infamy sings,
Here let me live, forlorn."

Mal sank to his knees at her feet, overcome by the words that echoed his own feelings. Never before had he realised how much he longed to return to England and reclaim his birthright, his family's estate in Derbyshire.

When the song was over, he felt a hand brush through his hair.

"So melancholy, Signore Catalin?"

He looked up. "It is a favourite of mine, but I had not heard words put to it before now."

"No? It was an Englishman who taught it to me." She tipped her head on one side. "Dowland. John Dowland."

"You met Dowland? Is he here in Venice?"

At her gesture, Mal took a seat on the bench beside her. The Venetian men, discreet as ever, melted away into the darkness.

"Signore Dowland came to Venice for a while," she said, "after seeking patronage in Rome. A brilliant musician..."

"Where did he go?"

"Who knows? To Milan, perhaps, or Florence." She leant closer, so that he could smell the scent of her, musk and roses and sweet creamy vanilla, like the lace around her bodice. "You like music?"

Mal cleared his throat. "What gentleman of taste does not? Though I cannot claim to play as well as you, *signorina*."

"You play the lute? Please, play for me."

"I–"

"Or perhaps you perform better in private," she said, so softly only he could hear.

Mal swallowed, unable to frame an answer. He looked around in search of Bragadin, praying this moment of intimacy with the courtesan was not a breach of etiquette. He had no desire to fight a duel, though a dagger in the back seemed more the Venetian style.

"Perhaps another time," she said. "We are both beholden to those wealthier and more powerful than ourselves, are we not?"

"Indeed, madam. I would not trespass on any man's property."

"Property?" She raised an eyebrow that had been plucked to the thinness of a pen stroke. "I am no man's property, *signore*, though sometimes it is wise to let others believe it."

"Then let us both keep up that pretence," he said, getting to his feet and bowing low. "Good evening, *signorina*."

CHAPTER XVII

Coby leant over the side of the ship, watching the glitter of moonlight on the waves. True to his word, Captain Hennaq had removed Sandy's spirit-guard and all their bonds in return for their good conduct. After all, where were they to go? The ship was provisioned for an Atlantic crossing and needed no further supplies until they reached Venice, which was now only a day or so's sail away.

She looked round as Gabriel joined her at the rail. He had grown thinner than ever on the voyage and his nose was peeling where it protruded from the shadow of his hat's brim, but he looked happier than she had seen him in a long time. No doubt he was looking forward to being reunited with Ned.

"Dalmatia," he said, pointing eastwards towards the barely visible mass of the distant coast. "We sail the narrow waters between Christian Europe and the Turks."

"Master Catlyn told me he fought the Turks, years ago. It must have been somewhere around here, I suppose."

A distant rumble of thunder sounded to the north of them. She looked up at the sky. Surely the night was too clear for a storm?

"Look, over there!" Gabriel tugged at her sleeve.

A flash of light, and then several moments later another low boom.

"Cannon? At night?"

The skrayling on watch silently roused the rest of the crew. In the lantern light their tattooed faces looked more inhuman than ever, and Coby could swear some of their eyes glowed like cats'.

She watched the distant battle get closer. A single large ship was surrounded by a swarm of smaller ones, too low in the water for its cannon to fire upon effectively. More than that was difficult to make out in the stark black-and-white of the moonlit waters. Then the beleaguered vessel turned a little towards them, and her heart skipped a beat. She knew that shape, had seen that same ship only a few months ago, waiting for them in the moonlight off the coast of Corsica.

She looked around for the captain. Hennaq had joined his first mate on the fo'c's'le and was watching the battle through a leather tube with glass in the end. Coby ran up the stairs, her feet slipping on the smooth treads in her haste.

"Captain Hennaq, we have to help that ship. Master Catlyn may well be on board."

The captain's amber eyes narrowed in suspicion. "Is this a trick?"

"No, sir," she lied. "Please, let me take a closer look."

He handed her the viewing tube. She gasped at how much closer the distant ship looked. There was the poop deck, with a tiny Captain Youssef directing his men. No sign of Mal, though. She cast around further, and could hardly believe her eyes. A familiar pennant fluttered from the *Hayreddin's* mast: five white diamonds in a diagonal row. Even if Mal wasn't aboard, this was no coincidence.

"They are flying Sir Walter Raleigh's colours," she said. "It must be them."

The captain hesitated for a moment, then turned and shouted orders to his men.

"Get below," he told her. "Now."

She ran back down to the weather-deck.

"Now may be our best chance to get away from here," she whispered to Gabriel.

"In the midst of a battle? How?"

"I don't know. But we have to try, don't we?" She looked around. "Keep an eye out for the captain, will you?"

Not waiting for Gabriel's reply, she ducked into the captain's cabin. *Now, if I were Hennaq, where would I stow a brace of confiscated pistols?*

Thankfully the cupboards lining the cabin were not locked. She searched one after another, and at last found the pistols, along with her powder flask and shot, her lock-pick roll and the book Sandy had stolen. With pockets and doublet front bulging she slipped back out onto the weather deck.

"All done?" Gabriel asked.

She nodded, and they dashed across to the hatch and down the ladder.

Down in the hold, Gabriel roused Sandy and gathered the rest of their belongings together. Coby handed over the book, stuffed the lock-pick roll in its usual place for safe-keeping, then primed and loaded both pistols. After a moment's thought she wedged them between a couple of sacks where they were easy to retrieve but wouldn't be spotted immediately if the skraylings came down here.

"Come on then, you two," Gabriel said, setting his foot on the ladder.

"Not yet," Coby replied, sitting down on her pile of bedding.

"What do you mean, not yet?"

"The ships are too far apart, and there are who knows how many pirate boats between them. We need to wait out this battle a little longer before we make our move."

He sighed, but did not leave his station at the foot of the ladder.

"Just because the *Hayreddin* is flying Raleigh's colours," she went on, "that doesn't mean Mal and Ned are on it. Surely they can't have completed their mission already."

"You think Raleigh left them behind in Venice?"

"It seems the most likely explanation. Still..." She turned to Sandy. "Could you find out if Mal is on that other ship?"

"I can try."

He wrapped his arms around his knees and closed his eyes. Long minutes passed. Gabriel clung to the ladder, staring up at the hatch as if it were a theatre trapdoor from which the gods themselves might descend to rescue them. At last Sandy let out a deep breath and rubbed a hand across his brow.

"Well?" Coby crouched down to his eye level. "Did you find Mal?"

"No."

She looked over at Gabriel and shrugged. "It's still our best chance of escape."

From the deck above came the rumbling of the strange glass cannons being rolled into place. Were they firing on the pirates – or the *Hayreddin*? Coby pushed Gabriel out of the way and ran up the ladder.

"What are you doing?" she yelled at the gunners. "Our friends could be on that ship."

One of the skraylings pointed through the gunport. "Look."

She followed his gaze, and blinked. The glass cannonballs had smashed on the galleass's sides, and yellowish smoke drifted down onto the surrounding boats. Sounds of coughing followed, and the pirates swarming up ropes dropped into the sea.

"There are other weapons than brute force," Sandy said, emerging from the hold.

They left the gunners to their work and went up on deck. The skrayling ship had now passed the *Hayreddin* and was unable to fire another broadside effectively, but the unexpected rescue appeared to have broken the pirates' resolve. The remaining craft were heading back towards the Dalmatian coast, abandoning the men who had fallen from the ship.

Hennaq came down from the upper deck.

"Forgive me," he said, "but I cannot let you escape."

He said something in Vinlandic to his men, who marched the captives back down to the hold, bound them hand and foot and gagged them. They lashed Sandy to the main mast, but before they could do the same to Coby and Gabriel, they were called back up on deck. The ship's timbers creaked in protest as it turned and began to tack in a wide arc back to the *Hayreddin*. Coby smiled behind her gag. The skraylings had not noticed the hidden pistols, and now all their attention would be focused on trying to capture Mal instead of guarding their prisoners.

She could just about make out her companions' features in the moonlight filtering down through the hatch. She shuffled over to Gabriel, working at the gag with her teeth until she could speak around it, albeit with difficulty.

"Ma'er Harrish? I meed you to goo somefing." She moved around behind him, to where his hands were tied. "Unghasten my hose an' reash infide."

"What?"

"Hlease, yust goo as I fay."

Gabriel crouched awkwardly to bring his hands down to the height of her groin, and clumsily undid her clothing. She forced herself to breathe slowly. It wasn't as though he was interested in her in that way, she told herself. There. She heard him gasp in surprise, then he pulled out the roll of canvas. She turned around so they were back to back.

"'ight, gig it to me."

She fumbled with the ties and carefully unrolled the miniature tool kit. She'd practised working with it by touch, in case she ever had to use it in the dark, but never in so awkward a way. *Ah, there you are!* She slid the narrow-bladed pen knife out of its pocket. *Carefully, carefully. Don't want to drop it.* "Ngow, kurn aroung again."

Gabriel obeyed, and she began to saw at the rope binding his wrist, taking care not to cut him at the same time. Within a few minutes he was free and able to take the knife and return the favour, then remove both their gags. Coby stifled a cough and swallowed several times to try and moisten her parched throat.

"I'll keep watch," she whispered to Gabriel, retrieving her pistols. "You free Sandy."

From the sounds of it they had circled back round and were drawing alongside the *Hayreddin*.

"Catlyn is there?" Hennaq's voice was just audible over the creak and groan of the ship.

There was a pause, then someone hollered back in English, "No, Catlyn stayed in the city. Who are you?"

Coby swore under her breath. If Mal wasn't on the *Hayreddin*, Hennaq would sail straight on and all would be lost. She turned and signalled to her two companions, then ran up the ladder, past the startled gunners, and pushed the main hatch open.

"Help!" she shouted in French as she emerged from below. "Captain Youssef! We have been taken prisoner!"

The crew of the *Hayreddin* erupted into curses, whilst the skraylings looked to their captain for further orders. A rumble below her feet told her the poison-smoke cannons were being wheeled back into position. Too late. The *Hayreddin's* cannon spoke, and the side of the skrayling ship erupted in splinters.

As Erishen stumbled up the stairs from the gun deck they exploded beneath his feet and he went sprawling. Something grabbed his calves, and he turned. Gabriel. Erishen crawled away across the rough planks of the weather deck, pulling the actor with him. Gabriel screamed, but his cries were drowned out by a second round of cannon fire.

Erishen looked around for help, but the girl was nowhere to be seen and the skraylings did not heed his cries. He rolled over and pulled himself upright. Gabriel lay on the deck, face deathly pale and a dark stain spreading across one stocking. Erishen crawled back towards the hatch and helped Gabriel up into a sitting position. Blood soaked the actor's stocking, but his leg did not look to be shattered.

"Do not be afraid," Erishen murmured in his ear. "The wound is not so bad."

He dragged Gabriel into the shelter of the awning and ran back out onto deck. The cannon fire had ceased, and both sides were watching one another warily. Edging around the mast, Erishen caught sight of the girl, Hendricks, on the fo'c's'le. She had both pistols drawn and pointed at Captain Hennaq, and was shouting to the captain of the other ship in a strange tongue. As he watched, the other ship lowered its boat and the girl began to back away, never taking her eyes – or weapons – off Hennaq.

Erishen took a lantern from the mast and ducked back under the awning. Gabriel lay on the matting, pale and unmoving. Erishen took a closer look at his leg wound. Lamplight glinted on slivers of curved glass protruding from his flesh. *Ulhantjaarr*. Unless Gabriel was treated quickly, he would die.

Coby edged down the stairs to the weather deck, one pistol still aimed behind her in the captain's general direction, one sweeping back and forth across the crew. Her arms were starting to tremble from the unaccustomed weight; if she didn't finish this soon, her plan – such as it was – would fall apart.

As she reached the bottom step, Sandy emerged from the awning carrying an unconscious Gabriel. He shouted something to the skraylings, and she thought she heard the name "Gaoh" amongst his words.

"What happened?" she said over her shoulder as she backed towards them.

"An exploding shell. He is poisoned."

Coby waved a pistol at the nearest skrayling.

"You! Get here Elder Gaoh, now!"

The sailor bowed and scurried off. Out of the corner of her eye she could see the *Hayreddin's* jolly-boat setting out across the gap between the two vessels. A few moments later the old physician appeared, clutching his medicine bag to his chest like a frightened girl-child with a doll. She jerked her head towards Gabriel.

"He die, you die," she told him. Tradetalk could be gratifyingly unsubtle at times.

Sandy lowered the unconscious actor to the deck, and Gaoh began fussing over him. After peeling back his patient's eyelids and feeling his pulse, Gaoh put his mouth over the young actor's and breathed into his lungs. He did this several times, then turned his attention to the wound, calling for a lantern.

Coby stood guard, arms crossed tight against her chest to stop them from shaking and pistols pointing in opposite directions. Out of the corner of her eye she could see the old skrayling pulling pieces of glass out of the wound. Gabriel never even flinched or cried out, which was worrying in itself. She turned back to the skrayling crew, scanning their features for any sign that they were about to attack. Her sudden appearance on deck had placed them at an impasse. If they tried to stop her, it would only confirm her story and spur on her rescuers, and if they did not, she would get away for certain. Captain Hennaq appeared to have opted for self-preservation over revenge. Very wise.

The splash of oars grew louder, and she heard someone shouting out to let down the rope ladder. After a moment's hesitation the skrayling sailors complied.

"Hurry," she told Gaoh. "We go. Now."

Gaoh chittered to himself and finished fastening a bandage around Gabriel's calf, then returned to his strange ritual of breathing into Gabriel's mouth. He paused and looked up at Coby.

"You do," the skrayling said. "I show."

"Very well, if you think it will help." She handed Sandy one of her pistols. "Try to look as though you know how to use this."

Gaoh showed her how to pinch Gabriel's nose and breathe into his mouth so that his lungs inflated like a bellows.

"Five times and then wait, then repeat," she said, as he explained as best he could in a mixture of Tradetalk and gestures.

The old skrayling rose and bowed. Coby got to her feet and took the pistol back off Sandy.

"Come on, time to go."

Sandy bent and lifted Gabriel's inert form once more. They backed towards the rail, just as a dark-skinned sailor's head popped up. He helped to manhandle Gabriel over the side, then Sandy followed with their baggage, leaving Coby alone on the deck. She waited for the skraylings to rush her, but they remained motionless and silent. With a prayer that the pistols would not go off, she thrust them through her belt and scrambled over the side of the ship and down to the waiting boat.

Coby sat on a stool next to the captain's bunk, watching Gabriel for any sign of improvement. She had blown into his mouth again and again until she was dizzy, and to her relief he appeared to be breathing on his own once more, but he was still as pale as a marble statue and almost as cold. She tucked the blanket in around him and brushed back the hair from his clammy brow, swallowing against the lump in her throat. If only she had waited until they were all safely above decks before alerting Youssef to their plight, this wouldn't have happened. The irony of losing one of the last surviving members of Suffolk's Men to another cannon, and through her own carelessness at that, was not lost on her. She wrapped her arms around her knees and blinked back tears.

She was roused from her misery a few minutes later by the cabin door opening. After wiping her eyes on her cuff, she looked up to see Sandy ducking through the doorway, carrying a wide-bottomed jug and a wad of damp linen. His face was flushed and his dark hair was damp and curling around his temples, like Mal's after a sparring match. He set the jug down on the floor next to the bunk, shook out the cloth and folded it neatly, then draped it over the top of the jug.

"What's that?" she asked.

"Boiled water. We have to let it cool before we wash his wounds, though."

"So why boil it in the first place?"

He gave her the kind of look one would bestow upon an ignorant child. "Because boiling drives off what you would call 'evil humours'. Using unboiled water would only make matters worse."

"Oh." She looked out through the open door. "Are the skraylings still following us?"

"Their ship is heading south, as we are, if that's what you mean." Sandy went and closed the door and then leant on it with his arms folded, a pose that reminded her even more of Mal. "They're keeping their distance, though."

"You don't think they'll attack again?"

"My people are not warlike," he said. "There are quarrels, of course, one man against another, but we do not take sides, nor fight in groups."

"But the skrayling ships have cannons, and Hennaq fired on the pirates."

"The cannons are for defence, not offence. It is one thing for Hennaq to frighten away pirates with a show of force, and quite another to attack a peaceful vessel."

"Good." She wrapped her arms about her knees again. "I was never afraid of the skraylings until now, no matter what people said about them."

"Never?" Sandy looked sceptical.

"No more than any other strangers," she said truthfully.

"So you're not afraid of me?" When she didn't answer, he nodded thoughtfully. "Hennaq was right. I am not like them, not any more."

Coby's hand strayed to the cross about her neck. Sandy smiled.

"Your God cannot protect you from things beyond His knowledge."

"Blasphemy," she whispered. "God knows all. He created everything."

"Did he create this ship? That jug? Men create also, and God has no hand in it."

"No, I cannot believe that."

"As you wish. I merely state the truth."

She got to her feet. "Will you sit with Gabriel for a while? I want to talk to Captain Youssef."

Without waiting for an answer she pushed past him and went out onto the deck. Mal needed her to be strong, now more than ever. If they could not rely on Sandy's sanity, she would have to lead them, and make better decisions than she had so far.

The sun was rising, gilding the hilltops of the Dalmatian coast and catching the red-and-white pennants on the mastheads of the *Hayreddin*. She drew a deep breath that turned into a yawn. Later. There would be time for sleep when she knew what prospects the day held.

The ship's bell clanged, and the sailors began to change watch, climbing down from the rigging as their fellows emerged from the hold to take their places. After a few minutes the captain climbed out of the hatch, looking as weary as Coby felt.

"How is our patient, my young friend?" he said, yawning and stretching in the sunlight.

"Much the same, sir. And your men?"

"We lost Fournier to one of their grenades and a few of the men are still weak from the smoke. Allah be praised, the gunners closed the ports before any more got inside."

"I'm sorry, sir."

"No matter." He patted her on the shoulder. "I could not let a friend remain a captive of those creatures. How did it come to pass that you were aboard their ship, anyway?"

She gave him a simplified account of their adventures, leaving out the details of the twins' true connection to the skraylings. A godly man like Youssef would not understand.

"But with Alexander safe in my hands," he said, "you think he dare not go through with the scheme, is that it?"

"Yes, but I dare not risk it. We have to get to Venice as soon as possible, to warn Master Catlyn." She stared at the shore. Colour was flowing down the hills, revealing a harsh, sun-baked land of scrubby forest and rocky outcrops. "Surely we should be sailing north, sir, not south?"

"Your friend Gabriel needs rest and care. A ship is no place for a sick man."

"You have somewhere in mind?"

"Spalato," he said. "It is ruled by Venice. If you want safe passage to the republic, I can think of no better place to start."

CHAPTER XVIII

Ned woke late and muzzy-headed the next morning, having had nothing better to do the night before but play cards with Berowne and drink strong Italian wine until he could barely see to make his way up to his attic bedchamber. He lay for a moment, probing the sticky recesses of his mouth with a furred tongue and listening to the sounds of the city stirring beyond the shuttered window, then rose and stretched.

Mal lay sprawled in the other bed, one black curl plastered to his cheek and smiling to himself in his sleep. Ned was sorely tempted to slip in beside him, but his stomach was demanding breakfast and his head was clanging like the bells of St Paul's. So he dressed as silently as he could and tiptoed out of the room in his stockinged feet, closing the door carefully behind him. He sat down on the bollock-shrivellingly cold top step and pulled on his shoes, then padded down to the ambassador's apartments.

The antechamber and parlour were both empty, but the great table was laid as if for dinner, with painted plates, napkins, and glasses with gilded rims. Two silver jugs stood near the head of the table, one of white wine, the other of water. Ned grimaced, wishing Berowne would serve ale like a good Englishman.

Shuffling footsteps sounded in the antechamber, and the door creaked open. Berowne's ancient manservant entered, preceded by a mouthwatering aroma of baking. Ned took the tray of hot pastries from the man's trembling hands and set it down on the table.

"Thank you, Master Faulkner," the old man wheezed. "Will your master be rising soon? I'll need to warm some more water for his shave."

"I hope so," Ned replied, trying to ignore the ache of hunger in his stomach. He went over to the window, to try and take his mind off the food.

The parlour offered a fine view across a little bridge and down the canal. To the left, brick walls enclosed gardens, dark foliage spilling over into the street and softening the hard edges of this most artificial of cities. To the right, tall houses ran along the *fondamenta*, some with shops or workshops at street level. Bathed in the thick honeyed light of early morning, the city glowed like a sated lover. Ned sighed, wishing Gabriel could be there to share the moment with him.

"Is there anywhere more beautiful?" Mal said, joining him at the window. "I think I would never tire of the view."

"Did I wake you?" Ned went back to the table, and as he hoped, Mal followed. "I thought you would sleep until noon. When did you get back? Before dawn, I hope."

"Long before," Mal said, picking up a pastry and tearing it in two.

Ned did likewise, resisting the urge to stuff the entire thing into his mouth. Instead he took a large bite, savouring the rich buttery sweetness. Say one thing about the Venetians, they knew how to cook. He finished it whilst Mal told him about the evening's entertainments, and helped himself to another.

"It was all very pleasant and courteous, but there's something going on in this city, something... unnatural. I heard rumours of an assassin they call *Il Mercante di Sogni*, 'the merchant of dreams'. I think he's a guiser."

"What? Are you sure?"

"No. I wish I were. But if there's even a sliver of a chance it's true… This changes everything."

"Witchcraft," Ned muttered. "I like this less and less."

They sat in silence for long moments, breakfast forgotten.

"So what do we do about it?" Ned said at last.

"Do? Nothing, at least for now. We shall continue with our business here, though I think I should stay away from Olivia and her patrician friends. Guisers are drawn to power like moths to a flame, and Olivia gathers some of the most powerful men in the city around her."

Ned shivered despite the growing warmth of the morning. "So, you have a plan for getting us in to see Lord Kiiren?" he said, trying to take his mind off the subject of guisers.

"Not exactly."

"What do you mean, not exactly?"

"I think we're being followed, or at least watched and reported on." He wiped his hands on a napkin and got to his feet.

"It's no more than we expected," Ned replied. "It's what I'd do if a foreigner moved into our street back home."

"Quite. So, I think it's time to apply the second rule of fencing."

"Which is…?"

"Make your opponent believe he knows where you will strike next. Then hit him somewhere quite different."

"What's the first rule?"

"Get him before he gets you."

"I like that rule better," Ned replied, grinning. "What do you have in mind?"

"I want to give them something to think about, something that will throw them off the scent for a while." He paused in the doorway. "I want them to think I'm in Venice to look for my brother Charles."

Whether through luck or a growing familiarity with the layout of the main streets, they eventually found themselves at their destination: a tavern on the main waterfront that Berowne said was frequented by Englishmen seeking news from home. Mal reckoned it was unlikely he would find Charles there, but on the other hand it would make his feigned search seem genuine enough, and in any case he had a more pressing reason to visit this establishment in particular.

"You know there's one small problem with this plan," Ned said as they approached the door.

"Oh, what's that?"

"What if you do find Charles? What then?"

Mal didn't answer. *Truth is, I don't know. Kicking the shit out of him would be a good start, though.*

The Mermaid looked much like any other Venetian house, having an elegant stucco facade painted a golden yellow, with arched windows and doorway picked out in white stone. Above the door hung a carved sign in the shape of a mermaid, with a gilded tail and hair and holding a real silvered mirror that flashed in the sunlight.

"Don't forget," Mal said in a low voice as they approached the door, "not a word about the skraylings unless someone else mentions them first. And if they do, don't sound too interested. We don't want Raleigh's name linked to them in any way."

"I haven't forgotten," Ned muttered. "You're not the only one to work for... our mutual acquaintance, you know."

"Good. Well then."

Stepping over the threshold, it was as if they had been magically transported back to London. The tavern was packed to bursting, and the combined stink of unwashed bodies, stale beer and tobacco smoke was enough to fell an ox.

"Quite the home away from home," Mal said, pushing his way through the crowd.

Contrary to Mal's first impression, no more than half the sailors were English. He heard snatches of French, German, mainland Italian dialects, Slavic, Greek and Turkish, and saw many swarthy faces – and not a few that were as dark as any Moor's. The city's black-clad natives stood out like crows in an aviary of parrots, sipping glasses of wine and looking nervous, whilst all around them the sailors laughed and sang and swore, making the most of their shore leave before the next voyage. There were plenty of whores to go round, even more than in a typical English tavern, and that was saying something. Venice's reputation as a city of vice was not undeserved.

He halted in the middle of the taproom.

"Gentlemen!" A few of the sailors looked around. Mal hooked a nearby stool with his foot and stepped onto it. It rocked a little, but that only served to attract the attention of a few more, some of whom laughed. *Perfect.* He stretched out his arms, like an actor addressing his audience. "Gentlemen, I am newly arrived from London and seeking my long-lost brother, Charles Catlyn. A beer to any man who can bring me news of him."

Before the crowd had time to react, he leapt down from the stool and beckoned to a skinny youth with the beginnings of a moustache.

"Boy, two pints of your best beer!" He gave him some coppers for the beer, and slipped in a silver lira amongst them. Lowering his voice, he added, "Tell Cinquedea a friend is here from London and would like to speak with him."

"Yes, sir."

"Master Catlyn?"

Mal turned to see three men in baggy hose and round hats seated a table by the wall. One of them, a short broad-shouldered fellow with a reddish beard, beckoned to Mal.

"Come and join our game, if you will, sir."

"I will, and gladly," Mal said, taking a seat beside him.

Ned took a seat next to one of the sailors and they made their introductions. The dealer grinned at the new arrivals with tobacco-stained teeth and began distributing cards. Mal scooped up his hand: five cards, Italian in design. The coins on the table were mostly *denari,* similar to English pennies in appearance but far lower in value. Perfect for a cheap evening's wager.

"Do you have change for one of these?" Mal pulled out the least valuable coin he could find in Raleigh's purse.

The dealer examined it briefly, then counted out two dozen *denari*. Mal gave half to Ned and placed one of his own in the central pool. The dealer turned the top card from the deck.

"Wands are trumps," he announced, and gestured for Ned to make the first play.

The pot-boy turned up with two tankards of beer, and gave Mal a nod as he set them down. Mal inclined his head in acknowledgement and settled down to wait.

"So, you are new come to Venice, sir?" one of the sailors asked.

"Aye, two days ago. And yourselves, good sirs?'

"Been here a week," one of them said. "Heading home soon, God willing. Though we do hear–" he leant forward across the table "–that Sir Walter Raleigh's in town, and looking for new crew."

"I fear you're mistook," Mal said. "Master Raleigh's ship left Venice just after we disembarked."

"That Will Frampton always were a liar," the dealer said. "Come on, Ben; play or renege."

A black-clad Venetian approached their table, his genial smile at odds with his sombre attire.

"May I join you, *signori*?" he asked, though his eyes never left Mal. When no one objected, he drew up a stool and sat down next to Mal. "Permit me to introduce myself. Marco da Canal, at your service."

"Good to meet you, Master da Canal."

Da Canal inclined his head. "The pleasure is all mine, *signore*."

"So, you have news of my brother?"

"Perhaps."

"Perhaps?" Mal glanced at his hand and discarded the two of coins.

"I do not know a man called..."

"Catlyn, Charles Catlyn. Though I'm told he goes by the name of Carlo Catalin these days."

"Catalin, quite so. I do not know a man by this name, and yet you have a familiar look. Perhaps if you told me a little more, I could match the face to a name."

Mal took a sip of beer. Was this Walsingham's man, or an intelligencer in the pay of... who knows whom?

"My brother is forty years old or so, about my height but with light brown hair. He left England four years ago, and I have not heard from him since."

Da Canal made a sympathetic noise. "And you are both from London?"

"No, Derbyshire. Place called Rushdale."

"But you have been to London?"

"Aye, I lived there for a while." He realised it was his turn, and played another card absentmindedly whilst watching the Venetian out of the corner of his eye. *Now he reveals himself...*

"Then you must be familiar with the *sanuti*," Da Canal said.

"Sanuti?" It was the name the gondolier had given to the skraylings' residence. *Il Fondaco dei Sanuti*.

"The strangers from the New World."

"The skraylings? I have seen them on occasion, certainly," Mal said.

"You know they are here in Venice?"

Mal feigned indifference, but he noticed that Da Canal leant fractionally closer, his eyes narrowing. *Well, two can play at that game.*

"I did think I saw one of their ships at anchor," Mal replied, slurring the words just a little, "but I wasn't certain." He drained his tankard with an exaggerated gesture, though in truth it was nearly empty, and beckoned to a serving man.

"Allow me," Da Canal said, and gave the servant a coin. "Never let it be said that we do not know how to welcome visitors to our city."

"You are too kind," Mal replied, holding up his tankard to be refilled.

"Here, are you playing or not?" One of the sailors leant across the table, jabbing the stem of his pipe at Mal.

"Nay." Mal threw down his cards, narrowly missing a puddle of beer. "My luck is all ill."

The dealer shrugged and slipped Mal's cards under the bottom of the deck. "Better odds for the rest of us, eh, lads?"

The sailors went back to their game, and Mal gestured to Ned to continue.

"I heard Signore Raleigh stayed behind in Venice after his ship departed," Da Canal murmured. "Is that so?"

"Aye. What of it?"

"Perhaps since you travelled with him, you know his purpose."

Mal leant forward, blinking at Da Canal in feigned drunkenness.

"Signore Raleigh, as you call him, thinks of only one thing," he said with a leer. "Her Divine Majesty. And her lack of a husband."

"Really? But she is much older than him, is she not?"

"When did that ever matter, where money and power is involved?"

"Then he would break up the skraylings' proposed alliance to win the favour of his queen?"

Mal laughed. *So that's da Canal's game*. "Sir Walter? He is no politician. He thinks only of wooing the Queen with fine gifts."

Da Canal leant back in his seat. "Then he has come to the right place."

Mal felt a hand on his shoulder, and turned. A skinny girl was smiling down at him, her face painted rose and white, with scarlet lips and pupils large as a cat at dusk. No, not a girl... a boy in girl's attire. The boy-whore leaned in and whispered in Mal's ear.

"*Cinquedea*."

Mal looked at him quizzically, and the boy beckoned.

"Excuse me, Signore da Canal," Mal said, and winked at the Venetian. "I think I have... business elsewhere."

Da Canal smiled thinly. "Of course."

Ned was looking daggers at him, but there was no time to explain. He followed the boy out of the taproom and up a rickety flight of stairs. By his companion's mincing walk and the clop-clop of his footsteps, Mal guessed he was wearing chopines, the high-soled overshoes that were so fashionable amongst ladies.

They emerged from the stairs into a large room divided into stalls by low wooden walls, more like a stable than a human dwelling. From several of the stalls came the sounds of the inn's other whores at business, and Mal began to wonder if he had misheard Walsingham after all.

The boy led him past the rutting couples to a door at the far end, and ushered him inside. The room was dark despite the early hour, and Mal paused on the threshold, hand on his dagger hilt. When no attack came, he breathed again. The door closed behind him, and he heard the boy's footsteps retreating.

"Signore Catalin." The sound came from the shadows; a young man's voice, steel-edged and deadly as its namesake.

"Cinquedea?"

"You asked to speak with me. So speak."

"I was given your name by Sir Francis Walsingham," Mal said. "He told me you work for an old friend of his, the Blind Lacemaker."

His eyes were starting to adjust to the gloom, and he could now make out a dark shape standing to one side of the shuttered window. Not a tall man, but solidly built. Was Cinquedea the Lacemaker? It would explain why they were meeting in the dark, where a blind man would have an advantage.

"A friend, is that how he describes her?"

Her?

"Still, they must be of an age, grandmama and he," Cinquedea went on. "I have often wondered if they were lovers, though my grandfather would have killed him if had found out."

"Your grandmother?" Mal was unable to keep the incredulity out of his voice.

"You have a queen in England. She is past her sixtieth year, I believe."

"Two years since," Mal replied.

"My grandmother is queen of her own little realm. But we digress. What business of England's brings you here?"

Mal cleared his throat. "I need to speak to the skrayling ambassador. Sir Francis is… concerned about their purpose here, and there seems no other way to discover it."

"I would have thought their purpose is obvious: to negotiate a trade agreement with the Doge and council."

"True. But my government wishes to be forewarned of any progress."

"Why should we help you? Increased trade will be of great benefit to Venice."

"I do not think Sir Francis would have told me about you unless he believed you would help."

Cinquedea stepped forward. He was not much older than Mal, though already greying at the temples. Handsome as his namesake as well, with an aquiline nose and deep-set eyes that were most certainly not blind.

"I will take the matter to my grandmother," the Venetian said, "and send you word of her decision. You are staying at the English embassy?"

"Yes."

"Very well. Expect my reply within a few days."

"Thank you."

Cinquedea bowed curtly and retreated into the shadows. Somewhere far off, a bell tinkled, and Mal heard the clop-clop of footsteps approach the door.

"Good day, Signore Catalin."

Mal followed the boy back down to the taproom, and signalled to Ned that it was time to leave.

"I think we should be going, gentlemen," Ned said loudly. "Captain Raleigh will be expecting us for dinner."

He made his farewells to the company and followed Mal out of the inn.

"What the hell was all that about?" he asked, as Mal paused to piss in an alley-mouth. "Have you been lying to me all these years? Is Hendricks really a boy after all?"

"The boy was just a messenger," Mal replied, just loud enough to be heard over the splashing noise. "I could hardly meet openly with… my hoped-for ally." He shook off the last drop and buttoned up his slops.

"And who is this ally? Christ's balls, Mal, you've become as close-mouthed as a banker's purse since you came back from France. We used to be the best of friends…"

"And still are." Mal put an arm around his shoulder. "If I keep secrets, it's only for your own safety."

As they walked along the quayside, a sleek gondola with a gilded prow drew up. A hand emerged from the gauzy curtains of the central cabin, and beckoned to Mal. An elegant, dark-skinned female hand. He swallowed, his mouth dry as tinder.

"What's she doing here?" Ned muttered.

The curtains parted to reveal Olivia, dressed in copper-coloured silk that shimmered like a last glimpse of the sun setting over the Grand Canal. She had shed her mask in favour of an ostrich-feather fan, which she fluttered over her breasts in a manner that didn't so much hide them as draw the eye to them like a needle to a lodestone.

"Signore Catalin, what a lovely surprise. Please, join me."

Mal swept a bow. "Alas, my lady, I wish I dared. But your patron would not look kindly upon it, I fear."

She pouted prettily and sighed. *"Je suis desolée."*

"As am I, my lady."

"Perhaps you would dare to attend another evening party? I have guests tonight; you need not fear visiting me alone."

Mal noted the ambiguity of her words, and smiled. "It would be my pleasure."

She raised her fan to cover her answering smile, but above it her jade-green eyes sparkled with triumph. Mal watched the gondola join the stream of craft heading towards the entrance to the Grand Canal, then turned back towards St Mark's Square.

"What are you doing?" Ned said, scurrying after him. "I thought you'd vowed to stay away from her?"

"I've changed my mind," he replied. "Machiavelli said: 'There is no avoiding war; it can only be postponed to the advantage of others.' I intend to take his advice."

CHAPTER XIX

Mal disembarked from the hired gondola and paused on the threshold of Ca' Ostreghe. It was over a year since Jathekkil had poked around in his head for memories he could use against him, and still it woke him in the middle of the night in a cold sweat. The prospect of coming up against another such monster made his stomach curdle, but he could not hide his head under the blankets like a frightened child and hope they went away. He adjusted his mask and stepped inside.

A cold wind was blowing down from the Alps tonight, and Olivia's garden was dark and empty. Instead the eunuch guard indicated wordlessly for Mal to follow him up to the *piano nobile,* where a log fire held the unseasonable chill at bay and dozens of candles bathed the room in a memory of sunlight. Olivia sat on a gilded chair reading poetry, whilst a number of admirers perched on stools around her. Bragadin leaned against the marble fireplace with an air of studied indifference; evidently he valued Olivia more as an ornament to his own reputation than for herself.

"Ah, Signore Catalin!" Bragadin stepped forward. With his face half-hidden behind the mask, his smile looked forced and insincere. "I did not know you had been invited."

"I chanced to meet La Margherita," Mal said, "whilst I was about my own business, and I confessed to her that I was weary of Raleigh's company after so many weeks at sea."

Bragadin's smile was more genuine this time. "Signore Raleigh is a simple man of action, I suppose."

"Alas so."

"And yet he comes all the way to Venice for a gift for your queen. A man of contradictions."

"I observed as much on first meeting him," Mal said. "But perhaps such grand gestures are of a piece with his temperament."

"May I ask what brings you to Venice, if you are not of his following?"

A liveried page appeared at Mal's elbow with a tray of steaming silver flagons. Mal took one, rolling the stem idly between his fingers.

"Vengeance," he said with a grin.

Bragadin looked taken aback. "I hope you do not bring a *vendetta* to our city, *signore*. We have strict laws against those who disturb the peace of La Serenissima."

"Nothing so dreadful, I assure you, sir. I seek my elder brother, who gambled away our family fortune. Perhaps you know him. He goes by the name of Carlo Catalin."

Mal watched Bragadin carefully, but this time the Venetian betrayed no sign of recognising the name.

"I am sorry, *signore,* but this is a large city and in any case state business occupies most of my time. If a man is not in the Golden Book or a notorious criminal, it is unlikely that I would have come across him."

"A pity. Perhaps I shall seek out this Mercante fellow. He seems to know everything that goes on in Venice."

Bragadin's eyes narrowed behind his mask, but before he could reply, a patter of applause marked the end of their hostess's recitation. Olivia's admirers hurried to make room for her as she rose from her seat. Like Venus from the waves, Mal thought, raising his flagon in silent salute. Olivia inclined her head in acknowledgement, then beckoned to him. He glanced back at Bragadin, who shrugged and motioned him to obey.

"Signore Catalin," Olivia said as Mal drew near, "I have a mind to play a duet. Would you oblige me?"

"I am sadly out of practice–"

"Come, I will not be denied." She snapped her fingers, and servants hurried forward with a pair of lutes.

After a last sip of wine to steady his nerves, Mal took one of the instruments and sat down on a stool near Olivia's seat. It took a while to get the lutes in tune with themselves and one another, then Olivia launched into a simple *ricercar*. Mal listened for a few stanzas then added a variation of his own, keeping the fingering simple to hide his lack of practice. He tried to observe the other guests out of the corner of his eye, but it was taking all his concentration to play without making a fool of himself. At last Olivia played a closing flourish and her hands stilled. Mal followed suit, relieved to be done.

"Another, *signore*?" she said, after the applause had died away.

"I have no wish to punish your guests further, *signorina*."

"Just one more, then." Her eyes sparkled with mischief behind her mask. "And you may take the lead this time."

"Since you are so fond of Dowland," he said, "how about this one…?"

He launched into the opening bars of *My Lord Willoughby's Welcome Home*, and was gratified when Olivia joined in the duet. It was a short song, thankfully, and he made it through to the end without fumbling more than a handful of notes. Olivia stood and curtsied, first to Mal and then to her audience. He bowed in turn, and excused himself. There had to be a piss-pot around here somewhere.

He wandered out onto the stairs, and was about to head down to the atrium when he heard voices below. He crouched by the balustrade, grateful that the rest of the house was not lit as extravagantly as the main chamber.

"What do you mean, you don't have it yet?"

The voices echoed around the marble stairwell, too indistinct to make out their owners.

"We were supposed to meet last night," the other man said, "under the *sottoportego* at the end of Calle di Mezzo, but he never arrived. I waited almost until curfew–"

"You did impress upon him the urgency of our situation?"

"Of course, but this business with Grimani must be filling his pockets right now. What need has he of our custom?"

Mal leant forward, pressing his ear between the cold stone balusters. Were they talking about Il Mercante?

"We had a contract. I–"

The rest of the sentence was lost as a large hand clamped over Mal's mouth, crushing the mask against his face, and he was dragged backwards away from the stairs. He struggled and tried to reach for his dagger but his assailant was too strong.

"Calm yourself, *signore,*" a deep voice whispered in his ear. "My lady means you no harm, but you cannot be seen here. Do you understand?"

Mal managed a nod. His captor released him, and Mal turned to see Hafiz, the eunuch slave.

"Please, come this way," Hafiz said, opening a door at the top of the stairs. "Quickly."

The voices in the atrium had stilled, but Mal had the uncomfortable feeling the men were listening now, perhaps even creeping up the stair towards him. His left hand groped for his absent rapier.

"Now, please!" the eunuch hissed.

With a last glance down the stairs Mal followed him into a small chamber, illuminated only by the moonlight coming in through an unglazed window. Hafiz lit a lamp and the shadows receded, revealing this to be an antechamber of some kind. Were these Olivia's own apartments?

"Who were those men?"

"Guests of Signorina Olivia. They come here to discuss business. Discreetly."

"And you ensure they are able to do so."

Hafiz inclined his head in acknowledgement and backed towards the door.

"Please wait here, *signore*."

For how long? Mal wanted to ask, but it felt like such a childish question. The door closed, and Mal heard the key turn in the lock. It was an answer of sorts, though not one he liked.

Long minutes passed whilst Mal waited, ear pressed to the door. He heard footsteps on the landing, one man only, followed at a long interval by another. The two conspirators returning separately to the company? He laid a hand on the doorknob but had more sense than to rattle it. If Olivia thought he needed keeping safe from her guests, he did not want to face them armed with naught but a dagger.

He crossed quietly to the window. The streetward façade of the palazzo was plainer than the canal-side one, but still offered enough footholds for a climb down to the garden. The gate was probably locked, but he recalled seeing a thick-limbed vine on the far wall, offering an easy climb into the street beyond. However he had come here to find out more, not to run away at the first sign of danger. Best to save this exit as a last resort.

He examined the rest of the room minutely, though there was little to see. Two doors led out of the room, in addition to the one he had entered by; he listened at both, but could hear nothing above the rumble of conversation from the parlour. A credenza stood against one wall, flanked by matching armless chairs. On the wall above it hung a fine silvered mirror, large enough for Mal to see his head and shoulders. He frowned at the trim of his beard and the length of his hair, and made a note to see a barber on the morrow. If he survived the night.

After a moment's hesitation he took up the lamp and searched the credenza's drawers and cupboards, but found only a sewing basket and a few items of the sort that a lady might want before leaving the house: gloves, masks and so on. One was the cream silk half-face mask that Olivia had worn the previous evening. So, this *was* her suite.

Intrigued now, he went back to the nearer of the two doors. The small room beyond was spartan even by Venetian standards, with whitewashed walls, marble floor and for furniture only a close-stool, a wash stand and a hip bath in the shape of an oyster shell. A room just for washing? Perhaps it was a Moorish custom.

He was about to try the other door when he heard the key rattle in the lock. Quickly he returned to the credenza, put down the lamp and adopted a nonchalant pose.

"Ah, so you are still here," Olivia said, crossing to the window with a graceful swaying walk and closing the shutters. "I was afraid you might have been alarmed by Hafiz's… intervention."

"Who were those men? Are you an accomplice of Il Mercante?"

She closed the space between them and put a finger to his lips. "So many questions. But first I think you owe me some answers, Signore Inglese."

"Oh?"

"Who are you–" she reached up and removed his mask "–and why are you here?"

"My name you already know, and I am here because you invited me."

"Come, *signore*, the time for games is over." She ran a

fingertip along the edge of his left ear and down to the lobe. "Put aside your pretty armour, and be your true self."

Mal prayed his surprise did not show in his face. She recognised the spirit-guard for what it was, which could mean only one thing.

"And what then?" he said, trying to keep his voice steady.

"We are two of a kind, you and I," she said. "Outcasts, for reasons not of our choosing. Is that why the *sanuti* are here? To track you down?"

Is that what she thinks I am, a renegade guiser? Perhaps I should play along. It is not so very far from the truth, after all.

He forced a laugh. "I arrived in Venice but two days ago."

"So you say. But perhaps you have been in hiding all this time, until your Sir Walter Raleigh came along and gave you a reason to visit me."

"You are very astute, *signorina*."

"In this city, one learns to see behind the mask if one wants to survive." She removed her own, and set it down on the credenza next to his. "Come, let us make ourselves comfortable, and you can tell me all."

She led him through the other door. Into her bedchamber. Mal hesitated on the threshold.

"What of Bragadin? Is he your partner? Is he Il Mercante?"

Olivia laughed. "He is naught but my puppet. A woman here has no station but that which a man gives her, so I must make the appearance of being a rich man's mistress." She turned and smiled. "As I told you before, I am no man's property."

Mal followed her inside, little reassured by this. If Bragadin were Il Mercante and she controlled him, what were her plans for himself?

An enormous canopied bed draped in crimson damask dominated the room, and a haphazard layer of Turkish rugs muffled Olivia's footfalls as she went about the room lighting candles. The window was his best chance for a hasty exit, since it opened onto the Grand Canal, though he was not a strong swimmer. Perhaps the door to the antechamber, then, and a climb down to the garden.

When all the candles were lit, Olivia blew out the taper and sat down on a couch by the window.

"Will you help me with these?"

She lifted her skirts to reveal the chopines. Mal knelt and unfastened the buckles and lacings that held them over her silk slippers, then eased them off her feet and put them aside. Olivia sighed and wiggled her toes, and patted the cushioned seat beside her. Mal sat down, arranging himself so that his hand was not too far from his dagger hilt.

"Who are you?" she whispered, twisting on the seat so that she could look him in the eyes. "Have the Christians taken to capturing our people once more?"

Mal shook his head. "I came here by choice, looking for you."

He held her gaze, willing himself not to look away and betray the lies. *Sandy should be here doing this, he has far more of Erishen's memories than I, he would know exactly what to say.*

"For me? Do I know you?"

"No, my lady. I am but newly stepped onto this path."

Her eyes narrowed. "Why should I trust you? The elders could have sent you to trap me."

"The elders would never approve such a step. You know it is against our law."

"And you broke that law," she said softly. "Why?"

He tried to imagine how Sandy would put it. "Because I think the elders are wrong," he said at last. "You are not evil. Becoming human is not evil."

"Ah, the confidence of youth," she said, smiling. "The elders are indeed wrong. And you, sweet boy, are the answer to my prayers."

"How so?"

"Tell your name," she purred, trailing a hand up his arm.

"You know my name. Mal."

"Your true name."

Mal hesitated. In many a fairytale, the true name of an elf or hobgoblin gave one power over them. Did the same apply to guisers?

"Does it matter?" he said at last.

"It is a matter of courtesy. But perhaps as the elder, I should begin. I am Ilianwe."

"My name is Erishen."

"It is a pleasure to meet you, Erishen." She smiled and said something in what sounded like a skrayling tongue.

"I am sorry. I remember little of our language. My transition was... painful."

That at least was no lie. The nightmares still troubled him from time to time, even now that he understood what they meant.

"No, it is I who should apologise," she said. "I was so glad to learn that another of my kind was in the city, I just thought..." She sighed. "You are not her."

Mal smiled. "Not *her*, certainly."

She smiled back. "Have you ever been female? Or are you one of those who prefers to be the same sex each lifetime?"

"I cannot remember."

"No matter. Though you really should try being female one day. These human bodies–" she guided his hands to her waist "–are pleasingly soft."

Before he could reply she shifted on the chaise and straddled his lap, draping her hands over his shoulders. Her breasts were level with his eyes now, and the silken curves of flesh spoke to his need more eloquently than words.

"No," he whispered. "I am pledged to another." He wasn't sure why he said it. He and Coby had exchanged no betrothal vows; indeed she rejected him at every turn. And yet he had always hoped...

"Then you are fortunate." She looked away but did not abandon her seat on his lap. "My *amayi* is dead. I am the last of our kind here in Venice."

Relief washed over him. If she was telling the truth, at least he did not have to worry about dealing with two guisers at once. The one in front of him was handful enough. Two hands full, at least. He chided himself for this unseemly thought, but she was after all very beautiful and he had been chaste these many months.

"When I die," she went on, "I must take my chances and hope to survive childhood, unprotected and unguided. Have you ever died in childhood?"

Mal shook his head. An odd question anywhere else, but here with her it made perfect sense.

"I have, many times. Plague, most often, though once my careless nurse let me fall into a canal and drown."

She spoke so matter-of-factly, but Mal could see the pain and loneliness in her eyes.

"How long have you been alone?"

"One hundred and forty-seven years," she said without hesitation. "My *amayi* was assassinated by a political rival. A human." She spat out the word.

"When did you come to Venice?"

"Four centuries ago, near enough. We fled to England after the Birch Men tried to sell us as slaves, but that was not far enough. They were everywhere in those days. Then we found this little group of islands in a lagoon, in a forgotten corner of Christendom. And so we made our home here."

She began to unbutton his doublet.

"Why don't you take this off?" she murmured.

"The doublet?"

"That too."

He slipped his hands under her skirts and up her thighs, expecting to feel the soft folds of stocking tops and then bare flesh, but instead his fingertips encountered smooth silken fabric, loose but enclosing, like–

"Breeches?"

She smiled and stood up, raising her skirts to waist-height to reveal rose-coloured breeches, like a boy's. Like Coby's. Mal shoved the guilty thought aside. This was business, even if it promised pleasure.

"Why do you think they call them Venetians?" Olivia said. "Even we women wear them, to protect our virtue."

Mal parted his knees so that he could pull her between them, and began unfastening the points that held the silken breeches in place. At last the flimsy garment fell away, sliding over the graceful curve of her hips to the floor. Mal swallowed as his prick stirred more insistently. Olivia ran her fingertips over his groin, making him gasp, then she unbuttoned his slops and tugged the waist-string of his drawers loose. As soon as his prick was free she climbed astride him once more and caught his gaze with her own as she lowered herself onto him. Gritting his teeth in an effort at self-control, he pulled her closer and bent his head to her bosom, tongue slipping between bodice and flesh to seek out her nipple like a bee questing for nectar. *Sweet Mother of God, it's been too long...*

"Take this out, and we can be as one," she whispered, fingering the pearl in his ear.

He made an affirmative noise, and felt her deftly unfasten his earring one-handed. He tensed, expecting some kind of magical assault. Nothing, only the warmth of her lips on his earlobe, her teeth nipping the edge of his ear... With a groan of pleasure he surrendered to the moment.

The world dissolved around him, not into the darkness of the dreamworld he knew so well, but a sunny glade by a brook. He and Olivia twined naked in the grass, the sun warm on their flesh. Above them, red and gold leaves fluttered in the breeze. She rolled over on top of him, silhouetted against the light. Her hair was short and spiky now, like Kiiren's… Mal's stomach constricted as he gazed up at her. Greyish skin and slit-pupilled yellow eyes. A skrayling. He pulled away.

"No!"

"What is wrong, my love?" She looked around the glade. "This is your dream, not mine."

"What have you done to me? Have you been haunting me from afar?"

He closed his eyes, trying to force himself awake. He was in Venice, in Ca' Ostreghe, not in an imaginary forest built of Erishen's memories. He blinked and opened his eyes.

Olivia sat sprawled on the floor where he had evidently pushed her off his lap, her eyes bright with tears. Mal hastily fastened his breeches and helped her up.

"Forgive me, my lady, I am unaccustomed to–"

"No, it is my fault." She dabbed at her eyes and nose with a lace handkerchief. "I intruded upon your thoughts, seeking to know you better. It was a great discourtesy."

He helped her onto the couch. "How… How do you do that? Pass into another's mind without going through… the dark places."

"Practice," she said. "And discipline. Do you really not remember anything of your former life?"

"Only what you have seen," he replied cautiously. "I am as ignorant of our ways as a child."

She glanced up at him through dark lashes. "I thought you said you were pledged to someone. You have an *amayi*, to take care of you in the end times and beginnings?"

"Not really. I have human friends, lovers, but…"

"But they cannot know what we are."

"No."

"Then how did you become one of the Unbound?"

Unbound? Was that the guisers' name for themselves? "I don't remember much of anything. It was dark and…" *And I was afraid.*

She took his hand and squeezed it. "Next time it will be different. Next time I will be there for you, and you for me."

He looked down into her green eyes. The pain and loneliness in her voice was genuine, he was sure of it. What would it be like to walk down the centuries together, man or woman, turn and turn about as they pleased? It was an intriguing prospect, but one that would make him the enemy of his brother, and of Kiiren. And yet he had to learn to control this thing inside him or he would never have peace, with Olivia or with Coby.

"Please, my lady, will you teach me?"

"How to dreamwalk?"

"Yes."

She smiled. "Of course."

She took him in her arms again, not as a lover but as a friend offering comfort. Mal laid his head upon her breast. *Dear Lady in Heaven, what am I doing?*

But reply came there none.

CHAPTER XX

They arrived in Spalato around dawn, and Youssef escorted them to an inn on the main square. Two of his men carried Gabriel on an improvised litter, causing many a sleepy-eyed stare from the women visiting the well in the centre of the marketplace. The captain also negotiated a fair price with the innkeeper and lent Coby some money to pay for it.

"We can't thank you enough, Captain Youssef," she stammered when he told her.

"You are most welcome. It is thanks to you that the painted demons drove off those pirates; otherwise I would have lost many men." He bade her farewell and left the inn.

Youssef must have made an impression on the innkeeper, for they had been given the finest room in the place, with a bed large enough for twice their party. Gabriel already occupied one side, tucked up in thick blankets despite the mild air. Sandy still had his cloak on, and his knapsack was slung over his shoulder.

"What are you doing?"

"Leaving."

"For Venice? It's not safe for you to go alone." She retreated to the door and stood before it, arms folded. "I swore to Mal I'd keep you out of trouble, and I won't break that promise." *Even though I have already failed once.*

"Then you will have to leave your friend behind."

She looked past him at Gabriel. The colour had returned to the actor's cheeks and he had even roused briefly when they moved him onto the litter, but he was a long way from being fit to travel.

"I can't leave him alone in a strange city, not like this. He could still die unless someone looks after him properly."

"Then you will have to choose between us."

He gave her that smug grin, the one that made him look so much like his brother. *Damn him.*

"No. It is you who have to choose," she said. "Stay here for a few days whilst we work out how we're going to get into Venice without Hennaq catching us first, or dash off and risk everything. You can't do it alone, you don't even speak the language."

"Neither do you."

"True, but I know my way around a city. Do you?"

His shoulders sagged, and she started to relax. A moment later he slammed both hands against the door, one either side of her head. The planks vibrated against her back in counterpoint to her pounding heart.

"I have seen more cities than you have seen new moons, youngling," he growled. "Now let me go."

She drew herself up to her full height and looked him in the eye. "No."

"No?"

"No."

From the bed came a groan. "Is it morning already?"

Coby wanted to run to Gabriel and soothe him back to sleep, but she knew that if she did that, Sandy would leave.

"How are you going to get there?" she said in a low voice. "You don't have any money."

"I will find a way."

"Give me a day," she said. "Just one day. If I don't have a better plan for you by this time tomorrow, you can go with my blessing."

He appeared to consider for a moment. "One day."

"And I have your word you won't run off, the moment my back is turned?"

"Yes."

"Thank you." She pushed past him and went over to the bed, but Gabriel was already asleep.

Exploring Spalato did not take long. Although it called itself a city, it was no bigger than many of the provincial towns Coby had visited whilst touring with Suffolk's Men: a market square with several streets leading off, a few churches, and a harbour. There were some buildings one did not find in an English town, including an office whose only purpose was the collection and delivery of letters, and a public bath where the citizens of Spalato resorted to wash themselves. If it had not been for the apparent respectability of the women going in and out of the building, and the separate entrances for each sex, she would have taken it to be a stew. The only whores she had seen so far had been in the common room of the inn, lounging around with bare breasts and bored expressions, much like their sisters back home.

She went down to the harbour and reassured herself there was no sign of Hennaq's ship, but still her heart was heavy as she made her way back to the market square. She had no idea how she was going to convince Sandy not to leave for Venice without her, nor how she could ensure Gabriel's safety if she left. Lost in this dilemma, she hardly noticed when a young man stepped out into the street in front of her. Passers-by laughed as wooden balls rained down around the two of them. Coby looked up into the eyes of a solemn young man a few years older than herself. He muttered an apology and bent to retrieve the balls. Over his head Coby spotted a large red-and-yellow striped tent that had not been in the marketplace when she left. She walked towards it slowly, a plan beginning to crystallise on the edge of her thoughts.

She found Gabriel sitting up in bed, pale but cheerful. He had managed to find paper, pen and ink from somewhere and was scratching away feverishly. Every so often he would pause and stare out of the window, then resume his writing.

"Sorry, am I disturbing you?" she said, when he laid his pen down.

"No, it's all right." He put the sheet of paper aside to dry. "My hand was starting to cramp anyway."

"How's it going?"

Gabriel sighed "The story has taken a strange turn. I'm not sure I'm in the right humour for comedy today."

"Perhaps a rest is a good thing, then." She looked around the room. Sandy's cloak was draped over the windowsill, but there was no sign of his knapsack. "Where's Sandy?"

"He said he was going down to the docks."

"I did not see him, and it is a small city. Faith, I hope he has not run off already. I need to speak to him."

She tried to suppress her grin of triumph and failed utterly.

"You have a plan?" Gabriel said, leaning forward.

"Later, when Sandy returns," she said. "But I will need your support."

He held out his hand. "Always."

She turned away, overcome by this unexpected show of loyalty. What had she done to deserve it, except get them out of the trouble she should have avoided in the first place?

"Come," she said. "Let me have a look at your wound."

Gabriel eased his left leg out of bed and sat patiently whilst she unwrapped the bandages. The deeper cuts had been stitched up neatly by Gaoh and were nicely scabbed over, and the flesh around them was less red and hot than it had been. Satisfied, she wound the bandages back around his calf and tied the ends.

"Have you tried walking yet?"

He shook his head.

"Why don't we give it a go? You can lean on me."

They made it to the window without much trouble, then Gabriel rested a while against the sill before attempting the return journey to the bed. By the time they reached it, he was white-faced and breathing heavily.

"Enough," Coby said. "We'll do it again after supper."

Gabriel forced a smile. "Thank you. I am in your debt."

"I think we are even," she replied. "I have long owed you and Ned for helping to rescue Master Catlyn from Ferrymead House."

"Still..."

Footsteps sounded outside. A moment later the door opened and Sandy entered, ducking under the lintel.

"So," he said, looking from one to the other, "do you have a plan to get us to Venice?"

"I do," Coby said.

Sandy drew up a stool. "I am listening."

She paced around the room, ticking off the points on her fingers.

"First, we send a letter to Mal, warning him about Hennaq. The Venetians have a very efficient postal service, and we know he intended to go to the English ambassador, so we have somewhere to send the letter. It could be with him even faster than we can get there."

"What if the Venetians open it?" Gabriel said. "Any mention of skraylings may cause them to suspect his purpose there."

"I will use a cipher, to make the contents seem innocent," Coby said. "But the point is, we can warn Mal swiftly, and still have time to make our own preparations. I have been gathering gossip, as best I can, and it seems the skraylings' embassy progresses slowly. No agreement has been reached, nor is likely to be, at least not this side of Ascension Day."

"What's so important about Ascension Day?" Gabriel asked.

"It is the day when the ruler of Venice, the Doge, celebrates the city's naval history with a grand ceremony out in the lagoon." She pulled a face. "Some heathen ritual involving a gold wedding ring, I'm told. Anyway, it's all about the power and might of Venice, so they're not going to overshadow that by admitting how much they need a foreign alliance."

"So we are to go to Venice after all."

"Of course. We cannot just go home, not after coming all this way."

"We will have to be careful," Sandy said. "We cannot count upon my people to protect us, not if Hennaq petitions them."

"Lord Kiiren would not betray us, would he?"

"Of course not, but it is not his choice alone."

"Then we will have to rely on stealth and guile," Coby said, "and hide our purpose from both the Venetians and the skraylings."

"What did you have in mind?" Gabriel asked.

"A phoenix."

"A phoenix?" His brow creased in puzzlement.

"Ascension Day isn't just about the Doge and the sea. There's a big procession, and entertainments all over the city, day and night. Musicians and players will be flocking to Venice, so no one will notice one more troupe. Our troupe." She bit her lip, hardly able to rein in her excitement. "Suffolk's Men will rise from the ashes."

• • • •

Erishen closed his eyes and let the night sounds wash over him: the girl snoring, the other one shifting on the flea-ridden mattress, mice scuttling across the rafters, the whisper of wings as a bat skimmed past the window. A dog barked, shaking him out of his reverie for a moment, then was silent. Down into sleep he drifted, dark waters pulling him under until his feet touched solid ground. Not water after all, but air, or at least the semblance of it. Not day or night, but a silver-grey twilight forever frozen, colourless, on the brink of dawn. He looked around at the dark landscape dotted with domes of faint golden light, the sleeping minds of the city. Though he scanned them carefully, he saw no sign of the brighter auras of his own people, white or violet in hue.

He stretched arms that became wings, and soared above the plain, wheeling over the barren darkness of the sea, heading north towards Venice. The cities were closer here than in the waking world, drawn together by bonds of blood and faith, and it took him only minutes to reach Venice, laid out beneath him like a jewelled carving. He drifted, letting his aura disperse a little so that he was just one more blur of light in the eternal firmament. It was harder to think clearly in this state, but also harder for anyone else to spot him. The lights below shimmered in an ever-changing pattern, flowing like water... For a moment he thought he caught sight of a blue-white spark amongst the gold, diamond-bright, but it winked out again. Did Kiiren stir in uneasy sleep? Or had some sharp-eyed enemy, spotting him, taken cover? The girl was right, he should not show his hand too soon.

With a sigh he skimmed southwards once more, picking up speed as he shaped himself into a falcon, bright and fierce. As the smaller city came into view, the temptation to plunge down and immerse himself in their memories and longings threatened to overwhelm him. It would not be as sweet as his communings with Kiiren, but there was a raw pleasure to be had from these mortals, playing upon their fears and desires until they woke in a cold sweat to the memory of his laughter. Only once before had he tried it, and then only to save his brother's life, but that had been enough to whet his appetite. He wheeled over the city, looking for a target. There. The girl's plan had been good, but with his help it would be even better.

Coby woke at dawn to find Sandy already up and dressed.

"You're not leaving, are you?" she said, sitting up and running her fingers through her tangled hair. She had slept in her clothes as usual, even though she knew neither man had any untoward interest in her. "I thought you agreed to my plan."

"So I do," he said. "But I need to bathe first. You Christians are filthy creatures."

"I can order hot water brought up here."

"I would prefer to swim, or at least immerse myself." He scratched his scalp. "No wonder you people are covered in lice. I will find a stream, or go down to the sea."

"You can't leave the city, it's not safe." A thought struck her, though it was a poor compromise. She dug in her purse and pulled out a couple of small coins. "There's a Turkish bath near the market square. I believe they have pools for bathing."

He looked sceptical, but took the proffered coins.

"Just be careful, all right?" she said. "I am not entirely sure those places are… respectable."

"I have no interest in rutting with one of your people," he said. "My *amayi* is all I desire."

"Well. Good."

He strode out of the room and shut the door sharply behind him, rattling the bolts. Gabriel twitched awake and groaned.

"What was that?"

"Just..." Sandy? She wasn't sure what to call him any more; he seemed less human with every passing day.

Gabriel struggled upright and swung his legs over the side of the bed, wincing as his left foot touched the floor.

"So," he said after a jaw-cracking yawn, "today's the day that Suffolk's Men are reborn."

Coby made an affirmative noise and turned her back whilst he dressed. Seeing men half-naked had never bothered her when she was in a tiring-house helping actors into their costumes, but in the intimacy of a bedchamber it felt quite wrong to stand and watch.

"Of course we can't call ourselves Suffolk's Men any more," she said over her shoulder. "Anyway, Grey is the last person I would want to claim as a patron."

"How about 'Raleigh's Men'? I dare say he's the one who'll be paying for all this, one way or another."

"No. We don't want anything to link us to Mal. How about..." She pondered for a moment. "Parrish's Men."

"What?"

"You have to be the leader of our troupe. You have the most experience, and we need to spare your leg. Sandy and I will do most of the work."

"What about the play itself? No one will understand a word."

"Doesn't matter. We're not going to be doing plays like the ones back in London." She paced the room, images crowding her mind's eye. "I was in the market square yesterday, and there was a troupe of Italian players. They call it *commedia all'improviso*. Very different from our own theatre: all bawdy comedy, mock fights and falling on their arses. As long as we're funny, I don't think it will matter if the audience understands us or not."

"And you think you can do that? Acting is not as easy as it looks, you know."

"I have been acting all my life," she said softly. "Just not on a stage."

She borrowed pen and paper from Gabriel and wrote the letter to Mal, then went downstairs in search of breakfast. To her surprise the *commedia* players were sitting round one of the tables in the courtyard, looking as miserable as a wet Sunday afternoon. The shy young juggler was turning a painted ball in his hands, staring at it as if it held the secrets of eternity, whilst their leader, a short curly-haired man in threadbare black-and-red motley, berated each of them in turn. The youngest of the troupe, a girl of about fifteen, was weeping loudly into a handkerchief.

"Did the play not go well last night?" she asked the landlord as he passed on his way back to the kitchen.

"Oh yes. But this morning they discovered that their Columbina and Il Capitano have run off to be wed, and taken a whole week's money with them."

"That is unfortunate," Coby replied. And strangely convenient. Two actors go missing, the very day after she had suggested taking to the stage. *Erishen*. She thanked the landlord and set off to post the enciphered letter.

"This was your doing, wasn't it?" She folded her arms and stared at Sandy, whose smug grin was good as an admission of guilt.

"The lovers had wanted to leave for a long time," he said, turning away abruptly so that droplets of water flew out from the ends of his damp hair. "I simply gave them a nudge."

"Don't tell me you...?" Coby wiped her face with her cuff. "No, I don't want to know. Whatever it is, it's between you and God." *If you still believe in Him*.

Gabriel looked from one to the other in confusion. "What's 'his doing'?"

Coby sighed. "The *commedia* players I saw yesterday are conveniently in need of two actors. A man and a woman."

"Women play on the Italian stage?" Gabriel asked.

"Oh yes. And in France too. It is only in England that women are forbidden to perform."

"The English honour skrayling custom in that regard," Sandy added.

"Whatever the reason," Coby went on, glaring at Sandy, "we now have a choice. Continue with my plan, or try to join the *commedia*."

"But there are three of us," Gabriel said. "And none of us speaks Italian."

"Which is all the more reason to join an existing troupe," Sandy said. "We will be less conspicuous amongst them than by ourselves."

"It's really up to Hendricks," Gabriel said with a sympathetic smile. "She is the one who must discard her current guise, as well as learn to act."

The two men looked at her expectantly.

"Very well," she said after a moment. "But only because I had been thinking about it already. And I will need your help, Master Parrish. I… I need to learn womanly manners if I am to do this properly."

"Of course."

"The gown I bought is rather plain; I think I should buy something to brighten it up a little before we approach the players. And you two ought to look a bit more like actors as well." She weighed the purse in her pocket. "If there's one thing I do know how to do, it's clothe a theatre company for next to nothing."

Choosing a pretty shawl for herself in the market was easy enough, but Venetian men's fashions were terribly sombre; not at all the sort of flamboyant clothing needed to make them look like actors. Eventually she found a couple of pairs of yellow stockings for the men, some dyed feathers to put in Gabriel's hat, and two striped and fringed scarves that would do for a number of uses. Satisfied at last, she returned to the inn with her haul and the two men began changing into their new clothes.

"These were the best I could find," she said, taking Gabriel's hat and pinning the feathers in place.

"They look splendid," Gabriel said with a smile. "I had a hat rather like that, back in Southwark."

He looked a lot stronger today, and was walking about the room unaided, though with a pronounced limp. The stockings did little to hide the bandages on his calf, however, and Coby prayed the wounds wouldn't bleed through.

Sandy finished dressing and struck a dramatic pose. Stripped to his shirt sleeves and with one of the scarves tied around his waist like a sash, he cut a dashing figure: an eastern prince, perhaps, or a noble bandit who, like Robin Hood, only stole from those who could afford it. She wondered if he had ever acted before, and if so, whether skrayling plays were very different from English or Italian ones. Mostly she prayed he would not embarrass them or cause trouble. He had done enough as it was.

"Out, out!" she said when they were done. "I'm not going to change into this gown in front of you, you know."

Gabriel apologised, and Sandy helped him down the stairs to the taproom. Coby bolted the door behind them and stripped down to her stockings and drawers. The latter she was not willing to discard, skirts or no, though she did extract the tool roll and stow it under the mattress. She slipped into the petticoat, thankful that she'd chosen a style that laced up the front. Halfway through the lacing she realised she ought to try and plump up her breasts, rather than flattening them as she usually did. Not that there was a lot to work with, but the bodice was surprisingly effective. She stared down at the unfamiliar prospect for several moments. *Sweet Jesu, what will Mal think when he sees me like this?*

She hurriedly pulled on the gown, and arranged the shawl to cover what the bodice exposed. There, much better.

She slipped into her shoes, drew the bolt and drew a deep breath before opening the door. *Well, nothing else for it.* Holding the edge of the scarf tight against her chest, she made her way down to the taproom.

CHAPTER XXI

Mal managed to deflect Ned's questions about his dealings with Olivia for two days, mostly by ensuring they were never alone together. He let Berowne take them on a tour of the city, including a visit to the basilica of St Mark's, which surpassed even Mal's expectations. The lower half of the building was splendid enough, with its fine marble paving and Herculean pillars, but when he looked up… Every inch of the ceiling was gilded, so that it gleamed in the candlelight like a treasure cave. Even the gilding itself was merely the backdrop to hundreds of mosaics depicting saints and Bible stories, their figures rendered in the flat Eastern style that betrayed the city's past connections with Constantinople.

"I used to think the preachers exaggerated," Ned muttered as they followed Berowne into yet another side chapel.

"Oh?"

"About the richness of the churches, before King Henry broke with Rome."

Mal smiled. "I doubt any English cathedral was ever a tenth as grand, even then."

Berowne launched into a description of the chapel ceiling, oblivious to the satiety of his companions.

"I suppose you're going to see *her* again tonight," Ned whispered.

"What of it?"

"We're supposed to be here on business, not pleasure."

"Can I not combine the two?"

"She has bewitched you, this guiser whore."

"Olivia is not a whore," Mal said, more loudly than he'd intended. An old woman who had been lighting a candle in the chapel glared at him and blew out her taper with a huff of disgust.

"So tell me what you've learned," Ned said, "and why this war has suddenly become a truce."

Mal sighed. "Very well. But not here. When we get back to the embassy, then I'll tell you."

"You swear."

"I swear. Now, look sharp. I think Berowne has found another interesting mosaic."

Ned rolled his eyes, and Mal chuckled in sympathy. This was going to be a long day.

Ned closed the attic door behind him.

"Well?"

Mal sat down on the end of the bed but immediately rose again, went to the window and closed the shutters against the noonday sun.

"Olivia's not our enemy," Mal said quietly. "In fact I think she may be our best ally in the city."

"What?"

"She has convinced me she has only good intentions–"

"Hah. And people say I'm the one who thinks with my prick."

"You think I trust her because I–"

"Because you're fucking her? Are you?"

Mal's expression was indistinct in the shadows, but the hunch of his shoulders implied guilt.

"I might have known," Ned muttered. When Mal made no reply, he added, "So, how is your new paramour going to help us?"

"She doesn't want the skraylings in Venice any more than England does. In fact she's terrified they're here to hunt her down. The only reason she trusts me is because..." He sighed. "I told her about Erishen."

"Sandy?"

"No, I've managed to keep that from her so far, though God knows for how much longer."

"And you?" Ned went over to him and, taking Mal's head between his hands, stared into his eyes. "What of you? Is the Mal I know and love still in there?"

"Of course."

His voice was as rough as his beard, and sent the same shiver down to Ned's groin. *Not now,* said the unwelcome voice of reason. Ned released him.

"You still haven't answered my question. How is she going to help us?"

"By getting the Venetians to look the other way whilst we conduct our business here."

"She can do that?"

"She's a guiser. An old one. And she is by no means mad, nor evil. She keeps the Grand Council and even the Ten in check; if she does so behind the scenes, well, can you fault her? No one in Christendom wants to hear they are being ruled by a five hundred year-old creature from the New World."

"Hmm." Ned chewed his lip. "Even if she does help us, what's the price? Your soul?"

"No price. I've told you, she wants the skraylings gone. But..." Ned's heart sank. *Here it comes...* "She has asked me to do her a small kindness–"

"Apart from the fucking?"

"Enough, for Christ's sake, Ned!"

Ned recoiled at the fury in Mal's voice. "Sorry. Go on."

"There is a man in her service, a patrician named Giambattista Bragadin. Through him she provides secrets to those requiring leverage over her enemies, and they share the fees."

"This is that Merchant fellow you were talking about?"

"Yes. Her problem is that she suspects Bragadin of plotting against her. She wants me to follow him and observe his dealings."

"So why doesn't she just use her sorcery to rummage around in his head? Guisers can do that, right?"

"That's why she suspects him. Bragadin has obtained a spirit-guard and is using it to keep her out of his dreams."

"So you're going to spy on him?"

"Yes."

"Sounds dangerous."

"Very."

"I'm in." Ned grinned at him.

"What?"

"I'm in. You don't think I'm going to sit at home and let you get into trouble all by yourself, do you?"

Mal sighed. "I don't suppose there's anything I can say to stop you?"

"Nothing."

"Very well. Meet me at sunset in the Winged Lion. It's a taverna in San Marco, not far from Palazzo Bragadin." Mal bent to unfasten his knapsack. "I have to see Olivia first."

"A daytime visit? Isn't that a little… conspicuous?"

"Why do you think I have this?" Mal held up a mask. "A convenient little fashion. Anyone would think this city was ruled through intrigue."

He picked up a long hooded cloak and headed for the door.

Ned rubbed his hands together, jealousy forgotten. A little night work, that was more like it. Best not to think who they were doing it for, only the ultimate goal. Finish their business here, and go home.

Mal walked through the Venetian dusk towards his rendezvous with Ned, exhausted in mind and body from his session with Olivia. Dreamwalking required practice and discipline as demanding as swordplay and, contrary to Ned's slurs, did not include any further carnal pleasures, at least not today. Olivia told him that for true mastery he needed to keep his thoughts and passions separate until he could command them both. Later, she promised, they could repeat the blissful experience of that first joining, and without unwelcome memories intruding.

As he crossed yet another little square, he caught movement out of the corner of his eye and halted. A squad of a dozen red-clad *sbirri*, the constables who patrolled Venice, were escorting several sullen young men in the direction of St Mark's. Seeing an open space, one of them tried to make a break for it but was brought down and beaten into submission before the procession continued on its way.

"Excuse me, sir," Mal said to a passing workman, "what was all that about?"

"Fighting on the bridges again. Those boys never learn." His voice was tinged with pride rather than condemnation. He looked Mal up and down and his eyes narrowed. "You a Castellano?"

Mal hesitated. Berowne had warned him about the factionalism dividing the city: the Nicoletti in the west and the Castellani in the east. From time to time fighting broke out between the young men of the two factions and could rapidly devolve into full-scale riots if not checked. San Marco was Castellani territory.

"I'm staying in Santa Croce," he said at last, "so I suppose that makes me one of the Nicoletti."

"You take care then, sir, if you know what's good for

you." The workman hoisted his bag of tools a little higher and went on his way.

Mal set off again, and a few minutes later found himself at the Winged Lion. The taverna was quiet, just a couple of old men playing chess and sipping wine. Mal had the feeling they came here every morning for the companionship and did not leave until curfew. Ned was in the opposite corner, playing a solo card game on a well-scrubbed table.

"You took your time," he said. "It's a good job these Venetians don't drink much. I'd have been thrown out of an English alehouse for nursing a flagon all afternoon." He gathered up his cards and drained his cup. "After you."

They made their way through the darkening streets of San Marco, Mal following the image of the route that Olivia had shown him at the end of their lesson. It had been strange to walk through a hazy simulacrum of the city, but less strange than walking the very real and solid streets and recognising places he had never been before. He began to see the true power of the skraylings, to communicate in ways that men scarcely dreamed of.

"No mask, then?" Ned asked as they trotted side by side up the steps of a small bridge.

"I thought it too noticeable," Mal replied. "It hides a man's face, but also marks him out as a person of note, since only patricians are allowed to wear them freely. This way we are just ordinary citizens going about our business."

"And what if we're recognised?"

"Bragadin has never seen you before, and I have my own defence." He pulled up the hood on his cloak.

Palazzo Bragadin was a substantial building on the far side of San Marco, deep into Castellani territory. Its façade overlooked one of the larger tributaries of the Grand Canal, whilst the rear entrance gave onto a small narrow square with a well in the centre.

"Should we not watch from the canal side?" Ned murmured as they strolled idly through the square. Around them, shopkeepers were dismantling stalls and barring their shutters. "I thought the grander folk of Venice travelled everywhere by boat."

"So they do. However, I would expect Bragadin to deal with this business through an intermediary, and whether here or elsewhere, that is best not done through the front door."

"He could conduct his negotiations through letters, and we'd be none the wiser."

Mal shook his head. "This is not the sort of matter one commits to paper, even enciphered. After all, a cipher common enough to be known by his clients would be as good as useless. So–" he glanced around, conscious of being overheard "–we watch the servants' entrance for any suspicious comings or goings."

"And how are we going to lie in wait? We should have disguised ourselves as beggars or something."

"No. The beggars are bound to know every one of their kind in the parish; our arrival on their territory would only spark trouble."

"So what do we do?"

Mal smiled. "The way has been prepared for us."

He paused at a door opposite the palazzo and knocked. After a few moments it opened and an old man squinted up at them, the lamplight gleaming on his bald pate.

"*Signori?*"

"We have come to visit our cousin," Mal said to him in Italian.

"Of course, sirs, come in."

They followed him inside, into a narrow passage smelling of mildew. Somewhere up above, a woman was singing, a repetitive song that sounded like a lullaby. The old man ushered them through a side door into a low-ceilinged room lit only by the faint glow of lanterns from the street. It appeared to be a disused storeroom, empty but for the remains of a wine barrel in one corner, rotting gently into the layer of must and slime that covered the tiled floor. Mal thanked the man, and he and Ned crossed carefully to the narrow barred window that looked out onto the street.

"Now we wait," Mal said softly. He peered through the grimy glass, resisting the temptation to clean it to get a better view. He wanted to leave no sign of their presence here, in case they had to return tomorrow night.

They did not have long to wait; before the bells had tolled the first hour after sunset, a small door just along the street opened, and a cloaked and hooded figure of Bragadin's height and build emerged. On such a mild night, there was only one reason to be going abroad so concealed. Mal led the way back to the front door of the house and opened it a crack. As soon as Bragadin turned into the square, Mal slipped out and beckoned for Ned to follow him. They padded to the end of the street and halted at the corner.

The square was still busy with men making their way home after work, so Mal stepped out and walked briskly in the same direction Bragadin was taking. Their quarry turned right and right again, then southwards towards St Mark's Square. Mal hunched his head as he walked, conscious that he was markedly taller than most Italians, though it did at least give him a good view over the crowds. Fortunate, since he almost missed Bragadin making a sharp right turn towards the Rialto Bridge.

"What... if we lose him?" Ned panted as they strode up the long low steps.

"Don't worry, I think I know where he might be going."

They followed Bragadin down the other side of the bridge and past the empty fish market, over a smaller bridge and left down a broad street, through a square and over another bridge, always heading north. For a moment

Mal wondered if he was wrong and Bragadin was heading for the skraylings' palazzo, though he couldn't think of a reason why he should. So intent was he on this idea that he nearly lost Bragadin again as the man turned west instead of continuing north. At least, Mal thought it was west, judging by the last faint glow of the sky ahead of them. It was hard to be certain in this city.

The stink of dyers' vats announced their arrival in one of the poorer parts of the city, somewhere on the border between San Polo and Santa Croce but far from the English embassy. The sort of place a patrician like Bragadin would never frequent, and therefore the perfect place for Il Mercante to conduct his business.

A few minutes later they emerged into a large square in front of a church composed mainly of round towers like a castle's. Halfway across the square Bragadin turned left down a narrow street.

"Now we have him," Mal whispered, halting by the well.

"How so?"

"If I'm right, this is the same place he was supposed to meet those men I overheard at Olivia's. I scouted it out in daylight, and that street ends at a canal. I think he intends to meet someone who will arrive by gondola."

"And if he leaves with them?"

"Then we have a problem. But I do not think he is fool enough to put himself into the hands of the men he is selling secrets to. He takes risks enough, dealing with them himself."

"Odd, that," Ned said. "I'd use a go-between, for fear of being recognised. These men know him, right?"

"Yes. But conspiracy makes men mistrustful. He cheats Olivia, and therefore does not trust any man not to do the same to him."

"Hmm. Well, we'll have to get a bit closer than this if we want to find anything out. So far he's not doing anything out of the ordinary, is he?"

"No, he's not. And I'm sure he's chosen this spot because it's somewhere his dealings cannot easily be overheard."

"That's no help to us, then," Ned muttered.

"True. But his attention will be on the canal, not the street. He cannot be looking behind him at every sound without drawing attention to himself. So, we walk calmly down the street as if we were visiting someone, and hope to find a place to conceal ourselves in the shadows."

"And if we can't?"

"We'll cross that bridge when we come to it. So to speak." He paused. "And speaking of speaking, don't say a word once we enter the street. If these men hear us speak English, they may put two and two together."

"Right you are," Ned replied, his expression comically serious. Mal prayed his friend would not forget himself, but there was nothing for it but to continue.

He wrapped his cloak around him and set off across the square, Ned at his heels. Though he would not admit it, he was glad he had not come alone. One man by himself looked more suspicious than two, and if it came down to it they could pretend to be having an assignation of their own. He smiled to himself. Ned would enjoy that, perhaps a little too much.

The street was dark at ground level, lit only by the faint glow of candles in the *piani nobili* above. Barred windows and closed doors lined both sides. At the far end Mal could make out a paler archway cutting through a tenement; the *sottoportego* that led to the canal. He strode as confidently as he dared through the darkness, finally pausing at a door fifteen yards or so from the archway, allowing his boots to scuff loudly on the worn paving stones. He laid his hand upon the door handle and pretended to fumble in his pockets for a key, meanwhile counting silently. One, two, three... When he reached twenty he stepped silently to one side and melted into a neighbouring doorway. A moment later Ned joined him, and they exchanged brief glances. Either it had worked and Bragadin thought them a pair of local men arriving home, or it hadn't. They would soon find out.

No sound came from the *sottoportego,* and at last Mal let out a slow breath. Now to wait. From the lights and noises above, the residents of this building were already home, and with any luck would stay there all night.

He was just beginning to fear he was wrong and their quarry had given them the slip, when a soft thud of wood on stone announced the arrival of a gondola at the nearby steps. Beside him, Ned tensed.

The scraping of shoe leather on uneven canal steps echoed down the passageway as someone disembarked, then the soft splash of an oar as the boat departed. No one was allowed to eavesdrop on this conversation, especially a garrulous gondolier.

"Good evening, sir." The speaker's voice was distorted, perhaps by a mask. Bragadin was evidently no fool. "I had not expected you to bring company."

"I had not expected to meet a second time. Do you have it?"

A pause.

"Alas–"

A scuffle and a thud, as of a man's body hitting a wall.

"I have been patient," Bragadin's client hissed. His next words were indistinct, whispered perhaps in Bragadin's ear. "I will be patient no longer."

"Please, you ask a great deal–"

"A great deal indeed, for I have paid you a thousand ducats already and seen naught for it."

A thousand ducats? What in God's name were these men asking Il Mercante to find out?

"I am close," Bragadin gasped. "It takes time to put

spies in place so that they will not be found out. Another week–"

"I don't have a week. You swore you could get me the information before the Doge's investiture. Your promises are worthless."

Bragadin laughed, his mask shaping the sound into a hollow cackle that raised the hairs on Mal's neck. "So is your house's name," he said softly, "if the Ten find out what you've been up to."

"Are you threatening me? You louse, you dungheap crawler–"

Bragadin cried out, the sound ending in a choking gurgle. Mal dashed forward, colliding with someone in the passageway. The man swore and Mal felt a blade catch in the folds of his cloak. He retreated a pace and drew his own dagger, sweeping it in a waist-high arc before him. Damn, but he hated fighting in the dark.

His vision began to clear a little. He could make out two figures between himself and the canal steps; the other was lying on the ground against the wall. Bragadin, he feared. The two men backed away, but they had nowhere to go until their gondola returned. Several minutes at least, he guessed.

"Who are you?" the nearer man asked. "We were to meet alone."

Mal said nothing. Whoever these men were, they had been at Olivia's supper parties, and would recognise him by his accent in an instant. The last thing he needed was for the courtesan to be connected to Il Mercante.

Long moments passed, the silence broken only by the rasping breath of Bragadin. So, he lived, for now.

"Where's that whoreson knave of a gondolier?" the other man muttered. Mal could tell by his stance that he was sizing up his chances of rushing past him into the street and getting away on foot.

"Calm yourself, Pietro," the nearer man said.

The words had the opposite of the desired effect. Pietro dashed towards the street, but Mal was there first and Pietro ran straight onto his dagger. He looked up at Mal wide-eyed, gasped a last curse, and fell dead at his feet.

Pietro's companion backed away until his boot-heels scraped on the edge of the canal.

"Peace, gentlemen." His eyes flicked left, along the canal. "We are done here."

At that moment the gondola slid into view and he leapt aboard. Mal watched him go, then sheathed his dagger and crouched to examine Bragadin. Blood soaked the man's doublet, leaving Mal's hands sticky. Bragadin no longer appeared to be breathing.

"There's nothing we can do for him," he told Ned, who stood pale-faced at the passageway's mouth. He wiped his hands on the dying man's cloak. "Come, let's get out of here."

As he stepped out into the street he realised it was brighter than before. Several of the windows on the upper stories were open, and people were leaning out. A man shouted. Mal broke into a run, cursing as his hood fell back. Rapid footsteps right behind him were Ned, he hoped, but he could hear doors opening now and more voices raised. He sprinted across the square in what he hoped was the right direction, halting in the shadows of the church to see if Ned had followed him.

Ned ran past, looking wildly around.

"Psst, this way!" Mal beckoned to him.

They ran down another narrow street, across a bridge, through a courtyard and under another passageway onto a broad *fondamenta*. No sound of pursuers. Perhaps the residents of Calle di Mezzo would not chase miscreants beyond the bounds of their own parish.

"What do we do now?" Ned gasped, leaning against the wall.

"We pray to God we can find our way home before curfew without encountering the constables," Mal said, "and that no one reports us to the Ten."

CHAPTER XXII

"I can't do this," Coby whispered, pressing herself against the back of the tent that formed their tiring house. She was dressed as Columbina, in a full calf-length skirt and a tightly laced bodice that would have shown far too much cleavage, if she had any. She twisted the mask in her fingers, wishing it were full-face to hide her blushes.

"Of course you can," Gabriel said. "You were very good in rehearsals, you know."

"Really?"

"Really. All those years watching me and Dickon didn't go to waste, that's obvious."

She forced a smile. Dickon Rudd, their old troupe's clown, had been killed in the same accident as Master Naismith.

Perhaps realising he had said the wrong thing, Gabriel struck a comic pose, sticking out his padded stomach and splaying his feet in their long slippers. He had been given the part of Il Dottore, since the character of the doctor would allow him to walk with a stick and talk elevated nonsense that no one was supposed to understand. Coby couldn't help but smile at Gabriel's antics; for such a handsome young fellow, he made a very convincing old man, all quavering voice and bowed legs.

"That's better," Gabriel said, clapping her on the shoulder. "Now go, before the audience gets restless. And don't forget what I told you."

She took a deep breath and ducked out of the tent. The low stage had been set up directly in front of it, with a wide circle of bare earth beyond that where the audience sat or stood. A hundred or more pairs of eyes gleamed in the light of the torches set on tall stands to either side of the stage, though the eyes were not on her but on the troupe's leader, Zancani. As Pantalone, he represented the archetypal Venetian merchant: rich, miserly and lecherous. Coby was sure she had bruises on her behind where the little Italian had taken his role rather too seriously during rehearsals. Fortunately her first scene was not with him.

She waited until Pantalone had made his speech and departed, then climbed the short flight of steps onto the stage. *You are not Coby Hendricks,* Gabriel's voice said in her head, *you are Columbina, young and lovely and full of mischief.*

"Arlecchino!" She put her hand beside her mouth, to emphasis the action. "Arlecchino?"

Someone in the audience laughed in anticipation. Coby crossed the stage.

"Arlecchino?"

Sandy emerged from the wings opposite, dressed as Il Capitano in his striped sash and a big-nosed mask. "Columbina?"

Coby made an extravagant gesture of mock alarm. "Capitano?"

Sandy bowed clumsily, then drew his sword. It was made of several jointed wooden sections and wobbled comically. The audience laughed at the bawdy image. Coby tutted and wagged her finger, and he put the sword away. Or tried to. It took several attempts, since the blade waved around as he moved it. The audience were helpless with laughter by now, and Coby began to relax. They were not watching her at all, she reminded herself. They were watching Columbina and Il Capitano.

Sandy began making gestures of love, kissing his hands and then stretching them out towards her. She folded her arms and shook her head. He advanced a step and repeated the pantomime. Still she refused him. He pulled a bunch of silk flowers out of his doublet and knelt, holding them out. She pouted, took them – and then hit him over the head with them. There followed a chase around the stage, with the audience cheering them both on.

"*Asino*! *Stupido*!" she yelled at Sandy. "*Bamboccio*!" When she ran out of the Italian insults she had learnt from Zancani, she added a few French ones for good measure. "*Bricon*! *Crapaud*!"

At last she paused for breath, fanning herself with the flowers, and Sandy pounced, taking her in his arms. She pretended to struggle until he bent her back over his arm and leant over her, feigning to kiss her. At least, that's what she expected from rehearsals. His dark eyes gleamed in the torchlight and his lips brushed hers, warm and wind-roughened. For a moment, memory of another stolen kiss took over and she kissed him back, then the audience's whoops and catcalls brought her to her senses. As she started to push him away, the juggler cartwheeled onto the stage as Arlecchino, Columbina's lover. Il Capitano took fright and dropped Columbina, who landed on her backside to more roars of laughter. Whilst the two men chased one another around the stage, Coby made a hasty retreat to the dressing-tent, biting back tears of pain and humiliation. How dare he kiss her like that, and in front of everyone!

Backstage the other players congratulated them on a scene well played, but Coby was in no mood for praise.

"What do you think you were doing?" she hissed at Sandy when they were alone again. "You only pretended to kiss me in rehearsal."

He shrugged. "This was not the rehearsal, it was the real thing."

"So that gives you the right to kiss me?"

"It is just a play."

"You're as bad as one another, you men," she muttered, and fought her way out of the tent. Zancani had arranged tonight's play so that his newest performers had only a couple of scenes each, and it would be a while before she was needed again.

She strode across the market square to the well, still hidden from the audience by the bulk of the actors' tent. Hauling up a bucket of water burnt off a little of her anger at Sandy. She pushed up her mask and splashed some of the water on her cheeks, which cooled her temper some more. Footsteps scuffed in the dust behind her.

"If you've come to apologise–"

It was not Sandy but a short stocky man in the rough garb of a farmer, perhaps one of the audience. He leered at her and said something in the local dialect.

"I suggest you leave before I call my friends," she told him in French, not expecting him to understand.

The man just leered again and stepped towards her. Without thinking she crouched in a fighting stance. The man laughed and made a lunge for her. She sidestepped and kicked him hard in the arse so that he stumbled. Cursing now, he turned to face her again.

He spat in the dust. *"Puttana!"*

"Don't you call me a whore," she muttered.

Stepping quickly forward she grasped his right arm in both hands and twisted it. The man cursed and lost his footing. Coby hooked a heel behind his ankle and threw him to the ground, releasing him as he fell. The man snatched at her leg. She brought the heel of her hand down sharply on his temple, and he slumped to the ground again, moaning.

She strode back towards the tent. Gabriel hurried to meet her halfway, stumbling in his overlong slippers.

"Are you hurt?"

"Only my dignity." She drew a ragged breath, let it out again. "I've been in fights before, you know. Dozens."

"So I see. That poor fellow had no chance."

They ducked back into the tent.

"He underestimated me," she said quietly. "Fighting in male guise is much harder, in a way. No quarter asked or given."

"So why not adopt women's guise all the time?" Gabriel said. "If it's easier."

"It's not really easier. Just different." She sat down on a crate. "And scarier. Fighting as a man, you know your opponent only wants to scare you, hurt you a bit, not..."

She swallowed, unable to say the words. Gabriel put an arm around her shoulders.

"Being a man is no protection, believe me," he murmured. "That's why I always warned you to be careful around men, even before I knew your true sex."

"I know. But it's not every man who has such intent towards boys. Sometimes it seems they all do towards women."

"Not all," Gabriel replied with a chuckle.

"No," she said, thinking of Mal. She smiled back. "Not all. Thank you."

"Come on, I'll walk you back to the inn and you can change into more suitable clothes, if that will make you feel better."

"No," she said. "I need to get used to it." *Or try to.*

Next morning Erishen left the inn early again, but instead of going to the bathhouse he headed out of the city, away from the noise and stink of humankind. Only a few minutes' walk brought him to a rocky headland with fine views out to sea. He sat down on a rock, basking in the growing warmth like the green water-lizard he had once had as a pet. He tried to remember the creature's name, but it was lost to him, like so much else.

As if summoned by his thoughts, a freckled bronze lizard about the length of his hand scuttled across a nearby rock, obsidian eyes blinking in the sunlight. Erishen watched it for a moment, until a hawk flew overhead and it disappeared into a crack in the rocks in a blur of motion. *Hide, little one. Perhaps I should be hiding too. Or at least keeping a better lookout.*

He lifted his gaze to the horizon. The sun glittered on the Adriatic, catching the peak of each lapis blue wave with a spark of gold dust. Below and to his right, the city was laid out like a painted map, all creamy-yellow stone and red tiles. Human vision was so much richer than skraylings', at least by daylight, with so many more colours to delight the eye; he never tired of it.

The players' red-and-yellow tent was being set up in the marketplace once more. Another performance tonight, another opportunity to kiss the girl. Of course she would slap him again, as the story demanded, but she seemed to enjoy it despite her protests. He congratulated himself on a plan well executed. At this rate, she would fall into his brother's arms at the first chance, and all would be well again.

He briefly considered visiting her dreams as well, to reinforce her feelings towards Mal, perhaps even scare her into a conviction that she must abandon her male guise forever, but he feared that such a blatant manipulation might arouse her suspicions. She was clever, this one, and must be handled with cunning. Which of course made the game so much more fun.

He turned his attention back to the sea. In the distance a white-sailed ship headed south before the wind, and another to the northwest of his lookout tacked elegantly towards the harbour. Any ship coming up from the south would make little headway in this wind – and yet one was trying. A familiar, red-sailed ship.

Erishen leapt to his feet and ran down the path to the city, small stones scattering before him as he went.

Coby sat in the inn yard, hemming another of the squares of linen. She refused to wear her stage costume during the day, even though her English gown was too hot and heavy for this climate. She still felt horribly naked in skirts, with the air moving freely around her bare legs, but at least this way most of her skin was hidden from view. A sudden movement in the corner of the courtyard drew her attention, and she looked up to see Sandy, breathless and dusty, walking towards her. She hastily secured her needle in the fabric and leapt to her feet.

"What's happened?"

"He is coming. Hennaq."

She beckoned urgently to Gabriel, who was practising a new routine with the juggler, Benetto. He excused himself and came over to join them. Sandy sat down on the bench next to her and told them what he had seen. Gabriel swore, more colourfully than Coby had heard him in a long time. She looked around the yard to see if anyone had noticed, but the players had gone inside.

"Skraylings? Are you sure?"

"You think I cannot recognise the ships of my own people?"

"It might not be Hennaq," she said. "Kiiren's wasn't the first skrayling ship to come to Venice, was it?"

"No," Gabriel said, "but what are the chances of it being someone else?"

"Then we have to leave, as soon as possible. How long do you think it will take them to get here, Sandy?"

Sandy cocked his head on one side, his eyes darting back and forth as if calculating the route.

"Several hours, perhaps a whole day. The wind is not in their favour."

"But it is not in ours, either," Coby said. "Not if we want to sail north, to Venice."

"Perhaps we can get away overland," Gabriel said.

Coby shook her head. "It would take us weeks to get to Venice that way. And the lands between here and Venice are overrun with those same brigands who attacked Captain Youssef's ship."

"We have to get away from Spalato somehow. Perhaps go north on foot and then get a ship as soon as the wind turns?"

"How? We have hardly any money, and the *Hayreddin* isn't due back here until the end of the week. Zancani will not leave Spalato on our say-so, not when there is still money to be had here."

"Leave Zancani to me," Sandy said. "You two pack up your belongings, in case we have to leave in a hurry."

Zancani always took a nap after dinner, a fact that Erishen was relying on. He instructed Coby and Gabriel to keep the other players occupied, then crept up to the maestro's chamber and silently let himself in. Zancani was lying on the bed fully clothed apart from his shoes, and snoring loudly. Erishen tiptoed over to the bed and drew up a stool. Placing one hand on the man's greasy curls he took a deep breath and let himself sink into that quiet place on the edge of sleep.

With physical contact the transfer was almost instantaneous. One moment he was crouched on a stool in an inn room; the next, he was in the darkened market square, sitting where the audience had been. Just in front of him stood Zancani in his nightshirt, watching the stage where the girl Hendricks danced alone. Round and round she spun, her skirts whirling higher and higher. Zancani drifted towards the stage, a rosy-pink erection peeping from the front hem of his nightshirt. Erishen snorted in disgust, but the maestro did not hear. Round and round the girl danced, showing the tops of her thighs now. This must stop. Erishen leaned over and whispered in Zancani's ear. At first nothing changed, except that the dance got faster and faster. The girl's skirts whirled up over her head to reveal a writhing knot of snakes, her legs now great pythons that twisted below. Zancani staggered back, whimpering, and the stage fell dark. Good. Now he had the man frightened. Malleable.

Erishen snapped his fingers, and torches flared all around them. Zancani seemed to notice Erishen at last.

"Wh…Who are you?" he quavered.

"Do you not know me? I am Il Capitano. And you are Pantalone."

Erishen gestured, and Zancani's nightgown lengthened and darkened until he was wearing Pantalone's costume of black gown, scarlet stockings and pointed yellow slippers.

"You are a wealthy merchant of Venice," Erishen went on. "In that city lies a fortune for the taking…"

A chest brimming with gold ducats appeared at Zancani's feet.

"Gold," the player whispered.

"But you must be swift!"

Zancani fell to his knees, but the chest of gold sprouted tiny oars and rowed away across the square.

"Summon your captain and sail after it!" Erishen told him. "Now, lest it fall into unworthy hands."

"Yes, yes!" Zancani scrabbled in the dust. "We must sail at once."

Erishen withdrew his presence, and a moment later blinked in the late afternoon sunlight. Zancani had rolled over and was cradling his pillow, smiling contentedly to himself and mumbling in his sleep. Erishen got to his feet and tiptoed from the room, confident that they would be away from Spalato by nightfall.

• • • •

As Sandy had predicted, Zancani awoke from his nap in a fever of urgency to leave for Venice. Amid much grumbling Benetto, Stefano and Valerio took down the tent and dismantled the stage, whilst Coby helped Valerio's sister Valentina to pack the costumes. When they were done, the men loaded everything onto a couple of handcarts.

"We're not going to push them all the way to Venice, are we?" Coby said.

Stefano laughed. "Of course not. We only take things down to the ship."

"But the wind is in the north still. How are we to sail there in this weather?"

"Maestro Zancani's cousin is in the navy. He can get us to Venice, no problem."

Gabriel and Sandy went back up to their room to fetch the bags. Coby was about to go and help them, but Gabriel took her aside.

"You're a young lady now, remember? Try to behave like one. That means letting us menfolk do the hard work."

"Sorry," she whispered. This was going to take some getting used to.

Zancani led them down to the quayside. Coby walked at Gabriel's side, feeling very odd at having nothing to do except look decorative. Not that she had any illusions about that. Any man with sense would be looking at Valentina, who had curves in all the right places and a nose that wasn't red as a strawberry from the sun.

She scanned the sea nervously, but could see no sign of red sails. Perhaps Sandy was wrong and the skraylings had not been heading for Spalato at all. Not that she minded. The sooner they were in Venice, the sooner she would see Mal again. That thought alone was enough to make all her other worries melt away.

Zancani's cousin's ship turned out to be a fearsome-looking galley bristling with oars. There were far more of them than the *Hayreddin* sported, enough to move a ship at great speed by the looks of it. That at least accounted for Benetto's confidence that they could sail into the wind, or rather row into it. She did not envy the men whose task that would be.

The stern end of the galley was covered by a red awning like a wagon, and banners bearing the winged lion of St Mark flew from its two masts. The central yardarm, its white sail tightly furled, stretched almost the entire length of the vessel. The muzzles of three cannon protruded from a wooden structure just behind the beak-like prow.

"Welcome aboard the *Bellerophon,"* Zancani's cousin said, ushering up the gangplank. He was taller than his kinsman but with the same dark eyes that lingered on Coby's face a little too long for courtesy. She was glad the voyage would be short.

As they stepped aboard she lifted her shawl to cover her nose and mouth. A stink like an open sewer rose from amidships, and she soon spotted the source. The men seated at the oars were chained in place, with nowhere to relieve themselves but the benches they sat on. Galley slaves.

"This way, *signorina*! You will be quite safe and comfortable back here."

They were soon settled under the awning, and within the hour the galley left harbour to the slow, steady beat of a drum. Coby sat hunched up by their luggage, torn between joy at finally being on her way to Venice, and pity for the poor wretches whose suffering would be the means of getting her there.

CHAPTER XXIII

Ned picked at his bread roll. Neither he nor Mal had slept much last night, and not for the reason he had hoped for when they first came to Venice. He had lain awake expecting the constables to come knocking on the door at any moment, though Mal repeatedly assured him they had not been followed, nor was the surviving Venetian likely to betray them even if he suspected. Indeed his friend seemed more worried that Bragadin's death in suspicious circumstances would lead some to connect this Mercante fellow with Olivia. For his own part he cared not; the guiser had what was coming to her. Perhaps now she might get her claws out of Mal.

He looked up briefly as the door opened. Berowne came in, looking worried.

"Have you heard the news, Catlyn?"

Mal yawned. "No."

"There's been a murder in the Calle di Mezzo, near San Giacomo's. Two men found dead. Some are saying it's Giambattista Bragadin and Pietro Trevisan."

"Really."

"Indeed. Didn't you meet them at the courtesan's house?"

"I suppose I must have," Mal said. "Though I don't remember half the men I was introduced to."

"Still, could just be gossip," Berowne said, sitting down at the head of the table. "I swear the Venetians are as bad as women when it comes to spreading salacious rumours. There's nothing they like better than a juicy scandal."

"It does seem unlikely that two important men would be in such a rough part of the city."

"You're probably right. Mind you, I dare say the lions will eat well today."

"Lions?" Ned asked.

"The *Bocce di Leoni*. Means 'lions' mouths'. They're collection boxes set in the walls of various buildings around Venice, including the Doge's Palace. Anyone who witnesses a crime is obliged to write a denunciation, countersigned by witnesses, and leave it in one of these boxes."

Ned kept his eyes on his own breakfast. Trust the Venetians to set their entire citizenry to spy on one another. No wonder Walsingham had warned them to be careful.

"An accusation cannot be made anonymously, then?" Mal asked.

"No. I believe that in past generations it was, but the system was too often exploited for petty revenge, and many false accusations were made."

Ned breathed a sigh of relief. Trevisan's friend was likely to keep quiet since he was the one who killed Bragadin, and no one else would have recognised them, would they? He glanced at Mal, who shrugged.

Jameson appeared at the door.

"Excuse me, gentlemen, but there's a messenger for Master Catlyn."

Mal looked around sharply. "For me?"

"He's waiting in the entrance hall."

Mal wiped his hands on his napkin. "Please excuse me, Sir Geoffrey."

"Oh, don't mind me," the ambassador muttered. "Good to see the place busy."

Mal patted Ned on the shoulder and followed Jameson out. Ned sighed and put down the remains of his own breakfast. He had no stomach for it anyway. Excusing himself to Berowne, he went back up to the attic and lay down on his bed to wait for Mal. After a while his eyelids fluttered shut and he fell asleep, to dream of disembodied lions' heads, their mouths open and slavering for his blood.

Mal clattered down to the atrium, glad of the distraction. A boy of about six or seven, barefoot and dressed in a ragged shirt and breeches, stood in the middle of the floor under the watchful eye of Jameson. He goggled up at Mal, who hunkered down so that they were eye to eye.

"You have a message for me?" Mal asked in Italian.

The boy nodded, hands clasped behind his back. "Yes, sir. Rio Tera degli Assassini, one hour after sunset."

"And who is this message from?"

The boy held up one hand, fingers splayed. Five. *Cinquedea*. Mal smiled. The scoundrel had a sense of humour, you had to give him that. Assassins' Canal Street, indeed.

"Thank you." Mal took out his purse and extracted a couple of small coins. "I shall be there."

The boy grinned and pocketed his reward. Mal got to his feet and showed him out, then turned back to the staircase.

"Master Catlyn?" Jameson quavered. "There is a letter for you as well."

"A letter?" Mal took it, expecting to see Olivia's hand – but it was Coby's writing. How had a letter from England reached here so soon? He went over to the little window by the front door to read it and broke the seal.

The letter was in cipher of course, but even once decoded it made little sense. *Beware skrayling Hennaq. Sandy and I will be in Venice soon.* Who was this Hennaq, and why should he be wary of him? And what in God's name was Coby doing, coming to Venice?

He thrust the letter into his pocket with a sigh of frustration. He had to see Olivia. She must have heard of the murder by now and be wondering about his own involvement. Better to go sooner rather than later. He headed upstairs to fetch his cloak and mask.

Mal rang the bell at the garden gate of Ca' Ostreghe. He had lain awake all night trying to decide what to say to Olivia about last night's venture, but he was no nearer an answer that did not make him look like a fool. And he was not fool enough to think she would be happy with his news. Coming here on foot had only delayed the confrontation a little while.

Hafiz showed him up to the main reception chamber, rather than Olivia's private apartments. Not an auspicious beginning. Olivia stood by the empty fireplace, clad in black silk, her hair covered with a long lace veil as if she were a respectable widow. Her expression was not one of sadness, however.

"Signore Catalin." She bit off every syllable. "How good to see you."

Mal swept a deep bow. "My lady, I can explain–"

"Explain? Oh I am sure you can. I allow you into my house, my bed, my heart – and this is how you repay me? With betrayal and murder?"

Mal said nothing, only sank to one knee and let her rage on. She was saying nothing he had not thought himself, although her accusations were couched in far more colourful terms. When the stream of invectives finally slowed he chanced a look up. Her eyes sparkled with unshed tears, though her expression was as stern as ever.

"You are right in all you say, my lady," he began. When

she did not interrupt him with another tirade, he got to his feet. "I have failed you. I found out nothing about Bragadin's dealings, except that he has perhaps been extorting more money than he told you."

He related the fragments of conversation he had overheard. Olivia's delicate brows drew together into a frown.

"The ungrateful cuckold! He owed his fortune to me."

"Indeed. However he would have died last night whether or not I had followed him. It is clear that his clients were not happy with the delays."

"It is my fault," Olivia said, and sank down on a stool. The anger had gone out of her, leaving her looking old and frail. "Since the *sanuti* came to Venice, I have been afraid to wander abroad in the dreamlands in search of the secrets Bragadin had promised. He was more patient with me than they were with him."

"He dared not kill the goose that laid the golden egg."

"And now he is dead. And Trevisan too." She got to her feet. "I have made my decision, *amayi*. This is over."

Mal's heart constricted, though with fear or relief he could not be sure. "What is over?"

She gestured around the room. "All of this. La Margherita Nera. I was growing tired of the game anyway."

"You're leaving Venice?"

She laughed. "Ah, my dear boy, I forget you are so new to this. No, now that I have you for an *amayi* I will seek rebirth. Everyone will say I died of grief for my beloved patron, and that will be an end to it."

"No!" Mal closed the space between them and took her in his arms. "You cannot do this."

"I must," she said, stroking his cheek. "I knew it could not last forever, that sooner or later Bragadin would be found out, or at least suspected. And now that I have you, I need not fear."

"It's not safe," Mal said. "At least let me try and get the

skraylings out of Venice first. You would not want to risk them interfering."

She looked thoughtful. "You have a point. But you must proceed without me, and you must not come back here until they are gone. I have to take great care in the coming days. Much gossip will fly my way, and the less that sticks, the better."

"And you swear you will not take your own life in the meantime?"

"I cannot swear, *amayi*. But it will be my last resort, that I can promise you."

Her lips were hot and sweet, and sent a flush of desire through his veins. After far too short a time, he let her go.

"Fare well, my lady. I hope we may meet again soon."

The galley rowed west and north around the island city, until Coby began to wonder if they were heading for the mainland after all. However just as the city's furthest northern limit came into view, they turned back eastwards into the Grand Canal. Narrower than the Thames, it was nonetheless a great waterway, wide enough for two such galleys to pass without tangling their oars. Their own vessel slowed after a few hundred yards and manoeuvred towards the bank, coming to a graceful stop just beyond a cluster of wooden posts that jutted out of the water.

The captain whistled to one of the nearby gondoliers, and the sleek black craft slid between the ship and the bank. Zancani haggled with the gondolier and at last climbed down into the boat, waving for the rest of them to join him. Coby was obliged to stand to one side whilst the men passed all their baggage from hand to hand and down into the gondola, then she and Valentina were helped aboard. It was all very irksome, having to behave like a fragile female, as if she hadn't spent her youth hauling chests of costumes and heaving wagons out of potholes with the other apprentices.

There was not a lot of space on the gondola once everything was loaded on board, and the little craft sat so low in the water that Coby, perching on one of the narrow seats that ran along either side, could easily reach out and touch the emerald-green water if she had wanted to. She was squeezed in between Gabriel and Benetto; the juggler smiled shyly at her and opened his mouth as if to say something, but then changed his mind.

The gondola began to move slowly on its way, wallowing somewhat from its heavy load. Coby stared up at the strange buildings that drifted past; every one was painted a different colour and had a different number and shape of windows, and yet they formed a harmonious pattern. Most of all they reminded her of the galleried façade of a tiring-house at the back of a stage, as if the entire city were one enormous theatre, and its people merely actors.

The gondola turned left into a side canal, then right and left again before halting at a smaller canal bank, no more than a walkway in front of the row of more modest buildings that lined the lesser canals. Their destination appeared to be an inn, although apart from the sign above the open front door – three leaping fishes with bulging glass eyes and gilded scales – there was little to distinguish it from the houses on either side.

Coby and Valentina were helped ashore, and the men began unloading their belongings. Passers-by gave them many curious glances, and a small child watched wide-eyed from the shadows of a doorway until its mother called it back inside.

"This reminds me of being on tour with Suffolk's Men," she said to Gabriel as he placed another bundle of canvas against the nearby wall. "People were always happy to see us arrive, but happy too to see us go."

"We brought spectacle and a glimpse of the outside world," he said, looking back down the canal. "And a disturbance of their quiet lives. Some people don't like that."

"Still, to see the same in a city like this, at the crossroads of the world." She shook her head. "It is… strange."

He shrugged and went back to work.

Zancani fussed around them until everything was unloaded from the gondola, then strode into the inn. Coby followed him, for want of anything better to do.

The inn was cool and shady after the heat of the afternoon, and at first Coby could make out little. As her eyes adjusted, she realised they were walking through a passageway with doors on either side. A moment later they emerged into a courtyard. The ground floor was colonnaded, with tables and benches laid out neatly, though unoccupied at this time of day; the floor above that was galleried like an English inn, with a staircase leading up from the back of the courtyard. The uppermost floor had many arched windows with shutters thrown back to let in the sunlight, and a roof of terracotta tiles. Somehow it looked far grander than the English inns that Suffolk's Men had stayed in, but it seemed even the humblest dwelling here was built of brick and stucco and tile, instead of the simple wood and thatch of England.

A stout, red-faced man hurried down the stairs, wiping his hands on his apron, and greeted Zancani warmly. A curly-haired lad of about twelve, the image of the innkeeper in skinny miniature, leaned over the balcony, gawping, until his father shouted up to him. Something about Zancani and "Mama".

By the time the players had finished carrying all the baggage up to their lodgings, the lady of the house had appeared, along with baskets of bread, bowls of olives and jugs of wine. The men settled down to talk business, whilst the innkeeper's wife ushered the two girls upstairs to their lodgings. Coby looked back wistfully over her shoulder; in the old days she would have been down there with them, not shuffled off to one side like a child.

"You are *Inglese*?" the innkeeper's wife asked in heavily accented English.

"Dutch," Coby replied. "But I lived in England for a while."

"*Si, Inghilterra*. I am Magdalena."

"Jacomina."

Magdalena grinned, gap-toothed. "Giacomina. Is very pretty name. I have the cousin named Giacomina."

She showed the girls into a small room on the top floor, not much more than an attic but neat and clean, with two cot beds and a shared nightstand. Coby thanked her and put down her knapsack. How she was going to get away from under Zancani's nose and visit Mal, she did not know, but she was determined to do it tonight. Otherwise she would never sleep, she was sure of it.

Valentina spoke neither French nor English, which rather limited their conversation. However this did not seem to deter the girl unduly. By dint of pantomime and a few words, she declared herself fascinated with Coby's blond hair and insisted on combing it. Coby sat dutifully and allowed herself to be fussed over like a doll, though she could not for the life of her see the point. She was quite capable of combing her own hair, after all.

She was spared any further feminine amusement by a knock on the door. Valentina leapt up and opened the door a crack to reveal the long face of Benetto the juggler. The two players chattered away to one another in Italian for several minutes, then Benetto went away.

"What was all that about?" Coby asked.

Valentina looked glum. She pointed to herself and then Coby, and mimed sewing. *Ah, the costumes*. That had always been Coby's first task when returning to London from a tour of the country. So much got damaged in use and would need mending before they could perform again. She followed Valentina down to the men's quarters, where all their equipment had been stored.

Mal took down his rapier from its peg, cinched the belt around his hips and threw the hooded cloak around his shoulders, adjusting its folds to conceal the weapon. *Might as well be hanged for a sheep as a lamb.*

"Expecting trouble?" Ned asked.

Mal closed the attic door.

"One can never be too careful around men like Cinquedea," he said quietly.

"You think he might betray us to the Ten."

"I don't know. I'd like to think not; after all, Walsingham surely wouldn't have led us astray on purpose."

"Walsingham's an old man, and hasn't been outside England in years. Things change."

"Exactly. Which is why we need to be on our guard."

They padded down the marble staircase and let themselves out into the street. There were few people about at this hour, since the Venetians preferred to eat supper late. The scent of garlic and hot oil drifted on the air. Ned's stomach rumbled loudly.

"I thought you already ate?" Mal said, leading the way towards the *traghetto* at San Toma.

"I did. And now I'm hungry again."

"Gabriel won't like it if you grow a paunch."

"I'll just lose it again in England, unless we have a better harvest this year."

By the time they reached Campo San Toma the sun was sinking behind the church, bathing the city in amber light. Several barefoot children were running around the stone wellhead, shrieking with laughter, but Mal looked about as cheerful as a man going to his own funeral.

"Strange, isn't it?" Ned said, trying to lighten the mood.

"What's strange?"

"Finding out Charles has been here all this time, alive and well. I remember you once saying you'd gladly slit his throat and dump his body on a midden for what he did to Sandy."

"I have more important things to think about than petty revenge."

"Still, when this is all over–"

"Never look beyond the next battle."

"Is that how you see this meeting with Lord Kiiren? As a battle?"

Mal halted in the blackness under a *sottoportego*. "Kiiren–"

He paused as two passing women broke off their gossip to eye them suspiciously. Ned slipped his arms around Mal's waist and pulled him closer, treating the women to his best salacious grin. The elder of the two muttered in disgust to her companion and turned pointedly away.

"Was that entirely necessary?" Mal asked when the women were out of earshot.

"It gave them something else to fix their suspicions on, didn't it? Anyway, what were you saying?"

"What I think I was going to say, before I was so..." He grimaced, extracted himself from Ned's embrace and set off again "...is: Kiiren is a foreign ambassador and puts his own people first, never forget that."

"But he will help us, right?"

"I certainly hope so."

The gondola ferry was waiting at its jetty, a lamp hanging from its stern. They paid the ferryman and climbed in. Mal hunched down, feeling horribly exposed out on the water. In the distance he could see a blaze of moving lights that indicated one of the *barche longhe*, the slender armed galleys in which the *sbirri* patrolled the canals. It was a relief to step ashore in San Marco before the galley reached them.

CHAPTER XXIV

Rio Tera degli Assassini turned out to be a short cobbled street with a fetid canal running across its far end. A gondola was moored to a rotting timber, a cloaked and hooded figure at its oar, like the ferryman of the underworld. Mal paused at the near end, his hand on the hilt of his rapier, and scanned the shadows. If this were a trap…

"Good evening, gentlemen." Another hooded figure rose from the gondola and stepped ashore. "Easy, there. We're all friends."

"Cinquedea?"

"The same."

Mal motioned to Ned to stay where he was and strode down the street, stopping a couple of sword-lengths from the man. Cinquedea threw back his hood.

"I see you brought a friend."

"As did you."

"Then we are even. This one here–" he gestured to the gondolier "–is Marco il Pessotelo."

Mal inclined his head in greeting. *Pessotelo* was not a word he knew, however; a Venetian surname, or another nickname?

"A great many Venetians seem to be called Marco," he said.

Cinquedea shrugged. "He is our patron saint. It is good luck to name your son after him. Now, if you will come with me…?"

"Where?" Mal asked, folding his arms.

"We cannot stand around in the street. Unless you wish everyone to hear your secrets?"

Mal glanced up at the surrounding buildings. Who knew who was listening, up there in the shadows?

"Very well. But we keep to the main canals, all right?" He beckoned to Ned. "The first sign that your man is turning down some little backwater, my man Faulkner here will plant a knife between his eyes." In English he added, "Won't you, Ned?"

"Uh, yes."

"Understood," Cinquedea said. "Please, after you."

Mal squeezed himself into the little cabin, wishing he were as small as most Venetians. Cinquedea joined him, and Pessotelo hauled on the oar.

"So, you'll help us?" Mal said as the gondola lurched into motion.

"For a price."

"I don't have a lot of money–"

"There are things more valuable than money, my friend. As well you know."

"What then?"

Cinquedea grinned in the darkness. "Truth."

"Truth is a false coin, oft clipped to worthlessness."

"And yet even the clippings have value. Tell me, who killed Bragadin and Trevisan?"

Mal stared levelly back at him. *No beating around the bush, then*. "Why do you think I know?"

"Because I have eyes amongst both Nicoletti and Castellani. And you, sir, were seen running through Santa Croce late last night."

"Very well, the truth. I don't know who killed Bragadin;

I saw it happen, but I did not see the fellow's face nor recognise his voice."

"And Trevisan?"

"I killed him myself, as he tried to run away."

"How did you happen upon this scene of slaughter?"

"I knew Trevisan and his friend were up to something. I overheard them talking a few days ago and thought the matter might impinge on my own business here, so I invited myself along, so to speak." It was close enough to the truth, and kept Olivia out of it.

"And Bragadin?"

"A fellow conspirator, perhaps," Mal said with a shrug. "At any rate their tryst soon became a quarrel; something to do with a great sum of money."

"Ah, money. Our oldest vice. We always want what we do not have, is this not so?"

"But Venice is rich, surely?"

"One would think so, but you must have discovered the true nature of our city by now."

Mal cocked an eyebrow and said nothing.

"Take that palace," Cinquedea said, pointing to one of the many beautiful buildings along the Grand Canal. "Exquisite rose marble, yes? Gilding, fine sculpture. Great windows filled with clear and coloured glass."

Mal made a noise of agreement.

"It is but a thin skin," his companion went on, "a layer of burnish upon a crude foundation. Every last building here is of timber and brick behind its façade. Go inside, and you will find dust and decay. It is all a show, a sham; but what an illusion, eh? The most beautiful city in the world, and she is a tawdry broken-down jade at heart."

Mal didn't know what to say. It matched his own impressions of the city, and yet as an outsider he dared not voice such a bold opinion.

"Of course if you repeat any of that, sir, I will have to

cut your throat. One does not insult a lady to her face, you know?"

"Absolutely," Mal said, trying to follow the Venetian's train of thought.

"Our patricians need new markets for their goods. Take that fine fellow Dandolo. He has his finger in many pies, as you English would say." Cinquedea laughed. "Spices, silk, salt of course, glass and porcelain... if you can buy it in Venice, the chances are high that it has been through one of Dandolo's warehouses. But storing and shipping all those goods costs a great deal of money. A very great deal."

"You're saying he's bankrupt?"

"That is the rumour. But who knows for certain? He may simply be trying to get out of paying his taxes."

Mal joined in Cinquedea's laughter. "Either way, an agreement with the skraylings will be most welcome."

"Yes."

"I thought you were in favour of these trade negotiations."

"I am. You mean to stop them?"

"I... No. Those were not my orders. Only to find out what I could, so that we can be prepared."

Cinquedea scanned his face. "I believe you. And we too wish to know, so that we can prepare."

"Don't you have sources inside the Great Council?"

Cinquedea muttered something obscene-sounding in the local dialect. "This Grimani has disrupted our entire operation with his pulling of strings. I need a truer source of information."

Mal smiled. With Bragadin dead those strings had been cut, but he wasn't about to tell Cinquedea that. Such valuable intelligence was better kept in reserve.

"You want me to share what I learn," he said, "in return for help in getting into the skrayling palace."

"Yes."

He considered for a moment. Walsingham had recommended the man, and surely it could do no harm to the English cause?

"Done."

Cinquedea rapped on the roof of the cabin, and Pessotelo turned the gondola back towards Rio Tera degli Assassini.

It felt like only a few moments later that they arrived at the street's end. Mal eased his cramped limbs out of the cabin and stepped ashore gratefully.

"Well?" Ned asked softly.

Mal simply grinned.

They were halfway down the street when a man stepped out of the shadows. A man in a red doublet and breeches, carrying a short pike.

"*Sbirri*!" Cinquedea hissed. "You betrayed us!"

"Not I," Mal said, drawing his rapier.

A squad of the red-clad constables appeared at the end of the street, cutting off their escape. Mal turned back to the gondola, but Pessotelo was already plying the oar. Cinquedea leapt aboard the departing vessel with enviable grace. Mal eyed the distance, but the moment's hesitation cost him. He turned to face the advancing constables. One of them uncovered a lantern.

"Put up your sword," a voice called from the darkness. "I have men with crossbows trained on you and your companion."

By sunset most of the sewing was done, but Coby feared she would have no time for her own business if she helped Valentina to finish it. She therefore went to find Gabriel and told him her plan.

"Why do I have to stay here and keep the girl amused?" He folded his arms like a petulant child. "I am just as anxious to see Ned as you are to see Mal. Let Sandy read to her, and we will go to the embassy together."

"Valentina doesn't like Sandy; I think she's afraid of him. No, she will tell Zancani I left her to finish my work, unless she is kept sweet."

"I hope you don't expect me to make love to her," he said with a sniff.

"Just tell her a story, or sing, or something. Anything."

She shooed him out of the room and began changing into her boy's clothes. Not only would it be safer, alone in a strange city, but the less connection between Zancani's players and the English ambassador the better, at least until she knew Mal's plans.

She slipped a purse containing the few coins Zancani had paid them into her pocket, and made her way out through the early evening crowds. It was a relief to be back in her familiar garb and free to move around without attracting unwelcome notice. Now there was just the small problem of finding her way to the English ambassador's house in a strange city where she did not speak the language. She decided the first thing to do was to get some distance from the inn before asking directions, so she set off in what she hoped was a southwards direction, towards the Grand Canal.

Half an hour later she was footsore and hopelessly lost. The Venetian streets appeared incapable of going in one direction for more than a hundred yards before turning a corner, opening into a square whose only streets led off in entirely the wrong direction, or ending abruptly at the edge of a canal, with no bank or bridge by which to continue. She tried asking for directions, but the few Venetians she could find who spoke English or French only smiled and nodded and said "straight on". There was nothing for it but to spend a little of her precious silver on a gondola.

She found her way to a busy canal-side and hailed a gondolier. He rattled off a price, and she only hoped that he had understood her directions. She scrambled aboard and entered the little cabin with a whispered prayer for God's protection. He had not failed her yet.

The bells were tolling the first hour after sunset as they navigated yet another small canal. This one described a dog-leg path under a bridge and around a red and white house, but the gondolier steered his craft to a set of weed-grown steps.

"We're here?" she asked.

The man gestured to the red-and-white house. "Inglese."

She handed over the money, praying he was telling the truth, and realised with a sinking heart that she did not have enough left to pay for a gondola back to the inn. Taking a deep breath to quell her panic, she walked up to the house and knocked on the door.

After a few moments, the door opened and a gaunt old man looked out.

"Si?"

"I'm looking for Master Catlyn. Is he here?" she asked in English.

The man paled. "N… no. I mean yes."

Coby's heart leapt in expectation.

"That is, he was," the servant added. "But he left about an hour ago."

"Did he say when he'd be back?"

The man looked away. He was hiding something, Coby was sure of it.

"Who is that, Jameson?"

The door opened wide to reveal the last person she wanted to see.

"Sir Walter."

Raleigh's wind-burned face was redder than usual, as if he had been drinking.

"The same," he said. "And who might you be?"

Coby sketched a bow.

"J... Jacob Hendricks. Master Catlyn's valet."

Raleigh frowned. "I thought Faulkner was his manservant."

"Yes, he is. In London. I served Master Catlyn in France."

"I see." He looked her up and down, his eyes narrowing. "Is he here?"

"Catlyn? No."

"Oh. But he was here?"

"Certainly."

Coby looked up and down the street. "May I come in a moment, sir?"

Raleigh raised an eyebrow, but stood aside for her to enter. Coby stepped into the darkened atrium. A lone candle glinted on gilded picture frames and a short flight of marble stairs, but little else was visible in the gloom.

"May I ask when he will be back?"

"I have no notion. Probably away with that Moorish whore; I doubt he'll be back before morning."

Coby felt sick. Mal, visiting a prostitute? Well, she supposed she could not blame him, since she had held him at arm's length for so long.

Behind Raleigh the old servant, Jameson, wrung his hands and would not meet her eye. Was that what he was concealing? But why would he be so embarrassed about it in front of another manservant?

"And Ned...?" she asked.

"Faulkner went with him," Raleigh replied.

Coby hesitated. She didn't want to confide in Raleigh, but neither was she willing to leave the embassy with so little achieved.

"Did he receive my letter?"

"There was a letter, just this morning," Jameson said, "though I do not know its contents."

"Could I have paper and pen?" she asked. "I would like to leave him another one, just in case."

Raleigh muttered something under his breath but sent Jameson for writing materials. These brought, Coby leant over the little table, composing the message in her head. She didn't want Raleigh to know the whole of her communication with Mal, but on the other hand asking for sealing wax would have made him suspicious. A cipher, on the other hand, might pass without notice if it were subtle enough.

"Make haste," Raleigh snapped. "I have no wish to stand here all night. Or can you not write?"

"One moment, sir. I am not practised in the art, and must get my thoughts in order first."

Raleigh made a contemptuous noise and began pacing the atrium. Trying to ignore him, Coby began to write.

If it please your good grace, your brother sends greeting. He is anxious to be here soon, and will come with all haste to take possession of three ells of fine gold brocade embroidered with fishes. Only the finest in any great city north of Rome suffices; Venice must provide. J H IV.

There, that would have to do. She blew on the ink to dry it, then folded the sheet and handed it to Raleigh.

"One last thing, if I may, sir?"

"Well?"

"I spent the last of my wages getting here. If I do not get back to my lodgings before curfew, I will be arrested. I would not wish to embarrass the ambassador or his guests."

"Is that a threat, boy?" Raleigh turned scarlet. "Get out, before I have you whipped all the way back to your lodgings."

"Yes, sir. My apologies, sir."

"Raleigh? What's all this about?" A stout man in a crumpled velvet doublet limped down the stair; the ambassador, she guessed. "Who is this boy?"

"A servant of Catlyn's. He was just leaving."

"I meant no offence, sir," Coby said. "I was so hoping to find my master here, I quite forgot myself."

"Stay a while," the man said. "Doubtless your master will return before curfew."

"Alas, I ought to pass on the news to my companions, who have come all the way from England to... to see him, with important news of their own. But as I was telling Sir Walter, I have not enough money to get back to my lodgings."

"Then you shall have the use of my gondola. Jameson!"

The servant reappeared.

"Roust out Giuseppe or one of those other ne'er-do-wells, and have him take this young fellow wheresoever he wishes. But be swift about it."

Raleigh gave Coby one last contemptuous look, and stamped off up the stairs.

"Thank you, my lord," she said to the ambassador, loud enough for Raleigh to hear. "You are most generous."

Mal shielded his eyes with his free hand. An armoured constable stood silhouetted against the lantern's light, a crossbow pointed at Mal's chest. To his left stood a wiry man of about thirty with thinning hair, wearing a blued steel breastplate over a crimson doublet, a sword hanging at his hip. Four more constables armed with pikes formed a cordon at the end of the street.

"Put up your sword, Master Catlyn," the captain said again, in perfect English with only the trace of an accent. "Or shall I have you shot somewhere painful but not fatal?"

After a moment's pause Mal slid the blade into its scabbard.

"Since you know my name, sir," he said, "perhaps you would do me the courtesy of telling me whom I address?"

"I am Francesco Venier, son of Lorenzo Venier. You and your servant are under arrest for the murder of Giambattista Bragadin and Pietro Trevisan."

Mal stared at Venier. Betrayed – but by whom? No one knew he was meeting Cinquedea here, no one except...

Jameson. He had been there when the urchin delivered Cinquedea's message. But the old man knew nothing about their connection to the murders, did he?

Venier gestured to Mal's sword. "Your weapons, please. Both of you."

Mal reluctantly unbuckled his belt and handed over rapier and dagger. After a moment, Ned contributed his own knife. Venier paused to admire the swept hilt of the rapier, holding it up to the torchlight.

"Very handsome," he murmured, and tucked the sword under his arm. "Against the wall, hands on your heads."

Out of the corner of his eye Mal saw the constable put down his crossbow. He briefly considered putting up a fight, but there were too many of them, most still armed.

The constable proceeded to search both prisoners for hidden weapons, turning out pockets and feeling down the sides of Mal's boots.

"Nothing?" Venier said, waving the man away. "Dear me, I expected better of Walsingham's men."

Mal kept a straight face. The barb about Walsingham was no doubt a lucky guess, or at least a fair assumption. Venier murmured instructions to his man, who motioned for Mal and Ned to precede him along the street. Mal hesitated, raising his left hand behind his back in a signal he hoped Ned could see in this light. Prepare to run.

"Might I ask where we are going?"

"The Doge's Palace," Venier said with a smile. "And do not think of trying to escape. There are *sbirri* in the surrounding streets also, with orders to shoot you on sight."

The streets were half-empty this close to curfew, but that only made their little procession more conspicuous. Passers-by stared at the two Englishmen, muttering curses or making obscene gestures. Mal ignored them; a few taunts were the least of his worries. He should have fought his way out of the ambush, damn it, even at the risk of death. But then what would happen to Coby, and his brother? They must surely be here soon, if that letter was to be believed. But even his resourceful young companion could surely not rescue them from the Doge's prisons. Nor could he count on Olivia, not after what had happened with Bragadin. This time they were on their own.

All too soon the palace came into view, its marble façade shining silver in the moonlight, its rows of arched windows dark as empty eye-sockets. They were escorted through the ground floor colonnade and into the palace itself. As they passed an inner doorway, a dreadful smell, worse than any canal, wafted out into the night air. Mal swallowed against the nausea roiling in his stomach.

"Ah yes, the Wells. I'm afraid the stench starts to get worse in the warm spring weather."

"Wells? That's your drinking water?"

Venier laughed. "No. It is what we call our lowest cells. You would know them as *oubliettes*." When Mal did not respond, he added: "Do not fear, *signore*. You and your… accomplice are not destined for the Wells. Not yet, anyway."

Venier led them towards a stair leading up into the palace.

"After you, gentlemen."

They were escorted across an echoing courtyard, into another marble-columned cloister and up a magnificent staircase lined with gilded bas-reliefs. They emerged into an antechamber, dark and empty at this time of night, and paused whilst the captain unlocked a small side-door opposite the entrance to the palace's grand apartments. Mal was pushed through into the darkness, scraping his scalp on the low lintel.

The rooms in this part of the palace were low and narrow, as if two floors had been fitted into the height of one palace storey and made to accommodate as many offices as possible. Walls of planking attached with parallel rows of wooden nails divided up the space, so that it looked more like the interior of a ship than a building. The captain led them into a cramped office that was barely large enough for his prisoners and the four guards restraining them. An elderly man sat at a desk at the far end, candle-light gilding his silver hair as he bent over a stack of papers. He looked up after a moment.

"Captain."

"Chancellor Surian." Venier gestured to Mal. "Our intelligence was correct."

"Good," the chancellor replied, looking Mal up and down with disinterest. "Put them in the lower cells. I will deal with them later."

"I don't know what you've been told, Your Excellency," Mal said, "but it's all lies."

"Then I look forward to hearing the truth. Later."

He went back to his documents, and the prisoners were hustled out of the tiny office, along a corridor and through another heavy studded door.

The room beyond was larger than any he had seen so far, a good twenty feet across and with a ceiling that rose to the full height of this storey. Near at hand stood a long desk with three high-backed chairs behind it, like a magistrate's bench. What drew the eye, however, was the massive rope, as thick as a child's arm, hanging over a pulley at the centre of the ceiling, its two ends stopping just short of a set of wooden steps like a mounting block. Two doors faced one another across the steps, and two more in a gallery that ran around three sides of the chamber, cutting its height in two. All four doors had large grilles at head height, giving them a good view of the rope and pulley. His guts tightened in terror.

One of the guards sneered and said something in the thick local dialect as he pushed Mal through the nearest door. The interior was barer than a monk's cell, scrubbed clean but with a lingering smell of soap, piss and vomit that was almost worse than the honest filth of an English prison. The door slammed shut and a key clicked smoothly in first one lock and then a second. The Venetians were taking no chances with their prisoners.

When their captors had gone, Mal peered out through the door grille. Fat candles had been left burning in cressets, carefully positioned to illuminate the rope but throw the rest of the chamber into shadows. He could just make out the pale circle of Ned's face at the grille in the opposite wall.

"That whoreson cur betrayed us." Ned's voice rose to a shout. "Just wait till I get my hands on him, I'll–"

"Quiet, Ned! We don't know who's listening."

"I don't care who's listening–"

"Ned, for the love of all the saints–" Mal drew a deep breath. "We are prisoners of the Doge. And this is his torture chamber."

In the appalled silence that followed, Mal knelt on the bare boards and began to pray. To Our Lady, the Archangel Michael, and every saint whose name he could remember.

CHAPTER XXV

When they reached the inn, Coby bade the servant wait for a few minutes. Sandy might want to send back a message of his own. She ran into the inn and up to her room. Valentina was lying on the bed with her back to the door, crying softly. Sweet Jesu, what had Gabriel done to upset her?

"Who are you?"

Coby turned round to see Zancani glowering at her.

"Jacomina?" He took a step closer. "What is this? Some new idea for the play?"

"Uh, yes." Coby's mind raced. "In England, it's traditional for boys to play women's roles. I thought it would be funny to do it the other way round."

"Perhaps, perhaps. We will try it out tomorrow."

"Have you seen Gabriel or Sandy?"

Zancani's expression changed. "Alessandro is in big trouble when I find him."

"What do you mean?"

"Ask your friend Gabriel. He's downstairs, drunk or crazy, I'm not sure which." Zancani walked away, muttering under his breath in Italian.

Gabriel, drunk? Gabriel never got drunk.

She found Gabriel at a table in the darkened courtyard, staring into a candle flame. There was an empty wine cup by his elbow, but the jug next to it was almost full.

"Gabe, what's happened?" she asked. "Why is Sandy in trouble?"

He blinked up at her.

"Sandy's gone," he said in a tight voice.

"What?"

"Vanished in a flash of light."

"Oh no. No no no..." She slumped down on the seat opposite. The last time this had happened, he had been spirited away by Kiiren, but this time? It was too much to hope that he had been so fortunate again. "Tell me everything," she said, refilling his cup.

"I did as you asked," he said, gazing into the depths of the wine like a fairground fortuneteller scrying the future, "and offered to read to Valentina as she did her sewing. She insisted on coming down to the men's chamber, as there was more light – at least, I think that's what young Benetto was saying, though he seemed to think it was more that she did not want to be alone with a young man in her own bedchamber–"

"Gabriel?" She laid a hand on his wrist. "What happened to Sandy?"

"Oh. Sorry. Well, Sandy was lying on his bed dozing and Benetto was trying to teach Valerio and Stefano a new three-way juggling pattern, so Valentina and I sat at the other end of the room out of their way. I was just acting out a scene from *The Jew of Malta* – you know, Rafe's favourite speech, where Barabas gets boiled in the cauldron – when there was a blinding light from behind me. I turn round to see Sandy walking towards a... a bright doorway that shouldn't have been there, then he vanishes and Valentina runs back to her room, screaming about witchcraft." He took a gulp of wine. "I managed to persuade Zancani that

Sandy was just experimenting with some skrayling fireworks and scared the girl out of her wits, but the whole troupe is rattled. Especially since Sandy is nowhere to be found."

"Perhaps it would be better if we left. Go and get your knapsack, and mine too."

She ran back out onto the canal bank. To her relief, the ambassador's servant was still there, chatting with a group of gondoliers.

"Please wait a little longer," she told him. "My companion and I want to go back to the embassy."

Gabriel emerged from the inn a couple of minutes later, glancing nervously back over his shoulder.

"Zancani will skin us alive for walking out like this," he said as they climbed into the gondola.

"Zancani can go to Hell," Coby muttered. "All that matters is finding Sandy before Mal gets back."

Mal's prayers were interrupted by the creak of a door and the shuffling of footsteps. He got stiffly to his feet and went over to the grille. Three men in black robes were making their way to the bench: the elderly chancellor and two slightly younger men. A secretary followed, carrying a pile of documents.

Mal looked across at the opposite cell. Ned's face was as pale as whey against the blackness within, but he managed a ghost of his habitual grin. Mal forced a smile in return, then turned his attention back to the new arrivals.

The three men had taken their places and were talking amongst themselves in low voices. The secretary placed the stack of documents in front of the chancellor, bowed, and left. The chancellor picked up the first item on the stack with palsied hands: a letter sealed with dark wax. He broke the seal, read its contents and then passed it to one of his colleagues, who then passed it to the third. After some discussion, one of the younger men made a note in a ledger, and they moved on to the next item.

Ned cleared his throat as if to speak and Mal shot him a warning glance, shaking his head. One of the clerks looked up briefly, then went back to his work. The chamber was silent but for the scratching of pen on paper. *Make them wait,* Walsingham had taught him on the subject of interrogation. *Anticipation is half the torture*. Perhaps his mentor had learned the technique from the Venetians.

At last the three men finished their business, and Mal could now only wish it had taken them longer. The chancellor rang a small bell that stood on the desk, and after a few moments two guards entered the room. The chancellor motioned towards Mal's cell. Mal made the sign of the cross and muttered a last prayer. The door of his cell was unlocked and the guard beckoned for him to come out. Mal decided to oblige him; if he struggled, it would not help his case and would only unman Ned entirely. He therefore stepped forth calmly and allowed the guards to escort him to the bench. The chancellor peered down at him with eyes yellowed and bloodshot by long years and too many late nights.

"Your name?"

"Maliverny Catlyn, sir."

The man to the chancellor's right began taking notes, glancing up at Mal from time to time.

"You are English?" the chancellor went on.

"On my father's side. My mother was French, but I was brought up in England."

"And what brings you to the Serene Republic?"

Mal swallowed. "I am looking for my elder brother, Charles. He fled overseas some years ago."

"It says here–" the chancellor picked up a letter "–that you were seen fleeing the scene of a murder. Yesterday evening, in Calle di Mezzo in Santa Croce."

"A lie," Mal said evenly. "Who so accuses me?"

The chancellor handed the letter to the guard, who gave it to Mal. The handwriting was uneven, the work of a man unaccustomed to it. The signature at the bottom was an illegible scrawl, countersigned by other hands equally hard to make out.

"Several citizens of the parish saw you," the chancellor said, "and did their civic duty."

Or were bribed to do so by Trevisan's friend? Once the identity of the dead men got out, it would not have been hard to link a tall silent stranger to Bragadin via Olivia, and a foreigner made an easy scapegoat.

"Do you still deny it?" Surian went on.

"I had no part in Signore Bragadin's death. That was the work of another man."

"His name."

"I don't know. He was with Trevisan, but it was dark–"

"How convenient, to lay the blame on a man of whom we have found no trace." Surian leaned forward. "You say you did not kill Bragadin. What about Trevisan?"

Mal said nothing, unwilling to condemn himself. The chancellor flicked a pale hand towards the guards, who took hold of Mal's arms and led him towards the steps.

"It is the truth, on my honour!" Mal could not help crying out as they pushed him to the foot of the steps.

His hands were pulled behind his back and bound tightly together, then he was shoved up the steps. He was now looking down on the inquisitors, but this was no vantage point.

"Again. What about Trevisan?" the chancellor asked in patient tones. "Did you kill him?"

"Yes," Mal whispered.

"A little louder, please. I fear my hearing is not what it was."

"Yes, I killed Pietro Trevisan. But it was an accident. He ran onto my dagger."

Surian chuckled, a dry sound like a rusty gallows-cage. "An accident. Ah, how many give that excuse."

The chancellor made a curt gesture, and one of the guards mounted the steps behind Mal and attached the rope around his wrists to the one hanging from the ceiling. Mal steeled himself for what would come next.

The *strappado* was a simple torture device, but highly effective. The victim was lifted by his bound arms until his entire weight hung from them, twisted up behind his back as they were. The pain was said to be unbearable. And even if he bore it, he did not trust Ned not to talk in order to spare him. His friend was too soft of heart for this business.

"Again. Why did you murder two of our eminent citizens? What is your purpose in our city?"

"I seek my brother, Charles, who fled England leaving our family ruined."

The guard pulled on the free end of the rope, lifting his arms higher. It was not yet tight, but still the anticipation left him trembling with dread. He tried to swallow, but his throat was drawn tight as a noose.

"One last time, Englishman. Why have you come to Venice?"

Mal shook his head, and the guard tugged on the rope. Mal stifled a grunt of pain as his arms were raised at an uncomfortable angle, forcing him to lean forward. He teetered on the top step, heart pounding, then regained his balance. He stood there, breathing heavily for a moment, knowing that far worse was about to come. The chancellor cleared his throat, ready to ask again.

"Stop! I'll tell you anything you want to know," Ned shouted.

The chancellor nodded at the guard, and Mal's breath caught in his throat as he was lifted onto the balls of his feet. The muscles of his shoulders and upper arms burned as they began to take his weight. The guard hauled on the rope and Mal screamed. A moment later the rope slackened just enough for his flailing feet to gain purchase on the steps once more. He sucked in a shuddering breath.

"I put it to you," the chancellor said, "that you are an English spy, perhaps even an assassin, sent to interfere with the negotiations between the Venetian Republic and the *sanuti*."

"No," Mal gasped. "I am here to find my brother and take him back to England. The murder was a chance meeting, an accident…"

The chancellor lifted his hand, but before the guard could respond, someone entered the chamber and crossed quickly to the bench. Mal looked up, blinking away tears of agony. The secretary had returned and now spoke in low tones to the chancellor and handed him a letter. The chancellor read it, his expression changing gradually from open irritation to barely concealed fury. At last he seemed to recall his surroundings, and made a chopping motion towards Mal. The guard let go of the rope and Mal tumbled from the steps to lie in a panting, shivering heap on the wooden floor.

Ned clung to the iron grille, heedless of the rough metal cutting into his fingers. There had to be some way to stop this. He shouted at the black-robed inquisitors, cursing them to Hell. Oddly, it appeared to have the desired effect. The ugly bastard who had been torturing Mal helped his victim to his feet and cut his bonds. Mal staggered against the steps, his face ashen. Ned released the bars and hammered on the door with both fists.

"Mal! What in Christ's name's going on?"

Mal looked up at him and shook his head briefly.

The other guard came over and unlocked Ned's cell door, waving curtly at him to come out. Ned shrank back into his cell, heart lurching in panic. Was it his turn now? The guard spat out what sounded like a curse, grabbed Ned by the arm and hauled him out into the torchlight.

Ned looked around him in panic. Mal was standing at the bench now, whilst the old man spoke to him in low tones. Mal nodded once or twice. Then the other guard opened the door and they were escorted out, to freedom. Ned drew a ragged breath, hardly daring to believe it was over. As they descended the staircase Mal stumbled and would have fallen, but Ned hurried down and caught him.

"Thank you," Mal said through gritted teeth.

Ned slipped an arm about Mal's waist and let his friend lean on him for support. They were shown to a gondola waiting at the nearby quayside. A dark-haired man with high cheekbones stood at the oar; from what land he hailed, Ned had no idea, but he did not look much like any of the Venetians they had seen so far.

He helped Mal down onto the bench, and soon they were slipping away through the night, to what destination he dared not guess. After a while he recalled that the republic's prison was next door to the palace, so perhaps they had truly been released after all.

At last the small craft stopped at a familiar-looking canal bank; the English embassy. Desperate as he was to get solid walls between himself and any servant of the Doge, Ned let Mal go ahead of him, fearing his friend might stumble once more. He didn't fancy fishing him out of a canal, not in pitch darkness.

Once ashore, he hurried ahead and knocked on the door of the embassy. No answer. Hardly surprising, since no one was expected to be out on the streets at this time of night. He pounded on the door harder.

"Open up, for God's sake!"

A shutter opened in a neighbouring building high above them, and a woman shouted curses before slamming it shut again. A few minutes later another shutter opened, this time directly above the door.

"Master Catlyn?"

"Aye, and Ned Faulkner," Ned called up. "Is that you, Hendricks?"

"Where have you been? I thought–"

"Just let us in." Ned looked up at Mal. His friend was deathly pale. "Now, for the love of Christ."

Coby ran down the marble staircase as fast as she could without blowing out the candle she was carrying. Hurriedly she put it down on the little table by the front door and pulled back the bolts. The key was stiff in the lock and her patience thin, and she fought with it for several long moments before it would turn. Hardly had she opened the door before Ned Faulkner barged inside. Coby opened her mouth to berate him, but stopped dead when she saw Mal. He looked like a man who had stared into the mouth of Hell.

"What happened?" she asked.

Mal stared at her wonderingly. "I could ask you the same."

At that moment Gabriel came running down the stairs.

"Ned? Mal? Christ in Heaven, what happened?"

"That's what I'm trying to find out," Coby said. "See if you can find any wine in the kitchen, will you?"

Gabriel disappeared through the door under the stairs, and Ned trailed after him like a man sleepwalking. Coby turned to Mal, suddenly hesitant. He gave her a weak smile and she slipped her arms around his waist, resting her cheek against his chest. When he gasped in pain, she drew back a little and gazed up at him.

"You're hurt," she said.

He made no answer, only gazed down at her with that haunted expression, then he awkwardly pulled her close and pressed his cheek against the top of her head. He trembled in her arms, hissing in pain as he pulled her tighter. *Sweet Jesu, I think he's weeping.* Tears pricked in her own eyes at the thought of what could have reduced him to such a condition.

"Come on, we can't stand here all night," she said, and led him gently towards the stair.

"I'm sorry," he whispered.

"For what?"

He shrugged, and gasped with pain again.

"Where is Ned with that wine?" she muttered. The stair was barely wide enough for the two of them side by side, but she was afraid to let Mal go lest he collapse entirely. At length they reached the upper floor. The door ahead of them opened.

"What is this?" Raleigh muttered, peering out.

"Just Master Catlyn returning," Coby said. "The worse for a late night. I'm just putting him to bed."

"Man after my own heart," Raleigh said. "Good night to you, sir."

Coby gave a sigh of relief as the door shut.

"Not far now," she said, guiding Mal up the next flight to the attic room. "Just like the old days in Thames Street. You never came there, did you, sir?"

"Only once."

"Of course. Master Naismith asked you to stay to dinner, then I took you to see the new theatre." She smiled. "That was when you found out my secret."

Mal didn't answer, only leant down and kissed the top of her head. She opened the door at the top of the stairs and they went inside, into the little attic room. She steadied Mal as he sat down on the bed, then put the candlestick down on the floor. Sitting down next to him, she took his hand in hers.

"Is... is it Sandy? Has something happened to him?"

Mal stared at her.

"I thought Sandy was with you."

"He was, but..." She sighed and began telling him about the events at the inn.

"Into a tunnel of light? Then he might be with Kiiren."

"That's what I thought. So, you haven't seen him?"

"No."

He stared down at their hands, entwined together, and told her of the murder, his rendezvous with Cinquedea and subsequent arrest. When it came to the *strappado*, however, words failed him. His fingers tightened around hers as the helpless panic threatened to overwhelm him again.

They sat for a long while in silence, heads pressed together. It was the longest he had ever spent this close to her, and he did not know whether to thank or curse his tormentors for it. Gritting his teeth he slipped his arm around her waist, though his torn muscles protested at the movement. If only they could go home to Provence right now, and forget all about guisers and skraylings and Venice. No chance of that, though, not until Sandy was found. As for telling her about Olivia… How was he to begin to explain that? He had allowed himself to be seduced by a guiser. She would never understand.

Footsteps sounded on the stairs, and Parrish appeared with two cups of wine.

"Sorry for taking so long," he said with a sheepish grin. "Here, this will help."

Coby jumped up from the bed, and Mal cried out as agony exploded through his abused sinews at the sudden movement. Parrish gave him a sympathetic smile, then said something to Coby, too quietly for Mal to hear, before departing.

She returned to the bed and held out one of the cups. Mal tried to raise a hand, but it lay on the coverlet, heavy as lead.

"Here, let me," she said, putting her own cup down.

She sat next to him and held the cup to his lips whilst he drank. Wine ran down his chin and soaked his beard, but he didn't care. He gulped it back, willing it to spread its numbing warmth through his veins as fast as it could.

"Careful, you'll choke," she said, laughing.

Mal managed a weak grin. The pain was subsiding, though he felt as weak as ever.

She took the cup away. "Would you like to lie down? You look exhausted."

When he did not gainsay her she knelt to pull off his boots. In the candlelight her hair looked like spun gold, each strand impossibly fine. After a few moments he realised that tears were streaming down his cheeks again.

"Ssh," she said, rising to sit next to him.

She started to unbutton his doublet, but he shook his head. The thought of trying to manoeuvre his arms out of the sleeves made him tremble anew.

"All right," she said, and helped to support his weight as he lay himself down on the bed.

After a moment's hesitation she lay down next to him, careful not to press against his arm. She reached down and took his hand in hers again, and lay there, gazing into his eyes.

"It's good to see you again," he whispered.

"And you. I'm... I'm sorry I failed you, sir."

"What happened? How did you come to be here, instead of France, and what did your letter mean? Who is Hennaq?"

"It's a long story; I'll tell you in the morning. Sleep now."

He closed his eyes obediently. One thing he had learnt in his soldiering days was the importance of snatching sleep whenever you could. Once he had dreaded the nightmares it could bring, but at last he felt in command of them. He had Olivia to thank for that, at least.

At that thought an idea came to him. His body might be broken, but his mind was still sound. He waited until Coby's breathing slowed into the rhythms of sleep, then lifted his hand inch by agonising inch until he could touch his earring. He unfastened it with trembling fingers and let it slither down onto the pillow beside him, then lay back, taking a deep shuddering breath. Now he could sleep, and find his brother.

CHAPTER XXVI

No longer did he begin in darkness. Olivia had taught him to make a haven for himself, a hollow in the landscape of dreams where he was safe and hidden from others, though it was not as strong as hers. He had based it upon the hill-fort he and Sandy had built on the slopes behind Rushdale Hall; a grassy dell ringed with the biggest rocks the twins could carry between them, the turf carefully cleared of thistles and smaller stones. The walls were lower than he remembered and yet they still hid the surrounding landscape. No bleating of sheep disturbed the silence, however, and the air hung still and hot, as on a midsummer day. The blue dome above was thin and hazy, and if he stared hard enough he could see the timeless sky beyond, nacreous grey like the inside of a mussel shell. But he must venture out there if he was to find Sandy. He stepped through the gap in the walls and immediately found himself on the dark moorland he remembered all too well. What next? He had never done this unaided. But he had to find Kiiren, if he could.

No sooner had he thought this than his feet began to move of their own accord. Now he could see the lights, hundreds upon hundreds of them, sleeping minds just waiting for his touch. He looked around, wondering which was Coby's, though tonight of all nights he had no desire to intrude upon her dreams. His own mood was too grim.

As if summoned by the thought, shapes began to coalesce out of the darkness, blacker than night, never showing themselves but lurking on the edge of vision. Following him, daring him to look back. Devourers. He swallowed and walked faster. *Ignore them, and they'll go away,* Olivia had told him. *Nightmares can't hurt you*. But it never felt like that when you were here, in their midst. He could hear their slavering breath, the scrape of claws as they scuttled up around the standing stones. *Don't run, they can run faster*. His feet wouldn't listen. In moments he was racing across the moor towards the nearest group of lights, breath rasping in his throat.

Flying, that was the way to escape them, but he couldn't remember how. Last time it had just happened: one moment running, the next soaring above the midnight plains. But his feet were as heavy as if his boots were full of water, and still the devourers followed.

On and on he staggered, dodging between the glowing domes that sprang from the grass like puffballs, each the gateway into the dreaming mind of one of Venice's citizens. Somewhere amongst these golden embers would be the white light he remembered from his first encounter with Kiiren, bright as new steel and reassuring as a blade in his hand. And on the other side of the city an answering violet glow, burning with the power of an ancient guiser's soul. Olivia. He wanted to run to her, find out if she had Sandy, but was afraid of the answer. Perhaps that was why the devourers were here. They smelled his fear.

The nightmare creatures were close behind him now, their rank breath hot on his back. One ran straight into a dream-sphere, which shattered as the dreamer awoke. A moment later the devourer leapt out of the dissolving remnants and resumed the chase, a faint scream echoing in its wake.

There was no sign of any white dome. Had Kiiren taken to wearing a spirit-guard himself, out of fear of guisers? Was he even in Venice at all?

Dream-spheres were exploding all around him now, their fractured light momentarily outlining images of the Venetians' worst fears: drowning, secret murder, humiliation. He slipped on the dry grass, fell on his hands and knees with his face mere inches from an intact sphere, his own reflection staring back at him from the glowing surface. Then he saw it, a violet-white corona like the midday sun, cresting a low rise in the distance. He got to his feet again and ran towards it.

As he drew near he skidded to a halt. The lights were blended together, swirling around one another in a way that reminded him all too much of his first night with Olivia. Kiiren and Erishen, joined in a blissful communion that transcended flesh. He backed away. He had his answer.

Turning back towards his sanctuary he felt rather than saw the devourers slip around him, towards the lovers.

"No!"

He backed carefully towards the pale dome and with an effort of will envisaged a blade in his hand, obsidian black as a rent in the dreamscape. The creatures hissed in frustration and he gripped the hilt more tightly, although his incorporeal arm ached in sympathy with his flesh. He stood guard for so long that he began to fear he would never leave the night realm, but at last the light behind him faded and was gone. The blade dissolved with it, and he began the long walk back. There was much to do tomorrow, and he feared he would have too little strength for it.

• • • •

Mal woke the next morning gritty-eyed and so stiff he could not move. Coby had gone, so he had no choice but to lie there with growling stomach and aching head, listening to the household stirring: Jameson's slow footsteps on the stair, Raleigh calling out for more hot water, and somewhere someone whistling a merry dance tune. Another fine spring day in the Serene Republic. Now he appreciated how that serenity was bought with a brutally efficient government.

The door opened and Coby came in. Her face fell when she saw him lying there, and she hurried over to help him up.

"Jameson is putting breakfast out," she said, retrieving his boots. "He's such a patient old thing, fussing over us like a mother hen."

She knelt at his feet and gently lifted one of his calves.

"Guilt," Mal replied with a bitter laugh.

"What?"

"Someone betrayed me to the *sbirri*. He's the only one who knew where I was going last night."

She looked up.

"I thought he looked guilty when I first arrived, but I never expected..."

"Could be worse. At least he wasn't the one who denounced me. Still, I don't want anyone speaking of our plans in front of him."

"I'll tell Master Parrish. And Master Faulkner, if you like."

She helped him to his feet. He still felt weak as water, but it was no worse than a bad night on campaign, or so he told himself. Breakfast and a cup or three of wine would make all better.

They went down to the dining parlour, where Jameson was setting out bread and cold meats. The old man's hands trembled more than ever, and he would not look Mal in the eye. As soon as he had finished laying the table he fled the room instead of waiting to ask if they had any further need of him.

Coby poured wine for them both, and Mal forced himself to lift the cup, though his hand shook almost as much as Jameson's. A few moments later Ned and Gabriel joined them, and Coby passed on Mal's warning.

"Well?" Ned asked, helping himself to several slices of ham. "What do we do now?"

"We still have find Sandy," Coby said. She took the platter from him and speared a slice for herself, then loaded Mal's plate.

Mal cleared his throat.

"No need. I know where he is."

Everyone stared at him.

"With Lord Kiiren?" Gabriel leant forward.

"Yes."

"You're sure? I know I saw something–"

"Yes, I'm sure." Thankfully no one seemed inclined to argue with him, although he could tell from their faces that they had doubts.

"Well, good," Gabriel said at last.

"Not so good," Ned told him. "We've been trying to get in to see the skraylings since we arrived, but they're locked up tighter than a maiden's virtue."

"At least we know he's safe," Coby said.

She put her hand over Mal's where it lay on the table, and for once Ned did not smirk.

"But how do we get in?" Ned asked. "The Venetians will be watching us like hawks after last night."

"You will not go," Mal told him. "Your task is to stay here. If anyone asks for me, tell them I am taken to my bed. Better still, go openly to an apothecary and buy medicine for easing pain. Let the chancellor's spies think I am too weak from their treatment of me to venture forth."

"And what will you do?" Ned asked. "Lie abed whilst I run errands?"

"No," Mal replied with a quiet smile. "I have a mind to become an actor."

Ned padded down the stairs to the atrium. Hendricks had given him an errand to run, but first he had business of his own.

The atrium was empty, as he had expected. He checked the storeroom where the gondola was kept, but there was no sign of anyone there either. Good. He crossed to the door under the stairs and laid his ear against it. A faint clatter of pans. He smiled to himself and lifted the latch.

He found Jameson in the kitchen, stirring a pot of gruel over the fire. Even this lowly room had an elegance not seen in humble English dwellings, with handsome if antique furniture and a carved stone hood over the hearth to channel smoke up into the chimney. The manservant did not even notice Ned until he was halfway across the room. With a feeble cry of alarm he shrank back, knocking the gruel all over the hearthstones.

"Feeling guilty about something?" Ned asked him.

"I… I… I'm sorry, sir, I had no choice. The constables came to the door asking for Master Catlyn, and when I said he wasn't here they accused me of lying s… s… so I–"

"So you betrayed us?" Ned stepped closer, hand straying to his knife hilt.

"They said they'd search the house from watergate to rafters. Sir Geoffrey wouldn't like that, not at all, so I… I told them where you were going." He began to weep.

Ned gave a grunt of disgust. Mal wouldn't thank him for harming their host's servant, especially when the old coot had only been doing his duty to his master.

"Just stay in here unless Berowne calls for you, all right?

If you don't see or hear anything, you can't tell anyone, can you?"

The old man shook his head, and Ned left him to clearing up the mess.

"Are you sure this will work?" Gabriel said as he and Mal followed Coby into the storeroom.

"Do you have a better plan?" she replied. "Two of us were seen arriving; only two must leave."

Gabriel opened the water gate with a hooked pole whilst Mal climbed into the gondola and curled up as best he could near the prow. Coby draped a grubby canvas over him then settled back in the cabin.

"We should have hired a gondolier," Gabriel muttered as he struggled with the oar.

"Master Catlyn said we shouldn't trust anyone. The servants have already betrayed him once."

She clung to the sides of the cabin as the gondola lurched out of the dock, bumping against the watergate. Poor Mal; this must be ten times worse for him. At last they were out into the daylight and weaving an unsteady course through Santa Croce towards the Grand Canal.

By dint of good luck they eventually found the inn where Zancani's troupe were lodged. At least their meandering route through the canals was likely to have deterred even the most persistent intelligencer.

"Master Catlyn? You can get up now."

Mal blinked up at her and coughed at the dust drifting down from the canvas sheet. She put out a hand to help him up, but he shook her off, climbing awkwardly to his feet as best he could without using his arms to bear his weight. It tore at her to see him so helpless, and she wondered what would happen if they had to fight their way out of another ambuscade. Could he even lift a sword in his present condition?

She left Gabriel tying up the gondola and led Mal through the courtyard of the inn and up to the room Zancani had rented.

"Where have you been all night?" the little man snapped in French. "I thought that you had been arrested for breaking the curfew."

"Our most profound apologies, maestro," she replied. "We went in search of our companion Alessandro, and see? Here he is."

Mal bowed stiffly on cue.

"You look terrible," Zancani said to him. "Did you spend all your silver on grappa and loose women?"

Mal merely smiled enigmatically which, Coby reflected, was no more than Sandy would have done.

"Well don't do it again," Zancani went on. "It is fortunate you will be wearing a mask on stage. Now, get into costume, all of you. You need to rehearse if we are to be ready for this afternoon's performance."

"Maestro Zancani," Mal said. "My evening was not entirely one of pleasure. I was pursuing your business advantage as well."

"Oh?"

"I have friends in Venice, friends with connections. They told me that the *sanuti* are growing tired of their seclusion in the *fondaco* and would welcome some entertainment. And what better to lift a melancholy heart than the antics of Harlequin and Columbine?"

Zancani frowned, his black eyebrows merging into one. "The *sanuti*?"

"They have silver to spend," Mal said, "and little to spend it on, until the Doge agrees to trade arrangements. But we should make haste, before another company hears of this and courts their favour."

"True, true. Gossip flies faster than pigeons." He clapped his hands. "Ready yourselves for a procession, everyone. We go to wait upon the ambassador from the New World."

When they had gone, Coby quickly changed into her own theatrical costume. It didn't feel any more natural now than it had then, and the thought of Mal seeing her like this turned her belly into a nest of writhing snakes. Wrapping the shawl around her, she took a deep breath and ventured out to find the men.

Mal raised an eyebrow when he saw her, but made no other comment. Coby tried to hide her disappointment. Did he not find her attractive like this? Or was she expecting too much? She chided herself for her selfishness. *The poor man has been tortured, and all you can think about is whether he lusts after you?*

Under Zancani's leadership, the players formed up in the little square behind the inn. At the front was Benetto, juggling his painted wooden clubs. Gabriel walked behind him, playing a simple rhythm on a pair of small drums hung around his waist, then Mal and Coby, and behind them Stefano playing the flute. Valerio and Valentina tumbled and cartwheeled on either side.

"Show some more tit, girl!" Zancani barked at Coby. "The Madonna knows your face ain't worth looking at."

Coby blushed scarlet but obediently removed her shawl, tying it about her hips instead to give her figure the semblance of womanly curves. She dare not meet Mal's eye.

Zancani took up his place at the head of the procession, and they began making their way southwards towards the Rialto Bridge.

As they approached the Fondaco dei Sanuti, Mal's gut tightened in apprehension. Sandy was no doubt welcome here, but what about himself? He was an agent of the English Crown and no friend of this mission. Apart from Kiiren, the other skraylings within were not likely to be pleased to see him. Especially this Hennaq, whoever he was. He had still not found an opportunity to ask Coby what that was all about.

Zancani bowed to the guard outside the street door: a Venetian soldier, not a skrayling. The maestro announced their business with many an obsequious bow, describing their company in glowing terms and gesturing to the players. The soldier looked them all up and down as if checking for weapons, then rapped on the gate.

A young skrayling dressed in a warrior's tunic peered out, his eyes widening at the sight of the players. The guard spoke to him in Italian, though evidently the skrayling understood none of it, for he merely stood there staring at them all. Coby glanced at Mal, seeking his permission to intervene, but he shook his head. The last thing they needed was for the Venetians to find out that someone who could speak Tradetalk was visiting the skraylings.

The young warrior disappeared back into the *fondaco*, and returned a few moments later with two silver-haired elders. Mal watched them carefully, wondering if either of them had been on Sark back in March. Even if none of them remembered Coby from their brief visit, surely many of the skraylings would have seen Sandy at some point. He was thankful for the masks concealing their features.

After a short debate amongst themselves the elders withdrew into the palazzo, and the players were ushered through the gate into a large courtyard. Mal looked up at the rows of arched windows, wondering if Sandy looked back down at him.

Zancani bade his players to show off their talents, and soon the little troupe were surrounded by two score or more wide-eyed skraylings. From out of the corner of his eye Mal caught a flash of azure blue, and then a tall figure striding along the shadowed cloister. A grin threatened to split his face.

As Sandy stepped out into the light, the Venetian players caught their collective breaths in surprise. One of Benetto's clubs fell to the ground, the hollow sound echoing loudly from the surrounding walls.

"What is this?" Zancani was the first to recover his voice. "There are two of you?"

"Forgive the deceit, maestro," Mal said, removing his mask. He nodded to Coby, who ran to the gate. "I'm afraid none of you can leave until our business here is done."

CHAPTER XXVII

Zancani and his players were shown into a side-chamber, little more than a store-room that had been swept clean and the floor laid with the matting the skraylings were so fond of. A flat-topped sea chest served as a table, and servants laid out jugs of wine and *aniig* and enough glasses for all.

"Please, come with me," Sandy said to Mal. He glanced at Coby. "The girl may come also."

The actor seemed unsurprised at being excluded and set about pouring drinks for the others. Sandy led the way around the cloister to a studded door and thence up a marble staircase and through a series of echoing rooms, each with a different coloured tiled floor. At last they reached a closed pair of double doors. Sandy opened one half and gestured for them to go inside.

The room beyond ran the length of the palazzo façade and commanded a magnificent view of the Grand Canal through the many arched windows along one wall. In the middle of the opposite wall stood an enormous white marble fireplace supported by caryatids. The hearth was cold, though the remains of a log fire crumbled in the iron grate, and matting had been placed in a semicircle around the hearthstone. A circular tabletop of multi-coloured stone inlay sat on four piles of bricks nearby, surrounded by large cushions.

Ambassador Kiiren stood on the far side of the table, hands folded in the sleeves of his formal azure blue robe. He looked tired, Mal thought, or perhaps it was just the bright Venetian sunlight emphasising the patches of grey skin under his eyes. As they approached, he broke off his formal pose and hurried towards them, embracing Mal like a long-lost friend.

"Catlyn-tuur!"

"Kii–"

Kiiren released him, eyes wide. "You are hurt, my friend."

"It's nothing. How are you?"

He took a seat on the cushions. About a dozen of the zigzag-folded sheets that the skraylings used instead of books lay scattered across the surface of the table, their pages covered in the tiny geometric glyphs of the Vinlandic language. A flask of *aniig* wallowed in a cistern of water, surrounded by half-melted chunks of ice. It must be dull indeed for Kiiren, shut up here for days on end with nothing to do but wait until he was needed.

"What did you think you were doing?" Mal said at last. He looked from his brother to the ambassador and back. "There is a guiser in this city, a powerful one."

"Are you sure?" Kiiren asked. "We have seen no sign of guisers."

"Olivia is no fool. She has been avoiding dreamwalking ever since you arrived."

"Olivia? This is name? You know who it is?"

"Her name is Olivia dalle Boccole, a courtesan." He forced himself not to catch Coby's eye. "We have become… well acquainted."

"You have consorted with the enemy?" Sandy slammed his glass on the table, shattering its delicate base.

"She is not what you think." He put his own glass down more carefully. "You told me to expect monsters, wicked corrupt creatures like Suffolk who would do anything–"

"Including lying and seducing?" Sandy replied. "Listen to yourself, brother. You have been led astray. The guisers are renegades and outcasts for a good reason–"

"Then so are we."

Silence fell, broken only by the drip-drip of *aniig* from the broken glass onto the floor.

"*Amayi,* Catlyn-tuur..." Kiiren stood and placed himself between them. "We are all friends here. No one is cast out for that which is not their fault."

"Tell that to Hennaq," Sandy muttered.

Mal looked at Coby. "You tried to warn me about a skrayling called Hennaq. Who is he?"

Coby explained about their attempted voyage from England to Provence and how it had been diverted by Hennaq. Mal listened in silence, torn between anger at Sandy for nearly getting himself shipped off to the New World, overwhelming gratitude to Coby for her resourcefulness, and shame at his own betrayal of her loyalty. At least that part of it was over. He would strive to be worthy of her from now on.

"Is this true, what Hennaq says?" Kiiren asked him when the story was done. "It was his heart-mate Tanijeel whom you and your brothers killed?"

"We – Sandy and I – didn't kill him," Mal said, staring at his hands clasped in his lap. "They smeared my face with his blood, as part of the initiation. But I did not lay a hand on him, nor did Sandy."

"And your brother Charles. What of him?"

"I don't know. I'd like to say not but... I was trying to protect Sandy. I didn't want to see, didn't want to hear..."

Coby put her hand on his, and he squeezed it.

"I'm sorry, sir," she whispered. "I should have taken more care in our choice of captain."

"You weren't to know." He looked up. "And this Hennaq is in Venice?"

"Not yet," Coby said, "or so we hope. But he is likely to come. He knows you are here, and is bound to suspect that we will seek you out and warn you."

"What will you do?" Mal asked Kiiren. "If Hennaq turns up demanding us both."

"I will not hand you over to him," Kiiren replied. "But I cannot speak for elders. They will want to examine your memories–"

"Then they will discover we are innocent," Sandy said.

Kiiren sighed. "Of murder, perhaps. But your brother speaks truth. You too are guisers, in eyes of many of our people, and for that alone you are subject to our laws."

"Which are?" Mal asked.

"If you wish forgiveness, you must be reborn into our people."

"They would take us back to the New World and kill us."

"No," Kiiren said. "Your own hand must do it. There are herbs–"

"Oh yes, there are always herbs." He smiled bitterly to himself. "I am not ready to die yet."

Coby squeezed his hand, and his heart lurched. No, he would not die yet, not for anyone.

"Why did Hennaq not bring his case when you were on Sark?" he said after a few moments.

"I do not know," Kiiren said. "Perhaps he feared my word would carry more weight with elders than his. Or perhaps he knew Erishen was not fully healed."

"Nor is he yet," Coby put in. "He became very ill on Hennaq's ship when he had the spirit-guard on all the time."

"And I will tell elders so." He looked from one brother

to the other, his amber eyes grave. "I do not wish to lose either of you."

Sandy excused himself, saying he wanted to speak to the players before they left. As soon as he had left the room, Mal seized his chance.

"I... I have a very great favour to ask of you, sir. One which I hope you will grant, in light of our past friendship." He paused, searching for the right words.

"Go on," Kiiren said.

He cleared his throat. "Our people have been allies for many years. Our ships harry the Spanish when they threaten your shores, and ofttimes escort your trade vessels across the Atlantic to England."

"This is true."

"And our Queen welcomed you into her realm, giving you the island of Sark for your sole use."

"For how much longer?" Kiiren asked.

Mal stared at him for a long moment. "You think the Crown will withdraw the lease?"

"You have been back to London. Are my people still welcome?"

Mal had no reply to that. When had England ever truly welcomed the skraylings? It had always been an uneasy alliance at best.

"Why Venice?" he said at last.

"They are great merchant nation, like us, and we hear they are no friends of Great Father in Rome."

"True enough, but their ships seldom venture outside the Mediterranean. If you want an alliance with a seafaring nation, the Dutch would be a better choice." He glanced at Coby, but his companion was staring at the skrayling books as if trying to decipher them by force of will alone.

"With respect to your friends," Kiiren said, "followers of Luther do not like my people either. They call us demons. No, we need friends who put profit before your God."

Mal laughed. "Then you've come to the right place after all."

"I wonder." Kiiren shook his head sadly.

"You must know why I was sent here," Mal said. "The Privy Council wishes to know what trade agreements have been made with the Venetians."

"Has not your Queen an ambassador for such things?"

"She does, but how much can he find out without endangering his position here? The truth may come out in due course, but the Council desires swifter news."

"And so you want me to tell you."

"Yes."

"There is little to tell," Kiiren said with a sigh. "We do not go forward as well as I hope."

"As well as *you* hope? This is not your clan's business."

"It is my people's business. Clans may vie for repute, but their successes benefit us all."

Mal frowned. None of this got him any further forward in his own mission.

"Will you at least tell me, sir, if you do make progress?"

"That will not be easy," Kiiren said. "Your game with actors cannot be repeated, I think."

"Can you not write to Master Catlyn, perhaps via a go-between?" Coby put in. She gestured to the sheets of skrayling writing. "These letters would be as good as any cipher, if you could but teach me their meaning."

"That would hide the contents, but declare the sender as clearly as if Kiiren had raised a signal flag from the roof of the *fondaco*." He smiled fondly at her. "But it is a good idea for a future cipher, in less troubled circumstances."

They sat in silence for long moments, each deep in thought.

"There is one way," Mal said at last. "In my dealings with the guiser, I learnt how to dreamwalk, or at least how to control it. You and I could talk at will, and the Venetians would be none the wiser."

"Apart from your guiser friend," Kiiren said. "She has sold others' secrets; can you trust her not to betray you?"

"Aye, there's the rub." He still did not know for certain that it was she who had saved him from the *strappado*. Sandy was right. He could have been deceived – or had deceived himself.

"If you were to be rid of her…" Kiiren spread his hands.

"That could be difficult," Mal said. "I told her I would get rid of the skraylings first."

"What?" Coby stared at him.

"She wants to be reborn here in Venice; start a new life, free of the Bragadin scandal. As a babe, she would not be able to eavesdrop on us. But…" He could not meet their eyes. "She wants me to be her *amayi*."

"*Amayi* to one of the ancients?" Sandy – or rather, Erishen – leant on the door jamb. Mal hadn't even heard him approach. "You have come on since we last met."

Mal ignored him. "If you could persuade the elders to leave the city, just for a while…"

"Alas, I cannot," Kiiren said. "I am but–"

"–a vessel for words. Yes, I know."

"There is a solution to both our problems," Sandy said.

"Oh?"

"Hennaq's case against us is not strong. He may be open to an alternative, one that will enhance his reputation far beyond anything he currently dreams of. To be the first among us to return one of the Lost Ones to her homeland…"

"You want to give him Olivia? No."

"Why not? Do you want to be her *amayi*?"

"No." He gave Coby a reassuring look, and she smiled wanly. "No, I do not."

"Then you leave her to die, alone and friendless. That is not a kindness, even to your enemy."

The argument was difficult to gainsay. "I should ask her–"

"And if she refuses? What then?" Sandy sighed, and came over to crouch by Mal, laying a hand on his shoulder. "Trust me, brother, it is for the best. For everyone."

Mal looked round at them all. Three against one, and two of them his elder by generations. How could he say no?

"Very well. But you must let me assist in her capture, and make Hennaq swear not to harm her. And we make no move unless he comes here and demands that Sandy and I go back to Vinland with him."

Kiiren nodded. "Then it is agreed."

Coby left the menfolk to discuss their next move. She did not want to hear any more about this Olivia woman, even though Mal had agreed to help be rid of her. It still meant he had to see her again.

She wandered along the gallery until she found a floor-length window that opened out onto a balcony. If only she could go out there! But someone would surely see her and report back to the mysterious Ten who kept the peace in Venice. True, Zancani's presence here would be reported anyway, but the less anyone knew of their activities inside the palazzo, the better.

"Time passes," Lord Kiiren said, getting to his feet. "You must leave, or Venetian guard will wonder what we do here. At least, Sandy must go now. You stay."

"Now wait a minute." Mal said. "Surely Sandy is safer here with you."

"I do not wish Hennaq to find either of you here, but you cannot leave together. The guard is certain to have counted you as you came in, in case someone tries to stay behind. He will be very suspicious if more humans come out than went in."

Mal grumbled something under his breath.

"I have to leave," Sandy said. "Now that I know Charles is in the city, I will not rest until I have found him."

"Why? Do you want revenge on him?"

"He has something of mine. Of ours, I should say. Something he stole long ago."

Coby turned around, intrigued now.

"If anyone goes chasing after Charles, it should be me," Mal said, "though I think it a good idea in any case. It will lend weight to what I told the chancellor."

"No." Kiiren held up his hands. "You are too hurt… No, do not deny. I study you all afternoon. You are still in much pain from trial."

"I am perfectly well, I assure you."

"Then hold out your hand."

Glowering, Mal stretched out his arm at chest height, but after only a few heartbeats his hand began to tremble. Cursing his disloyal flesh, he let his arm fall to his side.

"Lord Kiiren is right, sir," Coby said. "Sandy knows Charles as well as you, and he can even stand in for you at the embassy; with a haircut and a bit of barbering, you can be made so alike that even your mother could not tell you apart."

"No, it is not safe for him. Berowne is not that stupid."

"At least let me give something for pain," Kiiren said. "I would not have you leave here as you are."

"Very well."

Kiiren disappeared through a door at the far end of the room. They stood in awkward silence for several minutes, until the ambassador reappeared carrying a small cup.

"Drink this," he said, handing it to Mal.

Mal sniffed it and pulled a face. "Another of your evil brews?"

"Just drink quickly, and you may have some *aniig* to take taste away."

Mal drained the cup, then handed it back to Kiiren with a shaking hand.

"That tasted just as bad as the last…" He blinked, and stared down at Kiiren. "You false-dealing whoresss–"

Sandy caught him as he keeled over.

"You drugged him?" Coby stepped between her master and the skrayling.

"It was only way; he needs rest. Worry not, he will wake in few hours. Go now with your friends, and find this other brother. I will look after Catlyn-tuur."

Leaving Mal in Kiiren's care, Coby went back down to the chamber where the players were waiting. Benetto and Valerio were playing dice together, and Valentina was sprawled on the floor with her head in Stefano's lap. The air was thick with the smell of wine and something else, an acrid woody scent that Coby remembered from the ambassador's quarters at the Tower of London.

"Ah, Signorina Giacomiiina!" Zancani cried out as she entered. "What a wonderful performance today. *Bellissima! Bellissima!*"

Coby shot a glance at Gabriel, but the actor looked as cupshot as the rest of them. What had happened here?

"Ah yes, the performance," Sandy said in a loud voice. He winked at Coby. "Yes, the ambassador was very pleased with the show, and regrets he has no time for another. Sadly we must return to the inn."

"What are you talking about?" Coby whispered as the players prepared to leave.

"I, ah, convinced them that we put on a show for the skraylings, to much applause," Sandy replied. "I thought it best if they were not to suspect anything."

"You mean you've been poking around in people's heads again."

"You make it sound so sordid. I merely got them a little... befuddled and pushed their thoughts in a happy direction."

Coby rolled her eyes at him. It probably was for the best, but that didn't mean she had to like it.

They returned to the inn with the players, where Sandy

explained to Zancani that they were leaving the troupe and would not be able to perform with them after the Doge's ceremony the next day. The maestro was surprisingly unmoved by this announcement, and Coby wondered what other ideas Sandy had planted in his head before leaving the skraylings' palazzo. She made a note never to get drunk in Sandy's presence, and resolved to procure one of the protective necklaces at the earliest opportunity.

They bade farewell to Zancani and the players, though only Benetto seemed sorry to see them go, then Coby changed back into her familiar male garb. Now that it came to leaving, she felt surprisingly regretful. True, Zancani had been a dreadful lecher, and having to wear female clothes only served to confirm how much she hated being treated like a weak and useless woman, but being part of a theatrical company again had brought back so many happy memories. Even performing on stage had been less terrifying than she had imagined. She almost wished she could go back to her old job when they returned to England, but that was not very likely. With a heavy heart she joined Sandy and Gabriel in the gondola for the journey back to the embassy. Whatever happened when they left Venice, she would have to give something up.

CHAPTER XXVIII

"Ah, just the young fellow I wanted to see!"

Coby froze at the foot of the attic stairs. Raleigh was the last person she wanted to see right now. However she forced a polite smile and a bow.

"How may I help you, Sir Walter?"

Raleigh leant on the newel post, the sudden movement making the pearl pendant in his earlobe swing wildly. Coby was reminded of Mal's similar earring, and she swallowed past the lump in her throat. Now was not the time to break down in tears.

"I'm told you're a dab hand with all things mechanical," Raleigh said. "Is that true?"

"Well, I'm certainly interested…"

"Excellent, excellent. Then you can help me choose a gift for Northumberland."

"Me, my lord?"

"Certainly you. I know a little about astronomy and navigation, of course, but these new-fangled mechanical devices are beyond my ken." He took her by the arm and led her back through the antechamber. "Did you know that there are clocks so small, one can wear them on a bracelet, so you know the time wherever you are?"

"Really?" She was intrigued despite herself. "Have you seen such a device, sir?"

"More than one," Raleigh replied, looking pleased with himself. "So, will you accompany me to Quirin's shop this afternoon, and give me the benefit of your wisdom?"

"I would be honoured, my lord."

"Excellent. Be ready in an hour; I have engaged Berowne's boatman to take us there."

Ned took the stairs up to the attic two at a time. As he had expected Gabriel was back in their room, labouring away over his manuscript in the light from the little window overlooking the canal.

"You'll ruin your eyesight," Ned said, resting his chin on Gabe's shoulder and slipping his arms around his waist.

Gabriel put his pen down and got to his feet, turning to face Ned but still in his embrace.

"If I lose my sight, you can be my amanuensis," he murmured in Ned's ear. "As long as I can touch you and hear your voice, I will be content."

"You say the prettiest things," Ned replied, struggling to rein in his desire as Gabriel nibbled round the edge of his ear and down the side of his neck. "I have to go out. Sorry."

Gabriel pulled away, an expression of mock surprise on his delicate features.

"What's this? Ned Faulkner, turning down an afternoon of exquisite fuckery? Methinks thou hast been bewitched, love, or I am in a nightmare."

Ned sighed. "Believe me, Angel, I'd gladly stay here with you. But someone has to accompany Sandy on this hunt of his, and I seem to have drawn the short straw. Besides, you have a play to finish before we get back to England."

"True enough. I can't wait to see the look on Shakespeare's face." His smile faded. "Or perhaps I shall sell it to

Henslowe under a false name and see how it fares, before laying claim to it."

"Is it not going well?"

"Not well at all." Gabriel waved a hand at the pile of paper. Most of the lines were crossed out, written over and crossed out again. "Setting up all these obstacles and misunderstandings is easy enough, it's the resolving of them that's the tricky part."

"Sounds like real life." He pulled Gabriel close and kissed him. "I'm sure you'll work it all out in the end."

"You're probably right."

"Of course I'm right. Now, back to work!"

He released Gabriel and gave him a parting slap on the arse, then retreated before he could change his mind. Business first, pleasure later.

"It will not be easy to find my brother in a such a crowded city," Sandy said. "Especially when neither of us can speak the language."

"We can try the Mermaid again," Ned said. "Though after last time..."

"Who is this mermaid? I thought they were just stories."

"It's not a who, it's a what," Ned sighed. "A tavern, not far from the Doge's Palace. I think I can find my way there again."

"Very well. Take me to it."

Ned set off down Salizada San Pantalon, tracing the one familiar route that he knew would bring them to the ferry stop near San Toma. Although he was meant to be leading the way, Sandy often pulled ahead, his long strides eating up the ground.

"Slow down," Ned hissed, when Sandy paused to give way to a man pushing a barrow-load of vegetables. "We're no help to Mal if we lose anyone trying to follow us."

"You are right. I have waited many years for this; another hour or two makes little difference."

"Waited for what?" Ned asked, but Sandy was off again.

They crossed the Grand Canal by ferry, and from there it was only a short walk through San Marco to the quayside in front of the Doge's Palace. Ned scurried past, head hunched down, hoping none of the guards recognised him. He didn't trust these Venetians not to change their mind.

Though the sun had not yet set the lantern above the Mermaid's gilded sign was already lit, and the homely fug of beer fumes and tobacco smoke enveloped them as they entered the tavern.

"You have been here before?" Sandy asked.

"Yes." Ned dodged one of the tavern doxies before she could opportune him. "When we first came to Venice."

"You think Charles is here?"

"I doubt it, to be honest. We probably scared him away after Mal's performance last time. But there are usually plenty of Englishmen about. Perhaps someone will know him."

They found an empty table in a shadowy corner where they could watch the door. Ned waved one of the girls over and ordered two pints.

"Keep your eyes peeled," he said to Sandy, leaning across the table. He lowered his voice, so that he could only just be heard above the hubbub. "But don't stare at anyone. Keep it casual, all right?"

"You think there will be trouble."

Ned scanned the crowd.

"Mal told me Charles fled England with a great many debts. If I were such a man, I'd be worried right now. And if he's been here several years he must have money, or friends. Or perhaps both."

The crowd was little different from the last time they had been here, though perhaps fewer Venetians mingled with the foreigners tonight. Had rumour got out about his and Mal's arrest, or were the locals merely having an early night in preparation for tomorrow's festivities? He saw no sign of Cinquedea's boy-whore, nor the crow-like Venetian Mal had been talking to on their previous visit.

"So what does this brother of yours look like?"

Sandy shrugged. "About my height, perhaps a little less. Brown hair, though it may be going grey by now, like our father's."

"That's not much to go on," Ned grumbled.

"I'm sorry. It's been over ten years since last I saw him, and I was not exactly myself at the time."

And who are you now?

The beer arrived, and Ned looked pointedly at Sandy. "Money?"

Sandy dug in his pocket and pulled out a handful of coins, which he held out to the girl.

"Here, let me," Ned said, and seizing Sandy's wrist he picked through the silver looking for smaller denominations. "She'll have you paying porter prices for small ale."

He handed over a couple of *gazzette* to the girl, who eyed both men with evident disappointment. Ned was suddenly aware of Sandy's pulse under his fingertips, and he turned back to find the older man gazing at him intently with dark brown eyes, so like Mal's it never ceased to unnerve him. For a moment Ned wondered if Sandy was trying to bewitch him, then he saw him flick his gaze over Ned's shoulder and back.

"Charles?" He gently released Sandy's wrist.

He turned just in time to see a tall dark-haired man of about forty stare at them in horror before bolting for the tavern door. Ned was after him in an instant.

Their footfalls rang out as they crossed the square, echoing from the hard stone surfaces. Before Ned had got halfway across the square Sandy passed him, long strides eating up the ground. Charles disappeared under a low archway between a printer's shop and a cordwainer's, Sandy hard on his heels. Ned panted in their wake. What they were going to do when they caught up with Charles, he had no idea. Surely they couldn't get away with dragging him through the streets to the embassy?

By the time Ned entered the alley, Sandy was gone. Ned swore and redoubled his efforts, pounding around the corner just in time to see both men cross a bridge about fifty yards down the canal bank. He wondered if there was a shortcut he could take to head them off, but didn't trust his sense of direction in the labyrinth of Venetian streets. It was Charles who knew the lay of the land, far better than either of them, and Ned did not doubt he would evade them somehow.

He ran up the steps of the bridge, dodged around a water-seller in her brightly coloured skirts, and leapt down the other side, pelting down the street as if his life depended on it. His quarry came within sight again; what Sandy gained in length of leg, Ned made up for in long practice and dogged endurance. Nor was Charles likely to keep up a good pace for long. By all accounts the twins' elder brother was a drunkard and a gambler, and a good fifteen years older than either of them to boot. Ned grinned, anticipating that the chase would soon be over. He followed Sandy round a corner – and found himself teetering on the brink of slimy steps running down to another canal.

"Where is he?"

Sandy pointed to a gondola moving erratically down the canal. Charles stood in the stern heaving on the oar, his face scarlet with effort.

"God's teeth!"

Ned ran back out into the street and past the shops, until he found another alley leading towards the canal, this time with a bridge. He raced down the alley and onto the bridge, just in time to see the gondola's prow emerge from the far side. With a cry Ned dropped into the little craft, causing it to rock alarmingly. Charles cursed, let go of his oar and fell into the water. Ned looked on helplessly, clutching the gondola's sides; he could barely swim himself, never mind rescue a man of Charles' height and bulk.

"*Rehi!*"

Ned looked up to see Sandy dive from the bridge like a cormorant into the turbid green water.

"Sandy?" Christ's balls, Mal would have his guts for lute-strings if anything happened to his brother.

A few moments later two dark heads resurfaced, one towing the other towards the canal-side. Ned paddled the gondola towards the bank as best he could with his bare hands. A small crowd had gathered, and they helped Sandy heave Charles' inert body out of the water. Ned scrambled ashore.

"Is he dead?"

Sandy hauled his elder brother up by the back of his doublet, and Charles coughed up a little canal water. The bystanders, disappointed that the accident had ended without tragedy, began to drift away. Charles coughed again, looked around, and realised he had been caught. He scrabbled backwards until he fetched up against the wall of the nearest building.

"Mal?" He peered up at Sandy, blinking through the water that trickled down his forehead.

Sandy hunkered down, just out of arm's reach. "Guess again, brother."

"Alexander?" Charles made the sign of the cross. "Did you come all this way just to hunt me down?"

"It is no more than you deserve, after what you did to me."

"It was for your own safety, boy. Your brother was gone abroad, and I could not look after you–"

"Funny, that's exactly what Mal said."

"You've seen him? He's alive?"

"How many others did you murder, you and your friends?" Sandy asked in a low voice.

Ned looked around nervously. "Should we be having this conversation in the street?"

"Who are you?" Charles asked him.

"None of your business. Come on, Sandy, let's take him somewhere private."

Charles looked wildly from one to the other. "For the love of God, Alexander, I was trying to protect you. You don't know what's out there. Terrible things, in the darkness…"

Sandy paused, one hand on his brother's arm. "What do you mean?"

"Don't listen to him," Ned said. "He's probably just stalling for time."

"What do you mean?"

"Come with me to my house," Charles said, "and I'll tell you everything."

Mal awoke with a buzzing head and a mouth that tasted like he'd been drinking canal water laced with grappa. Or grappa laced with canal water. *Kiiren*. The devious little whoreson had drugged him, and Mal had taken the bait like a hawk pouncing on the lure. Strangers betraying him was bad enough, only to be expected really, but now he had to watch out for his so-called friends?

On the other hand his shoulders and arms were far less stiff and painful than they had any right to be, so perhaps he should thank Kiiren after all. He struggled upright and realised he was in bed. Naked. God's teeth! Did the skraylings have no decency at all? He shuddered at the thought of them pawing over him.

A soft golden light seeped through the gauze curtains that enclosed the bed. Dusk, or dawn?

Footsteps sounded on the tiles, and a shadow moved beyond the curtains.

"Good evening, Catlyn-tuur. Are you rested?"

"What time is it?"

"About one of your hours before sunset."

"And where are my friends?"

"Gone back to English ambassador's house, I believe."

Mal pulled back the bedclothes, fought his way through the gauzy drapes and strode over to where his clothes had been laid out neatly on a chair. Let Kiiren stare if he wanted to; he must have seen everything already.

"Where are you going?"

"Back to Berowne's." Mal pulled on his drawers and tied the waist-string. "You can't keep me a prisoner, you know."

"At least stay tonight, and rest some more. Please."

Mal paused. In truth he was not as well recovered as he would like. His muscles still ached despite the skrayling medicine, and he doubted he would pass Kiiren's test yet.

"Very well." He stuck his head through the neck-hole of his shirt. "But no more sleeping draughts. I need a clear head tomorrow."

Kiiren ducked his head in acknowledgement, though Mal noted he did not actually say yes.

He was left to finish dressing on his own. No weapons, but then he had come unarmed. Nor were these all his own clothes; he guessed his brother had exchanged their doublet and hose, the better to fool Berowne. At least they were a better fit for one another these days, though Sandy was still a little narrower across the shoulder. Too much time spent indoors instead of out fighting.

He went over to the window, which looked out onto the street at the side of the palazzo. It was not far down to the ground, and an adjacent windowsill gave easy access to a chimney-breast with convenient footholds. As soon as he had his strength back, he would be out of here in a matter of moments.

They followed Charles down the street, through an archway and along an alley to a plain door with tiny barred windows either side. Charles fished a key out of his pocket, unlocked the door and gestured for them to go inside.

"You first," said Ned.

Charles led them through a narrow damp-smelling passageway and up a flight of stairs with treads of worn red brick. The upper chambers were no better than the ground floor, with mouldering plaster and uneven, creaking floorboards. Stained mattresses and blankets piled here and there hinted at absent inhabitants, poor working men who only came back here to sleep. Charles stopped at a door with peeling green paint and unlocked it.

"Welcome to my palazzo, gentlemen," Charles said with a bow, and ushered them inside.

The chamber was only slightly less shabby than the rest, but at least had a proper bed and a window looking out over a narrow canal. Charles lit a tallow candle and motioned for his brother to sit down on the only chair in the room. In truth it was barely fit for firewood, though the faint sheen of gilding here and there suggested it had once been a rich man's possession.

"Thank you, I prefer to stand. I will not stay long." Sandy hugged his ribs, shivering a little. "You said you were trying to protect me, that you had seen things."

Charles began unbuttoning his doublet. Now that they were no longer running through the twilit streets of the city, Ned could see the family resemblance in the shape of the brow and the set of the mouth. Charles was fairer in colouring, though, with mousy brown hair, straight as a plumb-line where the twins' was inclined to curl, and a pale English complexion despite the sunny climate. His beard was full and untidy, as if he seldom bothered to visit the barber, and his clothes were more than a little threadbare. He matched the house rather well.

"I know your brother blames me for what happened that night, but it were necessary," Charles said, his native accent coming through. "The reason I wanted you and Maliverny to join the Huntsmen is that we need as many good and true men as we can get, for our secret war against Satan and his devils."

"Secret war?" Ned stifled a laugh as Charles glared at him.

"Aye. Thanks to the likes of me, the likes of you never get to hear on it." Charles peeled off his sodden doublet and draped it over the windowsill. "We Huntsmen get all the blame, though we are but martyrs to a righteous cause."

Righteous cause, my arse. The Huntsmen broke the law, and not just by riding hooded and masked.

"Mal and I never asked to join. We were tricked, coerced…" Sandy broke off, shuddering with more than cold.

"Wait a moment," Ned said. "You are all Huntsmen? You and Sandy and… and Mal too?"

"You mean they never told you?" Charles smiled thinly. "Who are you, anyway?"

"Ned Faulkner. A friend of your brother."

"Which one?"

"Does it matter?"

"You said something about devils," Sandy put in. "Is that what you think the skraylings are?"

"There's far worse things than skraylings," Charles said. "Nightmare creatures, fast and deadly, that lurk in the dark–" He stared at Sandy. "You've seen them."

"Only in dreams."

Charles pulled up his wet shirt. "Did I dream these?"

Ned stared. Four or five silvery lines, as wide as a man's finger and nearly a foot long, ran across the pale skin over Charles' ribs.

"How…?"

"Happened when I were a lad, just after my own welcome into the Huntsmen." He stripped off the shirt and hung it from the mantel to dry, weighting it with a couple of earthenware bottles. "Father's men heard rumours.

Sheep killed in places where no wolf had been seen in a generation. Children… missing. A gang of us went up into the hills, tracking it. Only me and him came back."

"I don't remember any of that."

"You two were naught but babes in arms," Charles said.

"No thanks to you," Sandy said. "If you had not murdered me, this might not have happened."

"What? Murdered you?" Charles laughed. "You look right lively enough to me."

"You murdered me. You and your friends, that night in the hills."

Charles looked at Ned. "Did you just let him out of Bedlam?"

Ned swallowed. Strictly speaking, he had indeed played a part in freeing Sandy from the asylum. "N… no, he's been free of that filthy den for over a year."

Sandy advanced on his brother. "What did you do with my necklace?"

"What necklace?"

"The clan-beads you stole from my corpse."

"He thinks he's a skrayling reborn," Ned said. "And since you're a Huntsman by your own confession, I think he blames you for it."

"You're both mad," Charles said, backing away. "Alexander, you are sick of mind, you need help–"

"My necklace," Sandy growled, seizing Charles and pinning him against the wall.

"I sold it." Charles gazed up into his brother's eyes. "Please, Alexander, I'm sorry…"

"Who did you sell it to?"

"Bragadin. Giambattista Bragadin."

Ned laughed. "Bragadin? He's dead."

Sandy turned to glare at him. "Dead?"

"Saw him killed myself."

"If you are lying–" Sandy pressed harder, grinding Charles' head against the rough plaster.

"I'm not, I swear on our father's immortal soul."

"If you are lying," Sandy went on, "I will come back and haunt your dreams. The creatures you spoke of are nothing compared to what I can do."

Charles blanched, and seemed to shrink inside his own skin.

Ned laid a hand on Sandy's arm. "Come on, you've got what you wanted. Let's leave him be."

Sandy let his brother go, but his face was still as hard as stone.

"I should turn you over to the elders for your crime," he said.

"And I should report you to the city authorities," Charles replied. "They have hospitals here too, you know, for the sick of mind. Out in the islands of the lagoon, where you can't escape."

Sandy went for Charles again, but Ned got between them. "Enough, the pair of you!" He dragged Sandy bodily to the other side of the room and pulled him close enough to whisper.

"We have to tell Mal," he said. "If this has anything to do with..." He broke off, not wanting to give anything further away in Charles' presence.

Sandy allowed himself to be led away, though he looked over his shoulder one last time as they left the shabby chamber. Ned muttered curses under his breath. Next time, Hendricks could look after the madman and he would stay at home with Gabriel.

CHAPTER XXIX

Mal rose before dawn and dressed as silently as he could. Twilight was the best time for such ventures, as he had explained to Ned; in the shadowless dusk between day and night, the eye struggled to make out shapes and outlines. At least, human eyes did; perhaps skraylings' were different. No matter. Once he was away from here it was the eyes of Surian's agents that Mal needed to hide from, not those of his skrayling captors.

A row of houses stood opposite this wing of the *palazzo*, any of which could conceal an informant. Mal scanned each one carefully whilst trying to remain unseen behind the shutters of his own window, but saw nothing untoward. He opened the window and threw Sandy's bundled-up cloak down into the shadow of the chimney breast then with a whispered prayer to Saint Michael climbed onto the sill.

For a moment he teetered there, regretting the idea, but then he turned to face the wall and forced himself to stretch out his right leg and feel for the ledge of the next window. There. He reached out his right arm and curled his fingers around the rough stone of the neighbouring window arch. Praying his abused flesh would not betray him, he shifted his weight to the right, gently at first until he was sure he had a firm footing, and then brought his left hand and foot across so that he was standing on the other windowsill. Not far now.

He sidled along the sill to the far side of the window, fingers clawing at the stonework in an effort to keep his balance. His shoulders were burning now, the effects of Kiiren's potions long worn off, and sweat was trickling down his back despite the dawn chill. Better get this over with before his arms failed him altogether. Quickly he reached out again with his right leg until he felt the side of the chimney, then flung himself across the gap, half sliding, half falling down the rough stone to land with a jolt on the pavement below. He looked around, heart pounding, expecting one of the Venetian guards to come running. Long moments passed, and they did not come. Perhaps they had gone home, or more likely were dozing at their posts.

It was starting to get light now, and he could hear shutters opening down the street and neighbours calling greetings to one another. Curfew was over, and soon the city would be busy enough that a man abroad would not be remarked upon. He waited in the shadow of the chimney as long as he dared, then shook out the cloak, wrapped it around him and sauntered off down the street without a backward glance.

Coby went down to breakfast, still in no better humour than she had gone to bed the night before. Whilst the visit to the clockmaker's shop had been fascinating, she had no desire to spend another moment in Raleigh's presence if she could help it. For all his claims to have needed her expertise, he had largely ignored her, or claimed her every idea as his own. It had been a frustrating, humiliating evening and she wanted nothing more to do with the man. If only they could eat in the servants' quarters... but ever since Jameson's betrayal they had been avoiding him. She couldn't fault the man for his loyalty to his master, but it made for uncomfortable mealtimes.

And then there was this business with Mal and his brother. She was glad they had a plan for getting rid of Hennaq and the courtesan in one fell swoop, but would it work? She still didn't entirely trust Lord Kiiren either. He might be devoted to the twins, but would his protection extend to the rest of them?

Distracted as she was by these thoughts, she didn't see Ned until she ran into him at the bottom of the stairs.

"And the same to you, Mistress Sour-breeches," Ned responded to her growled curse.

She grabbed him by the front of the doublet and leaned in until they were almost nose to nose.

"Don't. Call. Me. Mistress." She glared at him. "Berowne and Raleigh aren't supposed to know, remember?"

"All right, all right, keep your wig on. God's bones, you're in a foul humour this morning."

She released him with a sigh. "I'm just worried about Mal, that's all."

"He'll be fine. It's his brother you want to worry about."

"Sandy? What's wrong?"

"Not here." Ned looked around. "Come back upstairs. We need to talk."

The shops along the Rialto Bridge were just opening their shutters as Mal strode up the long shallow steps. He had thought it best not to go straight back to the embassy. Surian's men were doubtless watching it, and the later they discovered they were dealing with identical twins, the better. Let them concentrate their efforts on Sandy, and he could move about the city more freely.

Perhaps that was Kiiren's plan. He could hardly have put his prisoner in a better room to escape from, after all. Mal smiled to himself. Sometimes it was easy to forget that the young skrayling was older than his great-grandfather and thrice as cunning. Kiiren might pay lip service to the idea of obeying the skrayling elders, but he always put Erishen first. For that, Mal could not fault him.

The problem was, what to do if Hennaq did not come to Venice. What was he going to do about Olivia then? He could not communicate with Kiiren in secret with her still around. Unless... Cinquedea had offered his services before. And since Ned had confirmed it was Jameson who had betrayed them to the *sbirri*, not Cinquedea, perhaps he could persuade the man to resume their arrangement. It was certainly worth a try.

The Mercerie bustled with activity in preparation for the morning's customers. Servants swept the pavement outside each shop and shook tapestries from upper windows, whilst others swabbed the glass panes of the shopfronts and swore at their neighbours above for ruining their work. Men with delivery barrows hurried back and forth before the streets became too crowded, shouting *Permesso!* or the more brusque *Attentione!* as their humour took them. Mal dodged around them all and emerged at last in St Mark's Square. It was a relief to be in the open after the narrow streets of the city, and he whistled a old song as he crossed in front of the basilica. Even the sight of the Doge's Palace was not enough to dampen his spirits. Then he saw the ship.

It was a skrayling carrack, much like the one he had seen at anchor when he arrived. For a moment he convinced himself it was the same vessel, but a glance along the quay confirmed that there were now two of them. It might not be Hennaq, he told himself. Skrayling ships were hard to tell apart, since they bore no banners, nor were they even named. The skraylings seem to regard them as one would an oxcart: useful but unremarkable.

On the other hand if it really were Hennaq, this was an opportunity unlooked-for. Once the skraylings landed, they would no doubt be escorted to the *fondaco*, and if he wanted to negotiate for his own and Sandy's freedom, he'd have to find another way in. Cinquedea might still be able to help, but if he couldn't or wouldn't… Pulling his hood closer about his face Mal ran to the waterfront and hailed the nearest gondolier.

"Take me to that ship!"

The gondolier looked curiously at him but waved him aboard. The gondola had no cabin, only seats either side of its centre section. Mal sat down, clinging to the edge of the bench.

Upon reaching the ship, Mal did not climb aboard. Instead, he hailed one of the crewmen and asked to speak to the captain. A few minutes later a middle-aged skrayling with beads in his silvered hair appeared at the rail.

"Captain Hennaq?" Mal called up.

"Erishen?" Hennaq's eyes narrowed in suspicion and he said something in Vinlandic.

"No, not Sandy. I am his brother, Maliverny."

"And what is your purpose here, half-a-man?" Hennaq said, switching to Tradetalk.

Mal bridled at the insult, but swallowed his pride. "To offer you a far greater prize than myself and my brother."

"A prize? What prize?"

"I do not think you want it shouted across the water."

"Then come aboard." Hennaq gestured towards his cabin. "We can talk over a glass of *aniig*, like civilised men."

"You'll forgive me if I do not trust you," Mal said with a laugh. "Come down to the boat, and we can talk."

Hennaq hesitated. "Very well," he said at last. "But I warn you, I will tell my men to shoot if you try to row away."

Mal inclined his head in acquiescence and instructed the awestruck gondolier to row close to the ship. Skrayling bows did not have the range of European crossbows, but he knew he had no chance of getting away before they turned him into a porcupine.

Hennaq climbed gingerly down the rope ladder and stepped into the gondola. "Well?"

"I am not the only guiser in Venice. There is another, far older, whose return to our homeland would bring you great glory. Songs and stories would be written about you and spread throughout the clans."

Hennaq licked his lips. "Go on."

Mal told him. Hennaq's eyes widened, and his hand strayed upwards to touch his clan-beads.

"One of the Lost Ones?"

"Perhaps the last of the Lost Ones. The man who returned her to her people would win great fame. Women will vie amongst themselves to bear your daughters, and give you sons too."

"Why me? Why not claim this glory for yourself, if you know who she is and believe you can capture her?"

"Because we have wronged you, my brother and I. This is our recompense. I hope it is equal to our debt."

Hennaq nodded, his eyes unfocusing as if looking deep into memory.

"Nothing I do can bring back Tanijeel," Mal went on. "But I can make a sacrifice of my own, to balance his. I humbly ask that you accept."

For a long moment the captain did not reply, and Mal began to fear the skrayling would reject the offer. And what then?

"It is good trade," Hennaq said at last.

Mal drew in a slow breath and let it out again, hoping the skrayling did not guess how anxious he had been to secure this agreement. He held out his hand, palm up, and Hennaq placed his own hand over it. After a moment they both withdrew their hands and bowed as best they could, the boat rocking gently at the movement.

"Bring the human woman to me at the great house rented to our elders," Hennaq said. "All should see her and know what she has done, before I take her back to Vinland."

"To the *fondaco*? I'm not sure that will be possible–"

"You try to go back on our bargain?" Hennaq bared his teeth.

"No, it is the Venetian law. No visitors are allowed into the great house, as you call it." At least, not without a good disguise. Smuggling Olivia in there against her will was not something he wished to try in a hurry.

"Hmm. Then bring her to me here, tomorrow."

"Tomorrow?"

"I must either go ashore soon or leave. That is also the Venetian law. Tomorrow."

"Very well." Mal looked around. "It were best done after nightfall, when fewer eyes are around to see."

"Agreed."

They bowed again, and Hennaq disappeared up the rope ladder. Mal told the gondolier to return to shore. Tomorrow night. That did not give him a lot of time to work out a plan. On the other hand, the sooner this were over, the better. He did not trust himself to keep a secret from Olivia for long.

Coby sat on the end of the bed, listening in appalled horror to Sandy and Ned's story.

"You want to rob a dead man?" she said at last.

"It's not like he needs the necklace," Ned replied.

"Neither do you. Sandy has his own spirit-guard."

Sandy hefted the pouch, which rattled faintly. "This is naught but a makeshift substitute. What I seek are my clan-beads, taken from me when my last body was murdered."

"You could make more," Coby said. "That's what Ruviq said he would do, when he lost his."

"I am no child." Sandy's face was like thunder. "My clan-beads are centuries old, some of them, given to me by fathers long turned to dust. Wearing them marks me as *tjirzadhen*, one of the Many Times Born. They cannot be made anew."

"But how are you going to get them back, now Bragadin is dead?"

"I am sure I can persuade his widow–"

"Oh no. We've had enough of your magic, thank you. Besides, it's not safe with this Olivia woman around."

"Then what do you suggest?"

"We'll find a way." She looked at the two other men. "Won't we?"

Ned and Gabriel made noises of agreement.

"Very well," Sandy said. "I shall leave it to you to arrange it. I am going down to the garden to read, it is too hot in here."

When he had gone, Ned groaned.

"What did you say that for? I've had enough of sneaking around this city, I'm not going to risk being arrested again."

"We could just ask his widow, couldn't we?" Gabriel said. "She might be willing to sell it."

Ned broke into a grin. "Hendricks can ask her, one woman to another."

"Me?" Why did all her adventures of late turn on her adopting female guise?

"If you prefer, I could dress up," Gabriel said. "A good shave and a layer of ceruse, and I am sure I could pass."

"Don't be ridiculous," Coby said.

"It's not ridiculous," Ned said. "Venetian women never go anywhere alone. Gabriel could pretend to be a courtesan, and you his – I mean her – maidservant."

"Why must I be the maidservant? I am an actual woman, after all."

Ned gave her an old-fashioned look. "You're also a blushing virgin, whereas Gabe here..."

Gabriel threw a wadded up sheet of paper at him. "Are you calling me a strumpet? You can throw stones, Ned Faulkner–"

"Enough!" Coby glared at both of them.

"Anyway it'll never work," Gabriel said at last. "Neither of us speaks more than a few words of Italian, for a start."

"So you're an English courtesan, here to learn from your Venetian sisters."

"I still think it's a stupid idea," Coby muttered. "Anyway, why would an English courtesan be visiting Bragadin's widow?"

"Simple," Ned said. "Everyone knows that Olivia was Bragadin's mistress. But she's in mourning now too. So, she's sent one of her courtesan friends to request the return of the necklace Bragadin was having valued for her."

"It'll never work."

"Of course it will work. Won't it, Gabe?"

"We will do our best," the actor replied. "It can do no harm, at any rate."

"Very well, since I cannot dissuade you," Coby said. "Heaven forbid that Ned would shave off his beard and try to pass as your maidservant."

The lovers exchanged knowing glances, and Coby rolled her eyes. If only Mal would return and take charge of his wayward friends. She got more respect from the skraylings.

"Only one problem," Ned said. "Where are you going to get clothes from? You both need to look the part."

"That's the easy bit," Coby said. "Raleigh told me we are all invited to the Doge's investiture tomorrow, and to make a good show for England we must wear the finest clothes the Mercerie can provide. But he never said we had to dress as men."

When Mal stepped ashore, he half expected to be arrested. After all, he'd spoken to a skrayling captain in public, in full sight of the Doge's Palace. Perhaps Surian's men were only watching the embassy, or perhaps the skraylings were not subject to the full force of Venetian law unless they came ashore. Still, best not to push his luck. He wanted this business with Hennaq concluded quickly and efficiently, with as little danger to his friends as possible, and to be sure of that he needed help.

The Mermaid was empty this early in the morning. A pale-faced girl was scrubbing the tables; she looked up as Mal entered and forced a smile that turned into a yawn.

"Can I help you, sir?"

"I think he's looking for me." Cinquedea stood in the doorway leading to the upper storey.

At a glance from Cinquedea, the girl threw her scrubbing brush in her bucket and fled the common room.

"So..." Cinquedea drew up a bench and perched on one end, avoiding the wet tabletop. "You are a bold one, *signore*, coming here after what happened in Rio Tera degli Assassini."

"That was none of my doing," Mal replied, leaning on a neighbouring table. "The ambassador's servant overheard your messenger boy, and merely did his civic duty."

"Still, careless of you to let him overhear."

"I had no idea who the message came from. Perhaps it is your boys who need training in discretion."

Cinquedea raised an eyebrow. "As I said, a bold one. So, you still want passage into... a certain building?"

"No, I have a more urgent need." Mal glanced towards the tavern door and lowered his voice. "I need you to help me abduct the honest courtesan, Olivia dalle Boccole."

Cinquedea stared at him for a moment, then burst out laughing.

"You think I am Cupid, to help you in your amorous adventures?" He got to his feet.

"Please." Mal stood, ready to block the other man's exit. "This is no lover's whim. She is a dangerous woman. If you wish to work unhindered in this city, you would do well to be rid of her."

Cinquedea shook his head. "Our arrangement concerns the *sanuti*, not our citizens."

"So does this."

"How so?"

Mal drew a deep breath. Best to keep this simple. "She is not who she seems. She is a New World witch, and the *sanuti* have agreed to take her home with them."

"Do not lie to me, *signore*. Olivia dalle Boccole was born in this city. My mother's cousin in Cannaregio knows her mother."

"Olivia has a mother?"

"We all have mothers," Cinquedea said with a smile. "And fathers too, though not all know them."

Mal ignored the slur.

"She didn't mention a mother," he muttered to himself. It had never occurred to him that this scheme might leave an old woman bereft.

"It is hardly a fit subject for pillow talk, eh?" Cinquedea paused in the doorway. "Forget this woman who has wronged you. There are plenty more such. Bring me good information, and you may have your pick of my girls."

"Thank you," Mal replied with as much grace as he could muster. "Good day to you, *signore*."

He left the taverna in a far less cheerful humour than he had arrived. Why had he let the others talk him into this? Never mind, he could manage without them. All he had to do was kill Hafiz, bind and gag Olivia and bundle her into a gondola. How hard could that be?

Coby's stomach churned as their gondolier rapped on the door-knocker of Palazzo Bragadin. This was never going to work. Not because Gabriel did not look the part; on the contrary, once he had donned gown and makeup and Ned had fastened ribbons in his long pale hair, he made a remarkably convincing woman. But surely a respectable widow like Signora Bragadin would never admit them to her home?

Palazzo Bragadin looked like a much grander version of Berowne's house. The walls were painted a soft terracotta colour that contrasted prettily with windows edged in white stonework, and just above their heads a little balcony jutted out over the water, held up by carved lions and decorated with tiny male busts at intervals along the balustrade. After a few moments the door opened and a servant asked their names.

"Lady Elizabeth Raleigh," Gabriel said in haughty tones.

Coby hid her gasp of surprise with a feigned cough. Well, it was one way to get them through the front door. The servant ushered them inside, and after a short wait they were shown up to the *piano nobile*.

Signora Bragadin rose to greet them. A thin, handsome woman of forty or so, she was dressed in widow's black that made her look fashionably pale without the need for ceruse.

"Lady Elisabetta!" She chattered away for some moments in Italian, much to Gabriel's bemusement.

"Excuse me," Coby said in French. "My lady does not speak your language."

Signora Bragadin summoned her own maid, and between the four of them they managed a stilted conversation. A manservant brought coffee for the ladies, rather to Coby's surprise; she had seen Mal and Captain Youssef drink it together occasionally, but had not realised it had become a Christian habit. The scent was very enticing but the one time she had tried it, she had pulled a face at its bitter flavour and it had taken all her self-control not to spit it out. Gabriel's reaction was not dissimilar; she spotted him hastily ladling in sugar when their hostess was not looking.

Gabriel tried to keep up the pretence of being Raleigh's wife, but after a while he ran out of plausible answers to Signora Bragadin's questions and fell back on their original story, that he was a friend of Olivia dalle Boccole. Their hostess's expression turned to stone.

"I should have known," she said, looking Gabriel up and down. "Please leave."

"I meant no disrespect," Gabriel said. "Indeed, La Margherita sent me so as not to cause embarrassment. She only wants her necklace back, the one she lent your husband to have valued."

"I know of no such necklace. Now, be gone."

Gabriel rose to his feet and curtsied, and Coby did likewise though, she feared, with far less grace. The maidservant showed them to the stairs and then fled back to her mistress.

"What do we do now?" Coby said, glancing about them. Dared they risk sneaking back to try and steal the necklace?

Gabriel just shook his head. "Next time, Sandy does his own dirty work. Though I must say I haven't enjoyed myself so much in months."

As they reached the atrium, the manservant stepped out of the shadows. He held out his hand.

"The necklace!" Gabriel exclaimed softly.

The man gabbled something in the Venetian dialect and pressed the double string of beads into the actor's hands.

"Why, thank you!"

Gabriel passed it to Coby, then leaned closer to the man and murmured something in his ear, simultaneously reaching down to caress his groin. The manservant's eyes widened, then he grinned lasciviously. Gabriel swept past him, and he hurried to hold the door open for them. Thankfully the gondolier was still waiting.

"What was all that about?" Coby hissed as the gondola drew away.

"Just a handy phrase that Valerio taught me. Seems it works whether one is a man or a woman."

"You're as bad as Ned," she muttered.

"I'll take that as a compliment." He waved out of the window at a group of passing bravos, who leered and cat-called as they passed. "So, why do you think the servant gave us the necklace?"

"I don't know," she replied. "Perhaps he thought it some kind of black magic that had brought them bad luck. He must have found it rather odd when his master took to sleeping in a string of old beads inscribed with foreign-looking symbols."

She took the necklace out of her pocket. Some of the jade beads did indeed look ancient, their carvings worn to illegibility. She wondered again just how old Erishen was, but decided she was probably better off not knowing.

CHAPTER XXX

Mal climbed out of the hired gondola and paid the man. After a moment's hesitation, he raised his hand to the door knocker, a polished sphere that sat in the centre of a brass oyster shell like a giant pearl. The sound of its impact echoed along the canal, and he had to fight the urge to look about him to see if he had drawn undue attention. The door was opened by the eunuch slave, Hafiz.

"Signore Catalin." He bowed, his features politely impassive. "Is my mistress expecting you?"

"No," Mal said. "I… I hoped to surprise her."

"I will see if she wishes to be surprised." A glimmer of a smile crossed the eunuch's lips and was gone.

Mal readied himself for a long wait. Perhaps she would refuse to see him. After all, she had told him not to come back until the skraylings had left. Should he lie and say they were gone? No, even if she did not find out the truth, she would want him to assist in her self-slaughter, and that would throw all their plans into disarray. There was only one reason she would believe he had gone back on his word. He would have play the lovelorn swain to the hilt, despite his vow to be faithful to Coby from now on. This was just business, after all.

When the eunuch did finally return, he ushered Mal up to Olivia's private apartments. The courtesan was seated on the daybed near the doors to the balcony, her dark skin thrown into greater contrast by the sunlit glass behind her. Mal paused on the threshold and swept a low bow.

"*Signorina.*"

She beckoned for him to come closer.

"I did not expect to see you again so soon," she said. "Does all go to plan?"

"It progresses slowly. Rome was not built in a day."

"Nor Venice." She smiled. "Come, sit beside me. So, *amayi'a,* to what do I owe the honour of another visit so soon and unannounced?"

Ned strode across Saint Mark's Square, hands deep in pockets. The gilded angels on the façade of the basilica caught the last of the setting sun; they looked as if they were about to depart the earth and fly up to heaven, away from the sordid doings of the mortals below. He didn't blame them. If only his own Angel would do the same, and take Ned with him. Except without the dying part, of course.

Reaching the Mermaid meant passing the Doge's palace, though Ned gave it a wide a berth, averting his eyes and swallowing past the bile in his throat. The quayside was as crowded as ever: newly arrived visitors stepping off boats, their mouths sagging open at the wonders before them; citizens weaving through the throng on some urgent business or other; and of course the usual swarms of beggars and pickpockets buzzing around anyone who looked as though they might have a fatter purse than was strictly necessary. Ned ignored them all and slipped past the front of the palace as fast as he could.

Just as he approached the tavern a trio of drunken sailors lurched out of the door, singing a bawdy ballad. The words, about a man with a long "thing", cheered him up somewhat and he found himself humming the tune as he stepped through the door of the tavern and looked around. There was no sign of his quarry. He went over to the tap-man.

"Seen Charles Catlyn lately?"

The man looked him up and down, his solid features creasing with glacial slowness.

"Here, didn't I see you chase Catlyn out of here the other day? You and that tall fellow."

"Uh, yes."

"Owes you money, does he?"

"Something like that."

The tap-man laughed. "Good luck with getting it back."

"Have you seen him?"

The tap-man shook his head. "Most likely you'll find him in the Turk's Head, off the Campo San Giovanni."

"Another inn?" Ned asked.

"A *casino*: a private gambling house. Over the next bridge, turn left, and it's just before you get to the square. Got a dark green door with a knocker in the shape of a Turk's head. Knock twice, then twice again."

The *casino* was not hard to find; though it looked much like any other house in the street, the crowds eddied away from its door, as if an invisible fence kept them out. He stepped up to the door, feeling horribly conspicuous, and knocked as instructed. After a few moments the door opened, and he stepped inside.

The interior of the little gambling house was darker even than the streets, and the air thick with tobacco smoke and curses. Men sat at tables playing cards, or crouched on the floor to throw dice. Bare-breasted whores perched on customers' knees, shifting from one man to the next as the money changed hands, like sordid incarnations of Lady Luck. Ned weaved his way amongst the tables, trying to spot Charles without catching anyone's eye.

A man wearing rather better clothing than the rest of the patrons got up from his seat, directly into Ned's path and addressed him in Italian.

"I'm looking for a friend," Ned replied in English. "He recommended this place."

"His name, *signore*?"

"Charles Catlyn."

A few of the other players looked up at this. Ned tensed, expecting Charles to bolt again, but no one made a move.

"Over there." One of the patrons jerked a thumb towards the corner of the room.

Ned found his quarry seated at a table with three other men. He hung back and watched for a while, leaning on the wall. They were playing a game he did not know, one that appeared to require several dozen wooden counters in addition to the cards and the betted money. Some of the counters were marked "VI", and a small stack of darker counters sat at the dealer's left hand. At last the game ended and one of the players got up from the table with many complaints. Ned sauntered over.

"Mind if I join you, gentlemen?"

Charles appeared to notice him for the first time. He blanched and leapt up from his seat, staring wildly around the gambling-house with watery eyes.

"Where is he?"

"Sandy's not with me," Ned replied, taking the vacant seat. "Sit down, Charlie, I just came for a quiet game of... what is it you fellows are playing, anyway?"

"*Rovescino,*" one of the other players said, collecting up all the counters and sorting them into three piles. "You know it?"

Ned shook his head and grinned. "Why don't you show me?"

The crimson-draped bed was large enough for two at the very least. Mal pulled off his boots and then lay back, watching Olivia undress. The candlelight gilded her skin so that she looked like one of the icons adorning St Mark's basilica, complete with enigmatic eyes and a golden halo around her coiffure. Stripped to her corset and a pair of ivory silk breeches, she began to remove the strings of pearls and glass beads from her hair.

"Don't your lovers grow impatient?" he asked, swirling his coffee cup to dissolve the last dregs of precious sugar. "So many layers…"

"Are you impatient, my love?"

"Anticipation is half the torture." A lie; he could now vouch for that personally. "And half the pleasure."

She laughed, a deep throaty sound that send an echo through his veins. "You are a man after my own heart."

Free of her adornments at last, she drifted over to the bed, circling round to the far side before climbing onto the broad mattress, just out of arm's reach.

"Will you not undress?" she said, head cocked on one side. "You have the advantage of me."

"I was hoping you would help me."

She smiled. "I do not think you need my help."

With an exaggerated sigh he began to unbutton his doublet. Soon he was stripped to his linen drawers, the evening air cool on his bare skin. Once, he had dreamed of being naked with her; now he flinched at her touch, fearing could strip his very soul bare and betray his purpose.

"How often have you been a woman?" he asked as she sidled closer.

"Not often," she said. "It is not easy to be the weaker sex, even with our talents to protect us."

"Weaker?" He felt Erishen stir within him. "That is the human speaking."

"I have had to learn to work with the situation at hand. Here, women are allowed so little freedom. Did you know that Venetian noblewomen are scarcely allowed out of the house except to attend funerals or great state occasions?" She made a rude noise. "It is barbaric."

"Then you would prefer to be a man next time."

"Of course." She traced a line down his chest with her fingertip, and he suppressed a shiver of mingled fear and lust. "You would dislike that?"

"No. But I like you as you are. More like a skrayling woman than these pale Christians."

The lies came so easily, he felt guilt at every word but could not stop himself. It was as if Erishen was speaking through him. He tried to relax as Olivia kissed her way up his torso and across his chest, her unbound hair brushing his skin on either side of the kisses. Her lips brushed the knot of scar tissue on his left shoulder and began to trace a path down his arm.

"What is this?" she hissed, her body tensing as she crouched over him.

Mal realised she was staring at the tattoo on his shoulder: a triskelion of branched thorns surrounded by three five-petalled flowers. His mind raced, trying to concoct a story that would not betray his links to Kiiren. It would help if he knew what the sigil actually meant. Kiiren said it was for "remembering", but what did that signify?

"I had it done at a fair in England," he said at last. "I saw the design in the skraylings' pattern book and took a fancy to it. Why?"

"That is an ancient sigil; I have not seen its like in centuries. And you say someone was selling these to humans as mere decoration?"

Mal feigned innocence. "I can only tell you what I know. What does it mean?"

"I don't know." It seemed to bother her. "Perhaps you remember more than you realise..."

"Perhaps so." He ran his hands down her arms, then slipped them round her waist and pulled her close. "But enough of the past..."

"*Il mio tesoro,*" she whispered in his ear, and kissed the metal hoop where it pierced his earlobe. "Will you not take this off now? I think you are ready for a true joining."

He bent his head to kiss her shoulder, hoping that she mistook the pounding of his heart for lust. He had been afraid she would suggest this, now when it was impossible for him to allow it.

"I want to enjoy every inch of you with my waking eyes first," he said. "What's the hurry, when we have all eternity to look forward to?"

He pushed his fears to the back of his mind and let his body take over. This was a dance he knew of old, though never with so graceful a partner. Soon he forgot why he had ever been afraid of her.

They made love slowly, languorously, lingering over each caress until every nerve trembled like a lute-string at the merest touch. Her fingertips, hot as gledes, danced over his skin as he moved inside her, and the end came all too soon despite his best efforts to prolong their pleasure. He withdrew and rolled over, recalling his purpose here. Dare he stay the night? If so, should he take her captive as she slept and try to keep her hidden until tomorrow?

"Perhaps you are right," she murmured, propping herself up on one elbow behind him. "Sometimes the simple ways are the best."

She slipped a hand around his waist and down towards his navel, making his belly muscles tighten in anticipation. He sucked in a breath and pulled himself upright. Time to get out of here, before he did something stupid. Like doing that again, without the spirit-guard's protection this time. He could always come back.

"I don't suppose I'll see you tomorrow," he said, trying to sound casual. He retrieved his clothes and began dressing.

"You are leaving so soon?"

She shifted on the bed, candlelight gilding her curves. Mal turned his back and pulled on his shirt. It stuck to his clammy skin, but there was no helping it.

"I have business to attend to, and no desire to be arrested for breaking curfew." Mal looked back over his shoulder. "It was you, wasn't it, who gained us our reprieve?"

She grinned like a naughty child. "Was Surian very cross?"

"I thought as much." He pulled on his slops and boots, and picked up his doublet. "Until tomorrow, my lady."

"Until tomorrow, *amayi'a*. I will see you at the Doge's Palace."

"What?" He froze in the doorway.

"The grand reception at the Doge's Palace. Everyone has been invited, including your ambassador and Sir Walter Raleigh. There will be fireworks in Saint Mark's Square…"

"Yes, yes of course. I had quite forgotten."

He bowed to hide his discomfiture and made his way back downstairs. Damn it, how was he to abduct her and convey her to the skrayling ship with half the city on the quayside? This plan was going from bad to worse.

Coby took the hired gowns back to the Mercerie after supper, and spent some time at Quirin's afterwards. It was far pleasanter without Raleigh playing cock-of-the-walk, and she was able to discuss gears and movements with the clockmaker over a glass of wine. When the shop's gilded and enamelled clocks all began to strike the second hour after sunset, she remembered where she was and excused herself, running all the way back to the embassy to arrive out of breath but at least well within curfew.

She went straight up to her room, but paused at the top of the stairs when she heard whistling coming from behind the closed door. For a moment she considered going back down to the parlour, but she was in no mood for more conversation with Raleigh, so she knocked quietly. No response. She knocked again, a little louder. The whistling stopped, and footsteps approached the door. It opened to reveal Mal, stripped to the waist and rubbing his damp hair with a towel.

"Ah, Coby, about time," he said.

"Sir?"

She looked down at her feet. Though she had seen him half-dressed many times, in the wake of her recent thoughts it was particularly irksome of him to be flaunting his virility so.

"We need to talk." He opened the door wider and she made to go inside. "No, not in here. I want to talk to Sandy as well. And the others."

"Oh." Her cheeks became even hotter, if that were possible. *Idiot! Presuming he was talking about you, when—* "I'll… I'll just wait out here for you to finish washing, shall I?"

"I'll be out in a moment. Run down and see if Jameson has any of that Tuscan red left, will you?"

"Yes, sir." She hesitated. "What are you doing here? I thought Lord Kiiren wanted you to stay and be tended."

"He changed his mind and let me loose."

"Oh. Well, that's wonderful." She forced a smile. *Changed his mind, my foot!* The ambassador was up to something again, she would put a month's wages on it.

She ran down to the kitchen, where Jameson grudgingly handed out a flagon of wine and five glasses, all of them old and chipped, placing them one by one on a silver tray with a look that warned her not to drop them on the marble stairs or else. She dutifully took the tray and advanced slowly up to the attic, flinching at every wobble.

Mal was in the larger of the two attic rooms and now at least partially dressed, in a clean shirt and with his wet hair combed neatly back. Gabriel was lying on one of the beds, leafing through a stack of papers – probably his play – whilst Ned dealt cards on the counterpane at his side.

Sandy was staring out of the small window under the eaves. She set the tray down on the rickety table in a chime of glass and metal.

"Good, we're all here," Mal said, pouring out the wine. "I did not escape the *fondaco* this evening, as you may have been thinking. I have been out and about all day, trying to bring this sorry mission to a conclusion. And I have bad news."

"Hennaq is here," Coby said.

"You've seen his ship?"

She shook her head. "Just a guess."

"A good one. Anyway I've already spoken to him. He seemed quite amenable to taking Olivia in lieu of Sandy and I."

He caught Coby's eye and smiled, then handed her a glass of wine. Her fingers tightened on the smooth, fragile stem and she forced herself to relax. Soon they would be rid of both Hennaq and the courtesan, and could continue their mission in peace.

"That's good," Sandy said.

"It would be, but for one small difficulty: I swore I would do it tomorrow, and the lagoon will be busy with celebrations for the new Doge. How in the name of all that's holy am I to get her onto Hennaq's ship unseen?"

"That is the easy part," Sandy replied. "After all, you've done something like it before."

When Mal did not reply, Sandy stood with arms outstretched, like a man greeting a long-lost friend. Coby recalled the vision she had seen at the Tower of London. A magical tunnel through the dreamlands, with Sandy at the far end.

"No, I can't," Mal said.

"Yes you can. This woman has been training you, hasn't she?"

Mal nodded, his face a picture of guilt. Coby tried not

to think about what that training had involved. How often had they slept together, in body as well as spirit?

"Then it will be simple to deceive her," Sandy went on. "Let her believe it is just another dreamwalk, then I will make the link and you can bring her through."

"Through to where?"

"Hennaq's cabin would be the best place. Least chance of being seen."

"But that means you'll be on the ship as well," Mal said. "What's to stop him sailing away with you both?"

"You. As soon as Olivia steps through, I will come to you."

"I thought you needed a strong anchor," Coby said, the courtesan momentarily forgotten. "That was why you couldn't escape from Suffolk until Lord Kiiren drew near."

"We are both stronger now. It will suffice."

"Easy for you to say," Mal muttered. "Anyway, I'm not sure I know how. Last time, I was sleepwalking–"

"Exactly. Do not worry, brother, it will come as naturally as breathing, I promise you."

Gabriel put aside his sheaf of papers and got to his feet. "What are the rest of us to do in the meantime?"

"Stay out of harm's way," Sandy said.

"You can't exclude us," Ned put in. "We haven't come all this way to sit on our hands, you know."

Sandy crossed the room swiftly and leant over Ned. "This is beyond your skills, little man."

Gabriel took hold of Sandy's arm.

"Lay a finger on him and you'll have me to deal with."

Sandy turned and bared his teeth like a skrayling. Coby shot a desperate glance at Mal, but he was already there.

"Sandy, enough! You too, Parrish."

He glared at them until they resumed their places, then gestured for Coby to pour more wine. She wasn't sure that would help, but it was something to do.

"There is still the question of timing to be decided," Mal said. "Olivia will be surrounded by people all day, I am certain."

"We can do it after the reception," Sandy replied. "Surely you can contrive to go home with her?"

"The celebrations could go on all night, if they're anything like court masques back home." Mal sighed. "I'll have to go back to Hennaq and tell him there's been a delay."

"You cannot, if you have already pressed hands on the bargain. Hennaq would be entitled to go ahead with his original scheme and take us both to Vinland."

"He has to get hold of us first," Mal replied.

"Then we will have to do it at the reception."

Coby stared at them both. "What? Work magic in the middle of a gathering of Venice's most powerful men? Do you want to be burned for witchcraft?"

"We convinced people it was fireworks before," Gabriel said.

"A few gullible actors–"

"This time it will be real," Sandy said. "There is to be a display of fireworks in the square after dark. Amongst all the noise and bright lights, who will notice?"

"He has a point," Gabriel said. "All you need to do is lure Olivia into some quiet corner when everyone is distracted, and..."

"All right," Mal said. "But my first obligation is to protect Sandy. If I cannot find an opportunity to abduct Olivia before midnight, I will come back to the embassy and open a tunnel for you to escape Hennaq's ship. Swear to me you will come?"

"I swear," his brother replied.

Ned clapped Mal on the shoulder. "Don't worry, mate. Gabe, Hendricks and me can keep watch and make sure you're not disturbed."

Coby shot him a filthy look. She was relieved Mal would not be spending the evening alone with Olivia, and that toad Faulkner knew it, but he need not look so smug about it. She distracted herself by gathering up the glasses, though she did not trust herself to carry them downstairs without an accident.

"Here," she said, thrusting the tray at Ned. "You wanted to be useful. Take this down to the kitchen."

When he had gone she lingered in the doorway, hoping to hear the sound of breaking glass.

"Come, it's time we were all abed," Mal said, leaning over her.

She looked up into his dark eyes. "You will be careful?"

"Of course. You don't get rid of me that easily."

For a moment she thought – hoped – he was going to kiss her, but he just ruffled her hair and gave her a playful shove towards the little attic room. She bade him good night and plodded down the steps. Tomorrow. It would all be over, tomorrow.

CHAPTER XXXI

Coby slept badly that night, haunted by nightmares in which Mal burned on a pyre studded with fireworks whilst an unseen woman laughed and laughed. As dawn came she lay staring up at the rafters, watching their now-familiar lines coalesce out of the darkness, and wrestled with her conscience. There was no getting away from it; she had to at least try to persuade Mal not to go through with this idiotic plan, otherwise she would never forgive herself.

As soon as it was full light, she got out of bed, washed and dressed, then flung open the shutters. The street outside was quiet apart from a man with a handcart delivering sacks of flour to the nearby bakery. The city seemed to be holding its breath in anticipation of its greatest day of the year: the celebration of its independence as a self-ruled republic.

She could hear the men on the way down to breakfast. Opening the door she caught Mal's eye.

"May I have a word, sir?"

"Of course."

He waved the others ahead of him. Coby caught Ned winking at Mal, who shook his head. She pretended not to notice. Let them play their foolish games.

Mal closed the door at the top of the stairs.

"Well?"

She cleared her throat, summoning all her courage to say what she knew he did not want to hear.

"I know you know far more of these things than I do, sir, but I don't think this is a good idea. You only just prevailed against Suffolk, and if Master Alexander is to be believed, he was nothing compared to one of the ancients."

Mal put his hand on her shoulder.

"I know you're afraid for me," he said softly. "But I have to do this."

"Why?"

"What do you mean, why? If I don't, Hennaq will take Sandy and me back to the New World. Is that what you want?"

"Of course not. But surely there's another way? Why do you have to risk your life – your soul – to capture this guiser? Venice has managed perfectly well for centuries without our interference."

"I agree."

"You do?"

"Of course. But it is not my role to decide these things. I was sent here by Sir Francis to spy on the negotiations, and I can do that best with Olivia out of the way. Nor will it hurt to show the skraylings that I respect their ways, beginning with helping one of their lost sheep find her way home."

She shook her head. "I think you have become obsessed with this woman."

"I? I am not the one who blushes at every mention of her name."

Coby stared at him for a moment, then wrenched open the door and ran down the stairs, heedless of the tears streaming down her face. *Stupid, stupid, stupid!* She had let her jealousy derail her reasoned argument, and now he would never listen to her.

• • • •

After breakfast they dispersed to their chambers and reassembled half an hour later in the atrium. Berowne wore a heavily embroidered peascod doublet and an enormous ruff edged with Venetian lace, whilst Raleigh was dressed in the latest English fashion, in an oyster-coloured silk doublet with a simple collar of near-transparent lawn, and black-and-white striped trunk hose. Mal's borrowed finery was not unlike his former livery as Kiiren's bodyguard, all sable velvet discreetly slashed with matching silk, and the others were likewise dressed in traditional Venetian black. Coby's doing, no doubt; none of them wanted to attract attention tonight.

Berowne handed out masks.

"Damned foolish custom, if you ask me," he said, "but we'll look the fools for showing our bare faces on a festival day."

A sudden knock at the front door made Mal start. *Sbirri?* His heart pounded as Jameson shuffled over to the door, painfully slowly, and unfastened the locks and bolts.

"May I help you, sir?" he quavered through the gap.

"I damn well hope so," a half-familiar voice said. "I'm here to see my brothers."

Jameson opened the door a little further.

"Alexander! Maliverny! How good to see you again!"

Charles pushed past Jameson, beaming, but froze when he saw how many others were gathered in the atrium. To Mal's surprise his brother looked far less disreputable than Ned's description of him; evidently he had smartened himself up for the occasion.

"Sir Geoffrey, Sir Walter." Mal turned to his hosts. "This is my elder brother Charles, whom you mentioned when we arrived. Charles, this is Sir Walter Raleigh, Lord Warden of the Stannaries, and His Excellency Sir Geoffrey Berowne, the English Ambassador."

Charles swept a low bow, muttering apologies.

"You're very welcome here, Catlyn," Berowne replied. "Won't you join us in the gondola?"

"Delighted, Your Excellency, delighted!"

Mal forced a smile. "It's good to see you too, Charles."

Berowne led the way to the gondola dock and took his place in the cabin with Raleigh. The three brothers perched on side-benches in the prow of the gondola, whilst Coby, Ned and Gabriel sat in the stern. Fortunately two gondoliers had been hired today, one at the front and one at the back, otherwise the heavily laden craft would never have made it to the lagoon in time for the ceremony.

"Well, this is a happy day," Charles said as they set off. "All the family, together again at last."

"All that's left," Mal replied softly. "What brings you here so unexpectedly?"

"Your man Faulkner. He convinced me that you would be open to a reconciliation."

Mal frowned. What was Ned up to? "Well, I confess to being curious as to what you have to say."

"You shall know all in due course. But perhaps not here, eh?"

"Agreed." The last thing he wanted was for Charles to say something incriminating in front of Berowne. Or Raleigh. "Tomorrow, perhaps. We shall all be much occupied today."

Crouched in the back of an overladen gondola, Coby was reminded of the skrayling ambassador's arrival in London. Every boat in Venice, it appeared, was out on the lagoon, following the ducal galley as it rowed out to sea.

The *Bucentaur* was magnificent even by Venetian standards. Gilded carving covered every inch of the galley, so that it shone in the May sunlight like a new-minted angel. A scarlet canopy ran the length of the deck, shading its occupants from the heat of the sun, and an enormous banner bearing the lion of Saint Mark adorned its single mast.

Coby could just make out the tiny figure of the Doge himself, seated on a throne in the stern.

"The new Doge, Marino Grimani," Gabriel said, "The election was so tightly contested after the death of his predecessor, there almost wasn't a Doge in time for the ceremony."

"So what happened?"

Gabriel glanced around.

"The word is, someone helped him to sway the voters," he whispered. "Someone who knew a great many secrets that could ruin men if they did not change their minds."

"Olivia? Is that why Master Catlyn was so interested in her... business?"

"Why else?" He gave her a sly look. "I remember when you first confessed to being in love with him. We were in a boat then, too."

Coby felt herself blush. She remembered it all right, far too well.

"Do you think Grimani will be in favour of an alliance with the skraylings?" she said, trying to steer the conversation back on course.

"It's hard to tell. He's said to be no friend of the Pope, but that means little."

Just then their gondola was bumped by another craft and Coby had to cling to the gunwales as it rocked alarmingly. The *Bucentaur* had passed out into the Adriatic, leaving the rest of the city's boats trying to crowd through the bottleneck in its wake.

"We shall all drown at this rate," she muttered.

The gondola did not founder, but there was little to be seen at this distance, so Coby amused herself with watching the occupants of other vessels nearby. Everyone was in their Sunday best and most wore masks, from simple leather shapes like the one she had worn as Columbina, to elaborate full-face constructions, painted and gilded and trimmed with feathers. It was a most peculiar and eerie custom, and one she would not be sorry to leave behind.

After what felt like an age the ceremony was over and the boats turned back to the city.

"Now what?" she asked Gabriel.

"Now we go to the *Sensa,* the great Ascension Day fair, and pass our time in idleness until the masquerade this evening. I have a mind to see a proper *commedia* troupe perform. Care to join me?"

When Berowne's party disembarked at the quayside to visit the great fair, Mal took Erishen aside for a moment.

"Be on your guard around Hennaq," he said. "I have no wish to lose you."

"Do not fear. Last time, Hennaq was able to surprise me. Now I know his mind he will find me much harder to deceive."

"I hope you're right."

Erishen wished his brothers farewell and slipped away. Mal had been against it, but Erishen had convinced him that the best time to board Hennaq's ship was in broad daylight, when the water was at its busiest. With so many boats crowding around the quayside on their return from the ceremony, who would notice one approach the skrayling ship?

He waited for a moment until the others had disappeared into the crowd then made his way towards Hennaq's ship, which was anchored about halfway along the quay, equally distant from both the palace and the Arsenale. The broad quayside swarmed with merrymakers on their way to Saint Mark's Square, and the noise and smells – the strange foods and stranger tongues, the mingled stench of sweat, urine and perfume – threatened to overwhelm him as he struggled to make progress against the relentless flow of humanity. He would have turned and run, except that there was nowhere to run to. He took several deep breaths to calm his nerves and pressed on.

After what felt like an eternity he reached the midpoint of the quay and found a small gull-headed boat tied up amongst the gondolas. Some of Hennaq's crew had come ashore, then. Whether this was a good or bad thing, he could not decide. He jumped aboard, untied the painter and took up the oars.

Mal trailed after the others for a while, but his heart was not in merrymaking. Rather than spoil their enjoyment of the fair, he excused himself and went back to the embassy, where he could go over the plan without distractions. Olivia was ancient and powerful, far beyond his previous experience; how could Sandy be so sure they could capture her, even working together? He could only assume his brother had access to Erishen's knowledge of such matters.

Even if it worked, was he even doing the right thing? It would get rid of Hennaq, but going back to the New World probably wasn't what Olivia wanted. Venice was her home, and she had ruled it well enough for all these centuries, or at least, she and her kinfolk had. On the other hand, with the rest of the guisers dead her rule was beginning to falter. La Serenissima was no longer the great power it had been, and would sink further unless it gained the one thing Olivia could not allow: an alliance with the skraylings. Truly it was a kindness to everyone in Venice for her to admit defeat and go home.

It felt like an age until he heard movement downstairs and the sounds of the returning party. He went down to greet them, grateful for the distraction from his own conflicted thoughts.

"Did you enjoy the *Sensa*?" he asked Ned.

Ned shrugged. "You didn't miss anything, really. It was a lot like Bartholomew Fair, only with painted wooden booths instead of tents."

"Didn't miss anything?" Coby said, looking to her companions for confirmation. "What about the mechanical Saint George and the Dragon? It breathed smoke and rolled its eyes, and then… Saint George cut its head off."

"It sounds very impressive," Mal said. "However we ought to be getting ready for the reception."

"Of course, sir."

At last they were all washed and combed and ready to leave. Tonight the city would be freed of the guisers' insidious influence, and he would be able to complete his mission in safety. And then? Best not to look beyond the current action. Tonight he must focus on one thing alone: the capture of Olivia.

The Doge's Palace shone like a lamp, its façade rippling with the light reflected off the waters of the nearby lagoon. From its upper windows the well-to-do could look down upon the little square between St Mark's and the quayside, where stood a tiered wooden structure at least three times the height of a man. In the flickering light Coby could make out the shapes of fireworks: catherine wheels, fountains and other devices, individually quite small but together capable of making an impressive display. She tore her eyes away and followed Mal towards the palace entrance; when that lot went off, she wanted to be as far away as possible.

Lamps hung at intervals from the ceilings of the outer and inner cloisters, creating pools of light and shadow where guests gathered for whispered conversations. Berowne and his gentleman companions were escorted to the foot of the great stair leading up to the state rooms, whilst Coby, Ned and Gabriel were left to mingle in the courtyard with the other retainers.

"I don't like this," Coby muttered. "Sandy's been gone for hours. How do we know Hennaq hasn't got him trussed up in the hold again?"

"We don't," Gabriel said. "But if he has, he won't get Mal or Olivia, so what's the profit for him? He might as well have taken Sandy alone in the first place."

"Hardly alone." Ned slipped his arm through Gabriel's. "He would have taken you too."

Gabriel patted his hand. "I'm quite safe now, don't fret."

"So what are we going to do for the next hour?"

"In your case, keep out of trouble," Gabriel replied.

Ned punched him in the arm with his free hand.

"Enough, you two!" Coby frowned at them both. "Look, there are servants coming round with trays of sweetmeats."

Ned's eyes lit up, and he released Gabriel.

"Going to need both my hands free for this," he said with a grin.

Mal followed Berowne and Raleigh up the magnificent staircase and past the great statues of Mars and Neptune, trying not to think about the last time he was here. From the first floor they went further upwards, through a tunnel-like stair lined with gilding and white stucco, into an antechamber where the guests paused before being announced and presented to the Doge and council. To his left Mal could see the studded door he had been taken through after his arrest. He turned away, though he could not shake the feeling that he was being watched.

"Signori Geoffrey Berowne, Walter Raleigh *e* Maliverny Catlyn, *del'Inghilterra*!" a lackey announced.

Mal tried not to goggle as they entered the great chamber beyond. Like the Doge's barge, its every beam was carved and gilded, and every space between the beams was filled with paintings depicting the glory of Venice. Vast friezes with themes both secular and religious lined the walls between high windows overlooking the square; the chamber itself was of such enormous size that even with every nobleman in Venice present, it appeared half empty.

How the roof stayed up with no columns to support it, Mal could not imagine.

He left Berowne and Raleigh talking to a group of black-clad Venetians and moved casually through the throng, hoping to spot Olivia. There were many more women here than he had expected, all of them masked and clad in bright silks laden with gems and embroidery, but their skin was as fair as Olivia's was dark. Most, judging by their reserved air, were patricians' wives enjoying a rare venture into public life, but a few, no less richly dressed but with a certain sensuality of demeanour, were undoubtedly courtesans.

Alas, he could see no sign of his quarry, though it was early yet. Perhaps she had been delayed, or decided not to come after all. Mal cursed under his breath. He should have forced his brother to renegotiate with the skrayling captain.

The crowds parted for a moment, revealing a cluster of guests looking out of place amongst all this splendour. The skraylings. Only Kiiren in his azure silk robe seemed at ease; his companions, a handful of elders in patterned tunics and loose breeches, stood with folded arms, eyeing the humans uncertainly. None of the skraylings wore masks, though with their tattooed faces they might as well have been. Mal paused on the edge of the space surrounding the skraylings and bowed. Kiiren bowed back, but did not make a move to speak. Mal wondered if the ruling still held, that no one was permitted to speak to them, and if so, why they had been invited. The Venetians' approach to diplomacy was most perplexing.

He continued on his way, stopping now and again to exchange a few sentences with guests whom he thought he recognised from Olivia's house. At last he spotted the courtesan on the arm of a well-dressed man. Venier. The question was, how to get her alone?

"Signore Catalin, isn't it?" Venier said, leading Olivia towards him. "I thought I recognised you by your height. Perhaps you would be so kind as to look after my lovely companion for a short while? I have a mind to talk business with Dandolo, and I do not like to bore a lady."

"Of course, *signore*."

Mal bowed and held out his arm, paying more attention to Venier's departure than to Olivia. That had been a little too easy.

"Poor Lorenzo," Olivia said, her laugh muffled slightly by her full-face mask. "He really is too easy to manipulate."

"You wanted to get me alone?"

"What do you think?"

He could hear the wicked smile in her voice, even if he could not see it, and wondered if she had noticed he wasn't wearing his earring.

They discussed music for a while, then Olivia showed him round the room pointing out the more interesting paintings.

"This whole chamber was ravaged by fire, some twenty years ago," Olivia said. "Of course it was restored to even greater splendour than before, as you can see. Nothing but the finest artists in Italy for our greatest palazzo."

Mal nodded politely. He had never been terribly interested in painting, and it seemed to him that coating the interior of a building with canvas and thick layers of oil paint was just asking to have it burned down.

They were just approaching the far wall with its enormous frieze representing Paradise, when a murmur ran through the assembled guests. Fireworks. This was his chance. He took Olivia aside as the guests began to assemble around the windows overlooking the square.

"Let us leave them to their tawdry spectacles," he murmured. "Tell me more about the palace. You must have been here many times over the centuries."

She led him in the opposite direction to the crowd, through the antechamber and down the stair onto the gallery overlooking the courtyard.

"What is there to tell?" Olivia said, taking off her mask. "You have already visited the dark heart of the Venetian Republic."

Mal pushed his own mask onto the top of his head and took her in his arms. "There is only one heart I care for."

He brushed a stray curl back from her brow and kissed her. On the far side of the building, the first of the fireworks began to fizz and whine, and the crowds breathed out a great sigh of admiration. Now.

He closed his eyes, letting himself sink into that waking dream he had first experienced in the skrayling pavilion back in Southwark. The gilded splendour of the palace gave way to the twilit realm of the dreamworld, the woman in his arms at once translucent, made of violet light, and yet more real than ever. He looked over her shoulder into the darkness where Sandy was waiting. Should be waiting.

"My love?" Her voice was more hesitant now. She drew back, staring at him in panic. Silver light flashed overhead, then expanded into the mouth of a tunnel, green and gold like a tree-lined lane in summer.

"I'm sorry," he whispered, and taking hold of her wrists pulled her into the tunnel.

"No!" She writhed in his grasp, spat curses.

Shadows stirred In the darkness, circling. Mal hesitated and Olivia pulled one wrist from his grasp, pivoting away. He seized her elbow with his free hand, and pulled her across the slippery black grass, towards the waiting figure of Sandy. Olivia – Ilianwe – looked from one to the other.

"Two of you?" she whispered.

"We are Erishen," Sandy said, "of Shajiilrekhurrnasheth. By the law of our people we command you to submit to the authority of the elders."

She only laughed. "You are not my clan-fathers, you cannot command me. Abominations!"

"If you will not surrender, you leave us no choice." Mal gestured towards the far end of the tunnel. "Come with us, and we will return to your clan, to be reborn in our true form. A ship awaits us–"

"You think they will give me the choice?" She backed away, shaking her head. "They will throw me in the ocean to die rather than risk me returning to spread dissent."

"No."

"You are young, you do not know what they are like."

He hesitated. Images formed around them, stern figures pointing at Ilianwe in condemnation. Was this some illusion she was conjuring to sway him, or Erishen's own memories? Sandy pushed him aside and took hold of her.

"She lies," he said. "Come."

Mal let go, and watched the two of them shrink into the distance as the tunnel began to narrow and close. Time to make his own departure. He turned, only to find his way blocked by devourers. Their coal-black hides made them near-invisible in the darkness, so that they could only be seen when they moved. There had to be nearly a dozen of them.

From somewhere behind him, Ilianwe's voice rang out, faint but clear.

"Kill him."

Mal tried to summon the obsidian blade, but his hand remained frustratingly empty. As the creatures began to close in, he made a desperate dive for the hollow where all his dreamwalks began–

–And woke on the cold stone floor of the gallery with a start. The fireworks still popped and whined and lit the clouds with their man-made lightning, but the shrieks of awe had turned to screams of terror. Looking down into the courtyard, Mal saw bodies lying sprawled on the ground in pools of dark blood. Sweet Jesu, what had he done? He raced towards the staircase and followed the trail of destruction out into the night.

CHAPTER XXXII

St Mark's Square was as crowded as the palace, and the fair was still in full swing. Coby slipped through the shadows, trying to find a place to relieve herself in private. It was a good excuse to avoid the fireworks, but she had better be back before they finished, just in case Mal needed her.

For once she wished she was wearing women's clothes. At least that way she could use whatever facilities were provided for the noblewomen, or even squat in an alley without baring her nethers. Venetian men, on the other hand, pissed in the street wherever they pleased, including against the pillars outside the palace. It was all very irksome. She gritted her teeth and headed towards the basilica.

Around her, the citizens of the republic laughed and sang and ate, but there was surprisingly little drinking. Even so, or perhaps because of their normally abstemious habits, many of the faces were flushed, their owners unsteady on their feet and as lecherous as alley cats. Coby had her arse pinched more than once before she had gone ten yards, and one man had even groped her groin as she squeezed past a group of people watching a conjuror. Thankfully she was wearing a soft fake prick in her breeches, not the hard roll of lock-picks, but the man still leered at her, making what was presumably a lewd invitation in the local dialect. She smiled politely, not wanting to start a fight, and moved on.

Just beyond the mouth of the Mercerie an alley opened into darkness; empty, at least for the moment. She hurried down and ducked into a doorway, fumbling with the buttons on her breeches. Then she heard the screams, and nearly lost control of her bladder altogether. *What in Heaven...?* Rebuttoning her fly, she drew her knife and padded towards the alley mouth.

A mass of people surged down the narrow street like water along a storm drain, women screaming and men white-faced with terror. Something loped along beyond them, bigger than a wolfhound and moving with a sinuous grace. The screaming crowd passed the alley mouth. Coby pressed against the wall, her heart pounding. The high walls seemed to close in around her, like a nightmare, and she caught a glimpse of a wet maw with too many teeth and dead white eyes like a baked trout, then the creature was past her, spreading pandemonium in its wake. Two others followed, until the night was a swirling kaleidoscope of screams and the air thick with the scent of fresh blood.

Coby peered out of the alley, but her feet would not move. When she saw Mal heading towards her, she felt dizzy with mingled relief and panic. She stepped out of the alley mouth, and Mal stumbled to a halt.

"What are you doing here?"

"No time for that." She gestured back to the square. "There are creatures–"

"Devourers. I know. I let them out."

"What?"

"It was an accident." He manoeuvred past her; getting between her and the devourers, she noticed.

"So what do we do?"

"We find my brother."

"Sandy?"

"Charles."

Erishen staggered backwards, holding the woman by both arms. Skraylings surrounded them, iron shackles at the ready. Ilianwe screamed in fury as the manacles closed around her wrists, then collapsed to her knees to the floor.

"You are certain this is the Lost One?" Hennaq said, eyeing her doubtfully.

"Yes, certain," Erishen replied. "I saw her spirit-self and it is quite distinctive."

Hennaq's eyes narrowed. "If you are lying to me–"

"It is no lie. Ask her."

The captain cleared his throat. "Who are you?" Ilianwe merely stared into space. Hennaq looked at Erishen. "Well? Is she deaf or mute, or merely some poor human, ignorant of our business?"

"I suppose she has not spoken Vinlandic in many lifetimes, and in any case all tongues change with time." He crouched down and addressed Ilianwe in the ancient tongue. "Tell the captain your name."

"Ilianwe," she said, in tones befitting a queen. "Child of Maranë, of the Fourth City."

Erishen translated for the captain's benefit.

"Hennaq-tuur!" One of the sailors burst through the cabin door. "Come see, Hennaq-tuur, there is–" He shrugged helplessly.

Erishen followed Hennaq out onto the deck. The crowds of merrymakers on the quayside were no longer laughing and singing; they were dashing to and fro, screaming, and some flung themselves into the water as if desperate to escape.

"Human trouble," Hennaq said with a snort. "Nothing to bother us. But perhaps you would prefer to stay aboard for a while, Erishen-tuur, until peace returns?"

"No." Erishen felt the humans' unease. That blind terror was all too familiar. *Hrrith*. "No, I must go ashore now."

Hennaq bowed his acquiescence and signalled for the boat to be lowered. Erishen clambered down into it and was soon rowing himself back towards the palace. If the *hrrith* had managed to escape, they would slaughter everyone in their path, just as Charles had described. And Kiiren was right in the middle of it.

It felt like an eternity until the little boat's prow bumped against the mooring posts, an eternity in the Christians' Hell, all flickering torchlight and screams of terror. Erishen leapt ashore and began pushing his way through the crowd towards the nearest entrance to the palace. Two guards, their faces pale as porridge, barred his way. Beyond them he could see bodies strewn across the courtyard, the gruesome details of their fates intermittently revealed by the light of dying fireworks. He watched for any sign of *hrrith* lurking in the shadows of the outer cloister, but they would have fled the fireworks as blindly as their victims fled the *hrrith*.

Erishen closed his eyes and reached out with his mind. The dark plains were knee-deep in a swirling golden mist, exuded by the citizens' panicking minds as rationality gave way to nightmare terror. He waded through it, looking for Kiiren, and found his *amayi* at last, a pale solid presence amongst the chaos. He lived, then. Erishen opened his eyes, smiled at the two guards and punched them both in the stomach before they could react. With a murmured apology he strode past them into the palace.

"You must have some idea of what these creatures are and how to stop them," Mal said, pacing back and forth across the worn floorboards.

Charles glared up at them. He was seated on a rickety stool in the middle of the gambling house, fenced in by Ned and Parrish. The other patrons had fled into the night, and the owner had barricaded himself in the upstairs room. Coby was keeping watch on the street through one of the shutters.

"And why should I tell you?" Charles asked.

"Would you rather let these creatures have the run of the city?"

"No."

"So help us. You seemed very keen on a reconciliation yesterday. Brother."

"Aye, well, that were yesterday, before you let all Hell loose. You and your skrayling friends." Charles spat on the floor, narrowly missing Ned's foot. "Fuck the lot of 'em."

Mal hauled him upright by the front of his doublet. "Tell me what you know, or do I have to beat it out of you?"

"Why, little brother, you've grown balls since I last saw you."

Mal slapped him backhanded across the mouth. Charles raised a hand to his cut lip.

"Tell me," Mal said again.

"We gleaned some intelligence," Charles said at last. "But never enough. These creatures are fast, strong and tireless, and as cunning as a den of foxes."

"Sandy said you tracked them into the hills, back home. For how long?"

"Days, sometimes. Once, we found one... it had been roaming the hills for weeks, judging by the trail of dead sheep."

"It won't be sheep that get killed here."

"I know that."

"Then help us," Coby said, turning away from the window. "If not for our sakes, then for the sake of your friends and neighbours, and all the good Christian folk of Venice."

She glared at Mal, who reluctantly let Charles go.

"What business is it of yours, anyway?" Charles asked. "The Doge has soldiers, intelligencers, the machinery of an entire state at his disposal; let him deal with it."

Mal shook his head. "The Venetians have no idea what they're up against. You're the only man in the city who has ever faced one of these creatures, so…"

He left the threat hanging, and Charles reacted just as he'd hoped.

"Christ, no! Please, brother, you wouldn't hand me over to the Ten, would you?" He fell off the stool onto his knees and grovelled at Mal's feet. "You don't know what they do to traitors. Please…"

"Get up." Mal turned away in disgust, adding in a low voice, "I know exactly what they do."

Coby caught his eye and looked away, her features taut with sympathy. Mal turned back to his brother, who had ceased his grovelling but remained on his knees, shoulders slumped in defeat.

"Help me to clear up this mess," Mal said, "and we will both earn the Doge's gratitude. Perhaps even a reward."

Charles' head jerked up, and an avaricious smile spread across his features. "How many of the monsters did you say there were?"

"A good dozen."

"Christ's balls." Charles made the sign of the cross. "It'll take more than you four to kill that many. A lot more."

"Four is all we have," Mal replied. "Or should I say five?"

Charles turned pale. "No. You can't get me to face those things again." He raised a hand to clutch his side, as if his old wound had reopened.

"And you call me a coward. So, four. Mayhap with the aid of your knowledge it will be enough."

"Do we have to fight them?" Ned asked. "This city is full of churches and shrines. Perhaps we can find a priest, banish them back to Hell where they belong."

"They aren't demons," Charles said. "Not really. I don't know what they are. God knows they're as unholy as anything I can imagine, and yet…"

"Perhaps they answer to the gods or devils of the skraylings," Parrish said.

"They don't have any, as far as I've heard," Coby said. "Did you see any temples, sir, when you were in the skrayling compound?"

Mal shook his head. "I don't know what the skraylings believe in, but it's not gods or devils."

"In any case," Parrish said, "we are not wholly friendless. Surely the skraylings will help, if we can get a message to them?"

"Perhaps. But if Kiiren tells them how this happened, they may wash their hands of us."

"We must at least try," Coby said.

"What about your friend, Chinky-whatever-his-name-is?" Ned put in.

"Cinquedea?" Mal frowned. "I suppose we are allies of a sort, though I would not trust him further than I could throw him."

"You know Cinquedea?" Charles said with a laugh. "Well, well, little brother, you are full of surprises today."

"Oh? You know him?"

"I know of him. Nasty piece of work. They say he's one of the Lacemaker's lieutenants. And no one messes with her."

Mal picked up an abandoned gambling chip and turned it over and over in his fingers.

"We will hold that possibility in reserve," he said. "For now, we need to work out a stratagem for dealing with the devourers. What do you know of them, Charles? What are their habits, their weaknesses?"

"I know little enough," Charles replied. "They have few weaknesses, and their only habit is to kill without mercy."

"You must know something." Mal resisted the urge to slap his brother again.

Charles shrugged. "I only know what I've seen."

"Which is?"

"They don't like daylight. It weakens them, makes them... less real."

"There's no shortage of sunshine here," Ned said.

"But the streets are narrow, and the buildings tall," Coby said. "They may be able to find somewhere to hole up during the day."

"Then we must find these shadowy places and bring light to them."

"How?"

"That's one thing the skraylings are good at," Mal said. "I think we need to send a message to the skrayling merchants, find out if any of them can sell us a barrel or two of lightwater."

"Why lightwater?" Ned asked. "Wouldn't torches do as well?"

"Torches are too dangerous. The last thing we need is to save the city by burning it to the ground." He turned to Coby. "As soon as it's light, you and Parrish go to the skraylings' palazzo."

"What if the Venetians see us?" Gabriel asked.

"I think the Venetians have other things to worry about than someone talking to the skraylings," Mal replied. "Though if you can think of a ruse to get you in there, all the better."

"Sir?" Coby left her station at the window and drew him aside. "Do we even know if Lord Kiiren and the elders survived the attacks?"

Mal shook his head. "That's my other reason for sending you. Please, bring back news of Kiiren... and my brother."

She nodded, and after a moment's hesitation embraced him.

"I won't fail you," she whispered into his chest.

He kissed her hair, wondering what he had done to deserve such loyalty. If they survived the next few hours, he would find a way to make it up to her. Olivia was gone, and he had to deal with the consequences. All of them.

As dawn broke, Coby and Gabriel ventured out of the Turk's Head into a city more deserted than they'd ever seen it. Every window was shuttered, every door closed and bolted. Ranks of gondolas bobbed against their mooring posts, their elaborately carved oarlocks empty.

"Do we go on foot, or find a gondolier?" Coby asked.

"By water would seem the safest," Gabriel replied. "I for one would not willingly risk the city's alleyways this morning, certainly not until it is full light."

Coby could not disagree, but it chafed her to wait. Every minute that passed was a minute later in returning to Master Catlyn with news. It felt like an age until the rising sun burned away the morning mists and the citizens began venturing out of doors again. She pounced upon the first gondolier to set foot on the quay, and promised him twice his usual fee if he would take them via the Grand Canal instead of cutting through San Marco. He was more than happy to do so, and soon they were gliding westwards across the broad sun-dappled waters, safe – or so she hoped – from shadow-lurking monsters.

Closer to the Fondaco dei Sanuti, the silence of the cowed city gave way to an ominous rumble of voices. Dozens of gondolas were moored along the Grand Canal in front of the skraylings' palazzo, and a mob of angry citizens filled the portico, hammering on the bronze doors and shouting what sounded like demands for the skraylings to come out.

"Take the side-canal," Coby told the gondolier. "There's no chance of us getting in past that mob."

The gondolier hauled on his oar, and soon they were slipping down the small canal that formed the southern boundary of the skrayling compound. A narrow *fondamenta* ran along below the palazzo wall, and a few of the more intrepid protestors had made their way to the side entrance, where they were trying unsuccessfully to break the door down. A little further along, the *fondamenta* widened into the street that ran behind the palazzo, and this too was choked with a mob of Venetians, chanting and throwing stones at the windows. Coby caught only a brief glimpse, however, before they were past and heading deep into Santa Croce.

"You want to go back there?" the gondolier asked.

"Yes, but by a roundabout way," Coby said. There was nothing else for it, if they wanted to approach the palazzo unnoticed.

"I'll let you ashore, then." He pointed ahead, to where a small bridge spanned the canal. "Good luck to you, *signori*."

A few moments later the gondola bumped up against the canal bank and they scrambled ashore.

"I suppose the ordinary folk are blaming the skraylings for what happened last night," Gabriel said in a low voice as they hurried through the narrow backstreets of Santa Croce.

"It's hardly surprising," she replied. "The ambassador is finally invited to the Doge's palace after weeks in the city, fireworks go off – possibly even fireworks supplied by the skraylings – and shortly afterwards the city is overrun by slavering hellhounds. If I didn't know–" she lowered her voice to a whisper, "–if I didn't know who was really behind it, I'd suspect them too."

The crowd behind the palazzo were still in full voice, despite the occasional rain of broken glass as a stone hit one of the remaining intact windows. Coby heard many mentions of the word *diaboli*, and much calling on the name of Christ, the Madonna and various saints.

"How are we going to get inside?" Coby said, watching the crowd warily. "All the doors must be barricaded by now."

"If we can't get through the besiegers, we have to get rid of them."

"How?"

"Leave that to me. Give me your purse, and wait here a few minutes. If you see an opportunity to get inside, take it; otherwise just stay here and keep out of trouble."

She watched with a heavy heart as he jogged off down the street. After Mal, Gabriel was the best man to have at your side in a tight spot.

Not all the rioters were actively attacking the palazzo. Many, like herself, were content to observe from a distance. It provided cover, but it also made it impossible to get closer to the building without being noticed. Whatever Gabriel's plan was, it had better be good.

She found an empty doorway on the far side of the street. Either the inhabitants had sensibly locked themselves inside, or they were out here with the rioters; either way, they wouldn't be opening it any time soon. She leaned against the cool stone, trying to look nonchalant instead of terrified. Last time she had been near a mob like this was when the theatre burnt down, and then it was only frightened playgoers fleeing for their lives. This was something entirely different: ferocious and chaotic, like a fire in human form.

Where were the red-coated constables, for that matter? Defending the Doge and council, most likely. No one cared about a few skraylings, particularly if there was even a remote chance they were behind last night's unholy manifestations.

A higher-pitched note threaded through the shouting and was taken up by one voice after another. Screams. Like a swarm of bees the crowd began to turn and move towards Coby and the open street leading towards the Grand Canal. She flattened herself into the doorway, wondering if soldiers had turned up at last, though she had heard no gunfire nor any reason for the screaming. The fury that had been directed at the skraylings was now turned inwards as the fleeing rioters fought one another to get onto the gondolas. A few stragglers halted, weighed up their chances and headed down the street into Santa Croce.

As the last few rioters dispersed, Coby saw what had triggered the panic. Gabriel was staggering down the street, shirt torn and soaked in blood.

"No!" She ran to him, seized his arms, scanning his body for wounds. "Dear God, what happened?"

Gabriel groaned, but when she looked up into his eyes he winked and jerked his head towards the side door of the building.

"Quick," he said. "Before they discover this is all a sham and come back."

"You're not hurt?"

"Pig's blood," he said. "From the market. Now go!"

Coby needed no more prompting. She ran around the side of the palazzo, and sure enough the little *fondamenta* was empty, and the few gondolas that had been moored there were already gone. She knocked on the door, praying that the skraylings had not abandoned it.

"Hello! You in there! Friends! *Ingilanda!* Talk trade, get lightwater aid Kiiren-tuur!"

The garbled mix of English, Tradetalk and Vinlandic had the desired effect, and after a few moments the door opened a crack to reveal a sliver of tattooed face.

"*Ingilanda?*"

"Friends of Kiiren-tuur and Erishen-tuur. Please, let us in. We have to buy lightwater to fight the night-demons–"

The door opened a little further. Impatience getting the better of her, Coby pushed it wide. The skrayling porter goggled at the sight of Gabriel smeared in pig's blood but let them in.

"If you want to get out of this city alive," she told the porter in Tradetalk, "you have to take me to Lord Kiiren. Now."

CHAPTER XXXIII

Mal stood at the window of the Turk's Head, watching the city awake. Could he really ask his friends to lay down their lives to help mend his errors? Did he have a choice? He could hardly face the devourers alone. He slammed the side of his fist against the wall. Cowering here was not going to help. He needed to get out there, track the creatures down...

"Maliverny? There's something I have to tell you, before–" His brother looked around. "Not here, though."

Mal looked at him suspiciously. "What have you done, Charles?"

"Not here." He gestured towards a door in the back wall of the gambling house.

Mal glanced back at Ned and held up his hand in a "stay there" gesture, then followed Charles through the door into what turned out to be a large pantry-cum-buttery, well stocked with barrels of wine and jars of olives, along with stacks of plates, napkins and finger-bowls. Sausages the size of a man's arm hung from the rafters, filling the air with the scent of garlic. Mal's stomach grumbled, demanding breakfast.

"Well, out with it," he said, as soon as the door was shut.

Charles sat down on a barrel and stared at his clasped hands. "I don't expect you to forgive me, little brother–"

"For destroying our family? How can I?"

"Maliverny..." Charles got to his feet, though he still could not meet Mal's eye. "Rushdale Hall were never sold."

"What do you mean? I went there, some fellow named Frogmore has it now–"

"As a tenant. He rents it from me, through our lawyers."

"What? They told me–"

"They told you what they had been instructed to tell you. It was for your own good, yours and Sandy's–"

"I don't believe you. This is some ruse, to try and make peace."

"No, I swear. I had to raise the money to come here somehow, and my credit was hardly the best."

"Why Venice?"

"Because I found out that folk possessed by skraylings had come here long ago."

"You wanted to find Olivia?"

"No. I wanted to find others who'd fought these creatures – and won."

"And did you?"

Charles laughed bitterly. "No such luck. There were plenty of gossip and old stories, but no sign of either the possessed ones or their destroyers. And by the time I'd made certain of it, I were out of money. I could have returned to England in disgrace, but what would that have achieved?"

"You could have reclaimed your heritage," Mal said. "Rushdale Hall is still worth something, surely?"

"I cannot live there, not after everything... and neither should you. It's too dangerous."

"It seemed quiet enough when I visited, three years ago."

"Happen it does. But stay there long enough, and you'll see."

"Why are you telling me all this now?"

"Because neither of us might see tomorrow." He fumbled with the signet ring on his right hand. "Take this to our lawyers, and they'll tell you the truth."

Mal stared down at the heavy gold ring, remembering seeing it on their father's hand.

"Don't think this means I'll forgive you for what you did," he told Charles. "If you had seen Sandy in that place..."

"What's done is done; I'll face my sins when the time comes. God knows the account is long enough."

Ned waited, somewhat impatiently, for the brothers to finish whatever business Charles thought too private for his ears. He'd briefly been tempted to go over to the door and eavesdrop, but on reflection he'd had enough of prying into the Catlyns' business. Instead he took up Hendricks' former station at the window. The city was beginning to stir: a man hurried past, looking nervously at every doorway; a shutter opposite opened briefly and closed again. No one was going outside who didn't have to.

"So, are we going to stand around all morning, twiddling our thumbs?" he asked when Mal emerged from the pantry.

"Not at all. I mean to seek out Cinquedea and call upon whatever aid he and his... family are willing to give."

Charles snorted in derision. "Good luck with that. They say the Ten have been trying to infiltrate the Lacemaker's organisation for years, without success."

"I'm not talking about infiltration, merely an alliance," Mal replied. He scratched his chin. "I don't suppose Cinquedea will be at the Mermaid, not after last night. So where do we start looking?"

"Since you seem to be dead set on this scheme," Charles said, "I will give you one piece of advice. Go to the island of Burano."

"Burano? Ah, yes, that's where most of Venice's lace is made," Mal said.

"It's no idle nickname, 'the blind lacemaker'. The women who follow the craft often lose their sight from working every waking hour, dawn to dusk and then on by candlelight if need be."

"And you think I will find Cinquedea there?"

"I wouldn't be surprised. If there's trouble in Venice, the Lacemaker's boys are likely to retreat to home ground."

Mal thanked his brother and beckoned to Ned. "We'd better go back to Berowne's first. My rapier is there, and I would be reassured to know that our other friends escaped unhurt."

They bade Charles farewell and hurried through the empty streets of Venice. For once Ned had nothing to say. He could rail at Mal for being so besotted with this woman as to bring her wrath down on them all, but what good would that do? He just hoped Gabriel was all right. If anything happened to his darling boy, Mal would really feel his fury.

Mal hammered on the embassy door and shouted their names several times, but even so it took Jameson some minutes to open it. They ducked inside, and Mal ran up to the attic to fetch his weapons.

"Does your master have an old sword I could borrow?" Ned asked the manservant. "We're going back out there, and who knows what we'll have to face."

Jameson hesitated, but at last shuffled off into the depths of the house and returned with an old-fashioned sword, shorter and heavier than a rapier but easier to wield at close quarters. It would do very well. Ned thanked him and strapped the weapon to his hip, feeling at once safer and more conscious of the danger they were going into. A few moments later Mal clattered downstairs, his rapier's scabbard scraping the wall behind him.

"What's the best way to get to Burano?" Mal asked Jameson. "Should we ask to take the gondola?"

The old manservant smiled. "It's a bit far for that, sir. You want a proper boat, like a *caorlina*."

"And where would we find one of those?"

"Try the fish market, sir. Someone may have landed a catch this morning, not having heard of the troubles, and be glad to take you out into the lagoon."

The island of Burano was situated at the end of a small archipelago that jutted out from the mainland into the lagoon. Although lacking a harbour, its situation was such that ships could anchor close to its shore in the safety of the lagoon, and jetties provided mooring spots for smaller boats. The main town on the island lay on the south-east shore, little more than a cluster of white-washed houses along a single street.

Mal breathed a sigh of relief to be on solid ground again, and paused a moment to enjoy the spring sunshine. The city of Venice, with its dark, haunted alleys and terrified citizens, seemed a thousand miles away.

"So, we just wander round the island until we spot your friend?" Ned asked.

"Or until he spots us," Mal replied. "I think the latter more likely. The question is, will he approach us if he does see us?"

"And if he doesn't?"

"Then we keep our eyes and ears open. We're intelligencers, remember? Watching people is what we do."

Along either side of the broad, packed earth thoroughfare stood small whitewashed houses with tiled roofs and shuttered windows whose windowboxes were bright with spring crocus, anemones and cyclamen. Outside every one sat at a group of black-clad women of all ages, from white-haired grandmothers to little ones of five or six, all with pillows on their laps to which were pinned pieces of lace-work in progress. Mal was reminded of a flower garden thick with bumblebees, all hard at work.

"Do you think news has reached here yet?" Ned asked in a low voice. "Everything seems so… normal."

"Do the folk of Kent or Middlesex care about trouble in London? This island must be far safer, even though they are but an hour's boat-ride away."

They found a tavern at last, but it was deserted at this time of day and there was no sign of Cinquedea. After a swift cup of wine they moved on.

"We should be getting back," Ned muttered. "Gabriel will be wondering where we've got to."

"Just a little longer," Mal said. "It's barely noon. We still have the whole afternoon to prepare."

They turned and walked back down the street.

"Don't look now," Mal said in a low voice, "but I think I see the place we're looking for."

"Oh?"

He gestured discreetly towards one of the houses. It was indistinguishable from all the rest, except that one of the old women sitting near the door was unusually broad in the shoulder and the folds of her shawl did not quite conceal a dagger hilt. She appeared to have fallen asleep over her needlework, which looked tiny and fragile in her large, bony hands.

Mal beckoned to Ned, and they crossed the street. As they neared the door the sleeping woman seemingly woke up with a start and fixed them with her dark gaze. *His* dark gaze. Mal's initial suspicions had been correct.

"We are here to see the Lacemaker," Mal told the man. "My name is Maliverny Catlyn, and this is Ned Faulkner. We are friends of Cinquedea."

The man grunted.

"Your weapons," he drawled in the local dialect.

Mal reluctantly handed over his rapier and dagger, and motioned for Ned to do likewise, then they were waved inside. Mal blinked, hoping his eyes would adjust swiftly to the dimness of the interior after the dazzling light outside. After a few moments he could make out an ancient bedstead with faded, moth-eaten hangings, in which lay an old woman wearing a white lace cap and nightgown. Several young women sat on the floor around her, spinning the hair-fine thread used to make the famous Burano lace. Two more men, undisguised, played cards at a table by the window. One of them was Cinquedea. Mal breathed a sigh of relief.

"Who is that?" the old woman asked in a surprisingly steady voice.

She sat up and turned towards them, but did not quite look in their direction. Mal bowed and introduced himself and Ned.

"Is this true, Marco? They are… acquaintances of yours?"

"Yes, grandmama." The Venetian put down his cards. "Signore Catalin, this is my grandmother, Signora Petronilla."

Mal bowed again. "It is an honour to meet you, madam. Your reputation, and that of your family, precede you."

The old woman chuckled, and waved a hand at her young companions, who rose and filed out into the street to continue their work.

"I'm sure it does, young man," Signora Petronilla said. "But what is so important, that you come all this way to seek out my grandson?"

Mal cleared his throat, aware that he was in the presence of ruthless people who would cut him down in a heartbeat. The trick, as with a dangerous dog, was to show no fear. He forced himself to breathe slowly.

"You have heard about last night's trouble, after the *Sensa*?" he began.

"Of course." Cinquedea glanced at his grandmother. "Everyone is saying that the bronze lion of Saint Mark came to life and jumped down from its pillar, slaughtering sinners left and right."

"Not the saint's beast, but something worse," Mal replied. "Demonic creatures, loosed on the city by… by a witch."

Cinquedea crossed himself, and the old lady muttered something under her breath.

"The woman you tried to tell me about?" Cinquedea asked.

"The same."

"Then you have my apologies for not believing you. Still, what is that to do with us? Can these creatures swim?"

"I don't think so."

"The city is full of churches and priests," Signora Petronilla said. "Such evil cannot survive there long."

Cinquedea leaned over and muttered something in his grandmother's ear.

"Really? A bishop?" She shook her head and tutted. "Still, my men are not soldiers. Why should I throw their lives away?"

"I'm not asking for aid of that kind," Mal said. "I need knowledge. The creatures are most likely holed up somewhere, awaiting nightfall; my friends and I can lay siege to their lair and destroy any that emerge, but the city is too large to search before sunset. I need to know where to look."

"And that is all you need?"

"One more thing. We need as many clear glass flasks and bottles as you can lay your hands on."

"Then you have come to the right place. Marco, speak to your uncle about getting Signore Catalin the things he needs. You, my boy–" she beckoned to Mal "–sit down and tell me everything."

• • • •

They returned to the embassy later that afternoon to find Coby and Parrish waiting for them in the storeroom. A couple of dozen squat terracotta jars waited by the gondola dock, their stoppers sealed with wax.

"Lightwater?" Mal asked.

Coby grinned. "Every last demijohn in the skraylings' possession, almost."

"Almost?"

"We let them keep a couple for their own defence."

"Do you know where the devourers are?" Parrish asked.

"I believe so. According to Signora Petronilla's informants, they were last seen at the eastern end of the Dorsoduro district, just before sunrise. Since there's no way to leave except to double back or take a boat, it seems likely that they found a bolt-hole in some untenanted building or perhaps even a church."

"Even so, how do we find them?" Coby said.

"Follow the trail of bodies," Ned said with a ghoulish grin.

Coby pulled a face.

"Ned has a point," Mal said. "These creatures may be cunning, but they have made no attempt to hide their trail. Perhaps they are unfamiliar with cities; their native land, if you can call it that, is open moor. That is likely why they survived so long in the Peaklands."

"When do we make our move?" Parrish asked. "We surely want to have them surrounded well before sunset."

"I have arranged to meet Cinquedea in Campo San Vio at 5 o'clock."

"Will that give us enough time?"

Mal looked round at their worried faces. "It has to."

The square was already emptying by the time they arrived. Open to the water on two sides, it felt exposed to view but nonetheless safer than the suffocating closeness of most Venetian streets. Coby, Ned and Gabriel waited in a nervous huddle whilst Mal spoke to Cinquedea. The Lacemaker's grandson had brought the promised glass bottles, most of which had been rigged up with string handles around the necks. A few passers-by paused to stare at them as they unloaded the crates onto the *fondamenta*, but most were too busy hurrying home before it got dark.

"I hope to God Mal knows what he's doing," Ned muttered. "You should have seen those scars on his brother's body. Looked like a lion had tried to tear him in two."

"You're not helping," Coby said. Her guts felt like they were trying to find a way out of her belly by themselves.

Gabriel put his arms round both their shoulders and kissed each of them on the temple.

"We survived everything the Huntsmen and their lackeys threw at us, we'll survive this," he said.

"Aye, and this time we're fighting on the Huntsmen's side," Mal said, striding over. "Come. One of Cinquedea's gang thinks he knows where the devourers are."

He led them eastwards, through a dog-leg alley and over a bridge into a little square hemmed in by a canal on the nearest side and buildings on the other three. Ahead and to the right, small houses stood close-shuttered and silent, crosses hastily daubed on their doors for protection. To the left, blocking the view of the Grand Canal, stood a palazzo about twice the size of Berowne's house, with a walled garden in front. A vine had grown up the palazzo façade, reaching for the sunlight, and now half-covered the row of arched windows that marked the *piano nobile*.

"Ca' Dario," Mal said. "It used to be rented out to the Turkish ambassador, but it fell into disuse owing to the war between Venice and the Empire. No one's lived there in a generation."

"And you think they're in there?" Coby stared up at the building, imagining dead eyes staring back at her from the leaf-framed darkness.

"The gate is rusted up," Gabriel said. "Doesn't look like it's been opened in years."

"They wouldn't go in that way. See, along the wall?"

At the far end of the wall where it turned a corner to run alongside the canal, some of the stone coping was missing, and on either side of the gap fresh white score-marks stood out like wounds. The marks of enormous claws.

Several of Cinquedea's men had joined them in the square. Two started filling empty bottles with lightwater, and the rest went from house to house with these makeshift lanterns, offering them to any householder who dared to answer their knock, and hanging them up outside the doors and windows that remained shut. Soon the little square was as brightly lit as the skrayling compound, though the blue and yellow lanterns combined to cast an eerie underwater light on the façade of the palazzo.

Cinquedea came over and bowed to Mal. "We have fulfilled our side of the bargain, and more. Now, if you will excuse us, we have to return to our families, before..."

He jerked his head towards the darkened building.

"I understand," Mal said. "Thank you."

Cinquedea snorted. "You can thank me in the morning. Good luck, and may the saints watch over you this night."

He beckoned to his men, and they departed without a backward glance. Coby swallowed past the lump in her throat. They were alone now, with a dozen deadly creatures just waiting to come out and slaughter them all.

"Charles and I will go inside," Mal said. "Ned: you, Hendricks and Parrish will wait here and pick off any that try to flee back into the city."

"No!" Coby grabbed his sleeve. "You can't, not just two of you. It's too dangerous."

He took her in his arms. "This is my fault, love. I have to mend it."

He kissed her forehead, and she swallowed against the tears pricking her eyes. She clung to him for a long moment, not wanting it to end.

"One last thing," he said. "Wear this for me."

He held out Sandy's old spirit-guard.

"No, I cannot–"

"Please. I don't know what those creatures can do in this world, but you need this protection more than I." He looped the necklace behind her head and fastened the catch. "Be sure to wear it under your shirt, next to your skin."

She nodded, quite unable to speak. He bent and kissed her lips, and she melted into the embrace, cursing herself for all the times she had pushed him away. At last he withdrew, and wiped her tears away with a rough thumb.

"Go then," she whispered. "And may God be with you."

"And with thee."

CHAPTER XXXIV

Once Coby had retreated to a safe distance Mal prepared to enter the palazzo. He checked both his blades, and then removed his earring and stowed it in his pocket. Tonight he would need all his faculties, more than he needed the lodestone's protection. At least if the devourers ate his soul he would be spared the torments of Hell. A bitter laugh escaped his lips.

"What's so funny?" Ned asked.

Mal shook his head. "Give us a boost over the wall, will you?"

Ned crouched and laced his hands together.

"Just like old times," he said with a grin.

Mal vaulted onto the coping, sitting astride the wall, and Ned handed him up a lightwater lantern. What had once been an elegant paved courtyard surrounded by evergreen shrubs was now waist deep in weeds, its topiary outgrown and curtained in tangles of wild rose and woodbine. He scanned the shadows for movement. Nothing, not even a pigeon or rat disturbed by the light. He transferred the lantern to his left hand, swung his other leg over the wall and jumped down. Still nothing. He drew his rapier, slow and silent, then glanced back through the gate. Charles stood frozen, his face pale as the stucco'd wall.

"Art craven, brother?" Mal said quietly.

Charles pulled a face. "Don't teach thy grandame to suck eggs. I were hunting these creatures before you were breeched."

"Then come on over. And be quick about it."

Two hands appeared on the stone coping, then Charles hauled himself over the wall to land with a crunch on a frost-shattered flowerpot.

"Jesu–!"

"Quiet!" Mal glared at him. "Or would you fight them all at once?"

His brother gave him a sour look and drew his own sword. "After you."

Mal picked his way through the weeds and toppled statuary towards the palazzo entrance.

"Door's shut," Charles whispered. "Perhaps they climbed up the vine and went in through a window."

Mal followed his gaze.

"I don't think so. Take another look at the door. No–" he barred Charles' way with an arm. "Don't go any closer. Just look."

"It's slightly askew," his brother said. "And there are scrapes along one edge."

"Torn off its hinges by clawed hands," Mal said, "and put clumsily back in place to keep out the light. It'll be a bastard to open quietly."

"It's the only way in. Unless you fancy climbing that vine?"

"I think the time for stealth is over. Let's announce ourselves, shall we?"

He strode up to the door of the palazzo, planted one foot against it and pushed. The great bronze slab teetered for a moment then fell edgeways onto the marble floor with a deafening crunch. He tensed, blade at the ready, half-expecting the creatures to charge them, but no sound came from the palazzo except the dying echoes of the door's fall.

"They won't approach the light unless cornered," Charles said in a low voice. "Be careful."

Mal clambered over the fallen door, lantern held high. The swaying light reflected off polished marble surfaces, trailing dark shadows in its wake. Directly ahead an arched doorway gave access to the *piano terreno,* shrouded in darkness. To their left a flight of marble steps led up to the *piano nobile,* its treads half hidden by a thick layer of plaster debris and dead leaves. No tracks disturbed the carpet of decay. So, the devourers were down here. Mere feet away, perhaps. He took a deep breath and advanced through the archway.

The unearthly skrayling light gleamed on pale marble pillars veined with dark reddish brown like dried blood. Broken crates and barrels littered the store-room floor, but enough remained intact to hide a score of devourers. Mal held up his lantern, keeping it well out of his eye line. A dark smear of blood and fur halfway up a pillar suggested he wouldn't have to worry about rats.

"There!" Charles leant around him, pointing with his blade.

"Where? I saw nothing."

"A movement, I swear."

"It was probably just your lantern. Hold it by the neck, like this. It won't burn."

He advanced into the storeroom, yard by yard, the scraping of grit under the soles of his boots barely audible over the gentle lap of the canal outside. He drew in an unsteady breath and forced himself to loosen his grip on the rapier's hilt. Sweat trickled down his back and yet he felt cold as death, as if the damp air were leaching the life from his bones. Every movement became an effort, like wading through honey...

"Look sharp, lad!" His brother's voice cut through the fog in his head.

Mal tried to shake off his lethargy. They were here all right, their nightmare miasma bending nature to its will, making everything seem unreal. All the shadows in the room were moving now, and not just because of their lanterns. He tried to count the moving shapes but his eyes slid off them as if not wanting to see. Six? Eight? A dozen? It didn't really matter, as long as they didn't leave here alive.

"Hold the doorway," he called over his shoulder. "I'll try to flush them out of hiding."

He flung his left arm in a wide arc, sending glowing droplets of lightwater splashing across the wall. A devourer shrieked as if scalded and ran past Mal in a sooty blur. He heard Charles scream, though whether in pain or fury, he couldn't tell.

"Come on, then," Mal growled at the shadows, holding up the lantern, "who wants some?"

It was an empty threat; he could not spare much more and have enough light left for his own protection. He circled round the broken wreck of a gondola and lunged towards the darkness pooling inside its black-painted cabin. A shriek split the air as the point of the rapier penetrated something brittle, like a dried-up corpse. Maggots flowed out of the gondola cabin in a pale stream, spilling around his feet. Cursing, Mal stamped on a few before backing off. They squelched underfoot and disappeared.

"One down, methinks!" he called back to Charles.

"Two!" Charles replied. "But another got past me."

Coby crouched at the foot of the bridge steps, staring at the palazzo. She heard shouting from inside, and her stomach flipped over. It took all her self-control not to climb over the wall and join the fray, but she knew Mal was relying on her to hold the line. She glanced briefly towards Ned and Gabriel, who crouched shoulder to shoulder on the other side of the steps. Neither of them was a fighter, any more than she was. What use were any of them against demons as strong and deadly as lions?

A moment later a dark shape bounded across the garden and leapt up onto the wall. It hesitated for a moment in the glare of the lanterns. Coby raised her pistol and pulled the trigger.

For a horrible moment she thought the creature would move before the gunpowder caught, but then the pistol kicked in her hands and the devourer flew backwards off the wall as if punched. Coby blinked through the smoke, her ears ringing. Was it dead?

She laid the first pistol at her feet then drew the second. Not a moment too soon. The devourer reappeared on top of the wall. She cocked the pistol and fired. A thump and rattle of claws as the creature hit the cobbles – then it sprang up and bounded across the square, its neck snaking as it sought her out. She forced herself to stare at the ground. *It won't attack unless you look at it.* She didn't know how she knew this, but it felt right and true. Sweat prickled in her armpits and her heart beat so hard she thought it would burst from her ribs. Slowly she put the pistol on the ground next to its mate and reached for her dagger.

A flash of movement out of the corner of her eye, almost too fast to see. Unable to help herself she looked up. The devourer swiped at her with claws the size of meathooks. She rolled sideways, crying out with pain as a lock of hair was torn from her scalp, but came up in a fighting crouch, dagger in hand. The devourer gathered itself for a pounce. Too late. Ned ran up behind it and hacked at its neck with his sword. The heavy blade caught in the creature's flesh and the two figures struggled for a moment.

Ned tore his blade free and struck again, severing the devourer's head this time. Dark blood splashed across the cobbles and disappeared with a hiss like water on hot iron. The creature collapsed in a heap only inches from Coby and began to dissolve. She scuttled backwards up the steps as the pool of black fluid spread towards her, but it seeped away through the stones and was gone. Ned helped her to her feet.

"Thank you!" she gasped.

Ned inclined his head in acknowledgement and retreated up the steps to command the high ground. Coby went back to pick up her pistols, shaking her head in despair. If bullets were so little use against the devourers, what was she to defend herself with next time?

Mal spitted another devourer on his rapier and withdrew the blade as the creature collapsed into a tarry heap on the floor. He was breathing heavily now, and the sword felt like lead in his hand – no, that was just the illusion the devourers were trying to force upon him. He closed his eyes for a moment and brought to mind the hollow in the hills, the way Olivia had taught him, but the image would not come. Had the devourers destroyed it when they had come through? He opened his eyes again. If magic would not avail him, he must force his flesh to obey his own will and not theirs.

There was no time to put his earring back in. Blood and iron, that would break the spell just as easily. Gritting his teeth he swiped his left little finger down the rapier's blade, feeling metal grate on bone. The pain brought him wide awake. With an incoherent shout of fury he charged the thickest knot of shadows and the devourers fled from the cold light and colder steel. One, trapped between a crate and the far wall, folded in on itself until it was no bigger than a cat. Mal advanced on it, grinning, but as he prepared to lunge the creature flew up, claws slashing at his face. Mal raised the lantern, splashing them both with the glowing fluid, but the devourer was already gone. Blood streamed down into his left eye where one of its claws had opened a gash from eyebrow to scalp. Cursing, Mal wiped the blood away and turned to pursue his attacker.

A cry rent the air. Charles had dropped his sword and was now grappling with something that looked like an emaciated horse with the spiny carapace and eyestalks of a crab. Mal sprinted across the storeroom – too late. The creature's jaws snapped around Charles' throat and blood fountained over them both.

"No!"

Mal slid his rapier under the carapace, twisting the blade as he went. The creature squealed like a boiling lobster and released its prey, then dissolved into acrid smoke. Coughing, Mal knelt and tried to stem the blood flowing from his brother's neck.

Charles' eyes fluttered open, and his lips moved silently. Mal hushed him, swallowing past the lump in his own throat, but he knew it was hopeless. His hands were already slick with warm blood, and if he stayed here, another devourer might finish them both off.

"I have to go," he said. "Sleep well, brother."

Charles nodded and closed his eyes again. Mal wiped his bloody hands on his doublet, picked up his sword and lantern and got to his feet.

"Come on then, you craven skulking night-spawn! What are you waiting for?"

Only silence greeted him. After a moment he realised that the oppressive miasma was gone too. Four dead, but at least one had slipped past them in the chaos, probably more. He backed around towards the archway leading to the staircase. A clear trail now led through the debris, revealing cracked and worn treads, but the stairs looked sound enough. Well, there was only one way to find out. With a prayer to Saint Michael he made his way cautiously up to the *piano nobile*.

• • • •

Ned stood at the top of the bridge steps, watching for Mal to come out of the palazzo. He had to come out. They hadn't come all this way to die at the hands of some foreign witch's hell-spawn. He edged a little closer to Gabriel, wishing his lover had stayed behind at the embassy and yet glad he had not.

A scream, faint but all too human. Hendricks leapt to her feet and ran across the square to the palazzo gate.

"Come back, you stupid wench!" Ned shouted after her.

"Let her be," Gabriel said softly. "Would you hold back if it was me in there?"

"No, but – Christ's balls!"

Another devourer leapt over the wall, landing light as a cat halfway across the square. A second followed, and they flowed around one another in an eye-deceiving blur of smoky black, snaking across the open space towards the bridge.

Ned advanced down the steps, hefting his sword. "Come on then. Which of you's first, eh?"

"Don't be an idiot, Ned! Get back up here!"

Ned descended the last step into the square. Out of the corner of his eye he saw Gabriel leap down to stand beside him.

"What are you doing? Get behind me."

Instead Gabriel stepped forward, his cudgel held to one side as if about to discard it.

"Leave him alone," Gabriel said softly. "It's me you want."

"No!"

He dashed forward, putting himself between Gabriel and the devourers. The dark shapes swerved in opposite directions, curving round to try and slip past them and over the bridge. Standing shoulder-to-shoulder with his lover, Ned braced himself to stop the nearest one. The creature dodged his blade, claws scrabbling for purchase on the canal bank.

"Can't swim, eh?" Ned kicked it in the side of the jaw and followed up his attack with a roundhouse swing of the sword. More by luck than skill he severed a leg and it toppled into the water, squawking.

He turned to see if Gabriel need help with his own attacker, and something hit him square in the chest. A devourer. Ned fell backwards, winded. Teeth like daggers of ice closed around his right wrist and he dropped the sword with a scream.

"Ned!"

Gabriel's iron-shod cudgel smashed into the creature's eyeball, through its skull and out the other side. The cruel teeth withdrew as the devourer faded into nothingness, but Ned's arm still burned as if branded. Gabriel's pale face loomed over him.

"Ned? Ned? Don't die on me..."

Then he was falling into blissful oblivion, far from all pain.

Coby huddled against the palazzo wall, trying not to puke at the memory of that... thing crunching Ned's wrist like a dog with a new bone. She had failed to stop the demons and now her friends were suffering. Lead bullets were useless – but what about iron ones? She put down her guns and reached behind her neck, managing to unfasten the necklace on the third attempt. If lodestone protected against evil spirits, perhaps it would also kill them.

She swabbed out the still-warm barrel of each pistol and gingerly poured in a measure of black powder, then cut the waxed thread of the necklace and slid off two of the beads. The dark metal spheres were a bit smaller than her usual shot, but they had to be better than nothing. She shoved the rest of the necklace into her pocket and finished loading and priming the pistols. The next devourer to emerge from the palazzo would not be so lucky as the last.

• • • •

Mal ran through the main chambers of the *piano nobile*, but there was no sign of the devourers. Had they really killed them all? He leaned out of the window, hoping to get a good view of the square, and stopped, heart in mouth. Someone lay by the bridge steps, a pale-haired figure crouching over him... Blessed Lady, one down already? He ran back down the stairs and out into the garden.

"Master Catlyn, look out! Above you!"

Mal looked up, just in time to see a dark shape launch itself from the uppermost floor. It floated to the ground as if underwater, landing light as thistledown about halfway between Mal and the garden wall.

"Duck!" Coby shouted at him.

A moment later a pistol snapped and a bullet whistled overhead, far too close for comfort. The creature, undaunted, loped towards the wall. Mal ran after it, but as it leapt onto the coping a second pistol shot rang out around the square and the creature screamed and dissolved into smoke.

"Got it!"

Coby grinned at him through the gate. Her face was pale and smeared with grime, but she had never looked so beautiful to him.

"You're hurt," she said as he clambered awkwardly up the gate and dropped down beside her.

"Just a scratch. Looks worse than it is. At least I got out alive."

"Charles?"

Mal shook his head. "What about the... Sweet Jesu! Ned!"

Parrish was helping a white-faced Ned to his feet. Blood dripped onto the cobbles from Ned's mangled right arm, splinters of bones poking out of the raw mess. Mal had seen a few injuries like that on the battlefield, and there was only one treatment.

"Get him out of here," Mal called out to Gabriel. "Find Cinquedea, find a surgeon to–"

"I know," Parrish said quietly. He turned back to Ned, murmuring to him like a mother with her child, and together they limped up the steps of the bridge.

"Is that all of them?" Coby asked, looking up from reloading her pistols.

"We killed four inside, and yours makes five."

"Eight, then. Ned accounted for two, then Gabriel finished the one that..." She grimaced.

"We don't know for sure how many there were to begin with, though," he said, scanning the building. "There could still be some left, hiding in the shadows. The only way to be certain is to wait. If none emerge between now and dawn..."

"There is another way," a voice said behind them.

Mal looked round. "Sandy!"

"We came as fast as we could," his brother said.

"We?"

"Kiiren is here as well. He is fetching a sleeping draught for Ned."

"Lucky Ned." Mal pulled a face. "You said something about there being another way. You know how to destroy these creatures?"

"You already know that part. No, I meant that I can find out if there are any left here."

"How?"

"They cast shadows in the dreamworld, just as we cast light."

"Is there anything I can do to help?" *Assuming I still can.*

Sandy sat down with his back to the wall. "I need you to protect my earthly body; I cannot see into both places at once."

"Nothing will get past me, I swear."

Sandy closed his eyes, and within a few moments his

eyelids began to twitch as if he were asleep and dreaming. Mal peered through the gate, trying to ignore the returning ache in his shoulders. As soon as this was over, he would press Kiiren for another draught of that foul-tasting potion. Or get drunk. He hefted his rapier, and hissed through clenched teeth at the sudden movement. *Perhaps both.*

All was still within at first, then he heard a dry rattle, as of clawed feet on stone. Shadows pooled in the doorway. At least two of the beasts, perhaps three, it was impossible to tell. Mal hefted his rapier and stepped closer to Sandy. Coby cocked her pistol.

Two of the creatures rushed them in a smoky blur. One was felled by a pistol shot halfway across the garden, but the other reached the wall before Coby could fire again. Out of the corner of his eye Mal saw the third leap the wall in a single bound, heading for the bridge, but he had no time to pay it any further mind. A triangular head snaked down at him, jaws clashing, too close for blade-work. Mal turned his wrist and slammed the pommel of his rapier into the creature's snout. It hissed and snapped at him, dead-white eyes rolling in their sockets. He drew his dagger and thrust upwards into its soft under-jaw until the steel blade grated on the inside of its brainpan. The creature gave an inhuman scream and was gone. But the scream continued.

"*Amayiii!*"

Sandy pushed past him, heading for the bridge.

"Sandy, no!" Mal dashed after him. "Sandy!"

Two figures staggered from the street onto the bridge, locked in a deadly embrace: Kiiren with fists raised as though wielding a garrotte, and a nightmare beast, writhing in agony and clawing at its prey-turned-killer. Before anyone could reach them it had slashed open Kiiren's belly, even as it breathed its last and was gone. Kiiren's spirit-guard snapped between his hands, scattering jade and lodestone beads down the steps into the square.

Mal stumbled to a halt, all will seeming to drain from his limbs. Sandy ran up the steps and held his dying lover in his arms, crooning in the ancient tongue of the skraylings.

"Amayi'o anosennowe, amayi'o anodirowe, dedëhami anolessowe, acorro, accoro!"

Mal's hand went to his left shoulder, to the hawthorn tattoo Kiiren had given him when they first met. These were the same words Erishen spoke when he said farewell to Kiiren the last time the last time he died, in the hawthorn grove sacred to their clan. For remembering, Kiiren had said. And only now did he remember.

His own lips moved in time with the words. It was either that or scream Erishen's grief to the uncaring marble walls around them.

CHAPTER XXXV

Gloom had descended on the house, a melancholy wrought not by fashion but by real loss and grief. Gabriel refused to leave Ned's side, so Coby spent a lot of her time running up and down the stairs with jugs of hot water, or food for both patient and nurse. Meanwhile Mal sat bowed over a lute he had found somewhere in the embassy, playing the same few songs over and over, his face set like stone. Coby brought food for him too, but it sat ignored until, cold and congealed, it had to be taken back down to the kitchens, much to Jameson's disgust. Sandy just lay on his bed, staring at the ceiling in silence. After a few hours of this, Coby retreated to the relative congeniality of Berowne's parlour.

"An ill business altogether," Berowne muttered, leaning back in his chair and drawing on his pipe. "Though to fret so over the death of a foreigner… Doesn't seem right, if you ask me."

"No, sir."

Coby picked up a book lying on the table and began leafing through it, for want of anything better to do. It began as an interesting enough account of the travels of Marco Polo, but some of the pictures of fabulous beasts of the Orient reminded her far too much of the creatures they had fought outside Ca' Dario. She shuddered, and closed the book with a thud that caused Berowne to start.

"I suppose you will all be going back to England now," Berowne said, "what with the skrayling ambassador dead and the rest expelled from the city. Your master has done our country a great service."

"I suppose he has. Though at what cost?"

Berowne didn't seem to have heard, thankfully. She excused herself and went back up to the attic to see if Gabriel needed anything. Mal had put aside the lute and was staring at his hands as if they were a stranger's. Coby cleared her throat.

"I thought I'd go for a walk, to clear my head," she said. "If there's anything you need–"

Mal looked up. "I'll come with you."

She halted in the doorway, surprised but delighted at this evident improvement in his mood. They went down to the atrium in silence, and Mal opened the door to usher her out. Coby realised with a flush of pleasure that he was treating her like a woman despite her boy's garb. Still, she would have given anything to have the old Mal back. His present black humour tore at her heart.

As they crossed the little bridge heading towards San Toma, she ventured to break the silence.

"Sir Geoffrey is wondering when we will return to England."

"I dare say he is. We cannot outstay our welcome, and yet..." Mal sighed heavily. "For Sandy's sake, we cannot leave for a while yet."

She halted. "You think... Lord Kiiren...?"

Mal glanced around the street and lowered his voice.

"We have to allow that he may have been reborn, yes. And if so, we can hardly leave him here, to suffer the same fate as..."

The courtesan's name hung unspoken in the air.

"No, of course not," Coby said hurriedly, and walked on. "But how will you find him?"

"Sandy is looking, even now. But there are hundreds of women with child, and the trail gets fainter with every day that passes."

"What if he doesn't find him?"

"Then we must assume that he is dead in truth, and go home."

They walked on in silence for a while.

"It's not your fault," Coby said at last.

"No? If I had listened to your advice and not interfered, Kiiren would still be alive. Ned would still have his hand..." He shook his head. "Dear God, what is he to do? I have deprived my friend of his livelihood."

Coby had no answer to that.

"Do you suppose anyone else in Venice knows what really happened that night?" she said. "There must surely be rumours flying about the city by now."

"I don't doubt it. And none will contain more than a grain of truth, which is all to the good. I would rather not be suspected of causing trouble in Dorsoduro, would you?"

She grinned back at him. That was more like the old Mal. A moment later, however, his expression grew grave.

"There is something we needs must talk about," he said. "Something I have been meaning to say for a long time."

"Oh?" Her heart sank. This did not sound good.

He gestured to a nearby taverna. "It is not too early in the day for a drink, I reckon."

The taverna was empty of customers, though a delivery man sat talking to the landlord over a bowl of olives whilst his young assistant waited outside, ostensibly guarding the barrow but mostly flirting with any passing women. Mal ordered a flagon of wine and led Coby into the little courtyard out back. Strings of washing crisscrossed the sky above, and no doubt there were listeners up there, ears cocked for the latest gossip, but still it felt like they were alone.

"You are right," Mal said, filling two glasses. "I should have listened to you. I meddled where it was not needed, because I thought I was right, and because I wanted to gain Kiiren's approval."

He pushed one of the glasses towards her.

"However, there is no use crying over shed milk," he went on. "I must take responsibility for the outcome of my decision, as any commander must, as well as resolve to make better choices in future. And to do that, I need good advice. Your advice."

"You have it. Always."

"And shall make better use of it, I swear." He took a sip of his wine. "But I have need of your service in another capacity. If... If Sandy is right, we will have to take the child home with us. And I want to raise it as my own. My son and heir, if it be a boy."

"You are asking me to look after this child?" she said. "But I know nothing of infants. I helped my mother with Kees, true, but that was many years ago..."

"No. I'm not asking you to be a nursemaid. I can hire a woman for that. But... he will not be an ordinary child. And I fear he will not want to stay with us, once he remembers who he is."

"You think he will want to go back to the New World and be reborn as a skrayling?"

"I'm certain of it. And Sandy will want to go with him. I... I might never see them again."

Coby reached out her hand, and he took it, rubbing her knuckles with his thumb as if to assure himself of her solidity.

"But that won't be for years, surely?"

"I hope not," he whispered hoarsely.

They sat in silence for long moments, then Mal reached for his glass with his free hand and drained it in one go.

"The thing is..." He cleared his throat. "If he won't stay, I need a real heir, one born of my own flesh. And for that I need a wife."

He caught her gaze, held it. Realisation dawned, and she stared back at him, hardly able to believe what she was hearing.

"Jacomina Hendricksdochter, will you marry me?"

Coby nodded, her heart too full for words. Then the full implication of his offer struck her. To be a married woman, the respectable wife of a respectable gentleman, she would have to give everything up that she had worked for. Her life as Jacob Hendricks would be over.

"I know I ask a very great deal," he said, as if guessing her thoughts. "If you would rather seek your fortune elsewhere, then so can I." He looked more miserable than ever, if that were possible.

"No." The thought of him marrying someone else was too much to bear. "I accept your offer. On one condition."

"Anything."

The look on his face, of hope renewed beyond expectation, was so adorable, she almost burst into tears of laughter.

"I will be your faithful wife at home and in sight of our neighbours," she said carefully. "But if ever the Queen or Sir Francis Walsingham require your service, then I ask leave to become your servant Jacob for as long as you need me."

He laughed, and raised both her hands to his lips to kiss them.

"Agreed."

She got to her feet slowly and went round the other side of the table. For a moment she feared he would stop her, that he would remind her she was still dressed as a boy, but he only watched in silence. She sat down on the bench next to him, slipped her arm around his waist and pressed her forehead to his chin. His beard was scratchy on her skin, but she didn't mind as long as she could be this close to him. After a moment he took her in his arms and kissed her brow, her nose, her lips…

"You're not afraid someone will see us?" she murmured between kisses.

"This is Venice," he replied, "where even the women wear breeches."

She chuckled. "Perhaps we should stay, then."

Ned cursed as the nib splayed, spattering ink across the page.

"It's no good, I'll never get used to writing left-handed."

He threw the quill down and wiped his inky fingers on the rag as best he could. The stump of his right forearm ached, as if his missing hand had been clenched in frustration throughout the exercise. As well it might. He had known this was a stupid idea when Gabriel suggested it, but he hadn't the heart to refuse.

"Nonsense, it's my fault for cutting the nib poorly," Gabriel said. "You were doing very well with it."

He tried to kiss Ned's brow, but Ned pushed him away and got to his feet, pacing the attic room to ease his cramped muscles. The skraylings' potions had taken away the pain of surgery, but a week of lying drugged and immobile, and two more of being cooped up in this attic with nought to do but think, had left him both weak and restless.

"Much use I will be," he muttered. "A one-handed scrivener who can't even cut his own pens."

"Perhaps you could get work in a printer's shop," Gabriel replied. "I hear they need men with a keen eye to set the lettering."

Ned made a rude noise. "I'm too old for an apprenticeship. No, I shall have to rent out the house and hope that brings in enough to keep me."

"I shall earn enough to keep us both," Gabriel said cheerily. "Between my acting and what I can get for my plays–"

"You don't want to be bothered with an old cripple like me."

"No, I don't."

Ned turned to stare at his lover. Gabriel folded his arms and glowered. It made him look like one of the sterner archangels, barring sinners from the gates of Heaven.

"No?"

"Not if you're going to wallow in self-pity all day, I don't." Gabriel sighed. "You're alive, aren't you? That's more than can be said for some."

"Ah, but Kiiren's not really dead, is he?"

"You believe Sandy has found him, reborn as a Venetian child?"

Ned shrugged. "I leave all that uncanny business to him and Mal."

Footsteps sounded on the stairs outside, then came a knock at the door.

"Come in," they both cried out together.

Hendricks – or Mina, as they were now supposed to call her – came in, carrying a large wooden box. Ned still wasn't used to seeing her in women's clothes and kept expecting her to revert to her old ways, but seemingly Mal had tamed her after all.

"What's that?" Gabriel asked as she set the box down on one of the empty beds.

"A gift for Master Faulkner," she said with a grin. "Something for him to wear to the wedding."

The two men exchanged glances.

"Surely it's Gabe you should be buying the fine apparel for," Ned said at last. "No one wants to look at me."

"Oh, I think they will." She clicked open the two latches, then stepped to one side. "Go on, then. Don't you want to know what it is?"

"Very well, since you are so desperate to tell me." He walked over to the bed, lifted the lid, and whistled.

"What is it?" Gabriel peered over his shoulder. "Oh, sweet Jesu!"

It was an arm. Or rather, the lower half of an arm, with a hand attached. Made of brass and steel, all cunningly worked like fine armour.

"Well, what do you think?"

Ned shook his head in wonder. "Where did you get such a thing?"

"I designed it," she said. "Well, I borrowed some ideas from a book I read at Master Quirin the clockmaker's, and then Raleigh commissioned it from one of the best armorers in Venice."

She lifted it out of the box to demonstrate.

"See, you strap this end onto... your arm, and then with your other hand you can slide this lever–" she pointed to a protuberance on the inside of the prosthesis' forearm "–and the fingers close, thus."

The fingers did indeed fold into the palm with a clank.

"Ingenious," Gabriel said softly.

"Then slide it back and the hand opens again. It uses lodestones." She pointed out the cobbled appearance of the palm. "The armourer embedded the leftover beads from Sandy's old spirit-guard. It's not like he needs them any more, now he has his necklace back."

"Will it protect me from guisers?" Ned asked.

She laughed. "I don't think so. But you can always hit them with it and find out."

"It's... too princely a gift." He ran a finger over the smooth, cold metal. For an instant he felt an answering touch on his missing hand. Skrayling magic, or his imagination? "Surely it must have cost a fortune. I will never pay off such a debt."

"No need. I sold the drawings to Quirin for his collection, and Raleigh was so pleased with it that he's commissioned a life-sized automaton to give to the Queen."

"Thank you," Gabriel said, embracing her, and for once Ned felt no jealousy. Hendricks was just a girl, after all.

Getting married was all very well in theory, but there was the small issue that neither Coby nor Mal was a member of any parish in Venice. Nor did she wish to convert to Catholicism, despite Mal's assurance that being of the Old Faith was not in itself against the law in England. She had been raised a Lutheran, and she would not put aside her faith for any man, even a husband.

In the end it was agreed that they would follow English common law and make their vows before witnesses, then seek a church blessing once they were back in England. With an ambassador and a member of Parliament to vouch for them, no one could question the validity of the arrangement.

They assembled in the ambassador's tiny garden under the pomegranate tree. Coby wore a plain respectable gown and Mal his best doublet and hose. Berowne had put on courtly garb of silk brocade and velvet, and Gabriel and Ned had embellished their everyday outfits with new cloaks and plumed hats. Coby noted with satisfaction that Ned was wearing his false hand, though it was hardly noticeable with the sleeve of his doublet pulled down. She made a note to herself to suggest to Mal that they buy him a pair of gloves for Christmas.

"Is Raleigh not joining us?" Mal asked, looking around.

"He said he had an errand to run, and would be back forthwith," Berowne replied.

"Perhaps we ought to wait for him," Coby said reluctantly. She had no particular desire for Raleigh to be at her wedding, even if he did make an impeccable witness.

"He may be gone all day," Mal said. "Let us get on with it."

"Ah, the anxious bridegroom," Berowne said with a chuckle. "Afraid you'll change your mind if we don't get it over with?"

"Not at all," Mal said, and smiled down at Coby.

"Well, then, you have your witnesses. Make your vows."

Mal cleared his throat, then took Coby's hands in his. "Jacomina Hendricksdochter, do you marry me?"

"Yes." Her voice came out as a nervous squeak. She coughed. "Yes, I do."

"And I, Maliverny Catlyn, do marry thee."

"And I, Sir Geoffrey Berowne, bear witness to this contract, according to the ancient laws of England."

"And I, Gabriel Parrish."

"And I, Edmund Faulkner."

Mal shook hands with each of the men in turn, and they each kissed Coby on the mouth, Gabriel with a whispered "God bless you both" and Ned with another of his insufferable grins.

"Is that it?" Coby asked.

"One last thing." Raleigh appeared in the doorway. "Can't have a wedding without a ring, eh, Catlyn?"

He held out a small velvet pouch, and Mal took it from him. Mal's eyes widened as he loosened the strings and shook out the contents into his palm.

"You had it made smaller," he said, holding up the signet ring. "How did you even get hold of it?"

Raleigh nodded towards Ned, who looked sheepish.

"You stole it?"

"Borrowed," Ned replied. "It was Raleigh's idea."

"Since the mistress of the house seems so fond of wearing breeches," Raleigh said, "I thought she might as well be entrusted with the family seal also."

"I see."

"Well then, put it on her, man. I didn't spend half the morning running around Venice for naught."

Coby held out her hand, and Mal slipped the heavy gold ring onto her finger. She gazed down at it wonderingly.

"This is too fine a gift, sir..."

"Nonsense. You are the mistress of my household now, as well as of my heart." He kissed her. "And perhaps one day soon, the mistress of Rushdale Hall."

Sir Geoffrey insisted that they use his guest bedchamber for their wedding night, and sent Raleigh up to the attic. To Mal's surprise the captain did so with good grace, shaking Mal by the hand and congratulating him on making an honest woman out of her at last. Mal was not so sure; the new Coby was a mystery to him, an old friend turned stranger. It was none of her doing, but he felt strangely awkward now in her presence when he had never done so before. He prayed his nervousness would not entirely unman him tonight.

At last all their friends had bade them good night, and they were left alone together in the shadowy bedchamber. Coby fussed with the bed hangings, turned the counterpane back and plumped the bolsters. She seemed unable to meet his eye. He drew a deep breath. He was the master of the household, at least within this room; it was up to him to take charge of the situation.

He closed the space between them and put his arms around her waist.

"I have waited too long for this," he murmured in her ear.

She made a small frightened sound in her throat.

"Ssh, my sweet, I would never hurt you, you know that." He let her go, and began unbuttoning his doublet.

"Here, let me," she murmured. "That's one part I do know how to do."

She undid the rest of the buttons and helped him out of the doublet, then folded it and placed it over the back of a chair. He kicked off his shoes and unfastened his slops, and soon was down to shirt and drawers.

"Now you," he said.

She let him unlace the back of her gown, and he drew it over her shoulders and let it fall to the floor. Her chemise was cut longer than his and fuller, only hinting at the shape of her body beneath. He drew her close and kissed her. After a moment she returned his kiss with some of her former passion, and his prick stirred in anticipation. Best to take this slowly. He took her hand and led her to the bed.

"I believe," she said shakily, "that it is customary for the husband to… to uncover his wife's nakedness."

"So it is."

She pulled on the drawstring at her throat and loosened the neck of her chemise. Gently he pushed it over her shoulders so that it slid to the floor. He smiled. She was still wearing her linen drawers, like a boy. He unfastened his own shirt and pulled it over his head, then dropped his own drawers and stepped out of them. She swallowed hard, then did the same. In the candlelight the planes of her slender body reminded him of an alabaster saint, beautiful and vulnerable. It was some moments before he remembered to breathe.

Tearing his gaze away he threw back the bed-linens and lay down, inviting her to join him. After a moment she did so, her eyes never leaving his.

"Wh… What do we do next?"

"You mean you don't know?"

"Well, yes, but…" She sighed. "I have never done it myself. You must teach me."

He smiled. "It's not so different from fighting. Once you know the moves, it will all come as natural as breathing."

He reached out his hand and took hers, kissing the back, then the palm, then working his way up to her shoulder. That gave him an excuse to shuffle closer, until there was barely a finger's length between them. Or the length of another member. He took her hand and guided it down between them. Her eyes widened.

"Now you have me at your mercy," he whispered.

He propped himself up on one elbow and leant across her to blow out the candle. To her credit she did not shrink back, nor take her hand away. *Oh please God don't let her take her hand away*. As his eyes adjusted to the darkness he could make out her pale shape beside him. Smooth skin and strong hands. *Oh yes*.

"Is this what Gabriel does for Ned?" she asked after a few moments.

Mal nearly choked. "What?"

"Well, you know, since they can't..."

"Why are we even talking about them?"

"Sorry, I–"

He kissed her again. "It's all right. Just, keep doing that. *Aah*... gently."

He stroked the curve of her arse then slid his hand over her thigh and between her legs. She whimpered, this time more in pleasure than fear. *Sweet Jesu!* He took hold of her wrist.

"Enough for now, or God knows I'll spill my seed."

He drew a deep breath, then another. When he felt in command of himself again, he set to kissing and caressing her, letting her get used to this new intimacy. She trembled at his touch, but now out of desire, her breath coming as ragged as his own. He gently pushed her onto her back and climbed on top of her, pushing her knees apart with his own. There.

When she did not cry out, he paused.

"I thought you were a virgin."

"So I am, I swear." A pause. "You believe me, don't you my love?"

"I want to."

"I swear I was a pure maid, untouched by any man, until tonight. I swear it to be true, on my – on my mother's soul. May God keep her…"

It was the catch in her voice that convinced him. He knew she would not make such a vow lightly.

"I believe you," he murmured in her ear. "My own sweet Jacomina."

He thrust again, as gently as he could, though it cost him nearly all his self-control.

"I have been running around in breeches," she went on, "since I was a girl of twelve, and have ridden astride many times this past year. No wonder it is thought unseemly, if it damages a woman so–"

"Mistress Catlyn?"

"Yes?"

"Be a good wife and let your husband get on with the duties of the marriage bed. Please?"

"Yes, sir."

There were no more words between them, nor were any needed. Two souls, one flesh; it was all the magic he needed.

CHAPTER XXXVI

Mal picked up his cloak but did not put it on. They would need something to conceal the babe from curious eyes, but it was a warm day and he did not want to attract any more attention than necessary.

"Ready?" he asked Sandy.

"Of course." His brother's eyes gleamed with barely suppressed delight.

"And you're certain this boy-child is the one?"

"As certain as I have ever been. Kiiren's soul is reborn in him, it shines like a beacon in the night."

Mal turned to leave the attic, only to find his wife standing in the doorway, arms folded. In her severe linen coif and apron, she still looked like a stranger to him, and he realised he missed the boy he had known so long.

"You're not just going to steal the babe from its parents, are you?" she said, looking from one to the other.

"Well…"

"How could you think of such a thing? Those poor people…" She shook her head. "And what if you get caught? What help will you be to Kiiren then?"

"What do you suggest?"

"I don't know. Perhaps you could wait a little longer…"

"We cannot," Sandy said. "What if something happened to him? Gabriel has told me how infants that are sickly or seem… uncanny are suspected of being fairy changelings, and may be treated cruelly, even killed."

"I understand that. But–" She bit her lip. "Isn't there something Sandy can do? Like… like when he made Zancani and the others think they had performed for the skraylings. Make them forget the child's existence?"

Mal looked at his brother. Sandy shrugged.

"The father, perhaps; the mother, too, if I have time to work on her. But then there are the other family members, the neighbours… I cannot alter the memories of a whole community in one night."

"We'll think of something," Mal said firmly. "I won't just steal the child from under their noses and run away."

"Very well. But be careful, do you hear me?"

Mal crossed the room and bent to kiss her brow. "I promise. We will be back before dark, and in the morning we will hire a nursemaid to come back to England with us."

They took Berowne's gondola, though of course they did not inform the ambassador of their purpose. The gondolier set them ashore in Dorsoduro a couple of streets away from their destination, and was told to wait for their return. Mal led the way through the quiet streets. It was an hour after dinner, and the city drowsed in the summer heat, the heavy perfume of roses and lilac vying with the stink of the canals.

"Who are these people?" he asked Sandy. "You mentioned only that they were of the poorer sort, and live close to where Kiiren died."

"The father is a dockhand on the Zattere, the great quay where the city's timber is unloaded. The mother is a waterseller, when she is not laden down with an infant. It is only by the greatest luck and fortitude that she carried my *amayi* to term."

"Do they have other children?"

"Three. Two boys and a girl. They will not miss this one."

"I wouldn't be so sure," Mal said. "At any rate, it's not a risk we can take."

They paused on the corner of the street, where a shrine of the Madonna was set into the wall. A shrivelled bunch of anemones was thrust into the iron framework surrounding the carving. Mal made the sign of the cross and prayed silently for forgiveness. Sandy stood at his side, head bowed. After a few moments he raised his head.

"They are sleeping," he said. "In the house to the north of us. High up."

"That one?" Mal asked, cocking his head towards a shabby tenement.

Sandy nodded.

"I've been thinking," Mal said. "Olivia told me she had died in childhood more than once. If you could convince the parents something had happened to their infant, they would grieve over it and no one would be suspicious."

"It would have to be some method that did not leave a body," Sandy said.

"Falling into a canal?" Mal mused aloud. "No, the child is too young to crawl. Perhaps dropped in a canal by its careless mother?"

"She would have to take it outside first. It is easier to take the babe whilst they sleep." Sandy drummed his fingers on the wall. "It is but a matter of weeks since the devourers struck. What if there should be another such incident?"

Mal frowned. "I hope you're not suggesting slaughtering an entire family, just to cover up our deed?"

"Are you?" Sandy grinned.

"That's not funny." He glanced up and down the street. "You may be right, though. If we make it look like something ran off with it, they may conclude the poor child is dead. Wait there; I will be back in a few minutes."

He doubled back towards the quayside, hoping to find a market or a butcher's shop, but everywhere was closed for the midday break. Nor were there any middens to raid, as there would have been in London; the Venetians were frustratingly neat and tidy. Cursing under his breath, Mal jogged along the waterfront. If he didn't find something soon, they would have to go home and try again tomorrow. And that could be a day too late.

Just as he was about to give up, he saw a woman trudging along the quay with a basket of chickens. A few moments' haggling later, Mal was walking back towards the tenement with one of the birds tucked under his elbow. Thankfully Sandy was still waiting where he had left him.

"That is your plan?" his brother said. "It has claws, granted, but I fear no one will mistake it for a devourer."

The chicken cocked its head on one side and eyed them both malevolently.

"I need to kill it before we go in there," Mal said, "but they tend to make a lot of noise."

"Allow me."

Sandy took the bird under his own arm, placed his free hand on top of its head and closed his fingers around its skull. The bird went totally still.

"Now, do what you must," Sandy said.

Mal looked around, but there was no one to be seen. He took the chicken's neck firmly in both hands and yanked, severing the spine instantly. It shuddered briefly and went limp.

The front door of the tenement was not locked or bolted. Mal eased it open and peered inside. A stairwell smelling of piss and rotting vegetables led up into darkness. Mal crept up, all senses alert. He paused at the first floor. Hardly a *piano nobile*.

"This one?" he whispered.

"Higher."

They went up again, more slowly now. The stairs here were wooden and creaked betrayal at every step. By the time they reached the next floor Mal's heart was pounding. He pressed his ear to the nearest door. A little girl's voice was singing what sounded like a lullaby, though he could not make out the words. He turned back to Sandy.

"The children are awake," he whispered.

Sandy leant against the wall and closed his eyes. After a while Mal realised that the singing had stopped. Sandy straightened up with a grin.

"Children are so much easier," he said. "Come, we can go in now."

Mal eased the latch down, wincing as it slipped under his fingers and rattled slightly. The door opened into a one-room hovel with a large bed in one corner. The window was shuttered against the midday sun, throwing bars of light across the bed where both adults lay snoring loudly, with a couple of boys of about three or four snuggled between them like puppies. An older girl, perhaps seven years old, slumped against the wall next to a cradle. Hardly daring to breathe, Mal advanced into the room.

As he neared the cradle, the mother rolled over and muttered something in her sleep. She was not much older than Coby but already careworn, with a touch of silver in her raven hair. His wife was right, these people didn't deserve to have their child stolen, no matter who that child was. He turned back to Sandy.

"I can't do this."

"You perhaps cannot, but I can." Sandy marched over to the cradle. "You humans need to learn respect."

"Sandy!"

"I am not Sandy, I am Erishen." He reached into the cradle and lifted up the child. "And this is Kiiren of Shajiilrekhurrnasheth, my *amayi*."

He held out the babe.

"You want me to take him?" Mal asked.

"Just hold him a moment."

Mal put down the dead chicken and took the child in its place. The babe blinked up at him. He tried to see Kiiren in those dark blue eyes, to no avail. Perhaps it was too soon.

Sandy twisted the thin cradle-blanket into a sling with practised ease, then took the child back.

"Brother–" Mal reached out a hand.

Sandy's eyes narrowed in contempt. "If you wish to save us all, and spare this family further grief, you will finish what we came here to do."

Mal nodded numbly and picked up the dead chicken. He slit it open with his knife, pulled out the still-warm entrails and smeared some of the blood on the cradle. For further verisimilitude he took out his dagger and scraped parallel marks on the edge of the cradle, as of huge claws. He considered opening the shutters and repeating the process on the windowsill, but someone might see him and in any case it would add to the mystery if there was no sign of how the "devourer" got in or out. Instead he found a large rag and wiped his hands on it, then used it to bundle up the remains of the chicken, including all the stray feathers.

"Enough," Sandy said. "Let us away from here."

Mal threw the cloak about his brother's shoulders so that it all but concealed the sling, then followed him out of the house and into the deserted street. They walked back to the gondola in silence, Mal starting at every sound. What if someone saw them and sent for the *sbirri*? This time there would be no Olivia to save them.

They reached the gondola unchallenged, however, and Sandy ducked into the concealment of the cabin. The gondolier's thick eyebrows drew together. Mal took out his purse and gave the man several *lira*.

"For your silence."

"Of course, *signore*." He saluted Mal with a sly smile.

Mal scrambled aboard and crouched in the bow, watching nervously for any sign of the alarm being raised. The gondolier hauled on his oar, and they slid away towards the Grand Canal. Not a moment too soon. Shutters were opening here and there, neighbours calling out to one another as the city roused from its midday slumber. Very soon their ill deed would be discovered.

Somewhere on the journey back to Berowne's, Mal tossed his own bloody bundle into the water. It bobbed in their wake for a moment, then sank in a swirl of feathers and was gone.

"Signora Catalin?"

Coby looked up from her sewing to see the new nursemaid standing in the doorway.

"Yes, Susanna?"

The girl stammered something in her thick Venetian dialect. At Coby's frown of incomprehension she repeated it more slowly, then mimed sleeping.

"Yes," Coby replied in formal Italian. "The baby is sleeping."

The girl bobbed a curtsey, said something about laundry, and left. Coby sighed. She was going to have to teach the girl English on the way home, or it would be a very tiresome voyage. Still, Susanna was willing enough, and a hard worker. Mal said she was one of Cinquedea's girls who had recently lost her own babe to a fever, so no doubt anything was better than whoring, even sailing to a foreign land where she knew no one and could not speak the language. Coby smiled to herself. At least Susanna would not have to disguise herself as a boy to earn an honest living.

She finished off the hem of the baby gown and set it aside. Little children needed so much linen to keep them clean, it was no wonder that poor women let them run around naked. Unfortunately the son of a gentleman would not be allowed such liberties, which meant that Coby would be sewing napkins and smocks from dawn until dusk. Truly, a mother needed six pairs of hands and twice as many hours of daylight as everyone else.

She placed her hands on her own belly, wondering what it felt like to quicken with child. Thankfully nothing of that sort had happened yet. She did not relish the prospect of a sea voyage in such a state. There would be plenty of time later, when she had settled into her new role as mistress of her own household. And she could practise on her adopted son, with a little help from Susanna.

Her son. The thought thrilled and terrified her. She got to her feet and went over to the borrowed cradle. He was a handsome child, of that there was no doubt, with curly black hair and dark eyes. Perhaps he would grow up looking enough like his supposed father to fool people, but at such a young age, it was hard to tell.

"I thought we'd call him Christopher," Mal said. "Kit for short."

Coby turned to see him leaning in the doorway. He looked tired, as if the events of the past few weeks were a weight he could not put down.

"That's a good name," she said. "But is it not the English custom to name the eldest son after his father?"

Mal laughed. "I would not saddle him with a name like mine. You don't know how much I was mocked at school."

"For having a foreign name?"

He came over to the cradle and put an arm around her. "For having a girl's name. 'Mall' is short for Mary."

"I suppose it is. I'd never thought of it like that before."

"Anyway, I thought it would make slips of the tongue less obvious if we named him something similar to… his old self. And Christopher is the patron saint of travellers. It seemed appropriate, given how far he has to go."

"Christopher it is, then." She gazed down at the child. "Kit Catlyn. It has a pretty ring to it."

"We should leave soon, just in case someone recognises him. I know 'tis said that all babes look alike, but if by some ill chance his own mother or grandmother were to set eyes on him..."

"Very true. And we cannot be sure that his nurse will not gossip, either."

"Then it is settled. We will find passage on the next ship for France."

"We're not going back to England? What about Charles, and your family estate?"

"We'll go, but not yet. I don't know what else is waiting for me back there."

"What do you mean?"

She listened in horrified silence as he told her about the assassin on Raleigh's ship.

"Why didn't you tell me sooner?"

"What good would it have done? Whoever it was sent him, it would have been weeks until they heard the news of his failure, and even if they sent someone else it would take weeks more and I might have been on my way home by then. No, it makes far more sense for them to wait until I return to England."

"'Them' being the guisers, I suppose?"

"Who else? Suffolk must have had accomplices, allies..." An *amayi*. He swallowed, remembering the nightmare at Hampton Court.

"Will we be safe in Provence?"

"I don't know." He took her hand and kissed it. "I hope so. Safer than England, at any rate."

"What will you tell the servants back in France? They're bound to be curious."

"I'll tell them that my valet Jacob introduced me to his pretty cousin, Mina, and that I dismissed him from my service now that I have a wife to look after me."

"They won't believe you."

"What are they going to do about it? You are a woman, after all. I have proof on't." He grinned at her.

"You're as bad as Ned," she muttered, but she let him kiss her anyway.

"So," he said, "we shall all go back to Provence and make a home there together. You, me, and Kit."

"And Sandy."

To her surprise, Mal pulled a face. "Aye. And Sandy."

"What's wrong? I thought your brother meant the world to you?"

"He did. He does. But Kiiren was right." He sighed and shook his head. "Sandy isn't the brother I knew. He's Erishen now. A stranger."

"I'm so sorry." She laid her head on his chest.

"So am I. But I made my decision, that day in Southwark, and there is no going back. Our fates were decided before we were born, Sandy and me. And so it will be with this little one." He looked down at Kit and shook his head. "That's what so wrong. About the guisers. It's not that they pretend to be other than what they are, although that's bad enough. But they steal people's lives. Like this boy's. He'll never know his real family."

"He'll be an English gentleman, instead of a poor Venetian. Isn't that better?"

"I don't know. My head says yes, but my heart..." He kissed her forehead and released her. "Get your belongings together. I'll go and tell Ned and Gabriel. If there's a boat leaving for Marseille tonight, we'll be on it."

Venice shrank into the distance as the *Hayreddin* made its way out of the lagoon. Despite his determination to leave as soon as possible, Mal had let his wife talk him into waiting for Youssef's return. The Moor was going back to Marseille, after all, and it would be good to travel with someone they knew and trusted.

He turned away from the rail and went down to the weather deck to where his friends were waiting.

"Don't be a fool, Ned," Gabriel was saying. "You cannot possibly climb the rigging with that false hand, you'll fall and kill yourself."

"Then what am I to do with myself all voyage?" Ned scowled and folded the brass arm awkwardly under his unmaimed one.

"You can help me with my play," Gabriel said, taking his elbow. "I shall not be happy with it until I have heard the speeches read aloud, and I can hardly do them all myself."

"Sometimes I think they make a better couple than you and I," Coby said, watching them disappear into the cabin.

"Ned is probably a more obedient wife," Mal replied with a grin.

"Have I not always been obedient?" she asked, her attempt at innocence belied by the twinkle in her eyes.

"You didn't manage to keep my brother out of trouble whilst he was in London."

She looked crestfallen. "You have me there. But if we had not fled England in a rush, we would not have ended up in Venice, and none of this would have happened."

"Or it might," Mal said. "What happened, happened; it is all one."

"Did you love her?"

Mal paused. What answer to give to such a question? If he said yes, she would be angry; if he said no, he would be lying.

"Then you did love her."

He sighed. "I admired her. She was a clever, charming woman, but misguided. No one should hold power for centuries on end. Each generation must make its own way."

"You want to expel the guisers from England." It was not a question.

"Yes."

"They are many, and powerful. How can we hope to prevail against them?"

"We have Suffolk's book; perhaps some secrets can yet be gleaned from that."

"At least we won't have any of the ancients to deal with," she said. "If… If that woman did not lie about them all coming to Venice."

He smiled down at her. "I hope not. But whatever the truth of it, first we must make a safe home for Kit, so that he can return to his people when the time is right."

"And Sandy?"

"And Sandy. I will reconcile with Erishen, somehow. We are one and the same, after all."

EPILOGUE

Ilianwe woke from an uneasy sleep, memories of dreams fleeing even as she tried to grasp them. Was this what it felt like to be merely human? If so, she did not like it. Bad enough that she be chained like a slave, unable to stand or ease her aching limbs, but the iron that encircled her flesh caged her very soul. No wonder her dreams were full of panic and fear. No wonder she woke in cold sweats, her head pounding.

No, it was not her head. Heavy wheels rumbled overhead like thunder, then an answering boom shook the entire ship. Her captors were under attack. She scrambled across the deck to the full extent of her chains, trying to see up through the hatch. Shadows moved to and fro, orders were shouted, but the language of these sailors was strange to her: the speech of a clan distant in both space and time from her own kin.

Ilianwe was flung back against the mast as the ship took another hit. As she lay there, breathing shallowly to spare her battered ribs, she could hear the trickle of water coming through a breach in the hull. For the first time on this voyage she considered the very real possibility that she might drown whilst still chained and never be reborn. She twisted her hands in the manacles, wondering how much damage she would have to do to the bones to work them free. The seawater was swirling across the deck now, back and forth like the incoming tide as the ship rocked under fire. She spat on the iron, hoping saliva might provide enough lubrication to pull free, but her mouth was dry and only a few miserable drops spattered her flesh. Perhaps seawater would suffice?

Footstep sounded on the deck above, and other voices. Human voices, speaking… Arabic?

"Help!" she called out in that same language. "For the love of Allah, help me!"

The hatch creaked open and a man looked down into the hold. She could not make out his features, silhouetted as he was against the light.

"Who is that?"

"I am Islah bint Mehmed, a captive of these godless creatures." It was her mother's name, but would gain her more respect from these men than if they thought her a Christian.

Two men descended the ladder, dragging a skrayling with them. The skrayling unlocked Ilianwe's shackles, and one of the men helped her to her feet. She stretched her cramped limbs and allowed them to escort her up onto the main deck, blinking against the harsh sunlight. She smoothed her skirts, hoping she did not look too disreputable after so many days of captivity.

A tall, beturbaned figure strode up and down before the captive skraylings who knelt in a line before him. One of Ilianwe's escort spoke to him, and he looked round in evident surprise. When he caught sight of her, he lowered his gaze respectfully.

"Madam? My men tell me they found you chained in the hold."

"That is correct. Thank merciful Allah you rescued me."

He glanced up briefly, but did not meet her eye. "You give a Muslim name and call upon God, yet you dress as a Christian."

"They stole my hijab and forced me to dress like this," she said, letting her voice quaver a little. It was not hard, after the privations of the past few weeks. "I think they wanted to sell me as a slave in Christian lands."

"How did you come to be a captive of these demons?" he asked.

"I..." She thought quickly. "I am a widow, sir. My husband was a captain in the army of Telli Hasan Pasha, but was sadly killed in the retreat from Senj. I was making my way to Constantinople to rejoin my family when the ship I travelled on was attacked by these creatures."

The corsair captain muttered a lengthy curse on the skraylings and their descendants, then gestured towards his own ship.

"Please, madam, allow me to escort you to my vessel. I would be happy to set you ashore, perhaps in al-Jaza'ir?"

"Thank you. I am afraid I have no money with which to pay for my passage–"

"I do not need your money, madam." He grinned. "The price I will get for these painted demons will make me richer than the pasha himself."

Ilianwe ventured a coy smile in return. A rich corsair who had no idea who or what she was, and a new start in a country halfway to England. Catalin might have succeeded in betraying her, but he had been so intent on guarding his plans that he had not noticed her more subtle intrusions into his memories. There were others of his kind in England, other young upstarts from whom she could take her pick. If she could not rule her beloved republic, she would have a kingdom in its place.

Acknowledgments

As ever, I'd like to thank the Angry Robot crew for all their hard work in getting this book into your hands, and in particular Marc Gascoigne the AR publisher and Larry Rostant of Artist Partners for taking my ideas on board and turning them into the beautiful cover art for this second volume. It was important to me to have Coby on the cover of one of the Night's Masque books, and I'm hoping we'll start a trend for designs featuring young women who don't look like they're posing for a men's magazine!

A lot of research went into this book, requiring input from experts outside my own area of knowledge. I'd therefore like to thank Chiara Prezzavento and Francesca and Piermarco Terminiello for their help with Italian phrases (not all of which made it into the finished book - sorry!), and Fran in particular for a serendipitous picture of a sixteenth century boarding sword on Pinterest, which added a nice bit of period detail to one of my favourite action scenes. I also owe a debt of gratitude to Fatihah Iman for critiquing the scenes involving Muslim characters and setting me straight on a few points. Any remaining errors are my own, for which my apologies.

Still on the research front, I'd like to thank Nicholas Blair-Fish, owner of Ca' Malcanton, for allowing me and my husband to stay in his beautiful renovated medieval palazzo in Venice. It made a wonderful template for the English ambassador's house in my novel, albeit with some minor changes to fit the story. I did however keep the pomegranate tree in the garden; some details are too perfect to change.

All writers need their reality checks, and beta-readers Rebecca Payne, Alex Beecroft and Laura Lam gave me some food for thought, to put it mildly. I may not have agreed with everything you guys said, or altered the book as a result, but it was all taken into consideration. Marc also provided invaluable editorial feedback as usual, cutting to the heart of the story and pointing out where it needed fleshing out or tightening up.

A final thank-you is due to everyone who bought the first book, and I do hope you enjoy this one just as much, if not more. The lovely reviews, fan letters, emails and tweets have brought a smile to my face many a time when I was struggling through successive drafts of this second book, and I look forward to hearing from more of you; writing is an act of communication, and would therefore be pretty meaningless without you, the audience.

A.L.

About the author

Anne Lyle was born in what is known to the tourist industry as "Robin Hood Country", and grew up fascinated by English history, folklore, and swashbuckling heroes. Unfortunately there was little demand in 1970s Nottingham for diminutive swordswomen, so she studied sensible subjects like science and languages instead.

It appears that although you can take the girl out of Sherwood Forest, you can't take Sherwood Forest out of the girl. She now spends every spare hour writing (or at least planning) fantasy fiction about spies, actors, outlaws and other folk on the fringes of society.

Anne lives in Cambridge, a city full of medieval and Tudor buildings where cattle graze on the common land much as they did in Shakespeare's London. She prides herself on being able to ride a horse (badly), sew a sampler and cut a quill pen but hasn't the least idea how to drive one of those new-fangled automobile thingies.

annelyle.com
twitter.com/annelyle

"In *her* terrific debut novel Anne Lyle conjures up *a* magical Elizabethan England *of* seedy glamour, long shadows *and* heart-stopping adventure. THE ALCHEMIST OF SOULS *is the* calling card *of a* great new talent *in the* fantasy field."

Mark Chadbourn, *author of*
The Sword of Albion

THE
CLOCKWORK VAMPIRE
CHRONICLES
ANDY REMIC
KELL'S LEGEND · SOUL STEALERS · VAMPIRE WARLORDS

EMPIRE STATE
A NOVEL
ADAM CHRISTOPHER
"As captivating as a kaleidoscope." CORY DOCTOROW

ADAM CHRISTOPHER
SEVEN
WONDERS

LAVIE TIDHAR
THE
BOOKMAN

LAVIE TIDHAR
CAMERA
OBSCURA

LAVIE TIDHAR
The
GREAT GAME

The Collector Book One
Dead Harvest
Chris F. Holm

The Collector Book Two
The Wrong Goodbye
Chris F. Holm

TIM WAGGONER
THE
THE COMPLETE MATT RICHTER COLLECTION

SELL THE DOG

Collect the entire Angry Robot catalogue

DAN ABNETT
- ☐ Embedded
- ☐ Triumff: Her Majesty's Hero

GUY ADAMS
- ☐ The World House
- ☐ Restoration

JO ANDERTON
- ☐ Debris
- ☐ Suited

MADELINE ASHBY
- ☐ vN

LEE BATTERSBY
- ☐ The Corpse-Rat King

LAUREN BEUKES
- ☐ Moxyland
- ☐ Zoo City

THOMAS BLACKTHORNE
- ☐ Edge
- ☐ Point

MAURICE BROADDUS
- ☐ The Knights of Breton Court

ADAM CHRISTOPHER
- ☐ Empire State
- ☐ Seven Wonders

LEE COLLINS
- ☐ The Dead of Winter

PETER CROWTHER
- ☐ Darkness Falling

ALIETTE DE BODARD
- ☐ Obsidian & Blood

MATT FORBECK
- ☐ Amortals
- ☐ Carpathia
- ☐ Vegas Knights

JUSTIN GUSTAINIS
- ☐ Hard Spell
- ☐ Evil Dark

GUY HALEY
- ☐ Reality 36
- ☐ Omega Point

COLIN HARVEY
- ☐ Damage Time
- ☐ Winter Song

CHRIS F HOLM
- ☐ Dead Harvest
- ☐ The Wrong Goodbye

MATTHEW HUGHES
- ☐ The Damned Busters
- ☐ Costume Not Included

TRENT JAMIESON
- ☐ Roil
- ☐ Night's Engines

K W JETER
- ☐ Infernal Devices
- ☐ Morlock Night

PAUL S KEMP
- ☐ The Hammer & the Blade

J ROBERT KING
- ☐ Angel of Death
- ☐ Death's Disciples

ANNE LYLE
- ☐ The Alchemist of Souls

GARY McMAHON
- ☐ Pretty Little Dead Things
- ☐ Dead Bad Things

ANDY REMIC
- ☐ The Clockwork Vampire Chronicles

CHRIS ROBERSON
- ☐ Book of Secrets

MIKE SHEVDON
- ☐ Sixty-One Nails
- ☐ The Road to Bedlam
- ☐ Strangeness & Charm

DAVID TALLERMAN
- ☐ Giant Thief

GAV THORPE
- ☐ The Crown of the Blood
- ☐ The Crown of the Conqueror
- ☐ The Crown of the Usurper

LAVIE TIDHAR
- ☐ The Bookman Histories

TIM WAGGONER
- ☐ The Nekropolis Archives

KAARON WARREN
- ☐ Mistification
- ☐ Slights
- ☐ Walking the Tree

CHUCK WENDIG
- ☐ Blackbirds
- ☐ Mockingbird

IAN WHATES
- ☐ City of Dreams & Nightmare
- ☐ City of Hope & Despair
- ☐ City of Light & Shadow